USA TODAY bestselling author **Heidi Rice** lives in London, England. She is married with two teenage sons—which gives her rather too much of an insight into the male psyche—and also works as a film journalist. She adores her job, which involves getting swept up in a world of high emotion, sensual excitement, funny and feisty women, sexy and tortured men and glamorous locations where laundry doesn't exist. Once she turns off her computer she often does chores—usually involving laundry!

Amanda Cinelli was born into a large Irish Italian family and raised in the leafy green suburbs of County Dublin, Ireland. After dabbling in a few different careers, she finally found her calling as an author after winning an online writing competition with her first finished novel. With three small daughters at home, she usually spends her days doing school runs, changing nappies and writing romance. She still considers herself unbelievably lucky to be able to call it her day job.

D1589768

INNOCENT'S DESERT WEDDING CONTRACT

HEIDI RICE

RETURNING TO CLAIM HIS HEIR

AMANDA CINELLI

MILLS & BOON

First Published in Great Britain 2021
by Mills & Boon, an imprint of HarperCollins*Publishers*
1 London Bridge Street, London, SE1 9GF

Innocent's Desert Wedding Contract © 2021 Heidi Rice

Returning to Claim His Heir © 2021 Amanda Cinelli

ISBN: 978-0-263-28230-6

MIX
Paper from
responsible sources
FSC™ C007454

This book is produced from independently certified FSC™ paper
to ensure responsible forest management.
For more information visit www.harpercollins.co.uk/green.

Printed and bound in Spain
by CPI, Barcelona

INNOCENT'S DESERT WEDDING CONTRACT

HEIDI RICE

PROLOGUE

'WHY DON'T YOU just find yourself a wife, bro? That'll stop the old goat trying to force you into an arranged marriage.'

'No, thanks, *bro*,' said Karim Jamal Amari Khan, Crown Prince of Zafar, sarcastically as he knocked his brother Dane's booted feet off the coffee table, which his interior designer had probably paid a fortune for. 'Our father can't force me to do a damn thing.'

'Father's a rather loose term, don't you think?' Dane flashed a smile so sharp it could cut concrete. 'Seeing as his only participation in our upbringing was to get both our mothers pregnant?'

'True but irrelevant,' Karim lied smoothly. As the older son and nominal Crown Prince, he had been subjected to rather more attention from their father—including the horrendous summers he'd been forced to spend in Zafar after his mother's suicide. Summers Dane knew nothing about. 'The point is I have no desire to acquire a wife for our father's benefit. If he wants to disinherit me, he can.' In fact, Karim would be overjoyed at the prospect. The kingdom of Zafar held nothing but bad memories for him, which was precisely why he had carved his own path, building a billion-dollar business empire from the ground up by the age of thirty-two, and had not been back to the kingdom since the summer he turned sixteen.

'Which would leave me in the firing line,' Dane replied, the sharp smile taking on a rueful tilt. 'Gee thanks, bro.'

'Tough.' Karim chuckled. It would serve his father right to end up having to declare Dane his heir. His younger brother was reckless and undisciplined and had even less interest in their family heritage than he did. While Karim's mother, Cassandra Wainwright, had been a young British aristocrat, who had returned to the UK with him after the divorce and sent him to a series of tediously disciplinarian boarding schools, Dane's mother, Kitty Jones, had pursued a jet-set life as New York's premiere wild child after her divorce. And her son had reaped the whirlwind, living a life with no boundaries whatsoever. There were only four years between them but Dane had refused Karim's offer to join Amari Corp as an executive and set up his own hospitality brand five years ago, which had been surprisingly successful. If there was one thing Dane knew how to do, it was throw a party.

'I know something which might change your mind about acquiring a wife, pronto,' Dane said, the wicked glint in his eyes making Karim uneasy. There was nothing Dane enjoyed more than messing with him—which had to explain why he had turned up unannounced at Karim's mansion in Belgravia at eight this morning, after a red-eye flight from New York.

'Which is?' Karim asked impatiently, deciding to cut to the chase. He needed to start work, so he didn't have time for his brother's little joke.

'The old goat knows you're after the Calhoun stud,' Dane said as if he'd just scored a home run.

'How do you know that?' Karim demanded. His pursuit of the Calhoun stud was top secret.

Michael Calhoun had died nearly a year ago leaving the family's horse-racing bloodstock and training facility in Ireland with crippling debts. They'd sold a lot of their stock to stay afloat but he'd discovered a few days ago the business was finally being forced to go in to voluntary liquidation. And Karim had been preparing to go in for the kill as soon as it went up for auction.

'Overheard it at an event last night in Tribeca from one of Dad's many mistresses. Which was why I caught the last flight out. She told me he was…' Dane lifted his hands to do air quotes '…real thrilled about getting involved in racing by buying Calhouns. Which we both know is code for he plans to screw you over on the deal to force your hand on the marriage front.'

Karim swore under his breath.

'A phone call would have sufficed,' he murmured, knowing his brother's primary reason for catching the red-eye was probably to see him sweat in person. He refused to give him, or his father, the satisfaction. 'But thanks for the heads-up,' he added grudgingly.

He would have to lose the deal.

Which would hurt like hell. The Calhoun facility, even depleted and without Calhoun himself at the helm, represented a chance to enter the world of horse racing and build his own legacy—something he'd been planning for a while. The only thing he had enjoyed in Zafar was riding and training his father's Arabian stallions.

But he refused to engage with his father's games, on any level. The old bastard had pulled similar tricks in the past, forcing Karim to go head to head with him. Karim hadn't cared, in fact he'd enjoyed finding ways to best the bastard at first. To show him that he wasn't scared of him, that he had no power over him any more. And as he'd built his business, it had become easier to win. But as his father's attempts to blackmail him became more desperate, more deranged, he had become aware that every battle was taking a toll on Zafar's economy as well as his father's finances. Once one of the richest kingdoms in the region, Zafar was losing prominence because his father had been syphoning off money to spend on this war of attrition. Karim might not feel any connection with his heritage, but he didn't want to see the country's citizens punished. So, several years ago, he'd stopped engaging with his father—by keeping the deals he was involved in secret, or bowing out if his father showed an interest. It had taken a few strips off his pride, but he knew the non-engagement technique was working—his father hadn't been involved in any of his business in over a year. Ultimately, frustrating the bastard was more important than beating him, as it wasn't his father who would pay the price.

'Why not call his bluff, this time?' Dane said forcefully. 'Instead of dropping the deal.'

'I'm not getting married to close a deal...' Karim said, wondering if his half-brother had lost the plot.

'But what if you weren't *really* getting married?' Dane cut in. 'Why not acquire a wife in name only?' he continued. 'It would be the perfect revenge on the manipulative bastard. If you're not sleeping with her, you can't provide him with the heirs he wants.'

'And how would that work, exactly?' Karim snapped, annoyed now with Dane's nonsense. 'The main reason I do not wish to marry has nothing to do with our father. I simply do not want a wife.' He slept with women, he did not have long-term relationships with them. 'Even a fake wife would expect things… And make demands on my time.'

And could become as weak and needy and fragile as his mother.

He resisted the shudder as the memory of his mother's tear-stained face flitted across his consciousness. His mother's sadness had defined his childhood, he was not about to become responsible for another woman who needed things he could not give her.

Which was why he had a nicely appointed four-bedroom mews cottage in Kensington where he kept the woman he was currently sleeping with so she would be available when he wanted her, no messy emotions required. Maybe the place had been empty for a month—he frowned—or even two. But since paying off Alexandra, when she had begun to make noises about 'something more permanent', he simply hadn't had time to acquire another mistress.

'Bro, you're loaded,' Dane replied, with that charming, concrete-cutter grin.

It occurred to Karim, while his brother enjoyed messing with him, Dane liked to mess with their father a great deal more.

'Get your fancy legal team to put together an iron-clad prenup,' his brother continued. 'Then all you've gotta do is find yourself a woman who is greedy or desperate enough to be bought.'

CHAPTER ONE

'ORLA, ORLA, THERE'S a helicopter circling the farm. Gerry just gave them permission to land on the back pasture. Gerry says it's *him*, the sheikh who's going to put us all out on the street.'

Orla Calhoun paused while mucking out Aderyn's stall at her sister Dervla's panicked shout. The sleek black stallion jostled her as he shuffled his hooves. She pressed her hand to his nose, to soothe him. Unlike most retired racehorses, Aderyn was placid enough for her to muck him out while he was still in the stall. He liked the company, almost as much as she did, but even so...

'Shh, fella, it's okay, she's just stressed,' she whispered, before leaving the stall. She propped the rake beside the stall, latched the stable door, whipped off her work gloves and glared at her sister. 'For goodness' sake, Dervla, how many times have I told you not to raise your voice around the horses?' she hissed. 'You could spook them and someone could get hurt, or, worse, the animal could get hurt.'

They only had six horses left now, but each one of them meant everything to her—and she still mourned the loss of the horses they'd been forced to sell in the last year. Each one unique, with a personality and a purpose that had always meant more to Orla than just winning races or accruing stud fees. Perhaps that was why she had ultimately failed in her attempt to keep Calhouns going, not because she hadn't been good at training and caring for the horses, but because they had always meant more to her than just a business.

And now she was going to lose it all…

'All right, all right. I get you,' Dervla whispered back, grabbing her elbow to drag her away from the stall, and not sounding all that apologetic. 'But what are we going to do about *him*?'

Orla heard it then, the sound of a helicopter powering down. It was far enough away not to disturb the animals, but the sound would never be quiet enough not to disturb her.

'Are you sure it's him?' she asked. 'He's not due here till Friday.'

The liquidator had arranged to have Crown Prince Karim Jamal Amari Khan view the facility before the auction on Saturday. This must be a preliminary visit by one of his minions. Sure, it had to be. She wasn't ready for him.

She glanced down at her work boots and dirty jeans, the sweat-stained camisole that clung to her breasts. She'd been up at dawn to take Aderyn out on the gallops and had been mucking out the stalls ever since, because they'd laid off the last of the stable boys almost a month ago.

'Gerry said he spoke to him,' Dervla whispered. As if the man was standing behind them. 'He's piloting the helicopter! He came on his own, Gerry says.'

The anxiety that had gripped her stomach ever since she'd been forced to face the inevitable took another vicious twist.

She'd had a plan to have the house and herself spotless

when he arrived. When you were going to beg a favour from a playboy sheikh, you needed to look your best.

'Go keep him busy, then, while I wash up here,' Orla said, her mind racing. 'And get Maeve to bring over my best trousers, fresh underwear and the blouse I ironed yesterday in my wardrobe.'

She shoved her sister out of the stable entrance, then shot towards the washroom at the back of the stalls. Kicking off her boots, she ripped open the fly of her jeans. She could rinse herself here to get the stink off and then get changed before going to greet him.

Sophisticated and demure was out now, but she'd always been a tomboy and had never fitted into the racing high society her father frequented. She'd tried that by getting engaged to Patrick Quinn. And it had been a disaster.

What did you expect? Men have needs, Orla. And you're as frigid as a nun.

She flinched, remembering Patrick's parting words from five years back, and the sickening sight of him and Meghan O'Reilly wrapped around each other like superglue in the gazebo during their engagement party. Orla dumped her jeans by the sinks and ignored the shiver of humiliation that always accompanied the distressing memories.

Doesn't matter, you're well shot of him.

But Patrick had been right about one thing: she had never been any good at playing the flirtatious debutante. So trying to impress a playboy sheikh with her socialite credentials would always have been a stretch. Even if she'd had the time to prepare properly.

But if she changed into something not filthy, she could at least manage cool, calm and in control—something she needed to be to have any chance of persuading Karim Khan to let her stay at Calhouns.

The man knew their financial situation, that they were being forced to sell, so she didn't have much bargaining power.

She'd done a ton of Internet research on Khan last night, as soon as they'd got wind of Amari Corp's interest from the liquidator. From what she could tell their potential buyer was rich, entitled and arrogant, a royal prince who was used to having people like her at his beck and call and who was rich enough to think he could buy his way into a legacy that had taken her family ten generations to build. But she'd be damned if she'd let Crown Prince Whoever cut her out completely from the work she had dedicated her life to.

All she needed was a chance to prove to him she could still be useful at the stud. After all, she'd been as good as managing the place for five years now, ever since she turned seventeen and her father had become trapped in the well of grief left by her mother's death.

But she couldn't do that looking like Little Orphan Annie. From all the press reports she'd read, he was the sort of man who only paid attention to beautiful, sophisticated women with manicured nails, designer clothes and perfectly styled hair that reached down to their bums. The sort of woman she'd never been, even when she had fancied herself in love with the son of the neighbouring Quinn stud.

Standing in her camisole and panties, she grabbed the hose they used to wash the tack and turned it on. A whole body shiver raked her body as she doused her head with the frigid water. And cursed, loudly.

Why had Khan come five days early? Was he trying to catch her out?

A throat cleared loudly behind her.

'Ms Calhoun, I presume?' The deep, curt British accent had her swinging round so fast the hose flew out of her hand, sprinkling water everywhere.

Heat leapt into her cheeks and burned across her collarbone.

A tall man stood with his shoulder propped against the washroom door, his face cast into shadow by the sunshine, but she recognised him instantly from all the research.

What the ever-loving...?

She banded her arms across her chest to shield herself, but couldn't stop the humiliating shivers—as his cold assessing gaze set her freezing skin alight.

Seriously? Could she have made a worse impression? And how had he found her here so quickly?

Dervla, I'm going to strangle you.

'Mr... Mr Khan?' She stuck her chin out, trying to claw back a modicum of dignity, even though she knew she had to look like a drowned rat. 'We weren't expecting you until Friday. And what are you doing in the stables?'

He wore blue jeans, a black crew-neck sweater that clung to his impressively muscular chest, and black leather boots polished to a high gleam. His complexion was dark, his hair even darker. She had a sudden recollection of the villainous king in a book she'd read as a child who had been cruel and cold and all powerful, but also weirdly hot for the villain in a children's storybook. She'd loved that book once upon a time, reading it over and over again. And now she knew why.

'What am I doing here?' he said, the sarcastic tone cutting through her little reminiscence like a scalpel. 'I plan to buy your stud, Ms Calhoun. Today.'

Today?

Renewed panic sprinted up her spine, but then he turned into the light to grab the towel that hung from a peg on the washroom wall. And every thought flew out of her head bar one.

He's even hotter than the villainous king in Flinty O'Toole's Epic Quest.

Her lungs squeezed and the heat of mortification morphed into something a great deal more disturbing.

She already knew Karim Khan was stupidly handsome. She'd studied enough photographs of him last night at gala events, in tuxedos and designer suits, his hair perfectly styled as he paraded supermodels and actresses about as if they were accessories.

But the photos had not done him justice. In the flesh, and up close, and even without the luxury of a stylist, the man was quite simply breathtaking. Her heart literally stopped beating as she devoured the sight of firm, sensual lips, a strong jaw, high sculpted cheekbones and the long blade-like nose. The slight bump in the bridge and a sickle-shaped scar above his left eye marred the perfect symmetry of his face, but only made him look more rugged and masculine and overwhelming.

The burning heat in her cheeks shot through her veins, and her nipples, which were already like bullets, tightened into torpedoes. She squeezed her folded arms harder over her chest trying to quell the throbbing ache. She was more humiliated now than she'd been when she'd found her fiancé eating the face off another woman at her engagement party. And she'd always believed that humiliation could never be topped.

Wrong.

'Dry off,' he said, throwing her the towel.

She caught it one-handed, struggling to inflate her lungs when the light hit his face again and she saw the impatience in his eyes—which were a beautiful golden brown. Because, of course they were.

All the better to devastate you with, Orla. Because he's a god among men and you're a shivering, almost naked tomboy pauper.

As she frantically wrapped the towel around her nakedness, his gaze skimmed down, coasting over every inch of exposed skin until it got to the puddle of water forming at her bare feet.

'I'll meet you at the house in fifteen minutes,' he said, speaking to her as if she were a disobedient and particularly irritating ten-year-old. 'I need this deal finalised today.'

Despite her breathing difficulties, Orla felt her hackles rising.

Who did he think he was, speaking to her like that? Just because he was gorgeous and loaded and dry and fully clothed and she… Well… She wasn't.

But before she could come up with a suitably indignant reply, or gather enough courage—and breath—to actually enunciate it, the impossible man had strode back out of the stables and was gone.

CHAPTER TWO

'MR KHAN, I'M sorry to have kept you waiting. I hope Dervla offered you refreshments?'

Karim swung round from his lengthy contemplation of the impossibly green hills and hedgerows that surrounded the Calhoun stud to see the girl he had encountered twenty minutes ago in the stables crossing the faded rug towards him.

She had changed into a pair of simple black trousers and a white shirt, her damp red hair shoved back behind her ears. As she came into the light cast by the vast living room's bay windows, he realised she wore no make-up. He could still see the freckles sprinkled across her pale skin, which he had noticed earlier. She looked impossibly young and fresh-faced, even more so than she had dripping wet. He quashed the unbidden and unwanted spurt of heat at the memory of toned thighs, slender limbs and turgid nipples clearly visible through the wet fabric of her top.

He needed to find himself a new mistress if he was now responding to teenage tomboys.

'I don't have time for refreshments,' he said, leading with his impatience to disguise the inconvenient reaction that he knew had nothing to do with this fresh-faced, unsophisticated girl and everything to do with his recent sex drought. 'I have a proposal for purchasing the stud but to access it you need to agree to the sale today.'

The plan was a good one and foolproof and fairly straightforward. It hadn't taken him too long to figure out a better solution than dropping out of this deal—or the even more ludicrous solution Dane had outlined in Belgravia this morning—once he'd put his mind to it. He'd piloted the Puma himself to get here quickly and put the plan into action. Dane's prior warning was all he had needed to get ahead of his father.

He had also wanted to look over the property before he made his offer. But as soon as he'd walked into the stable yard he'd known. He wanted the Calhoun stud, whatever it took, because this was exactly what he had been looking for.

'I… I understand, Mr Khan, but I'm afraid I can't give you the agreement you seek.' Her eyes flickered with regret, even pain, but then she firmed her chin. 'The liquidators are handling the sale as this business is going under.'

He nodded. 'But you haven't yet, and you and your sister have inherited the business and the property, is this not correct?'

He'd already had his legal team double check the details while he was flying across the Irish Sea, so it was a rhetorical question, but she surprised him with the bluntness of her answer.

'Yes, we did, but we also inherited the debts. The property has already been remortgaged and we can't meet the interest payments any more.'

She and her sister would be left with less than nothing from the sale, by his calculation, because their father had frittered away the family business and more thanks to a gambling habit the family had kept secret for years.

'I understand you might want to get an even cheaper price by rushing the sale, but, believe me, you're already getting a bargain,' she said, the snap of pride in her voice suddenly making her seem older than her dewy skin and wide emerald eyes suggested.

'I'm not here to get a bargain, I'm here to offer you a chance to get out of this without debts still to pay.'

'How so?' she asked, the scepticism in her face making him realise that, however young she was, she was not naïve.

'I will pay off all your debts today, by bank transfer, a sum which is in excess of what the business is worth, by approximately five million euro,' he said. 'Thus leaving you free to sell the property to me, immediately afterwards, for the sum of one euro, and the liquidators will still get their cut.'

It was a fair deal, a smart deal, for her as well as for him. She and her sister would be free and clear of her father's debts to start a new life. They would still be homeless but, as the daughter of one of racing's first families, she would no doubt have opportunities if she was willing to work hard, and much to his surprise—because he would have expected her to be an idle, entitled debutante instead of the girl he had found mucking out a stable— she seemed willing to do that much at least.

But more importantly, the property would not be put up for auction, so his father would have no opportunity to bid against him.

He saw her shock at his proposal.

'So, do we have a deal?' he said, confident of her answer. She had to know it was her only chance to get out from under the mountain of debt her father had left her with.

'No,' she said.

'I beg your pardon?' he snapped, surprised by the swell of something in his gut at her stubborn expression.

Why should he be impressed by her stupidity?

'I…' Heat blossomed in her cheeks. 'I… I said no. We don't have a deal. I have a request.'

He frowned. Was she actually serious?

'I don't think you understand, Ms Calhoun. This isn't a negotiation. It's a time-limited offer. And by far the best offer you are going to get. If I walk out that door today and I am not the new owner of Calhouns, the business will be sold at auction on Saturday as already arranged by the liquidators for a great deal less money than I am offering to spend on acquiring it today.'

'I understand that, but you need the deal signed today. Which gives me some leverage—won't you at least hear my request?'

She was trying to appear calm, but the riot of colour that had flared across her collarbone, and was giving him more unfortunate recollections of the sight of her barely clothed and soaking wet, suggested she was far from composed. His impatience downgraded a notch. The woman was an enigma in many ways… Who would have expected to find her mucking out her own stable, sweaty from work she could get an employee to do? Or cleaning herself down with a hose? But then again, from the state of her home—the faded carpets, worn furniture and peeling paintwork—he was getting the definite impression the Calhoun stud had been struggling financially for a lot longer than anyone had realised. How many staff did they even have? He'd only met an old man called Gerry who seemed to be manning the phones and an elderly housekeeper named Maeve so far.

'I'm listening,' he said, surprising himself with the decision to at least hear her out.

'I… I want a job.'

'What job?' he demanded, but strangely, the moment he said it, Dane's foolish suggestion from earlier that day echoed across his consciousness.

All you've gotta do is find yourself a woman who is greedy or desperate enough to be bought.

'Any job that will keep me at Calhouns. I've been managing the stud for the last five years. I know racing and horses, including everything there is to know about the ones we have left here.' She paused and he saw sadness and possibly even shame cross her face. 'My… My father stopped working with the horses after my mother died… So the successes we've had on the track in the last five years have been down to the team I've put together here. I'd really like the opportunity to keep working with them…'

She carried on talking, rushing through a list of her credentials and successes, which might or might not be true, but he was only listening with half an ear now as he turned over the possibility forming in his head.

He'd dismissed Dane's suggestion he take a wife in name only out of hand four hours ago. It was extreme and unnecessary and frankly ludicrous. But the benefits of keeping his father off his back—perhaps with an arrangement slightly less extreme—and having a Calhoun on his arm when entering the world of racing began to appeal to him as he watched her breasts rise and fall under the utilitarian shirt. Her eyes had widened with expectation as she continued to plead for a role at the stud.

He would need a lot more than simply her say-so to give her a position in management here, but he had another position that she could well be perfectly suited for. His reaction to her in the stables had been an anathema. She was the exact opposite of the sort of woman he would

normally wish to have in his bed. Plain and unsophisticated, and far too slender… Although…

'How old are you?' he interrupted her frantic stream
of information about herself.

'Umm, twenty-two.'

Relief coursed through him. So not a teenager. Thank
God.

She might look fresh faced but from the awareness he
had seen flash into her eyes when he had first discovered her in the stables, and the way her body had visibly
responded to him, he suspected she was far from innocent. Even better.

'I'll consider giving you a job on my team here,' he
said, deciding he could offer her that much, once he no
longer had need of her. 'And throw in an extra million
euro to keep your sister and yourself solvent after the
sale goes through,' he added on the spur of the moment.
It was only money after all and he wanted her compliant
for what he had in mind. 'But I have a different position
in mind for now.'

'That… That would be incredible,' she said, the blush
turning her face to a becoming shade of pink. 'Whatever
the position is I'm sure I can do it. I'm very adaptable.
I realise you don't know me,' she said, getting ahead of
herself again as he continued to study her. 'I'm happy
to work a probation period, as long as I can keep working with our horses,' she added, a little frantically, the
leap of desperate hope sparkling in her deep green eyes.

Desperate was good, eager to please even more so,
it made her all but perfect for the role he had in mind.
Except…

He let his gaze drift over her slender frame again, the
boyish clothes, the lack of make-up and the wild hair
now beginning to curl around her ears, and still felt the

inexplicable ripple of arousal that had surprised him in the stables, annoyingly.

But perhaps it was easily explained. She was pretty enough and her gauche, guileless demeanour made her quite different from the women he usually dated. Her novelty value would soon wear off, though, making this inexplicable reaction easy to control going forward. Not only that, but he planned to make finding a new mistress a top priority as soon as he returned to London. Once he had another woman in his bed, his attraction for this only passably pretty, artless tomboy would surely cease altogether.

'What job did you have in mind for me, Mr Khan?' she said, having finally wound down long enough to ask.

'I want you to become my fiancée, Ms Calhoun.'

CHAPTER THREE

'W-What did you say?' Orla croaked, the shock blasting up her torso with a humiliating surge of heat.

Had he just proposed to her? No, he couldn't have. She must be having some kind of weird auditory hallucination to go with her even weirder physical reaction to his sharp, dispassionate gaze—which she'd imagined a moment ago was assessing her as if she were one of the stud's prize brood mares.

'I said, I want you to become my fiancée.' The words left his lips and reached her eardrums, bringing with them another surge of inappropriate heat. But they still didn't make any sense whatsoever.

Perhaps she had lapsed into a coma? Or was this some bizarre pseudo-erotic dream? Maybe she hadn't woken up at all this morning, hadn't spent an hour on the gallops exercising Aderyn and another five hours mucking out the stalls? Perhaps she was still in her bed upstairs, having fallen asleep scrolling through images of this man on the Internet…

'I… I…' she stuttered, wishing she could pinch herself to wake up. 'You want to marry me? But you don't even know me! We've never even dated.'

Or kissed, she thought irrationally, because that was all she could seem to focus on, along with his firm, sensual lips and that incredible face, which even with the inscrutable frown made him overwhelmingly gorgeous.

His eyebrows rose and then his mouth quirked in a wry smile. The once-over he gave her made every one of her pulse points pound, not to mention making the hot sweet spot between her thighs go molten—which had been overheating ever since she'd stood in front of him in the stables, soaking wet with torpedo nipples.

'I don't wish to marry you,' he said. 'Or date you,' he added as if she'd suggested something mildly amusing. She felt the bubble of anticipation she hadn't even realised was under her breastbone deflate and the renewed wash of humiliation roll over her. 'It would be an engagement in name only,' he continued. 'For which we would sign a binding contract. I would require you to be on my arm, and to act the dutiful, loving, soon-to-be wife, at any and all social and business events I frequent, to maintain the impression of a real relationship. We would have to establish that for the press—and for the racing fraternity, where I will use your connections to establish myself in the racing world…'

Connections? What connections?

She didn't have any connections in the racing world, because she'd always worked furiously behind the scenes, maintaining the fiction that the great Michael Calhoun was still the holder of the Calhoun legacy, long after he'd lost himself in his grief and his addiction. She had worked closely with the jockeys and the trainers and other stud managers, but she didn't know any of the big movers and shakers in the racing fraternity personally. Only the Quinns, the owners of the neighbouring stud, and after the devastating end of her engagement to Patrick they'd shunned her.

She'd been happy to remain anonymous, out of the

way. Doing the work she loved with the horses. The socialite aspects of the racing world were something she
had no interest in whatsoever and no aptitude for. Patrick
had made that very clear to her.

She chewed on her bottom lip, knowing she couldn't
tell Karim Khan the truth of the matter or he might withdraw his bizarre offer—which she was more than desperate enough to be seriously considering.

'But once everyone is convinced the engagement is
real,' he continued, with about as much emotion as if he
were discussing the weather, 'you will be free to carry
on your own affairs, as long as they remain discreet.'

Affairs!

Her blush incinerated as she registered what he was
saying. Somehow she managed to pluck a coherent question out of the fog of unwanted desire and utter confusion.

'How long would that be for?' she asked. 'That you'd
need us to pretend to be in love?'

He stared at her, his jaw tightening at the mention of
the L word, as if the reality of what he was asking her
to fake hadn't occurred to him. But then it occurred to
her, any man who would consider buying a fiancée probably didn't know the first thing about real relationships,
let alone love.

'Until it is no longer useful for me to have a fiancée…'
he said with supreme arrogance.

Right, of course, the parameters of this arrangement
would be dictated by him, because he would be paying
for the privilege.

'But, why would you be needing one?' she asked, curious now. If even the mention of love made him flinch,
why would a man like him consider such an arrangement? Sure, maybe he wanted to be accepted in the racing world, but the truth was buying the stud would do

that, he didn't need her. Even if she had the connections he thought she did. Money spoke louder than legacy in racing, just like any other sport. And surely he could have any woman he wanted on his arm? Why would he have to pay one to pretend to be in love with him? It was madness.

'A fake fiancée, that is?' she clarified, because the muscle in his jaw had only hardened.

'I'm paying you a million euros to do a job, Ms Calhoun, precisely because I have no desire to explain myself. Do you want it or not?'

She should tell him no. That she didn't want to be his fake fiancée. That she couldn't be bought. And that she would be terrible at it anyway. But somehow the words wouldn't come out of her mouth. Even though she now knew she definitely wasn't dreaming, this was actually real.

'Could Dervla and I keep the house? If we didn't take the money?' she asked. The old pile was the only home they'd ever known. And she didn't need a million euros, she just needed a chance.

He glanced around the room, probably taking in the ancient carpet, the few remaining pieces of furniture too old and worn to have any resale value, the damp patch in the corner by the dresser and the faded spots on the wallpaper where art had once been hung but had long since been sold—to pay for her father's gambling debts.

Michael Calhoun had needed an escape from the pain of losing the love of his life, her mother. Unfortunately his escape had eventually drained any semblance of the man she had once known, until all that was left was a shadow. The house reflected that.

'You can keep the property instead if you wish as I

have no need of it. But I will require you to be at my beck and call, and to travel with me for the events I mentioned.'

Her chest tightened, the sinking sensation in her stomach not making a lot of sense. This was a business deal effectively. She couldn't allow her emotions to get in the way. He didn't want *her*, he wanted her name, her heritage and, for reasons unknown, he needed a fiancée.

This was a chance, she told herself, to keep her family home, and to give her sister a place to live while she was at Trinity. Because Dervla could easily commute into Dublin from here. Of course, if Khan found out Orla was socially dyslexic and knew nothing about how to impress racing high society or any other high society, and that she was also a virgin, he might withdraw the offer. How was she supposed to behave like a woman in love when she'd never even taken a lover, and certainly not a man as—she drew in a deep breath—as far out of her league as him?

But even as all the things that could go wrong bombarded her, the hot ache between her thighs refused to go away.

'When would you need me to start?' she asked.

A rueful smile tilted his lips and his gaze sharpened. 'You would return with me to London tonight and we will sign the engagement contract first thing in the morning.'

So soon. Her mind began to race again, along with her pulse rate, the hot spot in her abdomen dropping deeper into her sex.

'I am attending the Jockeys' Ball at The Chesterton Hotel tomorrow evening,' he continued. 'We can announce our engagement and the sale of the stud at the same time.'

She blinked and swallowed around the wodge of panic working its way up her throat and threatening to gag her.

Of course, The Jockeys' Ball was tomorrow at the luxury six-star hotel in Soho. Everyone who was anyone in racing would be there, as it was the main social event to mark the middle of the racing calendar in Europe. She'd attended only once, with Patrick and her father, five years ago, and hated every minute of it. Feeling exposed and inadequate and out of her depth. How much more out of her depth would she be if she were there posing as Karim Khan's trophy fiancée? But even as the panic began to consume her, she forced herself to breathe. Once they had signed the contract, he wouldn't be able to change his mind. Would he?

She'd just have to wing it. And hope to heck he didn't find out how inadequate she was for the role he wanted her to play before tomorrow night—when it would become all too apparent.

'So, do we have a deal, Ms Calhoun?' he demanded. The tone was arrogant and commanding, those golden-brown eyes still doing diabolical things to her heart rate. She needed to get that reaction under control, asap. 'What is your first name, by the way?' he asked.

The question was so incongruous, she almost laughed. He'd just asked her to pretend to be madly in love with him, and he didn't even know her given name?

'It's Orla,' she said, feeling as if she were mounting a large, unbroken stallion for the first time—both terrified and yet also weirdly exhilarated.

She and Dervla would have their home, and she could continue to work with the horses. *Eventually.* All she had to do was cling on for the ride in the next few weeks and months—because surely he wouldn't want her for much longer than that—and hope to heck she didn't end up breaking her neck, metaphorically speaking.

'So, Orla, what's it to be?' he pushed, making no effort to hide his impatience.

'Yes,' she said, with a firmness and determination she didn't feel. 'Yes, we do have a deal, Mr Khan.'

'Call me Karim,' he said, although it sounded like an order rather than a request. He tugged his smartphone out of his pocket and she realised she had already been dismissed. 'You have half an hour to pack—don't forget your passport,' he said as he checked something on his phone. 'We can do all the necessary paperwork on the sale and the engagement contract after we get to London.' His gaze locked back on her face. 'I wish to take another look round the stud, so I'll meet you at the Puma at a quarter to two,' he said. 'Don't leave me waiting this time.'

Moments later, his footsteps had faded down the hallway.

Orla stood in the empty room and wrapped her arms round her midriff to hold in the shudder of panic and something a great deal more volatile. She walked to the window and gazed out on the land that had always been her home. The only place where she felt grounded and whole and significant.

What she'd just agreed to do was madness. The arrogant, entitled, overwhelming man had even refused to tell her why he needed a fake fiancée. And why on earth he might have picked her for such a role.

Karim Khan, Crown Prince of Zafar, held all the power in this situation and she none.

But beggars could not be choosers, and she refused to regret taking his devil's bargain—Dervla and the horses and their home were worth it.

To have a future free of debt, and the opportunity to continue living in the place she'd thought they'd lost, was something she couldn't even have dreamed of when she'd woken up this morning before dawn. Life had been so hard ever since her father passed in a car accident a year ago—much longer than that, truth be told, ever since her mother's tragic death while riding on the gallops five years ago had effectively robbed her and Dervla of their father too.

She and her sister deserved this chance.

All she had to do now was find a way to show everyone she had what it took to make a crown prince fall hopelessly in love with her—when she knew full well she didn't. Not even close.

This will be an adventure, she told herself staunchly.

But then the bottom dropped out of her stomach and heat careered through her veins as she spied the tall, indomitable, commanding man she had just agreed to attach herself to for the foreseeable future walk out of the house and take long strides across the lawn towards the stables.

She hadn't even managed to convince Patrick she would make him a good wife, and now she was going to have to pretend to be engaged to a man who could give her breathing difficulties and inappropriate goosebumps just by looking at her. A man she knew virtually nothing about. And what she did know only made him a hundred times more intimidating.

Orla Calhoun, what in the name of all that is holy have you gone and done now?

CHAPTER FOUR

'Miss Calhoun, you must wake up now. Mr Khan wishes to see you downstairs.'

Orla blinked furiously, waking from a particularly vivid dream, to find an older woman smiling at her. She jerked upright, taking in the feel of expensive cotton sheets and the bright sunlight streaming through the large multi-paned window opposite and shining onto a suite of luxury furniture.

'Hi,' she said, as the reality of where she was and what she had agreed to yesterday spun back through her groggy brain.

Standing in the stables, dripping wet, her nipples so hard they ached as Karim Khan's golden gaze awakened every one of her nerve-endings. His overpowering presence in her faded parlour, asking, no, *demanding* she become his fiancée. The mad scramble to ensure Dervla would look after the horses to her satisfaction before Khan's team arrived. The helicopter ride across the Irish Sea and the British countryside, before they'd flown over the nightlights of London to land on the rooftop heliport of Khan's mansion in Belgravia.

He'd hardly spoken to her since she had agreed to become his fake fiancée, spending the time while piloting the chopper talking to a series of subordinates through his headphones. Once they'd arrived, she'd been ushered into the house and served dinner alone in the suite of rooms she now occupied, and then she'd dropped into bed...

'Is it Mrs Williams?' she asked, trying to remember the woman's name from the night before. She was one of Mr Khan's staff. His housekeeper, Orla was fairly sure, but everything about the evening before had been a blur, the extravagant luxury of Khan's home and the thought of what she'd agreed to do making it hard for Orla to concentrate when she'd been introduced to about twenty people before being brought to her own luxury suite.

She'd dreamt of him, she realised, during the night. That intense gaze had woken her frequently causing the hot weight in her sex, and the tight ache in her breasts.

'Call me Edith, dear,' the woman said as she laid a breakfast tray on a table by the window with practised efficiency. 'Mr Khan has employed a stylist to acquire a new wardrobe for you. But I had your clothes from last night washed and pressed for the meeting this morning.' The housekeeper smiled. 'I hope that's okay, but I couldn't find anything else in your luggage that looked suitable when I unpacked it.'

'That's perfect,' Orla said, remembering the one humiliating conversation she'd had with Khan before boarding the helicopter in Kildare.

'Do you have any suitable clothing with you?' he'd asked, casting a cursory glance at the rucksack she'd packed hastily in the half-hour he'd given her.

'You didn't give me much time to pack,' she'd replied, not wanting to admit she had nothing suitable for the sort of rarefied social gatherings he was probably expecting her to attend. She hadn't had money for new clothes in years. Plus she lived in boots and jeans and T-shirts to work with the horses, and was already wearing her best clothing.

He'd nodded and lifted the rucksack into the helicopter. End of conversation. Obviously he had made a note of her lack of a decent wardrobe and arranged for new clothing.

She tried not to feel even more humiliated—at the thought of having to be dressed by him—as she climbed out of the bed and tugged on the silk robe that Edith had laid out at the end of the bed.

'The solicitor has already arrived to finalise the sale,' the housekeeper said. 'Mr Khan is keen to see you as soon as possible downstairs.' The woman sent Orla a warm, uncomplicated smile. 'He's even more impatient than usual. You two must be very much in love.'

Say what, now?

'Um, yes,' Orla murmured, struggling to control the full body blush that was currently incinerating her.

So the Crown Prince hadn't told his staff the truth about their engagement.

'Please call me Orla, by the way,' she added, unused to the formality with her own family's staff. The few she had been able to retain had become friends and allies over the last few years.

'Oh, I couldn't do that, Miss Calhoun. Mr Khan wouldn't approve,' the housekeeper replied. 'After all, you are going to become the Crown Princess of Zafar.'

The surreal unreality of the situation struck Orla again as she watched the housekeeper finish laying out the breakfast.

'Now, I must get back downstairs. Would you like me to send up one of the maids, to help you dress?' she asked.

'No, really, I'm good,' Orla replied.

'Can I tell the Crown Prince you'll be down in half an

hour?' Edith asked, the hopeful look making Orla wonder if the housekeeper was going to get chastised by her employer if she didn't get a move on.

'Yes, absolutely,' Orla said, even though the last thing she wanted to do was see him again. There wasn't much point in postponing the meeting, though, especially if it was going to get Edith into trouble.

The woman smiled then left Orla standing alone in the room.

Abandoning the breakfast, she headed for the suite's palatial bathroom. With her stomach churning she wouldn't be able to swallow a bite of the lavish display of fresh fruit, pastries, pancakes and eggs and bacon, laid out on the table.

Her stomach turned over again. And even if she could, she doubted she would be able to keep it down once she got downstairs.

Twenty-nine minutes later, Orla arrived downstairs, to be greeted by a butler who led her to Khan's study, a large, beautifully appointed room that looked onto the mansion's extensive gardens.

Her heart pummelled her tonsils as she spotted Khan's muscular frame silhouetted against the large mullioned window. In dark grey expertly tailored suit trousers and a white shirt rolled up at the sleeve, showing off the dark skin of his forearms, he looked like exactly what he was—a rich, powerful and supremely confident playboy prince. He turned as she entered the room. And her lungs squeezed.

Correction: a rich, powerful, supremely confident and impossibly hot playboy prince.

'Orla, at last,' he said. The familiarity of her name on his lips made her pulse rate accelerate as he strode across the thick carpeting to greet her. But when he took her hand and lifted her fingers, she jolted, the hot weight in her abdomen ready to detonate, as he skimmed her knuckles with his lips.

It was the first time he had touched her, let alone with such familiarity—the feel of his lips, firm and entitled, had sensation racing through her body. She struggled to relax as his eyes narrowed with displeasure.

Then she spotted the other man in the room for the first time.

The charade had begun, she realised, and she had already made a mess of things.

Was he angry with her? He had to be—he was paying her a great deal of money to play his besotted bride-to-be. But the slight frown had gone and all she could see in his gaze was something that looked like scepticism.

Taking her hand in a firm grip, he folded her arm over his, trapping her against his side to escort her across the room. Unwanted desire raced over her skin, but she forced herself to breathe.

Act natural, you're supposed to be lovers, you dope.

'This is the head of my legal team, Orla, Phillip Carstairs, who has some papers for you to sign,' he said, introducing her to the other man.

'Ms Calhoun.' The dignified man in his fifties greeted her with a warm smile. 'I'm so pleased to meet you at last. Karim has been telling me all about your whirlwind courtship. My wife will be starry-eyed when I give her the details,' the solicitor added, without a hint of sarcasm, as he held out his hand.

'Thank you, Mr Carstairs.' She shook his hand, trying to stop her own from shaking and look suitably excited—while wondering what the story was Khan had told his solicitor. It might have been nice if he'd bothered to clue her in.

'Yes, it all happened so very fast,' she added, directing an awestruck look at the man beside her.

Not surprisingly, that wasn't at all hard to fake, as she felt Khan's biceps flex and the warm skin of his bare forearm—lightly furred with hair—burned her fingertips.

Khan turned his searing gaze on her.

'Would you like Phillip to take you through the sales contract for the stud before you sign, Orla?' he asked. It seemed to be a genuine offer, even though she could sense his impatience.

'Does it contain everything we agreed?' she asked.

'Of course,' he said.

She nodded as Carstairs laid out the papers. 'I'm happy to sign it now,' she said, having skimmed through the details. Oddly she trusted him. The perfunctory nature of their relationship so far made it very clear he viewed her as nothing more than another of his employees. Bought and paid for. He hadn't quibbled about any of her requirements and had actually been much more generous than he needed to be. Money was clearly no object for him. She needed to view this situation as a job. And nothing more. A job she wanted to do well—she couldn't risk him changing his mind.

She could see she had pleased him when the wrinkle that had formed on his forehead when she reacted so violently to a simple hand buzz disappeared.

'Excellent,' he said.

'We'll have the contract couriered to your sister in Kildare to sign too. I understand she has already agreed to these terms as well?' Carstairs said as he handed her a gold pen.

'Yes, that's correct,' Orla said, recalling Dervla's joy

at the news they would be able to stay in their home with no debts to pay.

Orla signed her name in bold fluid strokes. The nuns who had schooled her would be proud, she thought, grateful that her fingers had finally stopped shaking.

It wasn't nearly as hard as she had assumed to sign away her heritage. The stud was just a business. It was the horses she loved, and her sister, and their home. The chance to get out of the shadow of debt that had been hanging over her for so long felt strangely liberating.

But then Carstairs laid out some more papers in both English and what looked like Arabic. 'Would you like to read through these, Ms Calhoun?' the solicitor asked. 'This is the English translation of the traditional Zafari Engagement Contract. I'm afraid it's a legal requirement in Mr Khan's country of origin that the Crown Prince's engagement must be accompanied by a binding contract, to ensure the cultural traditions as well as the economic interests of Zafar are observed and protected before the couple enter into a marriage.'

Orla nodded, then skimmed through the pages—the small type blurring before her eyes. She didn't need to read them, because they weren't ever going to get actually married. 'Great,' she said at last.

Khan's hand rested on the small of her back, rubbing absently as he signed the original first. He handed her the pen, still warm from his fingers, and Carstairs pointed out the places where she needed to sign and initial the paperwork. She could feel Khan's gaze focussed on her, the hand on her back like a heavy controlling weight. She doubted he was even aware of what he was doing, the caress as nonchalant as it was impersonal. But the sensation sprinting up her spine from his touch was anything but.

Her penmanship was forgotten this time as she dashed

off each signature and initial as quickly as possible. She needed to get this over, before she lost her nerve—or, worse, reacted in a way that would give away, not just her lack of familiarity with Khan and their so-called whirlwind courtship, but also her complete lack of sophistication when it came to being touched with such easy familiarity by a man.

She'd shared kisses with Patrick, of course, when they'd been engaged. But she'd been a girl then—naïve and eager, sheltered and completely untried. And Patrick, although having a great deal more sexual experience than she had at the time, had been a boy, not a man like Khan, who could light bonfires across her back with a simple caress.

At last all the paperwork was done.

But then she heard Mr Carstairs laugh and murmur, 'Perhaps you should kiss your new fiancée, Karim.'

'Yes,' the deep voice said beside her.

She tried to control her trembling, scared he might be able to feel it, as he turned her in his arms and rested his hands on her hips. He was studying her, the curiosity in his gaze both pragmatic and yet somehow exhilarating.

Could he see how inexperienced she was, and how much his nearness affected her? She hoped not, terrified he might annul the engagement before it had even begun.

He lifted his hand and placed it on her neck, holding her gently in place. The calluses on his palm, calluses she would not have expected, rasped across the sensitive skin, making her brutally aware of the light pressure. His thumb rubbed casually across the well in her collarbone, back and forth, as he watched her—the golden shards in the brown of his irises so vivid they mesmerised her. He lowered his head, gradually, allowing her to taste the toothpaste on his breath as it whispered across her lips.

His thumb paused, and pressed into her collarbone, trapping the frantic butterfly flutters of her pulse.

She suddenly had the vision of one of Calhouns' stable hands stroking their highly strung mare, Cliona, to quiet her for Aderyn to mount her. The thought turned the tremble into a violent shiver.

She stiffened. He had to have felt that now.

His other hand tightened on her hip, gentle, yet controlling, and even more overwhelming as he whispered for only her to hear, 'Shh, Orla. Breathe.'

Then his lips finally settled on hers, firm, seeking, confident, commanding.

Electricity seemed to arch through her body, the yearning so swift and so strong, she forgot everything but the scent, the taste, the touch of his lips. The solid wall of his chest pressed against her aching breasts as he dragged her closer.

Her hands flattened against his waist, grasping his linen shirt in greedy fists, and holding on for dear life as the storm of sensation battered her body, while her heart thumped her ribcage and sank deep into her abdomen, throbbing painfully between her thighs.

His tongue slid across her mouth demanding entry and she opened instinctively. His guttural groan of conquest matched her sob of surrender as she melted against him, her body softening and swelling in its most intimate places as his tongue swept in.

He explored in demanding delicious strokes, and she made tentative licks back, the yearning so intense now, the longing so real and overpowering she knew that whatever it was she wanted from him, she needed it now.

He tore his lips free, and stared down at her. His hands lifted to cradle her cheeks, and tilt her face up. She saw surprise flicker in his dark eyes as he studied her, but knew it was nothing compared with the shock careering through her body. Her breathing was so ragged her lungs felt trapped in her ribcage.

The loud throat-clearing from beside them had them both swinging round.

'Congratulations, you two,' Phillip Carstairs said with an avuncular smile on his face. 'I would suggest you start planning the wedding as soon as possible.'

The heat that still pounded between Orla's thighs and burned on her lips exploded into her cheeks like a mushroom cloud.

Khan let go of her face at last as he turned to his solicitor. 'Thanks, Phil, now perhaps you'd like to get lost, so my new fiancée and I can have some privacy.'

Carstairs gathered up the papers Orla had just signed, then sent them both a mocking bow. 'I'd say enjoy your engagement, Karim,' he said. 'But I can see there is really no need.' He held the papers up. 'I'll send the engagement contract through to the Zafari Ruling Council so they can inform your father of the good news.'

Orla felt Karim tense beside her, before Carstairs bid them both goodbye and left the room.

The door closed behind him.

'I should go too,' Orla murmured, brutally aware of the embarrassment scalding her cheeks and the heavy weight that had swollen to impossible proportions in her sex. Luckily Khan seemed a million miles away, his expression both strained and annoyed.

She had no idea what had caused his displeasure. But before she could make a quick getaway he snagged her wrist.

'Not so fast,' he said, drawing her to a halt. 'That kiss was unexpected.'

'I… I was just trying to be convincing,' she said, not even convincing herself with the desperate lie.

She could see she hadn't convinced him either, when his brows drew together, the puzzled expression doing nothing to cool the passionate intensity in the golden brown of his irises.

'You did an extremely thorough job,' he said, the mocking tone making it very clear he knew her response had been entirely genuine.

She tried to look away to hide the mortification running riot on her cheeks now, but he tucked a knuckle under her chin and forced her gaze back to his.

'Just tell me one thing—are you a virgin?' he demanded.

Her eyes widened. How had he guessed?

'Because if you are,' he continued, the dark frown on his face accusing her, 'we'll have to call this off.'

'I'm not a virgin,' she lied, finally managing to gather her wits enough to shake her head. 'I've had several lovers,' she added. 'Lots of lovers. I was… I was engaged five years ago,' she continued, desperately trying to dispel the scepticism lurking in his eyes. She couldn't lose this deal—the chance to stay at Calhouns, to secure a future free of debt, to continue to work with the horses she loved. But somehow those reasons seemed shallow and insignificant as the desire continued to spark and sizzle.

'Do you really think I would have kissed you like that if I was?' she finished.

Once upon a time, she'd been a terrible liar, but she'd had considerable practice in the last five years, convincing everyone from jockeys to trainers to racing managers that Calhouns wasn't struggling to stay afloat. She drew on every last ounce of that experience now to convince him.

He continued to study her, the desire he was making

no attempt to hide both disturbing and yet at the same time terrifyingly exciting.

'No, I suppose not,' he said finally.

He shook his head slightly, as if trying to jog something loose, then let go of her wrist abruptly.

Shoving his hands into the pockets of his suit trousers, he continued to stare at her, the penetrating gaze both intrusive and disturbingly intimate.

She folded her arms over her midriff, feeling exposed and desperately wary, far too aware of the stinging on her lips where their kiss had got so far out of control.

But she forced herself not to relinquish eye contact. If she was going to persuade him she wasn't a virgin, she needed to be bold now, even if her hormones were still rampaging through her body like toddlers on a sugar rush... And she'd never felt more insecure or unstable in her entire life.

She didn't know what the heck had happened to her. Maybe she didn't have very much experience, but she'd never responded like that to any of Patrick's kisses.

How had she forgotten so easily who he was, and that this 'engagement' was a charade? The minute his lips had claimed hers, even before that, the minute he had looked at her with that intense focus back at the stable yard, it was as if her body were no longer her own. That it belonged to him, and he could command it and destroy it at will.

She couldn't let that happen again, or she would lose. Not just this deal, but also her sense of self.

This engagement was a means to an end for him. A means to an end he hadn't even bothered to confide in her. She was bought and paid for, a fiancée in name only, until he no longer required her services, then she would be discarded.

He tugged his fingers through his hair, sending the expertly styled waves into disarray, still staring at her as if he were trying to decipher a particularly thorny problem.

At last he nodded. 'I'll see you tonight at seven,' he said.

Her breath gushed out as she realised she'd got away with her lie. For now anyhow.

'We'll go through the story I've made up to explain our relationship en route to the ball,' he added. 'So you don't trip up again.'

It was a reprimand. But she didn't care as she nodded and left, just so relieved to be out of the room.

As she raced up the stairs back to her suite, though, she wasn't sure any more if she was more concerned about Khan cancelling their contract, and leaving her sister and herself destitute, or her inexplicable and uncontrollable reaction to a simple kiss.

CHAPTER FIVE

'YOUR HIGHNESS, YOUR fiancée is waiting for you in the vestibule.'

Karim glanced up from his phone to find Muhammed, his butler, standing in the doorway to his study.

Your fiancée.

The words reverberated in his skull… and, unfortunately, his groin, reminding him of their kiss that morning. A kiss that was supposed to have been as false as everything else about this arrangement, and had been anything but. Orla Calhoun's artless eager reaction had been unexpected, but much more unexpected had been his own response. The fresh sweet taste of her lips, the sound of her stunned sob, the feel of her taut, trembling body softening against his, and her fingers gripping his shirt as if she were in a high wind and he were her only anchor. The combination had set fire to the heat already smouldering in his groin, ever since the day before.

All of which was a problem.

He had picked this woman precisely because he had expected his desire to die. Clearly that had been an error, because after that one taste of her he had not been able to forget the effect she'd had on him. Or the fact he wanted more of her. Desiring her could cause complications he did not need.

Thank God, at least she wasn't inexperienced, as he had at first suspected. Ever since their kiss he had been considering the problem, and decided that perhaps they could change the terms of their contract. However he needed to be absolutely sure this attraction was not going to get any more out of control. Already he did not appreciate the fact his reaction had been almost as uncontrolled as hers.

'Tell her I'll be with her in a moment,' he said, tucking the phone back into the breast pocket of his tuxedo.

Tonight's event would be long and tedious. Her racing connections would come in handy to smooth his passage into this world. It would also present a good chance to gauge exactly how volatile his reaction was to this woman.

'Yes, Your Highness,' the butler said, but then his usually formal expression softened. 'And can I congratulate you again on your engagement?' he added, his craggy face flushing. 'Your fiancée is indeed exquisite and so charming. I had no idea Michael Calhoun's daughter was such a beauty. No wonder he hid her away.'

What?

Karim frowned as his usually close-mouthed and now clearly besotted butler bowed and left. Orla, whatever the strange spell she seemed to have cast over him, could hardly be described as a great beauty. Could she? And what did Muhammed mean by Calhoun hiding her away? Karim had never attended any racing events, waiting for the right opportunity to buy into a pastime that had captivated him as a boy but which he'd had no time to indulge properly until now. Perhaps he should have done more homework before suggesting this association? The truth was it wasn't at all like him to make business decisions on the spur of the moment. That said, he always went with his gut instinct when opportunity arose, and Orla's circumstances had seemed perfect for what he had in mind.

He rebuttoned his tuxedo jacket and spotted, on the edge of his desk, the velvet ring box that had been delivered earlier in the day. He scooped up the box and stared at it. He'd had the engagement ring selected by the stylist. He shoved it into his trouser pocket without opening it, annoyed by the moment of hesitation. It hardly mattered what the ring looked like, as long as it fitted.

He marched out of his study, down the hallway towards the front entrance and then stopped dead as he spotted the woman standing with her back to him. The silver backless gown shimmered in the light from the chandelier, the iridescent material draping over her slender curves like water. The vibrant red waves of her hair had been pinned up with a series of diamonds, which glittered like stars in a sunset. The chignon should have looked supremely elegant… But somehow, the tendrils falling down against her nape made him think of the wild, untamed way she had returned his kiss.

Karim's breath backed up in his lungs, the shot of arousal so sudden it made him tense. He planted his hands in his pockets, the urge to slip the delicate straps off her shoulders and place his mouth on the smooth arch of her neck so strong he had to take a moment.

'Orla,' he murmured, and she spun round.

What the…?

Shock ricocheted through his system, swiftly followed by a need so sharp he couldn't contain it, let alone control it.

'What the hell are you wearing?' he growled before he could stop himself as the shot of desire detonated in his groin.

His gaze devoured her high breasts, the neckline of the

gown giving him a glimpse of her cleavage, which was as torturous as it was tantalising. She was not wearing a bra.

'You don't... You don't like it?' she asked as she crossed her arms over her waist, as if trying to shield herself from his view.

His gaze jerked away from her breasts to see the flush of embarrassment on her face. Smoky make-up had been deftly applied around her eyes and her full lips given a coating of something glossy, which only made the yearning to taste them again all the more compelling.

But beneath that, he could see the devastating combination of embarrassment and awareness in her expression.

He forced himself to move across the foyer, attempting to dial down his overreaction each step of the way. He'd seen other women wearing far less at the sort of society functions he attended. Hell, women he'd actually been dating had worn gowns that were a great deal more revealing, and he'd never had a problem with it.

Was this something to do with the fact she was his fiancée? But that was insane—this wasn't a real engagement. And even if it were, since when had he ever been possessive about a woman?

In truth there was nothing wrong with the dress, he tried to tell himself, as his gaze lingered again on the shimmering material. No doubt it was the height of fashion, probably made by some much-sought-after designer who charged a fortune to display his new fiancée's lush, coltish physique for everyone to see. In fact, it did exactly what he had asked the stylist to do: made the most of Orla's assets. Unfortunately, he had not realised when he requested such an approach quite how many assets she had, or how much he would not want to allow everyone else to enjoy them.

'It's okay, Orla, the dress is good,' he managed past the lump of lust forming in his throat.

Far too damn good.

He touched her elbow, her instinctive shudder of awareness reminiscent of the livewire moment he'd touched her for the first time that morning.

As she turned into the light, he became momentarily transfixed by the sprinkle of freckles across her cleavage and the glimpse of her naked breast visible at the edge of the gown. Her pulse pounded visibly against the hollow in her neck, giving him a lungful of her scent. The intoxicating aroma reminded him of a country garden, the subtle perfume of wild flowers and the earthy scent of freshly mown grass. He bit down on the urge to nuzzle the translucent skin and nibble kisses along the delectable line of her collarbone.

'Are you sure the dress is okay, Mr Khan?' she said, forcing him back to the present. 'The stylist might have another if you don't like it…' Small white teeth tugged on her bottom lip.

Was she really as sexually experienced as she claimed? he wondered, not for the first time. And why the hell did her guilelessness only intoxicate him more?

'I like it,' he said, which had to be the understatement of the millennium. 'You don't have time to change. And stop calling me Mr Khan. My name is Karim, Orla. Use it.'

Cupping her elbow, he led her out of the door to their waiting car. He needed to get this night over with, so he could think. He wasn't making any more rash decisions where this woman was concerned.

When was the last time a woman had affected him to this extent? The truth was his affairs had become jaded and dull in recent years, and while this livewire attraction was inconvenient, even unwanted, it also had the potential to be pleasurable for both of them.

But before he renegotiated the terms of their liaison, he needed to be sure his new fiancée wasn't going to spring any more unwanted surprises on him.

He held open the passenger door of the convertible he'd selected to drive to the venue tonight. As Orla climbed into the low-slung car, he noticed the split in the gown's skirt, revealing a generous glimpse of pale, toned thigh.

He cursed inwardly as the wave of heat shot straight back into his groin.

He slammed the door and walked around to the driver's side. First thing tomorrow, he was firing the damn stylist.

Mr Khan… Karim was angry with her, and she didn't know what she'd done wrong.

She'd done everything he'd asked. The dress had made her feel exposed and foolish—she'd never worn anything so skimpy before, or so beautiful. But the stylist had insisted it was perfect for her figure and would turn her new fiancé into her 'slave'—the stylist's words, not hers. Of course, the stylist—like the rest of Karim's employees—didn't know this wasn't a real engagement… And that even if she danced naked in front of him it wouldn't turn him into her slave.

But the minute she'd heard the gruff whisper behind her, and turned to see Karim standing staring at her in the vestibule, that intense gaze making her skin prickle and pulse beneath the sheer fabric of the glittery gown, she'd known something was terribly wrong. Because he didn't look pleased, he looked… Volatile.

His movements and his demeanour had been stiff and formal ever since, as if he were trying to hold onto his temper. The shock of seeing him in a tuxedo, his dark good looks somehow even more compelling and dangerous in the formal wear, hadn't helped.

She sat in the car, trying to gather her thoughts and figure out what she could do to make things better between them. If only she had more experience of intimate relationships she might have more of a clue.

He climbed into the car beside her, slammed the door, then pressed a button on the expensive car's state-of-the-art dashboard.

As the engine purred, he reached into his trouser pocket and produced a velvet box.

'Put this on,' he said, as he handed her the box.

She opened the small container. Her breathing slowed, the well-oiled vibrations of the powerful car amplifying the thundering in her ears.

Nestled in the box's black satin lining was an exquisite ring of interwoven rose-gold and silver bands, studded with diamonds but crowned by an emerald. The misty green of the gem reminded her of the colour of the fields in Kildare when the sun hit them for the first time on a summer morning.

'It's stunning,' she managed, round the strange swelling in her throat, as it occurred to her how different this moment was from the day Patrick Quinn had given her an engagement ring. Back then, of course, she'd believed Pat loved her, because she'd been a child with foolish romantic notions, instead of a woman with debts she couldn't repay.

Her heart hurt as the impact of what she'd done that morning—become engaged to a man for money—hit her solidly in the solar plexus.

She touched the ring, but her fingers were trembling too violently for her to pull it out of the box.

'Here,' he said, as he took the box from her. He plucked the engagement band out. 'Give me your hand.'

She placed her left hand in his, far too aware of the warmth of his palm as his fingers closed over hers, gently, in a silent gesture to stop the trembling. Remarkably it worked, his touch so compelling it seemed to command her obedience.

'Which finger does it go on?' he asked.

Her gaze lifted to his, to find him watching her, but instead of frustration or fury what she saw was contemplation, and something else, something that still looked remarkably volatile but not necessarily aimed at her.

'The ring finger,' she said. But when he went to thread the ring on, her finger wobbled.

'Is something wrong?' he asked.

His golden gaze was still fixed on her face. The warmth in her cheeks ignited, but she forced herself to remain pragmatic, even if the aching in her chest had got so much worse as a thought spun into her brain unbidden. What would it be like to have a man as passionate and powerful as Karim Khan truly care for you? To want to cherish and protect you?

'No, nothing,' she said hastily, dismissing the weak, pointless yearning as best she could. She didn't want to have this situation be real. She didn't need any man to cherish and protect her, and certainly not a man like Karim Khan. He might be rich and powerful, but he was also taciturn and cynical and cold... And far too overwhelming for the likes of her. Falling for a man like him would be even more fraught with danger than falling for a man like her skank of an ex-fiancé.

She squeezed her fingers into a fist then straightened them again to stop the trembling. She didn't want him to think she was some kind of foolish romantic, or, worse, that she had any kind of misconceptions about what this relationship was.

He stroked the ring finger with his thumb, then slipped the band on, pushing it down. His thumb slid back over the knuckle, then he let go of her hand. She missed the warmth of his touch instantly.

Her pulse began to punch her collarbone.

'Thank goodness it fits,' he said, his voice a husky murmur.

The tiny diamonds sparkled in the light from an overhead street lamp, exquisite and yet ethereal. She curled her fingers back into a fist and placed both her hands in her lap, painfully aware of the buzz of sensation his touch had ignited, and the cold weight of the ring that didn't really belong to her.

The engagement ring must have cost an absolute fortune, the insignia on the box from London's most exclusive jewellers. Perhaps it was the thought of possessing something so valuable, even for a little while, that was the problem, not the significance of having Karim Khan place his ring on her finger, when that had no real significance at all.

'I'll be sure to take good care of it for you,' she said. 'Until you need it back.'

'Why would I need it back?' he asked, the cutting edge back. Had she done something else wrong?

She stared at his face, the strong planes and angles even more striking cast into shadow by the street lamp. Was he serious? 'Won't you need it when you get engaged for real? It must have cost a fortune.'

He let out a harsh chuckle, as if she'd said something particularly stupid. 'Keep it. The stylist picked it out for you, so it's unlikely to suit any other woman.' He shifted the car into gear. 'And once this is over, I certainly don't intend to do it again.'

As the car peeled away from the kerb, the critical comment ripped through her show of confidence, to the neglected girl beneath.

The light summer breeze whipped at her skin. She squeezed her fist, determined to ignore the ring, and the lump of inadequacy forming in her throat.

This isn't about you, it's not personal. The engagement is a means to an end, he's made no secret of that.

But unfortunately, despite her frantic pep talk, there didn't seem to be much she could do about the heavy weight of his disapproval sinking into the pit of her stomach.

Getting through the next few hours pretending to belong in Karim Khan's rarefied world—and present the picture of a loving fiancée, when she knew she was no kind of fiancée—suddenly seemed insurmountable.

'I told Phillip Carstairs and my financial advisors we met when I visited the stud, and that my decision to pay off the estate's debts were a result of my affection for you.'

'I'm sorry, what?' she said, too preoccupied with her own evolving misery to take stock of what he'd said.

'The story of our whirlwind romance,' he clarified. 'I left it vague, but if anyone questions you simply say the engagement is based on our shared love of horse racing and our…' he paused '…our considerable chemistry.' He glanced her way, trapping her in that intense gaze for a second before he returned his attention to the road. Even so it was enough to reignite the familiar bonfire at her core. 'Which from this morning's evidence appears not to be a lie.'

She swallowed as the bonfire crackled and burned.

Why did knowing his response had been as genuine

and unguarded as hers only make her feel more insecure? And more unsettled?

'I'd say that's not much of a basis for a marriage,' she said, before she could think better of it. She wanted to grab the words back when he sent a sharp glance her way.

'What did you say?'

'I said, I don't think that's much of a basis for a marriage,' she managed, knowing she'd said it now, so no more harm could be done by explaining herself. And anyway, she was tired of worrying about saying or doing the wrong thing constantly. Perhaps if they talked more, he'd realise she was doing her best. 'A shared love of horse racing, that is… And…' She coughed to dislodge the sudden blockage in her throat. 'And chemistry.'

His brows drew down as he approached the traffic lights at Hyde Park Corner. The Corinthian columns of Wellington Arch at the centre of the roundabout and the galloping horses of the bronze statue on top looked particularly imposing illuminated from beneath as the dusk descended over central London. But it was nowhere near as imposing as the silence in the car or the man beside her. Orla's pulse accelerated and the weight in her belly grew. She could sense his disapproval again—seemed she was getting very good at noticing that much about him, at least—but she refused to apologise. Being timid and self-effacing was not a good way to deal with Karim Khan, she decided, because it only gave him more power. And made her feel more useless. If she was going to get through tonight without making some major *faux pas* she was going to need his help… Instead of his disapproval.

'I would have to disagree,' he said at last, finally breaking the agonising silence. 'Chemistry was the *only* element that compelled my father to marry all four of his wives.'

His father had been married four times!

Shock came first, followed by a strange ripple of regret as she acknowledged the bitterness in his tone. No wonder this man had such a jaundiced view of love and relationships if that was his role model.

'Well, you might say that proves my point, rather than disproves it,' she countered.

The lights changed and he drove past the arch.

'How so?' he asked, as he shifted down a gear to accelerate around a delivery truck and make the turn onto Piccadilly.

'Perhaps if he'd considered more than chemistry when choosing a wife, he might not have had four of them.'

The minute the comment had left her mouth his lips drew into a tight line.

She wanted to bite off her tongue. Why couldn't she learn to keep her opinions to herself? Starting an argument with him was hardly the way to go here.

And his father's four failed marriages were not her concern, any more than the bitter disillusionment in his tone was when he'd spoken of them.

But to her surprise, instead of telling her to mind her own business, his lips relaxed and he said, 'A good point. Although incorrect where my father is concerned.'

'How is that?' she asked, trying not to flinch when he sent her another assessing look.

Maybe he didn't want to talk about this, but she needed to know this stuff if she was going to pretend to be in love with him tonight with any degree of success.

Although her own parents' marriage had ended tragically, she could still remember the intimacy between them. Whenever they were together, it was the small possessive touches, the jokes only they shared, the secret looks they sent each other when they thought no one was watching, that announced their love, so much louder than any outward show of emotion or desire.

She suspected, from what Karim had just told her about his father's marriages and his scathing reaction to the L word yesterday, he would be unaware of how a connection like that manifested itself, so it would be up to her to fake that part... And there was no way she could do that if she didn't find out more about him. So surely the avid thundering of her pulse as she waited for him to give her an answer to her question was totally justified.

He sighed as if the question was an inconvenience rather than an intrusion, but when he spoke, she could hear more in his voice than impatience and it made her heart beat even harder.

'My father's reasons for marriage were two-fold: sexual gratification and the production of male heirs. Only two of his wives managed to achieve the latter—my mother and my younger brother Dane's mother—but he grew bored with them all after a few years, at which point they were always discarded.'

The bland, almost bored tone as he described a man who sounded like an arrogant, entitled monster shocked her. But then the car crossed Piccadilly Circus, and the red and gold lights from one of the junction's illuminated advertising hoardings highlighted the tension in his jaw.

Was he really as unaffected by his father's behaviour, or just very good at hiding it?

'He doesn't sound like much of a husband... Or father,' she commented.

'He's not.' His lips twisted into a hard smile. 'But the only wives who suffered were the ones who made the mistake of believing he wanted more,' he added.

Did that include his mother? It was hard to tell from the flat, unsentimental tone.

'What about his children?' she asked softly.

He let out a harsh laugh. 'Dane and I survived without him,' he said.

He sounded unmoved, almost amused by the suggestion any child would need a father—she found his attitude unbearably sad. No wonder Karim Khan could view a relationship as nothing more than a business deal. But didn't every child deserve a father who cared for them as a person—as well as simply a means to continue their legacy? As difficult as it had been to watch her own father change after her mother's death, allowing the grief and eventually the gambling to destroy all their lives, he had loved and nurtured her and her sister once. What would it be like never to have that support?

The silence stretched between them again until a question formed in her mind.

'Won't you have to marry to provide heirs eventually too?' she asked, wondering how he was going to square that with his avowed decision never to do so. 'Being the Crown Prince?'

'My father certainly thinks so,' he said, the coldness in his voice chilling. 'I do not.'

He glanced at her as he flicked up the indicator to turn the car into Seven Dials.

'His attempts to force my hand in the matter are the main reason I decided to acquire you, as it happens,' he added.

Orla blinked, his cynicism making her rub her arms despite the balmy summer evening.

So that was why he had needed a fake fiancée? To stop his father from trying to force him to marry. She supposed it made sense. But all it did was make her feel sadder for him. To have such a dysfunctional relationship with a parent—to know from a young age you had only ever been born for one purpose—couldn't be good for anyone.

But as he braked the car at the small roundabout in the middle of the Seven Dials, and handed his keys to a parking attendant, she tried to ignore the compassion tightening her throat and concentrate instead on the rigid line of his jaw.

Karim Khan, whatever the struggles of his childhood, was not the sort of man that inspired anyone's pity.

The road in front of The Chesterton Hotel had been closed off, and a red carpet laid on the centuries-old cobblestones flanked by a barrage of photographers. He escorted her through the mêlée, his hand once again doing diabolical things to her body temperature as the calluses skimmed across her naked back.

As they entered the hotel together, the anxiety in her gut twisted and burned and she forced herself to forget the glimmer of insight she had got into Karim's childhood during the drive.

Karim Khan wasn't an unloved boy, but a forceful, charismatic and extremely cynical man. Whatever had made him that man hardly mattered now, and she would do well to remember that. This wasn't a real relationship, despite the chemistry that had flared between them. It was a contract. And to hold up her end of the bargain, persuading everyone here she was the sort of woman Karim Khan, Crown Prince of Zafar, would choose to marry—was going to require an award-winning performance.

Unfortunately, getting to know more about Karim Khan hadn't helped at all in that endeavour—all it had done was make her feel even more out of her depth.

CHAPTER SIX

'WOULD YOU MIND if I went to the bathroom, Karim?'

At Orla's softly asked question, Karim turned from his conversation with a retired French champion jockey. Beneath the manufactured glow of affection, he could see the tiredness in her eyes and the strain around her mouth.

They'd been at the reception for over four hours, and she had played her role well. He had sensed her nerves at first, but he'd been impressed at her ability to talk with considerable knowledge and foresight about the business of racing. Even though she clearly hadn't socialised with the major players in the industry as he had originally assumed, she knew her stuff.

As the evening had progressed, though, it wasn't her knowledge of racing that had captivated him, but her attempts to appear the lovestruck fiancée. Where most women would have clung to his arm and fawned over him, she had blushed profusely every time anyone congratulated them on their engagement—which only made the story of their whirlwind courtship all the more credible.

In fact the charade had begun to feel so authentic he hadn't wanted to let her out of his sight.

And while the engagement might not be real, their physical connection had only become more tangible. The catch of her breathing every time he touched her and that instinctive shudder when he placed his arm around her waist to introduce her had begun to intoxicate him. But far worse had been the two times they had danced together and he had been forced to cut the experience short because her slender body, pliable and so responsive as she allowed him to lead, had a wholly uncontrollable effect on his as he pictured himself leading her in a very different dance.

All in all, the effect she had on him had become more disturbing as the evening progressed, making it next to impossible for him to keep his thoughts on what this engagement was actually supposed to achieve. And he wasn't happy about it, especially after the intrusive conversation they'd shared during the drive here.

He never normally responded to probing questions about his family—not even from women he was dating. So why had he revealed so much about his relationship with his father? He'd refused to see the bastard in over a decade, refused to return to Zafar for considerably longer. And while he was happy to use his royal title, if it gave him an advantage in business, he had no intention of ever taking up the throne and took no interest in affairs of state. His father had cut him off financially when he was eighteen, after he had refused to marry or produce heirs—so why the hell had he told Orla about a relationship he no longer had any interest in?

But as Karim had begun introducing Orla as his fiancée, he'd begun to realise why he might have let so much slip in the car… Her frankness had beguiled him, as had the strange look in her eyes when he'd told her the truth about his father's marriages.

What the hell did that look even mean?

Because whatever it meant, he was beginning to appreciate the effect it had on him less and less. Especially as the urge to remain by her side grew, alongside the annoyance as he watched every other man there become captivated by her.

Since when had he had a jealous streak? Especially for a woman he hadn't even slept with?

He lifted his hand from Orla's waist, annoyed anew by his reluctance to let her out of his sight.

'Of course,' he said. 'Perhaps we should leave soon?' he added.

Wary surprise crossed her features. 'I... Yes, Karim,' she said. 'If you wish.'

Perversely, the subdued reply only irritated him more as she headed off through the crowd. Where was the woman who had kissed him with such passion that morning, or argued with him so persuasively in the car? More than a few men tracked her progress, and he felt the familiar surge of possessiveness—bordering on jealousy—that had dogged him all night.

'You are a man of considerable patience, Monsieur Khan,' the former jockey, whose name Karim had forgotten, remarked wryly.

'How so?' he asked, his gaze still fixed on Orla as she disappeared into the ballroom.

'If I had such a woman, I would want to keep her in my bed, rather than spend hours allowing other men to admire her charms.'

Karim swung round, the older man's comment making the heat—and frustration—he had been trying to control all evening surge. His fingers curled into fists, so he could resist the urge to punch the smile off the much smaller man's mouth.

'What did you say?' he snapped.

'There is no need to look so indignant, monsieur.' The jockey lifted his hands—palms up—in the universal sign of surrender, but the mocking, almost pitying, smile remained. 'I meant no offence to you or your fiancée.'

'Then what did you mean?' he growled, knowing he was overreacting, but not quite able to stop the outrage.

'Only that Mademoiselle Calhoun is exquisite—not just fresh and beautiful but also intelligent and accomplished. I am an old man, and I am jealous of you, for having so much to look forward to with such a woman by your side for the rest of your life.'

Karim frowned at the hopelessly romantic statement.

Not exactly, she will be gone as soon as she has outlived her usefulness.

Thanking the man through gritted teeth, he made his excuses and walked away, still furious at the presumptuous comment and the surge of frustrated desire it had caused.

His annoyance increased as he acknowledged the twist of regret in his stomach at the thought that Orla wasn't his. He headed towards the ballroom—where the dance floor was packed with people. Maybe Orla wasn't his. But he didn't want to watch any more men 'admiring' her charms. As soon as she reappeared they would leave.

Then perhaps he could calm down enough to figure out how his fake fiancée had managed to complicate a perfectly simple business arrangement, tie his guts in knots, and turn him into a man he hardly recognised, in less than one night.

'Orla, dance with me...'

Orla barely had a moment to acknowledge the request before a damp palm clamped on her wrist and she was staring into a flushed freckled face she recognised.

'Patrick...!' She stiffened and reared back, as her former fiancé's now paunchy belly pressed into hers. But before she had a chance to extricate herself he had locked his other arm around her hips, like an iron band, and manoeuvred her onto the dance floor with him.

'Hello, Orla, don't you look good enough to eat...' His pale blue gaze dipped lasciviously to her breasts and his nostrils flared. A drop of sweat rolled down the side of his face to land on her shoulder. Funny to think that look had once made her feel special, when all it did now was make her flesh crawl.

She struggled, refusing to move her feet as he tried to sway with her in his arms.

'Patrick, let me go, you're locked,' she said, the stale scent of beer and whisky underlying the unpleasant smell of sweat.

She'd seen Patrick earlier in the crowd and had been beyond grateful he hadn't spotted her. But the truth was, she'd given him no more thought whatsoever, all her energies expended on dealing with the much bigger issue of not messing up the role she was playing for Karim tonight. And not letting any more of the destructive emotions that had assailed her in the car get the upper hand again.

As it happened, that hadn't been all that easy. Karim had remained by her side all night, which had only made her giddy, misguided reaction to him all the more intense and unpredictable. She'd tried to sound smart and authoritative when talking to racing industry figures she knew Karim had hired her to impress, her goal to persuade him she could do the job she'd begged him for the day before. But as the night had worn on and his unsettling effect on her had increased, she'd found it more and more difficult to string anything like a coherent sentence together.

Their dances together had been nothing short of excruciating. She didn't know how to dance, she hadn't socialised at all for five years and he had the smooth, easy grace of a man who was entirely in tune with his own body. The fact she had been far too aware of every spot where their bodies touched had only made her more clumsy. As a result, he'd called a halt, not once but twice in the middle of the dance.

Not only was she failing at the job he was paying her for but the more attentive—and intense—he became, the more difficult she was finding it to remember this was a job at all.

The suggestion they leave soon should have brought some relief, but instead it had increased the melting sensation between her thighs and the pulse of panic that they were about to be alone again.

'Don't be so high and mighty, Orla,' Patrick said, bringing her sharply back to the present. He squeezed her so tightly she realised he wasn't just locked, he was loaded too, the outline of an erection pushing against her belly. Nausea rose up her throat, and she began to struggle in earnest to get away from him.

Sure she didn't want to create a scene, but Patrick was and had always been a jerk, and it humiliated her to think she had ever fancied herself in love with him.

Unfortunately, the more she struggled, the more he tightened his grip.

'Patrick, this isn't funny, you need to let me go.'

'Ah, shut up, now, Miss Priss,' he said. The old nickname, which she had once thought was affectionate but had become aware was just another way to belittle her, had the spike of temper igniting. 'Just because you've nabbed some foreign royal now.' His eyes narrowed to slits and his fleshy lips quirked, the cruel smile one she recognised, because it had once had the power to cut her to the quick. 'Does he know you're frigid yet?' he sneered. 'Or did you finally put out for someone?'

Anger flowed through her, to cover the cruel cut of inadequacy.

The urge to slap his face was swift and undeniable.

She'd be damned if she'd let Patrick Quinn make her feel like dirt again, when he was the one who had cheated on her. But as she jerked her hand loose from his embrace, a roar from behind had them both turning.

'Get your hands off my fiancée.'

Karim cut through the swathe of dancers like Moses parting the Red Sea. The fury on his face sent a shot of adrenaline through her system so swift it made her light-headed.

The too tight band of Patrick's arms released her so suddenly she stumbled.

Karim grabbed her elbow, his hand firm and dry as he drew her close and prevented her from falling on her face.

The giddy rush that had been messing with her equilibrium all evening surged up her torso, but as his gaze roamed over her—assessing her well-being as if he actually cared for her—it became even harder to deny, or control.

'Are you okay?' he demanded, his voice low with barely leashed fury. 'Did he hurt you? I saw him grab you, but I couldn't get to you fast enough.'

'No… I'm fine,' she said.

Patrick—who had always been a coward—had already fled.

Was this all part of their act tonight? The possessive Crown Prince, defending the honour of his new fiancée? She tried to convince herself, as she became aware of all the guests staring at them, but her pulse refused to cooperate, the giddy tattoo hammering against her ribcage as his gaze remained focussed solely on her. Almost as if he couldn't see anyone else. Which was madness, clearly, but no less intoxicating all the same.

How long had it been since anyone had looked out for her? Had taken account of her welfare? Had cared enough about her to ride to her rescue as Karim Khan just had?

'Wait here,' he said, the terrifying moment of connection lost as he let her arm go. 'I'm going to teach that bastard a lesson he won't soon forget.'

'No, don't, Karim,' she said, grasping hold of his forearm, shocked when the muscle tensed beneath the sleeve of his jacket, sending a heady dart of delirious pleasure into her sex.

How could she be turned on? When this was a complete and utter disaster? Not only were they making a massive scene, but she was starting to lose her grip on reality. Not good.

'Pat's not worth it,' she added.

The frown became catastrophic again. 'Do you know that bastard?'

For a moment she debated lying to him. The last thing she wanted to do right now was talk about the man who had discarded her so callously all those years ago, when this man was making her feel even more needy. But she forced herself to tell him the truth.

'Yes. He's Patrick Quinn, the man I was engaged to,' she murmured, averting her face.

The light-headedness dropped into her stomach and turned her knees to wet noodles. A cold wave of shock mixed with the nerves to make the nausea rise up her throat as the reaction to Pat's assault set in.

'You're shaking.' Karim's deep voice seemed to come from miles away. 'Are you sure you're okay?'

'I think I'm going to be sick,' she blurted out.

'To hell with this,' he murmured, and she was scooped off the floor and into his arms.

'What are you doing?' she managed, as the scary feeling of being protected, cocooned, cherished wrapped around her torso.

It's not real, don't romanticise it.

But even as she tried to convince herself, she turned her face into his chest, to escape from the curious glances, the intrusive stares, that reminded her so much of that miserable April day when she'd had to announce to the engagement party her engagement was over.

'Getting us the hell out of here,' he growled as he marched through the crowd.

She pressed her nose into his collarbone, clung to his neck, and inhaled to give herself the moment she needed.

She breathed in his tantalising scent. The seductive aroma of soap and man cleared away the rancid smell of sweat and whisky.

At last the raging sea of shock and bitter memories calmed down.

But then his arms tightened around her, and the deep well of misguided emotion swelled into her throat.

What was she doing? Relying on his strength, even for a moment, would only make it harder for her to rely on her own. And that was one thing getting dumped by Patrick, losing her mother and then getting emotionally abandoned by her father had taught her, before she lost him too. Relying on anyone other than yourself would always lead to heartache.

So she shifted and tried to wiggle free of his arms. 'It's okay, Karim, really, I'm fine, you can put me down now.'

'In a minute.' Karim bit off the words, the rage still burning in his gut.

He walked down the steps of The Chesterton.

Patrick Quinn was going to regret touching her.

Quinn and his whole damn family, when he buried their business.

His hands tightened reflexively, but he made himself place Orla on her feet. Even so he kept a firm grip on her arm as she steadied herself.

'How's the stomach?' he asked.

'Good,' she said, tugging away from him.

He forced his hand into his pocket to resist the urge to touch her again. And tried to convince himself his fury would be just as strong if Quinn had treated any other woman there the same way.

'It's okay, Karim, he didn't mean to hurt me, his hand slipped.'

A memory flickered at the edges of his consciousness, of his mother, her face pale but for the livid bruise on her cheek.

He shut it out, as well as the brutal feeling of impotence and inadequacy that came with it.

Orla wasn't his mother. She wasn't even really his fiancée. She meant nothing to him. And the surge of fury that had assaulted him in the ballroom when he had spotted Quinn dragging her onto the dance floor and seen her stiffen and recoil had not been specific, but rather a natural reaction to the sight of any man treating a woman with such disrespect.

'I'm sorry for the scene,' she said as she looked down at her toes.

'Don't apologise,' he said, more curtly than he had intended, the rage burning under his breastbone again. And feeling more specific by the minute. For a moment there she'd clung to him. And instead of being shocked or annoyed, all he'd wanted to do was hold her.

He signalled the parking attendant. He needed to calm the hell down.

This. Is. Not. Personal.

'You're not responsible for Patrick Quinn's boorish behaviour,' he added.

She met his gaze at last. 'Thank you,' she said.

'What for?' he asked, his pulse accelerating again, despite his best efforts. He hated to see the shadows in her eyes. Wanted nothing more than to take them away, even though it shouldn't matter to him, this much.

What was going on here? Because he didn't like it, but he didn't seem able to stop it.

'For coming to my rescue,' she said, so simply and with so little expectation, his heart squeezed uncomfortably in his chest. 'And for not blaming me.'

'Why would I blame you for his actions?' he asked. Did she think he was some kind of monster? A monster like his...

He cut off the thought. He didn't want to think about his father, especially not now—when the woman he had effectively hired to dupe the bastard had somehow duped him into feeling things he did not want to feel.

The car arrived before she replied, and he took a moment to tip the parking attendant and open the door for her. She climbed into the passenger seat, giving him another flash of her thigh. Her breasts rose and fell—making the glittery fabric of her gown shimmer erratically—and it occurred to him she wasn't any calmer than he was.

The inevitable shot of heat hit as he skirted the car and got behind the wheel. Just as he was about to switch on the ignition though, she murmured, 'I made such a mess of things tonight, I wouldn't blame you a bit for wanting to sack me.'

He stared at her—the urge to defend her so swift and strong it was as confusing as everything else that had happened tonight.

But seriously, what on earth made her believe she had messed up? And at what exactly? Convincing people their engagement was real? Because she'd been too damn convincing at that, so convincing in fact he'd begun to believe it himself.

Even though a part of him knew he should take her up on her suggestion, and call a halt to this charade—because it had already become more complicated than it was ever meant to be—he couldn't do it.

So he turned on the ignition, peeled away from the kerb and asked the question that had been bugging him as soon as she had told him about her connection to Quinn.

'Why do you call him Pat? Do you still have feelings for that bastard?' Why the hell that should matter to him, he had no idea, but still, he wanted to know.

'Oh, no, not at all,' she said, the surprise in her voice and the instant reply mitigating at least some of his anger. 'The truth is I haven't thought about him in years.'

'How did it end?' Even as the probing question came out of his mouth, he knew he shouldn't have asked it—any more than he should want to know the answer. Her previous affairs were no business of his. But he'd be damned if he'd take it back.

Surely, he could be forgiven for being curious? After all, she had been engaged to that bastard when she was only seventeen. The man had most likely been her first lover.

He tapped his thumb on the steering wheel, jerked the gear shift into second to take the turn into Shaftesbury Avenue waiting for her reply—which didn't come nearly as quickly as her previous answer, he noted. His impatience mounted as the car sped past the row of theatres, their doors closed now, and the paper lanterns of Chinatown speckled light onto the hood.

'We were very young,' she said at last as he braked at the lights on the junction with Haymarket.

He glanced her way, hearing the hesitation in her voice.

'And we eventually figured out we just didn't suit,' she finished. But he could see the flags of vivid colour on her cheeks. She was lying, he was sure of it—there was more to it than that.

The questions cued up in his head.

How long were they together? Why did it really end? Had that bastard touched her roughly then too, the way he had tonight? But as the night air cooled at least some of the heat churning in his gut, he forced himself not to ask any of them.

Whatever had happened between Orla and Quinn in the past, once he had dealt with the man, Quinn certainly would not make the mistake of hurting her again.

And her past really did not concern him.

They made the rest of the drive in silence.

Unfortunately, as his fury began to cool, the hunger, and heat that had dogged him all night returned. He could sense the charge between them now like a living, breathing thing, and was sure she could feel it too.

Was it why he didn't want to let her go?

After he parked the car in the garage behind the house, she leapt out before he had a chance to open her door.

'Will you want me tomorrow?' she asked, backing away from him towards the house.

I want you tonight.

He cut the thought off, forced himself not to act on it. 'No,' he said.

Space and distance were necessary, until he could control his reaction to her in every respect.

'Would it be okay if I returned to Kildare for a few

days, then?' she asked, the colour on her cheeks still vivid as her back hit the door.

'No, it would not be okay,' he said, a lot more forcefully this time. Maybe space and distance were required, until they got this hunger under some semblance of control, but he'd be damned if he'd let her leave the country. 'We're supposed to be engaged, Orla,' he added. 'Leaving so soon won't fit the narrative.'

Nor would it improve his mood.

'But if you don't need me here, I'm sure there's lots I could be doing there...' Her breathing speeded up again and drew his gaze back to her cleavage, where the material shimmered and glowed and he could see the slope of her bare breast at the side of that damn gown that had been playing peek-a-boo with him all night... 'To brief your team when they—'

'I said no.' He interrupted the far too eager stream of suggestions. 'I'll be travelling to the stud next month, you can accompany me then. But I've already hired a new manager to take over the day-to-day running of the facility.'

'Oh.' She looked crestfallen. 'I see.'

He refused to feel guilty about it. This was what they'd agreed. She shifted out of his way as he approached the door—tense and skittish.

'I'll contact you when I require you to attend an event with me,' he said, trying to keep his mind on business and off the soft sway of her unfettered breasts.

She nodded. 'Okay. But what am I supposed to be doing in the meantime?' she asked.

He could think of far too many answers to that question. Every one of them only making the visceral need that had been riding him all evening increase, so his reply was sharp enough to make her jump.

'Waiting for my instructions.'

He unlocked the door and held it open for her, getting a lungful of that provocative scent for his pains that seemed to stroke the erection growing in his pants.

'Do you understand?' he asked.

He saw the mutinous expression in her eyes, and hated himself even more for noticing how it turned her irises to a rich emerald.

'Of course, Your Highness,' she said, but before he could take her to task for the mocking comment, she shot past him into the house.

He closed the door as he watched her disappear down the hallway.

The urge to go after her clawed at his gut. But just as vivid was the memory of her eyes—so wary, so vulnerable—as he'd carried her out of the ballroom. Something tightened in his chest as he remembered how she'd clung to him for that split second as trusting as a child.

As he made his own way through the dark house, the antique grandfather clock in the vestibule chimed midnight.

Taking this any further would be a mistake.

Sex was one thing, intimacy another, and he would never risk mixing the two.

CHAPTER SEVEN

'ORLA, I CAN'T believe you're actually engaged to a prince—that's mad.' Dervla's shocked voice made Orla's fingers tense on her phone in the upstairs lounge. 'I mean, I know he's super-hot and all, but I didn't think you were actually serious.'

'Dervla, I told you we're not really dating,' Orla whispered, worried that the staff might overhear her. Although she suspected they had realised she and Karim were not a real couple by now. After all, they had to have noticed the two of them had never shared a bed and she'd been living in his house for a week. 'It's not a proper engagement,' she added, even though it didn't feel entirely in name only either any more.

Not after their first—and only—event together as a couple.

'But I saw the pictures of him carrying you out of the Jockeys' Ball. It's in all the magazines over here.' Dervla sighed. 'It looks so romantic. Are you sure he hasn't fallen hopelessly in love with you by accident?'

Orla felt the familiar pang in her chest and swallowed down the foolish lump of emotion that had derailed her a week ago when he'd come to her rescue like an avenging angel... Or a protective fiancé. And the times she had run the memory of those moments through her head. But in the days since, it had become clear, whatever had happened that night, it wasn't going to be repeated. She'd hardly seen him—but for the two breakfasts they'd shared.

Karim had been distant and pragmatic both times she'd managed to catch him before he disappeared for the day, keeping any conversation to a minimum. And when he did speak to her, the discussion was about the horses, never anything more personal. He had been picking her brains for everything she knew about the sport and the stock at Calhouns. She'd found the two discussions they'd had surprisingly stimulating—Karim knew much more than she'd assumed, his decision to buy the stud and establish himself as an owner of superior bloodstock not a vanity project after all. As much as she had regretted having to sell her family business, she could see Karim was going to invest and build on the work they'd done there. That he had chosen to keep the Calhoun name had also pleased her. But those breakfast meetings had still been extremely disconcerting. She'd felt his gaze on her, and that masculine magnetism that had tripped her up before. The events at the Jockeys' Ball and even the one kiss they'd shared had played through her mind whenever she was with him—and the many hours she was not.

But it was three days now since she'd last seen him. And she'd felt the sharp sting of disappointment each morning as she'd walked into the breakfast room and found it empty.

She'd tried to be philosophical about that. It wasn't really him she missed, surely it was just that she felt so rootless here, her life in the last week so far removed from her daily routine in Kildare. When she'd agreed to this arrangement, she really hadn't factored in what it would mean to be the trophy fiancée of a man as rich and powerful as Karim Khan. She'd never felt so useless in her life. Not only did she miss the horses desperately, but Calhouns and the work there had given her life purpose and meaning, and it was clear she had no purpose or meaning here.

With no horses to exercise, no final demands to juggle, no stud business to deal with, no bank managers to placate or stalls to muck out, and no mention of any events to attend with Karim, she'd struggled to find anything to do. The house was run like a well-oiled machine, the staff so efficient all her offers to help out had been met with puzzled frowns followed by polite refusals.

The truth was, the yearning she felt when not seeing Karim at the breakfast table was probably just disappointment. Because without that shot of adrenaline to liven up her morning—and the chance to at least talk about the business she loved—she'd become unbelievably bored.

She had no idea what she was even doing here any more, or why Karim continued to refuse to allow her to return to Kildare.

'No, he hasn't fallen in love with me,' Orla murmured to her sister. She'd explained the circumstances of the engagement to Dervla a week ago—in the scant twenty minutes Karim had allowed her before they left—and every time she'd spoken to Dervla since. But Dervla didn't believe her.

Orla had always been the realist and Dervla the drama queen, but her sister's ludicrous romanticism—her determination to make this engagement something it wasn't—wasn't helping Orla keep everything in perspective.

As a result, she'd started screening her sister's calls—which was a pain. Because the conversations with Dervla, however aggravating her attitude towards the engagement, were one of the few bright spots in her monotonous days in London. She was desperate for news of what was going on at the stud, something she couldn't quiz Karim about—because he was never here.

'How's everything going at Calhouns?' she cut into Dervla's continued dreamy dialogue about how hot the photos of her and Karim were in her magazines. Time to change the subject before Dervla drove her totally nuts.

'Oh, it's marvellous,' Dervla said. 'They've started work on repairing and updating the stable block and the training facilities this morning. They even got an architect in to do designs for the remodelling. Can you believe it?' Dervla's voice was hushed with awe. 'I didn't even know there were architects for horse barns. Did you? It's gas.'

'Where are the horses while all this is going on?' Orla asked. She hadn't expected them to start work so soon. The stables had been in desperate need of repairs, that was true, but didn't the new manager know they had to be careful not to disturb the horses? These were thoroughbred, highly strung animals and any noise or disruption could seriously damage their—

'They're stabling them at the Quinns' until the work is finished,' Dervla interrupted Orla's panicked thoughts. 'They moved them all yesterday.'

'Oh, I see, that makes sense.' Orla frowned, the twist of disappointment in her belly making her feel small and petty. Why should she begrudge her neighbours the business, just because Patrick had acted so appallingly at the ball? Karim had no loyalty to her, not really, especially where his business was concerned. 'I expect the Quinns'll be glad of the business,' she added, knowing the family had struggled in recent years because their horses hadn't had the same results as Calhouns on the track.

'I expect they would if they still owned the place,' Dervla said.

'What?' Orla asked.

'Didn't I tell you already? Someone bought their business in a hostile takeover… And kicked them off the land. Two days ago.'

'No, you did not mention it,' Orla said, her fingers gripping the handset. How could Dervla have forgotten to mention something so important? The Quinns had been a premier Kildare racing family for generations, just like the Calhouns.

'Ah, damn, I meant to tell you all about it yesterday. It was all over the pub on Sunday night, happened very suddenly, Maeve said. Her husband works at Quinns, you know. Apparently they kept all the staff on. Even increased their wages as a loyalty bonus. Maeve said Dermot's pleased, he thought Patrick had been running the place all wrong for years. The new owner's already made improvements.'

'Who is the new owner?' Orla asked, shocked despite the fact she would have agreed with Dermot on Patrick's handling of the stud since he'd taken over.

'Didn't I tell you now, the best bit of gossip?' Dervla said, her voice rising with excitement.

'No, what?' Orla asked, thinking her sister was going to give her an aneurysm if she didn't get to the point.

'So no one knows who the new owner is for sure—it was all done in a secret sale. But the very next day, Carly, the new manager here, announced Calhouns horses were being rehoused there, during the remodelling, so everyone got to thinking, it must be *him*.'

'Him who?' Orla asked, thoroughly frustrated now. Why couldn't Dervla ever give her a straight answer about anything without dressing it up in loads of fanciful nonsense?

'Him as in your fiancé. Maeve and Dermot and everyone else think he's the new owner for sure.' Dervla's voice lowered with even more unnecessary drama. 'And that he probably did it for revenge—isn't that so cool?'

'Revenge for what now?' Orla asked, but the weight in her stomach had already begun to twist and turn at the memory of Karim's fury, and the words he'd ground out.

'I'm going to teach that bastard a lesson he won't soon forget.'

'Don't be dense,' Dervla cut back in. 'For revenge against Patrick Quinn, of course, for daring to put his hands on you at the ball. And you keep saying he doesn't love you.' Dervla scoffed. 'Why would he do such a thing if he wasn't mad about you?'

'That... It can't be true...' Orla said, so shocked she didn't know what to think let alone say—the weight in her stomach now dancing a jig. Would Karim really have done such a thing? He'd talked about retribution at the ball for Patrick's behaviour, in the heat of the moment, but he'd calmed down once they were in the car on the way home. And after she'd told him an edited version of her break-up with Patrick, he hadn't mentioned the incident, or her former fiancé, again.

What shocked her more though was the spurt of something heady and exciting at the thought he might have done such a thing for her. But as soon as she acknowledged the feeling, she felt ashamed of it.

If Karim really had done this, it wasn't because of his feelings for her, because he clearly didn't have any. He'd barely acknowledged her presence in the last week. She hadn't even seen him for three days now. In truth, he didn't even seem interested in maintaining the charade any more that they were actually an item.

And while it was true Patrick had been unnecessarily cruel to her all those years ago, cheating on her the whole time they were engaged, Karim knew nothing of that. Patrick might have behaved very badly at the ball too, but he'd been drunk. And yes, his family had blamed her for the breakdown of the engagement, but did they really deserve to lose a family business they'd spent years building because Patrick had had one too many whiskies?

'Well, I reckon it's true. And I think it's super romantic,' Dervla added, unhelpfully. 'It's just what Patrick deserves—he was never as good with the horses as you are. And he knew it, that's why he was so mean to you. And now he's out of racing for good. No one will give him a job if they think your fella won't like it. So he'll have to find something else to be bad at. At least you won't ever have to see him at another official event. Are you sure you don't know anything about it? I told Maeve I'd ask you.'

It took several minutes of deflecting Dervla's increasingly probing questions, but Orla finally managed to get her sister off the phone. She put the receiver down, her fingers trembling as the confusion and anxiety built under her breastbone and began to tangle with the weight in her stomach.

Surely Karim couldn't have done something so… Well, so vengeful? And for a woman he didn't really care about. It made no sense. But even as she tried to reassure herself, her heart began to beat two to the dozen.

Should she ask him? If he had bought Quinns? How could she not? And yet how did she even bring up a question like that? When the last thing she wanted to do was discuss Patrick with him again? And, anyway, when was she even likely to see him next?

She stared at the phone she'd been given by his personal assistant a week ago, a phone that was supposed to alert her to any events she might need to attend with Karim. The phone that hadn't rung or buzzed once since he'd insisted she stay in London—and then given her nothing to do.

She picked it up and scrolled through the numbers stored in the contacts. There were only two. One listed Khan—which had to be Karim. And the other with the name of the personal assistant. She didn't quite have the guts to ring Karim and ask him outright. But would it be so wrong to find out from the personal assistant where he was today?

She called the number. The assistant picked up on the second ring.

'Ms Calhoun, what can I do for you?' he asked politely.

'Hi, I was just wondering where Mr Khan is today?' she asked before she lost her nerve.

'Would you like me to give him a message?' the PA asked, rather evasively, she thought. Had he been instructed not to tell her Karim's whereabouts?

Damn.

'No that's fine, I have his number here, but I didn't want to disturb him if he's busy,' she said. 'Is he? Busy?' she added, then felt like a fool. Of course Karim was busy, he was always busy, the man ran a multibillion-dollar business empire, single-handedly from what she could gather given the amount of time he spent out of the house or locked in his study.

She was just debating whether to hang up, when the PA replied.

'We're going to be at Hammonds Sale this afternoon

in Kensington Palace Gardens, which kicks off at three, so I would suggest contacting Mr Khan before it starts as he will be bidding on the lots.'

She thanked the man and then hung up.

Her heartbeat accelerated into her throat, the familiar tangle of nerves jumping and jiggling in the pit of her belly joined by the definite spike of irritation.

Karim had gone to Hammonds Sale without her? If he was planning to buy any stock there, why hadn't he taken her with him? She was the one who knew the horses Calhouns would need to buy, better than anyone.

She glanced at her watch.

A quarter to two. Instinct and the definite bubble of excitement drowned out the jangle of nerves and the prickle of irritation. She picked up the house phone and ordered one of the cars to be brought round to take her to the event.

She'd never had the chance to go to Hammonds Sale but she had always wanted to. They held it every year in the grounds of Kensington Palace. Everyone who was anyone in racing would be there and, while most of the big sales happened in private, occasionally there were some good horses up for auction. She'd forgotten it was today, probably because she'd forgotten what day it was entirely. But she had studied the catalogue herself months ago when it had been issued, as she did every year, imagining what it would be like if she had money to invest. She could give Karim her advice about the best prospects, and maybe… *Maybe* she'd get up the courage to ask him about Quinns. But more importantly, it was way past time she stopped sitting on her backside and waiting for Karim to give her something to do.

She rushed out of the study and up the stairs to her suite, to hunt through her wardrobe of new clothes and find something fancy enough to wear for the super-posh event.

As she stepped into the car half an hour later, her fingers trembled round the clutch purse she'd found in the wardrobe. Then the jumps and jiggles settled low in her abdomen and began to throb at the prospect of seeing Karim again.

She ignored them. Her excitement wasn't about Karim, and her ludicrous over reaction to him, it was about this chance to prove to him that while she might be hopeless as a fake fiancée she could be a real asset when it came to buying bloodstock for Calhouns.

'You drive a hard bargain, Khan. But one I think we will both benefit from immensely. Your knowledge of bloodstock is much better than I anticipated. More champagne?'

'I'm good, thanks.' Karim declined the offer of a top-up from Piers Devereaux—a racing legend who had established himself as the premier stud owner in England—and dismissed the condescending tone.

He had expected as much from doyens of the racing establishment such as Devereaux—which was precisely why he had spent several years doing his homework and waiting for the perfect purchase before making an assault on the higher echelons of the sport. The prestigious racehorse sale organised by Hammonds each year was a gala event. The auction itself was more of a social occasion than a business opportunity, because the real business was done as the movers and shakers chatted privately over vintage champagne and cordon bleu canapés. Karim had prepared carefully for this event, knowing he wanted to match Calhouns' top stallion Aderyn with one of Devereaux's mares. But as he listened to Devereaux, a question that had been tormenting him consistently for a week tormented him again. Given all his careful planning over the last few years to enter this arena, why the hell had he been so damn impulsive when choosing a fake fiancée? And why hadn't he brought Orla with him to this event? When she knew so much about Calhouns stock?

'I have heard your father has an amazing stock of thoroughbreds, but I never knew you were so interested in the Sport of Kings,' Piers continued. 'So what's the story on Quinns?' the older man asked bluntly. 'Did you destroy them as penance for young Pat's diabolical treatment of your new fiancée—and his former fiancée—as everyone believes?'

Karim clenched his teeth and held onto his temper, with an effort. Devereaux was the first person to have the audacity to actually ask the question. But he wasn't the first to think it. Hammonds was buzzing with the latest gossip—he'd noted the questioning glances as soon as he'd arrived. But he'd be damned if he'd explain or deny his actions to these people. Taking over the Quinn farm had been a sound business move, once he'd discovered they were ripe for a takeover.

But even as he told himself that, he knew it wasn't the whole truth.

Destroying Patrick Quinn's standing in the community had been more than business. And he'd been trying to justify the impulse to himself ever since.

'The Quinn land borders on Calhouns, and I intend to expand the operation considerably,' he answered calmly, deciding not to deny he was the new owner. 'Figure out my motives for yourself.'

Maybe his motives had more to do with Orla—and the sight of her being manhandled by that bastard—than they should. But he refused to regret the impulse. No woman deserved to be touched without her consent.

Devereaux chuckled, as Karim knew he would, because loyalty came a distant second to power and success in this community. 'Touché, Khan. Now I've met you, it's clear the rumours circulating about your hot-headedness are unfounded.'

Karim ignored the familiar prickle of unease at the comment. A week ago, Devereaux would have been correct. He'd never been a hothead, and certainly not over a woman, until he'd met Orla Calhoun. And he'd never had a problem controlling his impulses or his temper, but now he couldn't seem to keep a handle on either of them. And he didn't like it.

'I'm looking forward to working with you and competing against you,' Devereaux added. 'With Calhoun stock and your own considerable expertise you could well become a force to be reckoned with in a few years. Such a shame Michael passed when he did. The man knew horses like no other, even if he had trouble passing a betting shop.'

Karim bristled at the latent sexism of the man's assumptions. His in-depth conversations with Orla earlier in the week had proved to him conclusively she hadn't lied about her influence at Calhouns in the last few years. Although the racing community were blissfully unaware of her talents, it wasn't her father who had managed to steer Calhouns to so many successes despite the crippling debt the man's addiction had landed her with.

Thoughts of Orla though awakened the familiar pulse of yearning. Infuriatingly.

He'd been avoiding her for three days now. Ever since their impromptu breakfast meetings had given him a burning desire that had nothing whatsoever to do with mining her extensive knowledge of Calhouns' strengths and weaknesses.

How could he still want her so much? Even more now than he had the night of the ball? Why was the hunger only getting worse? And why couldn't he control it?

Almost as if he'd conjured her up by magic, his fiancée appeared at the tented opening to the event. He blinked several times. Was he hallucinating now? This was intolerable—weren't the dreams of her every damn night since she'd arrived in his home enough?

But as his gaze locked on her slender, willowy figure and high breasts, displayed to perfection in a floaty, fluid sundress the same rich, striking green as her eyes, it became clear she was not an apparition.

The moment of relief though—that he wasn't going totally insane—was followed by the brutal shaft of heat. He tensed, furious with the unbidden and uncontrolled reaction.

What was she doing here? He certainly had not requested her presence, for precisely this reason. Because she distracted him. A lot.

But even knowing he ought to fight the disturbing effect she had on him, he found himself tuning out Devereaux's small talk as he watched her pick her way across the grass in her heels. She kept her head down, and her hands gripped the auction brochure she had been handed when she entered. She declined the offer of a glass of champagne from a passing waiter, pausing to look around.

He resisted the urge to go to her immediately, attempting to swallow down the ball of lust… Not very successfully.

Calm down, dammit. She'll spot you in a minute and then you can demand to know what she is doing here.

Looking too eager was not his style, and having a domestic dispute in full view of everyone would hardly keep up the pretence that he was in love with this woman.

But as he battled the desire to storm through the crowd—and reignite the rumours about his being a hot-head where this woman was concerned—a young man in a designer suit waylaid her. Orla paused, clearly disconcerted by the attention, especially when her admirer began to flirt with her in that way the English aristocracy had of being loud and annoying and thinking it was charming.

The possessive rage that had blindsided him at the ball a week ago surged.

And he had the answer to a question he hadn't even acknowledged... Avoiding her hadn't worked, if anything it had only made the hunger, and the inexplicable emotions that went with it—jealousy, envy, need—all the more volatile.

He made his excuses to Devereaux, dumped his empty glass on the tray of a passing waiter and headed towards his fiancée, ready to extricate her from the attentions of that obnoxious toff who had his eyes glued to her cleavage.

'So you're Irish? I should have guessed from the charming accent. And the red hair.' The young man grinned flirtatiously as his gaze finally lifted from Orla's breasts to her face. 'Are you dating one of the Irish breeders, then?' he said, putting enough emphasis on the word breeders to be less than charming.

She tried not to be insulted. While racing had always been a male-dominated sport, women were making their mark as both breeders and trainers, so this idiot's assumption that she was some airhead who knew nothing about the sport had just given away his ignorance.

'No, I'm Orla Calhoun, of the Calhoun stud…'

'Orla, you're here.' Her explanation of who she was dried up as Karim appeared from nowhere. Dressed in a grey linen suit, he looked dominant and powerful and stupidly gorgeous. So what else was new?

Heat suffused her cheeks, and sank deep into her sex, as he clasped her elbow in strong fingers. 'This is a surprise,' he said, the edge in his voice unmistakeable.

He didn't sound too pleased to see her, but before she could reply he pressed his lips to her cheek in a fleeting but somehow possessive kiss.

Fire ignited in her belly and spread up her collarbone.

It was the first time he had touched her since the ball. His dark gaze seared her skin, the intensity so vivid and compelling it felt as if they were alone—cocooned by the live-wire chemistry that flared between them so easily.

The jiggle of nerves she had tried to explain away during the drive to West London became turbocharged. Why did she feel as if she had just been branded? How did he do that? Make her feel as if she belonged to him? When she knew she didn't?

'Um, Karim, hi,' she managed, clearing her throat while desperately trying to get her bearings again—and remind herself that she was here to prove to him she could be useful. 'I heard you were at the auction and thought you could use my help with the bidding,' she managed, desperately trying not to get derailed again by his disapproval. He should have invited her, why hadn't he?

The young man beside her cleared his throat obviously waiting for an introduction.

'Karim, this… This is, um…' She turned to the young

man, but even though he had introduced himself to her less than five seconds ago, his name totally escaped her.

'Miles, Miles Johnson at your service,' he said and offered his hand to Karim, managing to collect himself quicker than she had.

Karim merely glanced at the offered hand, which was hastily withdrawn. 'Hello,' he said.

'I'm honoured to meet you, Your Highness,' the boy continued—for he suddenly seemed like a boy rather than a man as his confidence visibly disintegrated under Karim's focussed disdain. 'E-everyone's t-talking about y-your acquisition of Quinns,' he stammered. 'What a bold move that was. And how you're set to be the most exciting thing to happen to racing in years...'

Orla shivered. So Karim *had* bought out the Quinns. And he hadn't bothered to tell her. All the questions she'd had before about the purchase came hurtling back, along with that weird feeling of vindication.

'Are they really?' Karim remarked, but he already sounded bored.

His thumb stroked her inner elbow, the light touch controlling enough to send her heartbeat catapulting into her sex.

'Yes, sir, they—' Miles began again. But this time Karim cut him off.

'Miles, do you think you could leave us alone? I'd like to speak to my fiancée in private.'

'Your fiancée?' The boy's face went bright red, but it was the flash of panic in his eyes that spoke volumes. 'I'll be off, then,' he said and left so fast Orla felt sure the rumours Dervla had repeated about Karim's motivations for destroying the Quinns, while they couldn't be true, had certainly travelled far and wide in the racing world.

'That's quite a trick,' she murmured, aware of the

flicker of panic in her own body—but for very different reasons—as Karim pulled her round to face him.

'What trick?' he asked as he drew her closer, so close she could smell his cologne, and the subtle scent of his soap, which had haunted her dreams for days.

'The ability to make annoying people disappear. I wish I had that knack,' she said.

The slow smile that curled his lips was so sensual and so arrogant her breathing became distressingly ragged. 'I'll teach you it,' he said. 'But first you need to answer a question for me.'

'Yes,' she said, fairly sure they weren't talking about Miles What's-His-Name anymore.

'What the hell are you doing here?'

The question was delivered calmly but with enough of an edge for Orla to know he was holding onto his temper for the benefit of their audience. But while the nerves in her belly were now doing back flips she refused to apologise. He'd left her alone for a whole week, with nothing to do. After refusing to let her return to Kildare. She needed a role in London, or she'd go mad.

'I knew my knowledge of the lots could be useful. I've studied the catalogue and I know what Calhouns needs to purchase…' The frantic explanation trailed into silence as he continued to stare at her. One dark brow rose up his forehead, making his scepticism clear. And suddenly she found herself blurting out, 'Why did you buy out the Quinns? And destroy Patrick's reputation? Was it…?' She sucked in a breath, determined to continue despite the way both his brows lowered ominously—this was not a conversation he wanted to have. But she needed to know. 'Was it because of what happened at the ball?'

'You think I spent fifteen million euros to buy a stud

farm neighbouring Calhouns to defend your honour?'
he asked.

The mocking tone and the glitter of cynicism in his
eyes were unmistakeable. But she could still detect that
edge. And before she could stop herself she asked the
question that had been burning in her gut since her conversation with Dervla. 'Well, did you?'

The minute she'd said it, she felt like a fool. Of course
he hadn't—why would he really care about that, if he
didn't care about her?

The rueful smile remained fixed on his lips, but his
eyes narrowed.

'No,' he said.

Her chest deflated, and hot colour flared in her cheeks,
making her feel hideously exposed. But then he stroked
the side of her face with his thumb, the callused skin
sending darts of sensation everywhere. His touch was
light but so intimate her breath caught when he added,
'Or not entirely.'

She gulped down the lump forming in her throat. And
began to feel light-headed. Was it the intensity in his
gaze? That misguided yearning to be sheltered and cherished by this man—that had overwhelmed her when he
had rescued her from Patrick that night? Or was it the
visceral desire tugging at her sex and making every one
of her pulse points pound? Because she was fairly sure
the excitement racing through her veins right now wasn't
to do with her desire to find a way to be useful when it
came to buying bloodstock for Calhouns anymore.

The stunned awareness in Orla's eyes turned the bright
emerald to a compelling jade and sent a renewed shaft of
longing through Karim's system… And he was finally
forced to confront the lie he'd been telling himself for a

week, that somehow by avoiding her he would be able to control the effect she had on him.

He'd never gone back on a contract, never reneged on an agreement. That wasn't how he did business. But this had stopped being a business deal a week ago. This was about need and desire and chemistry as well as expediency now.

This hunger was visceral and real and all-consuming. For them both. And if they didn't feed it soon it would only become more so.

He could hear the speeches being made by the director at Hammonds and then the auction began. The auctioneer listed the first horse up for sale: a two-year-old filly who had run some good races.

Orla's gaze flickered away from his face. She looked down at the brochure in her hands, avoiding his eyes. 'You should buy her. She's a good prospect.' She flicked through the pages, her fingers trembling. 'And number five, Debonair Boy, is a good colt,' she said, her cheeks glowing as she struggled to fulfil the role he'd once given her... A role that he now didn't give a damn about. It wasn't her expert racing advice he wanted. If it had ever been.

He signalled to his assistant, who was hovering nearby. The man appeared by his side instantly. 'Jason, buy this filly. And the fifth horse on the docket,' he said, not taking his gaze off his fiancée.

'Yes, Mr Khan,' the man replied.

'And make my excuses to Devereaux,' he added, surprised he could even remember the commitment he'd made earlier when all he could seem to focus on was the staggered rise and fall of Orla's breathing, the sultry scent of her perfume and how much he wanted to strip her out of the summer dress and lick every inch of her fragrant flesh. 'I won't be joining him for dinner after all.'

His assistant nodded and left. Karim gripped Orla's elbow and began to direct her through the crowd, back towards the entrance she'd come out of less than fifteen minutes before.

'Karim, is everything okay?' she asked, the nervousness in her voice only making him more aware of the arousal darkening her gaze.

'No, everything's not okay,' he managed. 'But it soon will be.'

He walked past the cloakroom set up by the entrance. 'Wait, Karim, I left my—'

'I'll get Jason to collect it,' he snapped. He could feel her pulse battering his thumb as he pressed it into the soft inner flesh of her elbow—trying not to grip her too hard.

'Tell my driver we're ready to leave,' he said to one of the doormen.

'But, Karim, we're going to miss the auction,' Orla said, then chewed her damn lip.

His gaze fixed on the plump flesh trapped between small white teeth. The desire to touch his tongue to the reddened skin was so strong he spoke through gritted teeth.

'Are there any more horses you think we should bid on?' he asked.

She shook her head, but the flush of pleasure—because he had asked for her advice—only made him feel more on edge.

'Good,' he said. 'Then there is no need for us to remain here.'

He stood on the grassy verge at the entrance to Kensington Gardens waiting for the chauffeur-driven Mercedes to arrive, aware of her starting to tremble beside him. He probably ought to reassure her. But how could he, when he couldn't even reassure himself?

He was behaving like a madman, the way he had at

the ball. But he couldn't wait any longer to get this damn desire out of his system. Why hadn't he done this a week ago? Or any of the nights since? Instead of torturing himself for days? He would be over this driving hunger now if he had… Surely.

The car pulled into the park gates what felt like several eternities later.

After they were finally inside, cocooned in the leather interior, he tapped on the driver's window. 'Take us back to the house, Mark, park in the back and don't disturb us.'

The driver nodded, then closed the partition.

Finally they were alone. The spurt of adrenaline—and anticipation—had his heart beating heavily as the car drove off.

'Are you angry that I came?' she asked as she reached for her seat belt.

'No,' he said. 'Come here,' he added, gripping her arm before she could anchor the belt.

He dragged her up, and over him, until she straddled his lap. Her knees dug into the leather on either side of his hips, her fingers grasped his shoulders and the colour on her face intensified as he ran his hands up her thighs, felt the shudder of reaction. And caught the musky scent of her arousal.

Shock flickered across her face, but did nothing to lessen the vivid desire he could see in her eyes. Or the rush of blood pounding into his pants and thickening his shaft.

'Karim, what are you doing?' she gasped.

He caressed the glorious curve of her bottom through her panties and tugged her closer to murmur against the pummelling pulse in her neck: 'Changing the terms of our agreement.'

CHAPTER EIGHT

NEED RUSHED THROUGH Orla's system like wildfire, scorching everything in its wake, the hard press of his erection against her thigh only increasing the giddy sense of desperation—and validation—at his murmured comment.

His thumb glided beneath the leg of her panties, finding the slick seam of her sex as his lips devoured her neck, her collarbone.

'Tell me you want me, too,' he growled, his voice a husky rasp of command.

'Yes, yes, I do,' she said.

'This changes nothing,' he said as he deftly undid the buttons at the front of her dress, exposing the white lace bra. 'Tell me you understand that.'

She nodded, unable to speak now, the anticipation starting to choke her as she heard the snap of her bra releasing in the quiet interior of the car.

They struggled for a moment, as he adjusted her on his lap, so he could release her arms from the confines of the dress, and free her breasts.

Her nipples throbbed, so hard they were already begging for his attention.

She sat on his lap, topless and exposed and so needy she thought she might actually die from the desperate need to feel his lips on her. The solid erection felt huge trapped between her legs, but only increased her desire. She wriggled, instinctively trying to alleviate the pressure against the hard ridge.

He groaned, the raw sound a sop to her ego, making her feel powerful... Or at least less powerless.

His dark eyes met hers as he cradled the swollen weight of her breasts in his palms, traced the edges of the areolae. 'Don't move, Orla. Or this will be over far too soon.'

She stilled, the agony intensifying.

Then he bent forward and licked across the turgid tip of one nipple. She moaned, bucked, unable to do as he demanded, rubbing against the ridge trapped in his pants. The exquisite torture continued as he captured the stiff peak with his mouth and suckled hard. The pressure built and twisted at her core, her skin tight, raw, aching, her breasts on fire as he tormented one nipple, then the other.

Her soft, guttural moans echoed around the car, flagrant, uninhibited, desperate.

He bucked his hips, and finally released her from the torture, rearing back to press his hands to her burning cheeks.

'Release me,' he said.

She nodded, eager and yet unsure. Aware of him watching her, she tried to look as if she knew what she was about as she fumbled with his zip, concentrating hard. At last she managed to locate the tab and draw it down, her fingers shaking. As she undid the zip, revealing black boxer briefs, the defined outline of his erection took her breath away.

Good Lord, that's... Impressive.

She pulled the waistband down and the erection leapt free, so hard, so long, so thick, so beautiful.

Her breathing clogged in her lungs, the air conditioning chilling her damp breasts only adding to the barrage of sensations as she stared at the magnificent length.

Had she done that to him? Did he want her that much?

'Does it hurt?' she said, then realised her mistake when he gave a strained chuckle.

'Yes, it does. I'd love nothing more than for you to ride me right now,' he said, the explicit language only making her feel more needy, more desperate and like more of a fraud. 'But I don't have protection with me. So we'll have to be creative.'

She wanted to ask his permission, to touch him, but forced herself to trail a finger down the solid length, gasping when it jumped, bending towards her touch.

'Hold me,' he said, his voice a tortured husk of breath. It was all the encouragement she needed, fascinated and so turned on her thoughts were no longer her own.

She wrapped trembling fingers around the thick girth, marvelling at how soft and strong he felt—like steel encased in the finest velvet. Her thumb captured the bead of moisture leaking from the crown, lubricating her fingers, allowing her to slide them up, then down.

'Ah, yes...' He shuddered, shifted. The feeling of power built but then he moved the hand he still had in her panties. She bucked against his hold, his touch sure and firm and unflinching as he pressed the heel of his palm into her vulva then teased the swollen nub. He circled and stroked, expertly stoking the fire until it burned and stung.

But even as the rush of desire hit her, so did the terrifying rush of emotion.

'Tell me what you want,' he demanded.

So many things, too many to count.

'I...'

I don't know...

'Is this good?' he asked.

She nodded, round a choking sob, just as he swirled and stroked over the very heart of her.

She jolted, panting now, trying to concentrate on him, but too aware of his devious, devastating touch. She was caught in a battle of power, and passion and submission. A battle she was desperate to wage, but soon realised she didn't know how to win.

For while her movements became more clumsy, his were sure and true—torturing, tantalising, tormenting her.

She bowed back, forced to release her hold on him as the shattered sobs gathered in her lungs. The waves were building too fast for her to breathe, to think, to concentrate, to focus on anything but the tumultuous swell of pleasure. She moaned as the pulsing heat rose up from her core like a tsunami, destroying everything in its path.

He planted a hand on her back to bring her forward, to suckle her nipple, deep into his mouth at the exact moment the wave crashed through her.

She cried out, seeming to ride on the crest for what felt like an eternity. His fingers driving her up, and over, again.

At last she collapsed against him. Tears stung her eyes and she blinked them back furiously.

Don't cry, or he'll know you've never done this before.

'Shh…' he murmured against her cheek. He gathered her hair in a tail with one hand and gently tugged, forcing her to raise her head, so he could stare at her with those dark eyes.

But where she had expected to see accusation, disgust—she hadn't upheld her part of the bargain after all, had left him wanting—instead a sensual smile curved his lips.

'Are you okay?' he asked.

'Yes, that was…' she had no words, she realised '… really hot.'

He barked out a laugh.

'Good,' he said. 'Because it was really hot to watch.'

'You're not angry?' she blurted out, still confused by his reaction.

His shaft was still so hard, so huge, pressed into her belly.

Patrick had been furious with her, when she had failed to get him off once, while they necked. Although that had been nothing like this. Patrick had never touched her, or tasted her the way Karim had, had never even seen her naked, or semi naked. But he'd told her men had expectations, surely Karim would have them too—why wasn't he mad at her? For prioritising her own pleasure?

'Are you joking?' he said. The puzzled frown only made him look more seductive and made her feel more insecure.

'I didn't…' She glanced down, seeing the hard length still trapped between them. 'I didn't take care of you.'

He chuckled, the sound strained but no less amused. The sound reverberated off the leather seats, making her both painfully embarrassed, but also strangely comforted. At least he definitely wasn't mad with her.

'You're such a surprise,' he said when the chuckles had finally stopped.

For a heartbeat, maybe even two, she thought she saw genuine affection in his eyes, as he ran a thumb down the side of her face and stared into her eyes. Her heart swelled painfully into her throat, with a yearning far stronger than the one she'd just experienced.

'It's not an obligation, Orla. Or a race. We can easily remedy that once we're in a bed and I can take you properly. This was just a taste. Suffice it to say, what you did do will probably keep me hard until then.'

She nodded, the yearning, and the fear that went with it, starting to choke her.

Don't need more from him, Orla. Don't you dare. This is just sex. No biggie.

The sudden tap on the door had them both jumping. It was only then she realised the car had stopped moving. When had that happened?

Mortification hit and she scrambled off his lap, trying to tug up her dress.

Karim chuckled again before shouting, 'Mark, I told you not to disturb us.'

He readjusted his own clothing, with a nonchalance that suggested how commonplace the experience they'd just shared must be for him. She tried not to let it derail all her happy thoughts, or the endorphins still charging through her system.

He probably turned women to mush in the back seat of his limo every other day of the week. Didn't mean this couldn't be special, precious, for her.

Still just sex, remember.

'I'm sorry, Your Highness, it's not Mark, it's Muhammed,' came the reply from outside the car. 'We have just received urgent news from Zafar. News I thought you should hear immediately.'

The atmosphere in the car changed, a dark frown marring Karim's brow, the smile dying on his lips. 'Okay, wait there.'

He glanced at her as she struggled to do up her bra. 'Do you need help?'

'No, I'm… I'm grand,' she said as the damn thing finally snapped into place, the mortification starting to outweigh the endorphins.

He nodded, then, grasping her neck, he tugged her towards him for a kiss.

'Stay here,' he said. Then opened the door. He slammed it shut again after stepping out of the car and she acknowledged the pulse of regret that, whatever had just happened between them…nothing had really changed. She still wasn't an important part of his life. Certainly not important enough to know what had put that dark frown on his face.

But as she buttoned the front of her dress, her nipples still raw from his ministrations, she could overhear the conversation outside.

'What is it, Muhammed?' Karim commanded. 'I told you I don't receive my father's calls and I don't want to be bothered with his messages or demands.'

'I'm sorry, Your Highness,' the butler replied. 'But this was a message from the head of Zafar's Ruling Council. The news will be released tomorrow morning to the world's press, but Mr Abdallah wished to inform you immediately, your father died twenty minutes ago, and you are now the new King of Zafar.'

CHAPTER NINE

'KARIM, HOW ARE YOU?'

Karim looked up from his desk to see Orla silhouetted in the doorway of his study.

Heat surged, inevitably, making him tense, but the sight of her also lifted the weight that had been sitting on his chest since yesterday, ever since he had walked away from her—and into a nightmare.

'Good,' he lied.

He dropped the papers he had been reading—the contents of which had begun to blur in front of his eyes about half an hour ago—and thrust his fingers through his hair. He hadn't slept in close to thirty-six hours. Probably not the best time to have her in his office.

Orla was a problem, just like every other damn thing in his life right now, and he still hadn't decided what to do about her. By rights he didn't need her any more—or their fake engagement—his father was dead. And he was going to have to take his place on the throne, for the next few months at least—which meant he was being forced to return to Zafar tomorrow.

He had sworn he would never return to the desert kingdom, had never intended to succeed his father. But the old bastard had had the last laugh, his untimely and unexpected death at only sixty making it impossible for Karim to escape the responsibility.

A delegation had arrived that morning from Zafar, explaining that a constitutional crisis would engulf the country if he did not take his place on the throne. His father had ruled Zafar for years with an iron fist—as a result the institutions of state, including the Ruling Council, were no longer fit for purpose. Karim planned to bring democratic rule back to the kingdom, as soon as possible, but until that was done—and it could take months, given the state of the country's infrastructure and institutions—he would have to be a monarch in a lot more than name.

As she stood on the threshold of his study, the spark of attraction—and something more, that strange yearning that seemed to go beyond the physical—spread through his system.

Leaving his life behind in the UK, turning the management of his businesses over to his board while he concentrated on freeing Zafar from his father's brutal legacy, was going to be tough enough. But more than that, it wasn't going to be easy to explain Orla's sudden disappearance to the council members he'd spoken to that morning, who had suggested the engagement was something that would move the country forward.

Of course, he knew it wouldn't, because it was not going to lead to marriage, but ending it so abruptly and sending Orla back to Kildare might well be premature.

'What time is it?' he asked, his voice husky to his own ears as he got up from the desk and moved towards her. 'Shouldn't you be in bed?'

'I couldn't sleep,' she said. 'I just wanted to come and check you were okay. And give you my condolences.'

'What for?' he asked, his mind groggy as he took in

the simple jeans and T-shirt she wore. When had her tomboy attire become so damn appealing? The memory from yesterday, the echo of staggered sobs, the feel of her flesh, slick, swollen, ready for him as the orgasm he controlled ripped through her body, assailed him all over again. When had everything about her begun to intoxicate him?

Had it always been so? He wondered, his tired mind not quite able to figure out a coherent answer. His hand lifted out of his pocket, the urge to touch her again unstoppable, but then she turned into the light.

'For your father, Karim,' she said, the deep well of compassion in her eyes making him stiffen and drop his hand. 'I'm so sorry for your loss.'

The brutal feeling of exposure at the softly spoken words washed through him like acid. He wanted *her*, not her pity.

He shrugged, the movement stiff. 'Don't be, I'm not.'

If she was appalled by the bitter remark, she didn't show it, her gaze still containing that tender glow—almost as if she could see into his soul and knew he was lying.

He shouldn't want her compassion, shouldn't care about the sympathy she offered. He had not loved his father; he certainly wouldn't miss the man, and he had survived very well without anyone's care or compassion since he was a child of ten. So why on earth should he respond to that look now? Or be comforted in some weird way by the simple fact of her presence in his home? He hadn't spoken to her since hearing of his father's death, although he'd thought about her often while being inundated with the responsibilities involved in sorting out his business affairs to make tomorrow's trip.

'You should go to bed,' he said, keeping his hands

firmly in his pockets as he returned to his desk. He hated the feelings churning in his gut, making him do and say things that would make the turmoil inside him visible.

'Okay,' she said softly, still standing in the doorway. 'Mrs Williams told me you're leaving for Zafar at noon tomorrow. If I don't get to see you, I hope… I hope everything goes well.'

His head jerked round, the vicious twist of longing making the hollow ache drop into his stomach. And suddenly he knew he wasn't ready to let her go.

'You need not worry about seeing me tomorrow,' he said. 'As you shall be accompanying me to Zafar.'

'I… I don't understand.' Orla was so shocked by Karim's bold statement she stuttered over the words.

She'd been standing in the doorway to his office watching him, for several minutes, before alerting him to her presence. He'd looked shattered. His shoulders bowed, his dark hair dishevelled, his eyes staring at the papers in his hand but clearly not reading them.

He had seemed so different from the harsh, indomitable man she had come to know, her heart had pulsed painfully in her chest.

She had no right to care about him, or what he was going through. But he'd looked so different too, from the vital, playful man who had whipped her senses into a frenzy the day before, that she hadn't been able to control the wave of sympathy.

He'd been locked in his office ever since learning of his father's death with a series of assistants and delegates, diplomats and executives. This was the first moment she'd been able to get him alone… Had he even slept since getting the news yesterday? The bruised shadows under his eyes made it seem unlikely.

'I didn't think you'd need me any more,' she blurted out when he didn't say anything, just pinned her with that intense glare that made her nerve-endings sizzle and spark.

Although she'd been told nothing about her situation, she'd assumed she would be returning to Kildare. Now his father was dead, why would he need a fake fiancée?

'Did you read the engagement contract you signed?' he said, his voice gruff.

'Yes, but...' The truth was she hadn't read the contract's every detail, but she knew what it contained.

'Then you know the Ruling Council are expecting me to travel to Zafar with my future Queen. Breaking off the engagement so soon after my father's death is a disruption the country can do without while it is already facing a constitutional crisis.' He paused, and she could sense his frustration. But then his gaze met hers, and the stark challenge in his eyes made heat flush into her cheeks. 'And I think we both know there is unfinished business between us.'

She nodded, trying to ignore the bubble of something building under her breastbone.

She'd been prepared for him to discard her, had been ready to leave his home tomorrow, perhaps never to see him again. But the truth was, her reaction to that possibility hadn't been nearly as simple or straightforward as it should have been. She had tried to convince herself that was because he had introduced her to a world of physical pleasure she hadn't even known existed. But as she stared back at him now, his eyes shadowed with fatigue and frustration and a grief he refused to acknowledge, she knew her reluctance to leave him was about more than just the physical connection they shared.

'Okay, if you're sure you need me,' she said. 'I'll make sure I'm ready.'

The bubble under her breastbone turned into something that felt suspiciously like tenderness when she watched the rigid line of his shoulders soften.

Had he been expecting her to argue? To refuse to honour the terms of their agreement? Perhaps she should have. After all, there had been no mention of her travelling all the way to Zafar. And a part of her had wanted to return to Kildare, where everything was so much more simple and straightforward.

But they both knew this wasn't just about maintaining their charade any more. Or avoiding making the constitutional crisis of his father's death any worse.

He was right, there was unfinished business between them. And she wanted to finish it.

'I'll have Jason give you all the details first thing in the morning,' he said, picking up the papers again. 'Get a good night's sleep. It's a long journey through the desert to the Palace of Kings.'

'Will do,' she murmured, then added impulsively, 'Perhaps you should do the same. You look exhausted.'

He stared at her for a long moment and she wondered if she'd overstepped the mark. After all, his welfare wasn't really supposed to be her concern. But then his lips quirked in a rueful smile. 'Point taken,' he said.

But as she turned to leave, stupidly pleased by the oddly domestic moment, he added, 'By the way, Orla. Don't worry, I won't expect you to actually marry me once we're there.'

She paused and turned back. The smile had disappeared, and the intense stare had returned, almost as if he was trying to gauge her reaction. She forced herself to stifle the tiny flicker of disappointment, knowing it had nothing to do with the thought of not marrying him, but rather the sudden loss of that precious moment of camaraderie.

Was he concerned that she was getting the wrong idea? That by agreeing to go with him without complaint, she was expecting more? She forced a smile to her lips and said, 'That's a relief. As I'm sure I'd make a disastrous queen.'

He choked out a rough chuckle and the odd sense of elation returned as the tension eased. 'I doubt you'd make a worse queen than I will make a king,' he said.

She knew that wasn't true. She'd seen how hard he had been working already and how seriously he took his responsibility, to do the right thing, for his country and his people—even though he had professed a week ago to have no loyalty to either. And she couldn't think of a man who was more confident or decisive, who wielded such an air of command or authority the way he did—all of which surely made him the perfect candidate to lead any country out of a constitutional crisis.

But she could see the weary cynicism in his eyes, and had heard the bitter edge in his tone… And she doubted anything she had to say on the subject would convince him, so she simply smiled and decided to lighten the mood instead.

'Whatever you say, Your Majesty. I'll see you at noon tomorrow. If nothing else this should be a grand adventure,' she finished, pleased when she heard another tired chuckle.

'Yeah, right,' he murmured.

When she got back to her suite, she sent Dervla a text, telling her she was heading to Zafar, then switched off her phone.

She did not need to be bombarded with a ton of fanciful nonsense by her sister right now.

But as she put the phone down and got ready for bed, the bubble of exhilaration she hadn't really acknowledged until this moment expanded.

Going to Zafar with Karim *would* be a grand adventure. So much about Karim fascinated and excited her.

Here was a chance to discover more about him, and to see where this *thing*, this connection, or whatever it was between them, might lead. She would be well outside her comfort zone again, but was that really a bad thing? She'd spent so many years making a place for herself—finding a purpose—in Kildare, in some ways her work there had become a prison. She'd become scared to try anything new, to move away from the comfortable, the familiar and take a chance. She'd allowed her weaknesses as well as her strengths to define her, but Karim had already shown he had confidence in her abilities. Now she just needed to be brave again. And bold. And see where this new adventure might lead her.

She sobered, recalling the flash of confusion, even vulnerability on Karim's face when he'd lifted his head earlier to find her standing in the doorway of his study.

The death of his father had hurt Karim in ways she was fairly sure he wasn't even aware of.

He needed her support. Even if he refused to admit it. Because however short, or fake, or fleeting their relationship, she understood what he was going through because she'd been through it herself when her own father had died a year ago. She'd had to pick herself up, deal with the conflicting emotions she felt towards a man she'd once loved and looked up to who had let her and her sister down terribly in the end. Coping with her grief in the midst of all that had been next to impossible—and the only way she'd survived it was by immersing herself in work, in caring for the horses she loved, and by leaning on Dervla and Maeve and Gerry and her other friends and colleagues.

Karim had more than enough work to keep him busy, but he didn't seem to have any friends, anyone who could lift his spirits or look out for him when the going got really tough.

And maybe she wasn't his friend—and he didn't want her support—but he had rescued her once. Was it really so wrong to want to rescue him in return?

CHAPTER TEN

As the chauffeur-driven cavalcade of vehicles crested the rocky terrain and the minarets of Zafar's Palace of the Kings sparkled in the setting sun in the distance, the dark thoughts that had defined so much of Karim's boyhood and adolescence crowded into his mind.

His mother's pale, drawn face—which looked so young now from the distance of twenty-two years. The tight thin line of his father's lips, the spark of anger in his golden eyes—signals that Karim had displeased him again and would be punished.

Karim tensed, humiliated by the dropping sensation in his stomach—the echo of that long-ago fear—as the car rolled through the palace gates, and made its way past the honour guard of tribesmen and uniformed officers in Zafar's red and gold livery.

A soft gasp beside him yanked him free from the bitter memories. And he turned to see Orla, her vibrant hair contrasting with her pale skin as she stared in awe at the palace's golden walls. They passed into the lavish inner sanctum of lush planting, exotic birds and trees, elaborate fountains and deep pools of blue-green water created in defiant contrast to the barren desert that surrounded them.

'It's so beautiful,' she remarked, those wide emerald eyes meeting his.

'Is it?' he said as the familiar spike of desire and yearning—and something more debilitating, an emotion he couldn't and wouldn't name—accosted him. He quashed it, as he had so many times in the last ten hours, ever since he'd met her on the heliport in Belgravia.

Just knowing she was with him, tucked in a seat at the back of the private jet reading a book, had helped to calm him down while he worked with his advisors during the long plane journey. But being in this damn car with her for two hours, for the drive from Zafar's main airport, had been nothing short of torture. The phantom sound of soft sobs, the very real scent of her permeating his senses, had put his whole body on high alert while he was supposed to be concentrating on how the hell to navigate the next few days, weeks, God help him, probably even months...

She'd caught him at a weak moment the night before, and he'd given in to the need coursing through his body—to have her by his side while he dealt with this new reality. But it wasn't just the familiar surge of heat that accosted him as she stared back at him, her eyes seeing so much more than he wanted her to see. Just as they had last night.

'I'm sorry you don't think so,' she said.

The intuitive remark made the vice around his ribs—which had dogged him ever since he'd learned of his father's death—tighten.

Why had he really wanted her here? Was it just to finally satisfy the sweaty erotic dreams that had pursued him for days now? Or the expediency of not creating a diplomatic incident by terminating the engagement too soon...? Or was it more than that?

Why had he been incapable of leaving her behind,

when he'd never had a problem facing his demons alone before now?

One thing was for sure. He would have her tonight—and put at least one damn demon to rest.

'Once the official introductions are concluded, I'll have you escorted to my quarters,' he said, the tightness in his chest joined by the much more familiar spike of desire.

The blush hit her cheeks. 'Okay,' she said softly.

The breath he hadn't even realised he was holding gushed out at the indication that she was still willing.

Perhaps he hadn't been wrong to bring her with him. His motives didn't have to be that complicated. It *would* have been hard to explain her absence to the Ruling Council. And Orla, with her wide eyes, wild hair, lush lips and glorious body, had always been an excellent distraction. Perhaps she was smarter and funnier and more engaging than he had realised, her wry wit and willingness to challenge him a turn-on he hadn't expected. But he was going to need some light relief over the next few days, maybe even weeks, and Orla seemed the ideal person to supply it—in so many ways.

'I have no doubt the Ruling Council will have lined up a series of tedious meetings and briefings which I will be unable to escape today,' he said.

He lifted her hand, allowing himself to touch her for the first time since their escapade two long days ago in the car journey back from Hammonds. She jerked, as he brought her fingers to his lips and kissed the knuckles. A rueful smile tilted his lips as he released her and registered her heightened breathing. Good to know he wasn't the only one being tortured by the enforced celibacy of the last few days. 'But I'll join you as soon as I can,' he finished, unable to disguise the husky promise in his voice.

She nodded, her cheeks now a beguiling shade of scarlet.

He had to bite his tongue, to contain the rough chuckle of satisfaction that wanted to burst out of his mouth.

Damn but he wanted her. So much. Surely satisfying this driving hunger would simplify his feelings for her? Feelings that had become unnecessarily complicated, just like every other thing in his life right now.

'The madness should settle down in a couple of days,' he added, or maybe in a couple of weeks. 'Then we can discuss your future.'

After this much anticipation, he doubted either one of them would be satisfied too quickly. He wanted to explore every inch of her fragrant flesh, to see her lose herself again, but this time while he was embedded inside the tight wet warmth of… He dragged his mind away from the thoughts that had been crucifying him for days.

Not helping, Karim. Not when you have several hours ahead of you of tedious bureaucracy before you can finally make her yours.

He cleared the blockage in his throat. 'I expect you'll want to return to Kildare?' he said, trying to keep the conversation on practicalities to drown the heat.

Something flickered across her face that looked oddly like disappointment. He dismissed it, along with the idiotic leap in his chest. They'd already agreed that this was a temporary arrangement, which suited them both.

'Yes,' she said.

He nodded, glad when the car finally cruised to a stop, in front of the dramatic Moorish structure that towered above them like a glowering giant.

A row of dignitaries and diplomats, including the delegation who had turned up in London two days ago, stood in their ceremonial robes waiting to greet him.

One of the palace servants rushed forward to open the door.

The traditional wailing cries of the local tribesmen, punctuated by the ceremonial cannon fire from outside the palace walls to celebrate the arrival of the new King, became deafening as he struggled to ignore the provocative promise in Orla's eyes and step out of the car.

She joined him a few moments later. He had to place his hand on her hip, far too aware of her tremble of response and the effect it had on him, as he guided her through the introductions to a never-ending line of dignitaries.

As they finally neared the end, and approached the line of palace staff, he knew he'd had enough. The journey had been tiring for them both, and, even though he'd managed to get some much-needed sleep last night, having her so close was taxing his resolve, not to mention the last remaining reserves of his patience. He needed to get Orla safely ensconced in his rooms, if he were to have any hope of surviving the next few hours without sporting an erection the size of the tower above them.

Drawing the introductions to a halt, he called over the man whom they'd already been introduced to as his father's former head of household.

'Um… Saed,' he said, glad he'd managed to remember the man's name as he pressed his hand to Orla's hip. Now he'd begun touching her it was becoming harder and harder to stop. 'Could you take my fiancée to my chambers?' Apart from anything else, he wanted Orla well rested, because he planned to keep her very busy tonight. 'And make sure she has everything she needs.'

The older man's brows shot up his forehead, his expression a picture of shock, his skin darkening as he flushed. 'But, Your Majesty, it will bring much dishonour on yourself and Mistress Calhoun for such an arrangement before the wedding on Friday.'

'The… *What* wedding?' he snapped. Orla stiffened beside him, obviously as horrified as he was by this information. 'I didn't authorise a wedding,' he said, his voice raw with fury.

What the hell was going on? He'd never been informed of any such arrangement. Certainly hadn't sanctioned it.

'The Ruling Council made arrangements for your convenience, Your Majesty,' the man said, his eyes darting towards the council members who were standing on the other side of the courtyard, out of earshot.

'What…?' Karim bit off the swear word as the man flinched. 'What convenience?'

This was intolerable, inconceivable. He had never given any indication he wished for a wedding to be arranged on his behalf.

He could feel Orla beside him, trembling. Did she think he had engineered this, lured her here to trap her into marriage?

The fury was tempered by the brutal stab of guilt… And the hazy pain of memory. His mother's face dragged him back to the darkest days of his childhood, the words she had uttered so many times in her distress, before she took her own life.

He didn't love me, Karim. He used me, he tricked me, and then he discarded me, because he never really wanted me.

Other memories, ones he'd blocked for so long, clawed at the edges of his consciousness as Saed continued talking.

'For Your Majesty's convenience,' the man said, his face getting redder as his confusion and concern increased at Karim's reaction. 'The Ruling Council believed…' He trailed off, his gaze darting to Orla, who had gone painfully still beside him.

Why did that only make this worse? That she hadn't asked him to explain? What did she think was happening here?

'What did they believe?' he snapped through gritted teeth, trying to control his temper, and the bitter pulse of guilt.

'It was always your father's way, to arrange a wedding as soon as possible so that…' Saed trailed off again.

His father? The mention of the man he had always despised had the fury galloping into his throat. The bastard had tried to manipulate him in life and now he was managing to do it from beyond the grave? He wasn't going to tolerate this.

'So that *what*?' he demanded, his voice rising, but he suspected he already knew the answer.

'So that he wouldn't have to wait,' the man replied so softly Karim could barely hear him. 'To consummate the marriage.'

Of course.

His father had enjoyed exploiting women. He had used them and discarded them. Sometimes he married then, sometimes he didn't, but when he wanted a woman one thing he never did was wait.

'The Ruling Council have arranged for Mistress Calhoun to be housed in the Women's Quarters, as is tradition, to honour her as your betrothed, until the marriage is performed,' Saed continued, practically quaking now.

Karim felt sick—as the implications of what had happened began to sink in—and shame engulfed him. This catastrophe wasn't Saed's fault. Any more than it was the fault of the Ruling Council. They had simply assumed he was as much of an entitled, insatiable bastard where women were concerned as his father—and they had been trying to honour Orla as his betrothed while also giving him what they had assumed he would demand, this woman in his bed as soon as possible.

The irony—that he had brought Orla to Zafar intending to do exactly that without actually marrying her—only made this situation more screwed up.

But the truth was, the only person to blame for this catastrophe, other than a dead man, was himself.

'It's okay, Karim. I can go to the Women's Quarters now, if that works best for everyone.'

At the quietly spoken words, he turned to Orla. But where he had been prepared to see accusation and disgust, maybe even fear, all he saw was concern... And something far worse—trust.

Why did that only make him feel like more of a bastard?

What had he ever really done to deserve her trust? How could she have so much faith in him and his motives, when he had done nothing to earn it?

The look in her eyes reminded him for one agonising moment of the woman who had clung to him, after he had marched across a ballroom to protect her from the unwanted advances of another man. In that moment, as her fingers gripped his neck and her face pressed into his shirt, she had seemed more like a girl than a woman. An innocent, vulnerable girl who deserved to be cherished and had needed his protection.

The pulse of guilt and shame threatened to engulf him again at the disturbing thought that the man she needed protecting from now was him.

'That would probably be for the best, until I can get this sorted out,' he said, his voice so rough it scraped against his throat like sandpaper.

'I will have Mistress Calhoun escorted to the Women's Quarters immediately,' Saed announced, clicking his fingers to summon two women over from the line of palace staff. The manservant looked so relieved at this new turn of events, it was almost funny.

Although Karim had never felt less like laughing.

If he'd been angry at the prospect of being forced to take his father's place on the throne of Zafar, now he felt sickened by his own actions.

He'd always believed he was a much better man than the man who had sired him. Had always taken his moral superiority for granted, but when had it ever really been tested until now? And already he'd been found wanting.

He'd brought Orla with him to Zafar because it had been the expedient thing to do politically, but also because he had wanted her for himself. He had convinced himself his sexual needs took precedence over everything else—and had quite possibly put her into an untenable position as a result. Because getting this wedding stopped now might well be impossible.

How the hell was he going to explain to the Ruling Council he did not wish the wedding to go ahead as planned without also cluing them into the fact the engagement had simply been a ruse to frustrate his father? Whatever he did now, he realised, with a bitter sense of regret, Orla and he would not be able to feed the hunger tonight.

How could he have her brought to his chambers without raising lots of questions about his own integrity, not to mention the integrity of their engagement?

He tried to remain as dispassionate as possible while

Saed introduced Orla to the two women who were about to take her away from him, for God only knew how long. One was an older woman called Ameera, who was Orla's most senior lady-in-waiting, while the younger woman, Jamilla, had been hired as the new Queen's PA.

As the older woman fussed over Orla, Karim was finally forced to lift his hand from her hip. Before she could leave him though, he snagged her wrist and tugged her round to face him. Tucking a knuckle under her chin, he lifted her face to his.

'Don't panic, Orla,' he murmured, so only she could hear him, before he placed a parting kiss on her lips. He'd compromised both of them enough already by reacting so violently to Saed's mention of the wedding. He needed to calm down and work out a solution. 'I'll figure this out.'

He forced himself to draw back and let her go. Perhaps having her safely ensconced in the Women's Quarters wasn't such a bad thing. At least it ought to stop him thinking with a part of his anatomy that wasn't his brain. Something he'd been doing way too much of recently.

To his surprise, given how badly he'd messed up, instead of looking anxious or annoyed, she sent him another uncomplicated, far too trusting smile—the shadow of desire in her eyes undimmed. 'It's grand, Karim. I'm not panicking. I have faith in you.'

But as he watched her walk away, the sway of her hips doing nothing to dim the hunger that had got them both into this fix in the first place, he realised it wasn't her faith in him that was the problem.

It was his faith in himself.

He'd strived his whole life not to be a man like his father. Had always been sure to be honest and open in his relationships with women. To let them know what he could offer and what he could not. But with Orla, nothing had ever been that easy or uncomplicated. And now he'd crossed a line he wasn't sure he had the strength, or the integrity, to uncross.

CHAPTER ELEVEN

'YOUR HAIR IS like flame, Orla. Is it real, or from a bottle?'

'It's real.' Orla choked out a strained laugh at the typically forthright comment from Ameera, as the older woman washed her hair. Thank goodness for Ameera's chatty, friendly presence or she would probably have lost her mind completely in the last two days.

She'd been in Zafar for nearly seventy-two hours now, most of it cocooned in the palace's lavish women's quarters.

The morning after she'd arrived she'd been given a tour of the stables by Karim's stable manager, who had told her the new King wanted her advice on the care of the beautiful Arabian stallions that had once belonged to his father. She'd been flattered by Karim's faith in her, and at least it had given her something to do, but she'd also been disappointed that she hadn't had a chance to see him herself. So far the only contact she'd had with Karim personally was a two-line note yesterday morning, thanking her for her feedback on the horses, which he had said was invaluable, and then a cryptic mention of how he was working on 'resolving their situation to everyone's satisfaction'.

But since then she'd heard nothing—and the wedding was tonight. Ameera, though, and the other ladies-in-waiting, seemed convinced it was going ahead—in approximately four hours' time—because they had arrived in her suite of rooms that morning and insisted on beginning the seemingly endless process of preparing her to become the new Queen of Zafar.

Orla had never felt more embarrassed or confused or anxious in her life.

But she'd had no choice but to try and force herself to relax.

Whatever was going on diplomatically, she hadn't lied to Karim, she trusted him. He'd sounded as shocked as she had felt when Saed had informed him of the planned event, and she had no doubt he had probably been trying to prevent it from happening. But it had dawned on her this morning, when Ameera and the other women had begun gossiping, brimming with excitement at the prospect of the wedding—and all the guests who had begun to arrive—that getting it stopped might have turned out to be an impossible feat. Not least because how was Karim going to do that without admitting to everyone theirs was not a real engagement?

It was a humongous mess, she could see that, and possibly not one he was best placed to deal with when his whole life had already been thrown into turmoil by the huge challenges the country faced in the wake of his father's death—something that had also been a hot topic of discussion among the women.

'You are very tense,' Ameera said, massaging Orla's scalp with a fragrant shampoo scented with bergamot and orange. 'You must not be nervous. The wedding will be a glorious event. The whole of Zafar is excited to greet our new Queen as well as our new King.'

Orla swallowed down the hysterical laugh that had been threatening to pop out of her mouth all morning at

Ameera's generous words—the flush of guilt, though, was impossible to contain.

What would Ameera and the rest of Zafar's population think if they knew she and Karim hardly knew each other? And that this whole engagement was a total fraud?

The flush intensified, though, as she remembered Karim's bold kiss when they had parted and the fierce possessiveness in his gaze as she'd been led away.

Okay, maybe they weren't a *total* fraud any more. She cared about him, and what he was going through. Probably more than she should. And she still wanted him, desperately. As the minutes had ticked by over the last forty-eight hours and she'd got no more word from him about whether the wedding had been cancelled, she'd come to the conclusion that maybe going through with it wouldn't be so terrible. Especially if it meant they could finally deal with the driving hunger that had consumed them both—well, certainly her anyway—for days now.

After all, if they could fake an engagement, why couldn't they fake a marriage?

'You blush very prettily,' Ameera said, grinning, as she finished rinsing Orla's hair.

Orla felt the blush ignite. *Terrific.* As if this situation weren't awkward enough, now everyone could see how eager she was to end up in Karim's bed.

Way to go, Orla, it's official, you're a total hussy.

'The new King is very handsome…' Ameera murmured, the indulgent smile in her voice only making Orla feel more exposed. But then the woman added, 'From the way he kissed you in the courtyard, so tender and so much in love, I think he is not a man like his father—and you are nothing like his mother—so your wedding night should be a good one.'

Ameera laughed as she draped a linen cloth over Orla's head to dry her hair.

Orla straightened in her chair and turned to meet Ameera's gaze, surprised by the mention of Karim's parents.

She had been in the quarters for three days now, and she'd got the definite impression no one wanted to talk about the dead King. Because every time his name was mentioned in front of her, looks were exchanged and the subject was changed. Which, now she thought about it, was beyond weird. After all, he had died less than a week ago.

All she knew about Karim's mother were the things she'd discovered while trawling the Internet for information about him the day before she had met him. By reading old press reports, she had discovered that Cassandra Wainwright had been a young British heiress, who had married and divorced King Abdullah, returned to England with her son and then died five years later when Karim was still only ten years old… Which was perhaps why he had never mentioned her. But why was there so little information about her? Orla had been able to find virtually nothing out about the death of the former Queen of Zafar, or why the marriage had ended.

Until Ameera's cryptic comment.

'I think he is not a man like his father—and you are nothing like his mother—so your wedding night should be a good one.'

She probably shouldn't ask Ameera about Karim's parents. His past was none of her business. But she was desperately curious about them both. She knew Karim hadn't had a good relationship with his father, but she also knew how much he was struggling with his death, even if he didn't want to admit it. And now she was wondering about what had happened to his mother on her wedding night, too.

Was being curious about Karim's parents and their relationship so wrong? After all, she might well have to actually marry Karim this evening, because they were running out of time to have the wedding stopped.

'Did you know Karim's mother, Ameera?' Orla blurted out.

Ameera's smile faltered, and her eyes lost the twinkle of amusement that had been an essential part of her personality over the last few days. Did she regret letting the information slip? Orla felt sure she did, but just when she was convinced Ameera would refuse to answer, the lady-in-waiting nodded. 'Yes, I knew the King's second wife. I was a maid in the palace, when she first arrived here and they married.'

'What was she like?' Orla asked.

'The King has not spoken of his mother to you?' the woman asked, her gaze kind, but also probing.

Orla blushed at the perceptive comment, but the lady-in-waiting's gaze remained kind and knowing.

'Karim and I haven't known each other that long,' Orla said, carefully. That definitely wasn't a lie. 'He's never talked to me about his mother, but I know he didn't get on very well with his father.'

Ameera let out a sad laugh. 'The new King has not visited Zafar since he was a boy, and has not seen his father in over a decade, so, yes, it is true. They did not get on well.' The sad smile flattened to be replaced with a guarded expression. 'I am afraid I cannot tell you about what went on in the marriage, because Cassandra swore me to secrecy many years ago. And it is a vow I have never broken. His Majesty was only five when he left Zafar with his mother, but I think if he was aware...' She paused, sighed. 'Then he would not wish me to speak of it either.'

Orla's pulse pounded heavily at Ameera's statement—and the sadness in her eyes, which was so unlike her usually cheerful demeanour.

So something had been terribly wrong in the marriage before the divorce, and Karim might have witnessed it? Was that where the haunted look had come from when they drove through the walls of the palace into the grounds?

He'd insisted he had no feelings for his father, but it had been obvious then, as well as the night she had gone to his study, that the truth was more complex. Perhaps it wasn't that he didn't have feelings for his father, but that he didn't want to have feelings for him.

'Do you...? Do you know why Karim and his father didn't get along?' she asked.

He had seemed so alone in his study that night, but also during the flight over and the journey to the palace. So closed off and wary and tense. Karim had always been dominant, commanding, pragmatic rather than demonstrative, so it hadn't really surprised her that he hadn't wanted to lean on anyone, let alone her. But she knew he could also be playful, and unbelievably hot—because she'd glimpsed that man too during the heated moments they'd shared in the car—before all this had happened.

And she wanted to help him find that man again. Somehow.

But how could she do that, when she had no idea what he was struggling with? She knew he needed a friend, but how could she be a good friend if she didn't know more about where that haunted look came from?

'All I can tell you,' Ameera began, 'although you must not repeat this to anyone, for it is disrespectful to talk so of a king...'

Orla nodded, realising that Ameera was taking a risk by speaking to her so candidly about her former employer.

'Is that King Abdullah, His Majesty's father, was not a man made for marriage…' Ameera paused as if looking for the right words. 'Or, I think, for fatherhood. He could be harsh, as a husband. And also as a father. During the summers His Majesty Karim came back here to Zafar as part of the divorce settlement, they clashed often—especially as His Majesty got older—and the old King would have him punished severely for his disrespect.'

'Oh, no.' Orla felt her throat closing. Poor Karim, no wonder he was so conflicted now about assuming the throne. And still so angry with his father.

Although her relationship with her own father had become increasingly difficult after her mother's death, he'd never been a violent man, or a cruel one, or not intentionally so—just increasingly absent.

She was getting the impression King Abdullah Zakar Amari Khan had been both.

'It must be such a struggle for him to assume the throne if that's his only role model,' she murmured.

'The new King's advisors say he is very competent and has already made many good changes that are long overdue,' Ameera interrupted Orla's thoughts.

Orla's heart stuttered at the odd wave of pride.

She could well imagine Karim would make a good monarch, he certainly made an extremely efficient businessman, although it wasn't really what she'd meant.

As if guessing as much though, Ameera added, 'But his manservant tells me he does not sleep well at night. That he wakes from nightmares and paces his chamber. They believe he is troubled, yes, but it is not their place to understand what is in His Majesty's heart,' she finished and Orla heard the soft note of censure.

No, it wasn't the place of Karim's advisors or servants to understand what was in his heart—nor could they help him wrestle his demons, whatever they were—because that wasn't a job of an employee, it was a job of the woman he loved.

And okay, maybe she wasn't actually that woman. But she was all he had at the moment.

Over the last seventy-two hours she'd been panicking about her own situation. Worrying about what it would mean if she and Karim were forced to go through with this wedding.

But she could see clearly now that Karim was the one who needed an anchor—even more than she did right now. Perhaps it was time to show Karim she could help out with more than just his father's Arabian stallions.

'I need to see the King now,' she said.

Ameera frowned. 'That is not good luck for your marriage, to see him so soon before the wedding.'

Right. So they had the same silly superstitions in Zafar as they did in Kildare. She sighed. 'How about if I wrote a note?' she asked. 'Could someone deliver it?'

'That would be very romantic.' Ameera smiled, obviously pleased with the idea of her and Karim sending each other love notes. 'I can deliver it, while the ladies prepare your bath.'

'Grand,' Orla said.

Now all she had to do was figure out what to write, so Karim would know she was ready to go along with the wedding if that was what he needed. And she was here for him, if that was what he needed, too.

'Sheikh Zane and Queen Catherine of Narabia and Prince Kasim and Princess Kasia of the Kholadi tribal lands have just arrived at the palace with their entourages.

Would you like me to have them taken to their rooms before you greet them?'

Karim glared at Saed Khouri, his head of household, and tried not to snap at the man—especially when the older man flinched and bowed deeply.

Perhaps it was time he admitted defeat. He'd been in negotiations with the Ruling Council for three days now, trying to be diplomatic as he arranged to postpone or cancel this damn wedding while also dealing with a million and one other issues—some large, some small, all urgent—and he'd got absolutely nowhere. While carrying out all his other orders and decrees, the council had effectively steamrollered over all his suggestions to do with the wedding, and now apparently they hadn't even got around to cancelling the invitations to the neighbouring rulers and other VIP guests that had been sent without his permission.

No way was he going to be able to stop the wedding now.

'Sure, you do that, Saed,' he said, not making much of an effort to hide his frustration. 'I'll greet them properly in an hour,' he said, distracted by the thought of the conversation he was going to have to have now with Orla. 'Make sure they have everything they need in the meantime.'

Karim had met Zane Khan, a distant cousin, and his British wife, Catherine, a few times at events in London and New York and he'd had a few business dealings with Zane's half-brother, Raif, aka Prince Kasim, but knowing both men and their wives and children had been invited to witness this fake event was not improving his temper.

Karim's frontal lobe started to pulse as Saed left his study.

Somehow or other he was going to have to explain this

whole mess to Orla, and ask her to go through with the wedding. Perhaps he could offer her the job she'd asked for at Calhouns, or something similar. And include the payment she'd originally turned down? A million euros would surely sweeten the prospect of having to pretend to be his Queen for any length of time. But even as he contemplated doing that, he felt the bitter taste in his mouth. How could he offer her money? When he still planned to have a wedding night with her? It was the only damn thing that made the thought of going through with this farce tolerable. Wouldn't offering her money now be like paying her for sex? Of course, he'd had mistresses in the past, who he had supported financially… But his situation with Orla was not the same. Something about her had always been different from the other women he'd dated. He would certainly never have contemplated going through a marriage ceremony with any of them. Would never have trusted them not to take advantage of the situation. But strangely he did trust Orla. And he wasn't even sure why.

Maybe it was that moment when she had told him she trusted him? Or maybe it had happened before that, perhaps when she had responded with such artless abandon in his arms in the car journey from Hammonds? Or was it that first night, when she had clung to him and looked to him for protection? And for one terrifying moment, all he'd wanted to do was keep her safe.

It would be deeply ironic—that a woman he was being forced to marry had come to mean more to him than any other woman before her—if it weren't so damn disturbing. How did you tell someone you actually respected, and who you cared enough about not to use, that you were going to have to use them anyway? He had no idea, as he'd never allowed anyone to get so close to him before. And now he was going to be forced—thanks to what he was sure was the deliberate intransigence of his Ruling Council—to let Orla get closer still.

Karim paced the length of the ornate room, and finally let go of the curse word that had been building inside him.

He had forced himself not to see Orla again before he could give her a definitive answer about the wedding. But he wasn't sure going to her now was a good idea. After the agony of spending eight hours in a plane with her and two hours in a car—on the journey here—and not being able to put his hands on her, perhaps they both deserved the chance to savour the moment, to spend a long, indulgent night together once this farce was done with?

The knock on the door of his chambers dragged his attention back to the present, but did nothing to stem the hot pulse of heat that tormented him whenever he thought of her.

'Who is it?' he shouted out.

'Your Majesty, it is Hakim,' his young manservant called out. 'I have a message for you delivered by Ameera, your fiancée's lady-in-waiting.'

Karim frowned. This had to be from Orla, demanding to know what the hell was going on. And how could he blame her? 'Bring it in.'

The young man came in and bowed, then handed him a handwritten note. He recognised Orla's swirling handwriting on the envelope, even though he'd only seen it once—when she had signed their engagement contract.

How had so much changed, in so short a time?

The ache in his crotch throbbed as he took the envelope off the silver salver and caught a lungful of her scent, which clung to the paper. He ripped open the envelope. He read the message and felt the vice around his ribs squeeze.

Karim,

I know you're super-busy at the moment, but I just wanted to tell you however you need to handle our 'situation' today, I'm good with it.

BTW, I'm also a great listener. I know ours is not a conventional engagement, but sometimes grief can surprise us and we need a friend.

Orla x

Karim stared at the note. The simple compassion in the words made the hollow ache that had dogged him ever since he had learned of his father's sudden death turn into a gaping hole in the pit of his stomach.

How did Orla know that he needed her?

He tensed—suddenly feeling more transparent, more vulnerable than he had since he was a boy. And he'd sat in the cold church, staring at the wicket casket covered in flowers, the heavy perfume of the late summer blooms masking the musty smell of old hymnals, his legs dangling from the pew, as tears stung his eyes and he tried to figure out why his mother had left him, when he'd tried so hard to make her happy.

'Your Majesty, do you have a reply I can give Ameera?'

He looked up to find the young man watching him expectantly. The brutal heat flared into his cheeks as he recognised the hollow ache for what it was. A weakness he could not afford to indulge. And could not allow anyone to see.

He crushed the note in his fist. Leaning on Orla was not an option.

He shouldn't want her care or her compassion. He couldn't accept it. Because it would turn him into that defenceless child again—frightened and alone.

'Yes,' he said, the grim determination in his words not

helping to fill the hole in his stomach. Returning to his desk, he jotted down a note on a piece of paper and folded it, sealed it in an envelope and handed it to the servant.

'Tell Ameera to give this to Miss Calhoun.'

As Hakim nodded and left, Karim picked up the phone and asked to have his call connected to Carstairs in London.

He needed to arrange to have Orla returned to Kildare as soon as possible after the ceremony. He could then have the marriage annulled discreetly in a few months' time. There would be questions at first about the Queen's absence, but his course was clear. He was being forced to go through with this ceremony, but that was all he could go through with. He couldn't risk making this relationship any more real than it already was. She'd slipped under his guard somehow. And he had to minimise the damage.

She had come to mean too much to him.

Perhaps it was just sexual frustration, the rare chemistry that he had struggled to control, the strange circumstances of their situation, or simply the stress of being forced to assume a legacy he had always believed he would be able to avoid—and the nightmares that had assailed him ever since his return to his father's home. But whatever the reason, Orla was not the solution to controlling emotions he had thought dead and buried a lifetime ago.

He explained the situation to Carstairs and listened to the man's stunned surprise at his decision to end his contract with Orla—'Damn, that's a shame, Karim, you two looked so good together.'

But the hollow ache, and the inconvenient heat, refused to subside, convincing him that tonight was going to be the longest, most agonising night of his life.

CHAPTER TWELVE

'YOU LOOK BEAUTIFUL, ORLA,' Ameera murmured as she rolled the veil over Orla's face.

Orla breathed out a nervous sigh, far too aware of the butterflies going berserk in her stomach as the sound of the waiting guests and dignitaries could be heard in the courtyard beyond. Night had fallen a few minutes before, casting a golden glow over the large antechamber where she had spent several hours being dressed and primped and perfumed and styled to within an inch of her life by a small army of hair and make-up professionals.

'Thanks, Ameera,' she said, catching a glimpse of herself in the silver standing mirror near the door.

Her gaze stared through the veil at the stunning red and gold silk dress embroidered with a thousand tiny gems that draped over her figure like a whisper, to reveal the fitted bodice and skirt beneath of traditional Zafari royal wedding attire. Her usually mad hair had somehow been tamed into a cascade of curls, while her eyes had been made up with black kohl to look huge. The make-up artist might as well not have bothered, because her eyes widened to the size of saucers all on their own when she heard the crowd being quietened in the courtyard beyond. A crowd packed with kings and queens, princes and princesses, heads of state and dignitaries from Zafar and its neighbouring countries—all people she didn't know, and who didn't know her.

She could hear the announcement of the wedding being made in Zafari and then English by the man who had come to speak to her in detail about the ceremony a few hours ago—right after Karim's note had arrived, the contents of which continued to whirl round and round in her head.

Orla,

I'm afraid we will have to go through with this farce of a wedding, but I have already made arrangements for your return to Kildare.

In the circumstances, I think it best we don't share a chamber after the ceremony, so that we may obtain an annulment quickly.

K

The butterflies turned into dive-bombers in her stomach as she forced herself to draw several steadying breaths and ignore the foolish well of disappointment and sadness.

Why was she getting so freaked out?

He hadn't rejected her, he'd simply stated how things would have to proceed.

But why then couldn't she get rid of the sharp stab of inadequacy?

Ameera finished adjusting the veil, as the wedding music began and the dive-bombing butterflies threatened to explode out of the top of her head.

'It is time, Your Highness,' Ameera squeezed her hand. 'Do not fear, you will make His Majesty a wonderful bride.'

Except he doesn't want me as a bride, or anything else.

'Thank you, Ameera,' she said, gripping her friend's fingers back.

The huge brass-panelled doors to the room opened and she was forced to let Ameera go.

Clasping her hands together, she stepped out into the courtyard, flanked by the Queen's honour guard—who were dressed in long red robes embroidered with gold thread.

Just keep going. And don't trip.

She forced her feet to move in the red silk slippers along a path lit by torchlight and strewn with rose blossoms leading into the palace's central garden. She could see faces, so many faces staring back at her. She tried to take some of them in to calm down the dive-bombing butterflies and the pain in her stomach.

A striking man dressed in black tribal wear cradling a beautiful toddler in his arms bowed his head as she passed, while his equally stunning and heavily pregnant wife, who held an identical toddler's hand, curtsied and sent her a sunny smile.

That smile helped to get Orla past the next line of lavishly dressed diplomats and dignitaries, their critical gaze making her certain they must be able to see what a fraud she was. Then she passed another equally handsome man and his three children of varying ages—who had to be royal too—and his beautiful wife. The woman winked at her as she curtsied and whispered in a British accent, 'Keep going, Your Highness, you're nearly there.'

A nervous smile tugged at Orla's lips, but then she rounded the corner, and the smile died.

Her breath caught in her lungs and her steps faltered as her gaze landed on Karim standing at the end of the line of guests.

He stole the last of her breath; his tall, muscular build

made even more overwhelming, if that were possible, by the gold and silver robes of the King and the fierce planes and angles of his face only made more dramatic by the ceremonial headdress.

Royalty totally suited him, she thought, desperately trying to tame the giddy leap of her heart and the now flame-grilled dive-bombing butterflies.

His golden eyes locked on her face, then flared with heat as she approached. The weight of arousal dropped deep into her sex and tangled with the stabbing pain of his rejection.

His shoulders tensed, his sensual lips pressed into a firm line and a muscle in his jaw twitched as he reached out a hand and captured her trembling fingers.

'Orla…' he murmured, his voice so husky it seemed to stroke every inch of exposed skin. He blinked as if collecting himself then said so low only she could hear it, 'This won't take long.'

But I don't want it to end.

She stifled the foolish romantic thought.

What was wrong with her? Why couldn't she get this whole thing in perspective? How could she wish for more when she'd always known this wasn't real?

He drew her to his side and folded his arm under hers to hold her steady, as the officiant began to read out the marriage rites. She had been told the ceremony itself would be brief, but somehow she lost track of time, the force of him beside her completely overwhelming her senses.

She couldn't hear the officiant's words over the punch of her own heartbeat. Couldn't smell the delicate garden perfumes of orange and jasmine and rose over the intoxicating musk of man and soap. Couldn't feel anything but the strength of his big body next to hers, his thumb absently stroking her knuckles and making the pounding in her sex painful. And couldn't see anything but the blur of colours through the jewelled veil and the commanding aura of this man who was about to become her husband... And yet not.

After what felt like several millennia, the words she hadn't understood had all been said. Turning, he lifted the veil and she saw the slash of colour highlight his cheekbones before his eyes flared with a fierce longing that detonated in her sex.

He swore—his expression full of frustration—then captured her face in callused palms and bent to cover her lips with his.

Applause and cheering, gunfire and the pop of fire-crackers surrounded them, but as he feasted on her mouth, delving deep, the possessive kiss destroyed the last of her sanity. She clung to his waist in a desperate attempt to anchor herself and the only sound she could hear was them both, surrendering to the storm of need.

She wanted this, she wanted him, and God help her that was one thing she couldn't fake.

'Thank you so much for winking when you did. It helped me get the rest of the way down the aisle,' Orla said to the staggeringly beautiful and insanely smart woman she had just been introduced to.

Queen Catherine of Narabia was a British scholar originally, but as she stood next to her husband Sheikh Zane, who had their youngest child on his hip while the other two chased each other in the garden behind them, it was hard not to see how well she had adjusted to life as the wife of a desert king.

Catherine laughed. 'You looked absolutely exquisite but also terrified and I knew exactly how you felt, so it was my duty as a woman to do *something*.'

Orla found herself smiling back, despite the nerves running riot in her stomach. Karim's arm remained around her waist, as it had been ever since their kiss had caused such a stir an hour ago. The heavy weight felt possessive and strangely protective, as he had introduced her to all the guests, but she was brutally aware of the tension rippling through his body, every time she moved. And the thought that this might well be the last time she would ever be this close to him.

'How did you two meet?' Catherine's husband, Sheikh Zane, asked casually. But Orla could sense the intelligence behind his questioning gaze.

Was it obvious, she wondered, how fraudulent this marriage really was?

Ever since the ceremony itself had finished, Karim had made a point of shepherding her around the reception with him, which she had to believe was as torturous for him as it was for her.

He looked drawn, she had discovered, once she'd managed to calm down enough after the ceremony to gather her senses. Not just drawn, but tense and on edge.

'His manservant tells me he does not sleep well at night. That he wakes from nightmares and paces his chamber.'

Orla's heart pulsed in her throat as she recalled what Ameera had told her about Karim's sleepless nights that morning. But the wave of sympathy only made the heat that continued to ripple at her core—every time she got a lungful of his scent—more torturous.

She tried to remember the story they'd worked out to give Zane a coherent answer, when Karim's hand moved to her hip and her emotions cartwheeled into her throat again.

'I bought her family's stud in Kildare. We met while I was considering the sale,' Karim supplied.

'You know about horses, Orla?' Catherine asked, thankfully changing the subject.

Orla nodded, suspecting that Catherine had detected the unease between her and Karim, from the kindness in her eyes, and was trying to alleviate it. Why did that only make it worse?

'Yes, I… I managed the stud for a number of years,' Orla replied. 'Racing and horses are my passion,' she added.

They were putting up a good show. No one need know what was really going on… But still his response to her note tormented her.

Had she done something wrong, by reaching out to him? Was that the real reason why he had decided not to share a bed chamber with her tonight?

'Our daughter Kaliah would love to meet you. She's passionate about horses too,' Catherine added with a gentle smile, as she pointed out the stunning pre-teen girl across the courtyard who was dressed in an elegant trouser suit speckled with mud while she raced around with her younger brother.

'And far too much of a daredevil.' Her father shuddered theatrically, but Orla could sense the Sheikh's fierce pride in his oldest child.

'Not unlike her cousin Jazmin,' the tall man dressed in magnificent tribal wear who Orla had noticed with his pregnant wife earlier announced as he joined them. He looked slightly harassed, probably because he had one of his toddler daughters perched on his hip—who Orla suspected was the aforementioned Jazmin because she was bouncing up and down shouting, 'Giddy-up, Daddy.' An identical little girl gripped his hand and hid behind his legs.

This had to be the fearsome Chief of the Kholadi tribe, Prince Kasim, known to his friends as Raif, if Orla remembered correctly. Although he looked a lot less fearsome with his daughters in tow.

'Hey, Raif.' Zane slapped him on the back. 'I see you got left holding the babies again,' he added with a smile, before the little boy on his own hip started to chatter to the bouncing Jazmin.

The children were cousins, Orla realised, as she recalled that the etiquette advisor—while going over the guest list with her—had told her the Kholadi Chief Prince Kasim and the Sheikh of Narabia were half-brothers. The man had also mentioned that Queen Catherine and Princess Kasia, Raif's wife, were best friends.

It wasn't hard to tell, as the brothers shared a knowing look while their toddler children jabbered to each other.

These people were family, the unit they made so obviously strong and bonded. The boulder of emotion that had been dogging Orla all day—especially since receiving Karim's note—swelled in her throat. She blinked, trying to control the pain in her eyes.

Don't you dare cry.

But then Karim's hand shifted on her hip again, and the boulder that had been expanding all day settled in the centre of her chest as she glanced up at him. He was staring at her, his gaze so intense, the boulder felt as if it were about to crush her ribs. She looked away, knowing how foolish it was to regret the fact she and Karim would never make a family like the Khan brothers and their wives and children.

Why should that derail her emotions now, when this relationship had always been a business arrangement? This lavish ceremony didn't change that, no matter how significant it had felt as she had walked down the aisle towards him. And he had branded her with that incendiary kiss.

'Has anyone seen Kasia?' Raif's question interrupted Orla's troubled thoughts. His gaze roamed around the garden, his anxiety obvious as he searched for his wife. 'She was only supposed to be going to the restroom, but I think I may have to insist we retire. She looked tired and I don't want her on her feet too long.'

Karim clicked his fingers, signalling a servant boy over. 'I'll have her found immediately,' he said to Raif. He gave the servant instructions. As the boy raced off to do his new King's bidding, Karim added, 'Would you like me to arrange for a nurse to take your children to your rooms and put them to bed while we locate Princess Kasia?'

Raif smiled a warm but weary smile that softened his rugged features and made his eyes glow.

The boulder ripped a hole in Orla's chest.

No man had ever looked at her like that... Except Kasim. But that had always been a lie.

'It's okay, I've got them,' Raif replied. 'We always put the girls to bed ourselves. Can't even imagine what chaos that is going to cause when the next two arrive,' he added with a sigh. 'But I guess we're going to find out pretty soon.'

Two? So his wife was having *another* set of twins. No wonder the Kholadi chief looked so anxious, and his wife had been so enormous.

'Perhaps you should stop impregnating her with more than one baby at a time, then, bro,' Zane said, the affectionately smug tone getting a rueful eyebrow quirk from his half-brother.

'Don't worry, *bro*. I am not going to let Kasia talk me into impregnating her again *ever* after this,' he said bluntly, before bidding them all goodbye and leaving with his daughters to locate his wife.

A few moments later, a man Orla recognised as one of Karim's many personal assistants arrived and whispered something in his ear.

Karim cleared his throat and nodded, then turned back to her and the Narabian royal couple. 'Apparently the feasting is about to begin, and my...' His gaze locked on her face, the glance so fierce and penetrating she felt the answering tug in her sex. 'And my wife needs to retire.'

'We should leave you to say your farewells,' Catherine remarked, her gaze alight with humour and something compelling that looked like understanding as she touched Orla's trembling hand. 'I'm so glad to have met you, Orla. I hope you can come to visit us in Narabia very soon.'

'That would be grand,' Orla said, blinking back tears again as the royal couple left with their children.

She wouldn't be going to Narabia or anywhere else.

She had been told by the etiquette consultant she would be asked to leave the festivities early to prepare her for the bridal bed... But Karim had already made it clear he would not be joining her tonight, or any night.

There were so many things she wanted to ask him, she realised. So many things which had been too private to bring up with an audience.

A courtier announced the feasting and the guests began to head towards the palace's banqueting hall—finally giving them a moment alone.

'Why don't you want to join me tonight, Karim?' she whispered, before she lost her nerve. 'Did I...? Did I do something wrong?'

'No, of course not,' he said, but something shadowed his eyes before his face became an impenetrable mask. 'I have arranged for you to return to Kildare in the next few days and the marriage to be annulled in a few months' time.'

'But I thought we'd agreed we wanted to finish what we started?' she blurted out, before she could stop herself. Maybe she had no power to control this relationship at the moment, but if he felt nothing at all for her, why had he brought her with him to Zafar, why had he kissed her with such passion and purpose an hour ago and why had he kept her anchored to his hip ever since?

His eyes flashed with a fire that seemed to sear her right down to her soul, and his hand gripped her waist for a second, almost as if he were struggling with the same yearning she seemed incapable of controlling, but then he dropped his hand, and his voice when he spoke was rough with command. 'It would only confuse things between us even more, Orla, and you know it. And it could make an annulment more complicated.'

Before she could question him further, demand a real explanation, the personal assistant reappeared with two of the women who had helped prepare her for the ceremony. 'Goodbye, Orla,' he said.

As she was led away, the brutal yearning tore at her insides along with the painful feeling of inadequacy. She forced herself not to look back.

She went through the motions as the women took her to a luxury suite of rooms at the back of the palace that overlooked a secluded courtyard. She was presented with a tray of lavish dishes, some of which she tried to eat, so as not to offend them, but the last thing she felt like right now was food. The women then insisted on bathing her in essentials oils.

Where was Ameera? She wanted her friend here, but at the same time she decided it was probably good she wasn't. Keeping up appearances was the only thing that mattered now. And holding back the tears that had been building all day.

After the women had insisted on brushing out her hair and dressing her in a ridiculously suggestive diaphanous robe, Orla finally managed to persuade them to leave.

All of this was for show too, she realised, to convince the palace staff this was a real marriage. When it wasn't and it never had been. But as she found the suite's only bedroom and climbed into the huge mahogany bed, she allowed the tears to finally fall.

She didn't even know why she was so upset. Was it the disappointment of a passion unfulfilled, was it the perfunctory note he'd sent her, was it simply emotional exhaustion from the confusion of the last few days and the stress of the ceremony itself, or was it the fact she had somehow ended up investing something in a relationship that wasn't real?

The tears finally stopped as the sky lit up with flares of colourful fire and the distant crackle and pop as the guests finished celebrating the wedding of Zafar's new King and Queen.

When the sky returned to black, she finally sank into a restless and troubled sleep.

CHAPTER THIRTEEN

KARIM DRAGGED OFF the heavy keffiyeh he'd been wearing all day and ran his fingers through his sweaty hair. He dumped the headgear onto the lounging sofa in his suite's bathing chamber, then sat down to yank off his boots, aware of the lingering scent of summer flowers.

Damn it, even her scent is haunting me now.

He threw one boot, then the other across the room, in a vain attempt to use up some of the energy that had been pounding through his veins for four hours now, ever since he had turned to see Orla in the traditional Zafari wedding gown, her curves clearly visible through the gossamer material, her wild hair tamed by sparkling jewelled pins, and her eyes—brimming with awareness and need and understanding—crucifying him.

He tore off his tunic—the vicious arousal still pulsing through him.

By rights he should be exhausted. He'd barely slept since arriving in Zafar, the nightmares he'd thought he'd conquered so many years ago returning to disturb his sleep each night. But as well as the nightmares there had been dreams of her—his so-called wife—not just her live-wire response, her lush curves, the taste of innocence and arousal that had tricked him in the limo so many days ago, but also her smile and those emerald eyes, the same honest green of her homeland.

He shouldn't have kissed her tonight, shouldn't have given in to the urge to mark her as his in front of their guests, because she wasn't his. But something had happened when he'd lifted her veil and she'd stared back at him with a desperate yearning that matched his own—that damn compassion shining in her eyes, which had tormented him and made him weak. And suddenly his lips had been on hers, and her instinctive shudder of surrender had reverberated through his body as he devoured her.

He'd been hard, or semi hard, ever since. Even after she'd left the ceremony—through about thirty courses of rich food, which he hadn't been able to swallow, and almost as many toasts, which he hadn't been able to drink because he knew if he started he would never be able to stop.

He kicked off his trousers and stood naked in the large tiled room, aware of the bathing pool that had been prepared for him—and the blood coursing through his rampant erection.

What he needed was a cold shower, and to forget her. She would be gone in a few days. He'd already made the arrangements, knew he couldn't see her again or he would break.

He headed into the tiled shower area. Thank God one of his father's many luxury expenditures had included adding state-of-the-art plumbing to the traditional network of pools in the King's bathing suite. He switched the dial down to frigid and stepped in. The needle-sharp spray pummelled his tired muscles and refreshed his sweaty skin.

He wrapped a sheet of linen around his midriff and

headed out onto the balcony that overlooked his private gardens. The scent of water tinkling below in the fountains, and the mix of rose and jasmine and white musk from the garden's exotic foliage, permeated the night, but still all he could smell was Orla.

Was he actually going mad? From sexual frustration and the battle to keep the endless thoughts, the desperate need to give her more, to take more, under control until he had finally sent her away? And this painful longing—the terrifying vulnerability that haunted his dreams?

He entered the bed chamber, ripped off the towel, then slammed the door shut to close out the scents of the night garden.

But then he stopped dead, as a figure rose on the bed.

'Karim?' The soft, seductive Irish accent—lilting and confused—was thick with sleep.

His eyes adjusted to the moonlight streaming through the open windows, the light breeze from the desert stirring the still air in the stuffy room. And his flesh stiffened so fast, the vicious pulse of need pushed him towards madness.

She was like a vision kneeling on the bed, her naked body draped in a gossamer veil that caressed her slender curves, framing the flare of her hips, the turgid jut of her nipples, the curls between her legs where he could remember her slick and swollen, and the mass of red hair falling over her shoulders like fire.

His erection turned to iron.

Why is she here? Who brought her to my rooms when I told them not to?

The puzzling questions drifted in and then out of his brain, but he couldn't grab hold of them, didn't care any more about the answers, the wave of need and desire and longing so swift and unforgiving it propelled him across the room towards her.

She was his. And he wanted her. And he didn't care any more about the consequences. He'd done his best, but he would go mad now if he didn't have her.

He touched her hair as he climbed onto the bed, felt the soft silky strands curl around his questing fingers, then tugged her closer. He cradled her face, tilted her head so he could drown in those fathomless eyes—now dazed with need. He pressed the painful erection into the soft swell of her belly and brought her mouth to his.

'Orla,' he whispered across her lips. 'I need you so damn much. Tell me you need me too.'

It was more demand than question, but he waited—the anticipation building like a volcano—as her wide eyes filled with desire.

'Yes,' she whispered.

It was all the answer he needed as his mouth swooped down to claim hers, and his hands fisted in the misty garment.

He ripped it off her body, the sound of rending fabric joined by the shattered pants of their breathing.

He cradled her breasts, rejoiced in the heavy weight. He rubbed his thumbs across the rigid nipples, the hunger pounding through his veins as he felt them pebble and swell under his touch. He shook violently, determined to savour rather than devour the fragrant flesh he had waited so long to own. He thrust his tongue into her mouth—in deep, demanding strokes—as he cupped her sex at last, trailed his finger through the wet curls and found the proud nub of her clitoris.

She jolted, panting in broken sobs, as her body danced to his touch. Her back bowed, instinctively offering him her breasts.

He worked the spot as he captured one rigid peak then the other and suckled, forcing her to orgasm.

She shuddered and moaned as she crested. And finally collapsed into his arms.

He pushed her down onto the bed.

He couldn't wait a moment longer. The need so fierce, so brutal now he was scared it might rip him apart.

Holding her thighs, he angled her hips and pressed his shaft at her entrance, then thrust deep.

She flinched, as he tore through the slight resistance and plunged into the all-encompassing heat.

Is she...?

The horrifying question formed... But as the wave began to overwhelm him, he let it go, too dazed, too desperate to engage with anything but the feel of her—so hot, so devastating, welcoming him in.

He buried himself to the hilt, moving out and then rocking back, giving her the full measure of him, feeling her milk him as she reached another climax. The battle to hold on, to hold back, became impossible, as the swell of pleasure clawed at the base of his spine.

He flung his head back, shouted out his pain, and poured himself into her—as he surrendered to the exquisite pain. And let himself fall.

Am I dreaming? It feels like a dream. A brutally hot, wild, frantic dream.

As Orla floated down through the blissful cloud of afterglow, the dream turned into something too earthy, too intense, too sore to be anything but real.

The weight of Karim's body pressed her into the linen sheets, his heavy length still stretching her tender flesh. The salty musk of sex and sweat surrounded her. She could still taste the frenzied desperation of his kisses, feel his lips on her nipples, his touch, so sure and perfect, driving her to one titanic orgasm, then another.

The sound of his rough breathing, and the thundering beat of her heart, were deafening. They lay like that for seconds, maybe even minutes, as she tried to hold back the storm of emotion threatening to engulf her.

She'd seen the desperation in his face, heard the need in his voice, felt the exquisite stab of pleasure combine with the deep well of something she knew she had no right to feel.

The fierce longing contracted around her ribs and she struggled to draw a steady breath. What did this mean? Were they really married now?

Don't be an eejit.

The promises they'd made to each other tonight had all been false. Nothing had changed, not really.

This was just the sex talking. Raw, epic, far too intimate, long-overdue sex, but still just sex.

Karim had been her first. And she'd been fascinated with him for a while now. But sex didn't mean intimacy. Or even affection.

A warm desert breeze played over her skin. She shuddered, aware of her nakedness, and his. He'd torn off the negligee, suckled her breasts, worked her clitoris with a focus and purpose that had shattered her in seconds. The echoes of sensation still caressed her skin. She'd had no time to deal with the emotional impact, but it started to besiege her now.

'Karim?' she whispered into the darkness. He didn't reply.

She slid her palms down his back and realised his rough breathing had fallen into a deeper rhythm.

Was he...? Was he asleep?

She blinked rapidly, aware of the dark silky waves of

his hair tickling her nose, and the ridge of his collarbone digging into her shoulder.

She shifted, managing to get her hands underneath his shoulder blade, and gave him a gentle shove.

He rolled off her onto his back. She gathered the thin sheet up to cover her nakedness, aware of the sticky residue between her thighs and the memory of him plunging into her so hard, so fast, so furiously. He was a large man, in every respect, but it had only hurt for a moment. Even so she had seen the stunned question in his eyes, and regretted the lie she'd told him about her experience.

She glanced across at him. His usually harsh features looked relaxed and almost boyish in sleep, the smudges under his eyes shadowed by the long eyelashes resting against his cheeks.

Why had he come to her? Had it been an accident? Had her attendants put her in his rooms by mistake? It had to be so, he had looked as shocked as her, when she'd woken—dazed and disorientated—to find him standing at the end of the bed, so powerful and compelling and irresistible. Everything she'd imagined and a lot she hadn't.

It had all happened so fast, and yet the memories now spun through her mind on a loop. The dance of his tongue, branding her, owning her. The touch of his fingers, finding the heart of her pleasure and exploiting it ruthlessly. The fierce frown on his face as he plunged inside her and made her his.

Except she wasn't his. He was sending her home in a few days. And the only reason this had happened was because the palace staff seemed to have their own agenda, which had nothing to do with what Karim wanted.

She let out a guttered breath, tried to keep a firm grip on the sinking sadness in her heart.

She shouldn't stay in his bed, shouldn't encourage

any more intimacy between them. This was about self-preservation now, because she was very much afraid she was falling in love with this taciturn, intense, unattainable man, who also happened to be her husband.

And all that would lead to was devastation.

But as she scooted to the edge of the bed, she heard movement behind her and then a muscular arm banded around her waist and drew her back into the cradle of his big body. She found herself anchored to him, his hot chest pressing against her back, his thighs cradling hers.

He buried his face in her hair, his arm tightening as he held her close—possessive, protective, unyielding.

'Don't…' The gruff words were groggy with exhaustion but no less demanding. 'I need you… Tonight.'

Just like that her heart tumbled into the abyss. And the tears of misery she had shed earlier turned to tears of tenderness as his breathing descended again into the rhythm of exhausted sleep.

After what felt like for ever, the emotion clogging her throat finally cleared enough that all she could hear was the strong steady beat of his heart at her back—safe, secure, all-consuming—beckoning her into oblivion too.

'No… No… Don't.'

Orla woke with a start, to see dawn lightening the sky outside the bed chamber. The gruff shouts—so full of pain—were echoing in her ear.

Karim.

The events of the night came flooding back, as she became aware of the soreness in her sex, the reddened skin where he had touched and suckled her. And his arm still wrapped around her midriff.

'No… Don't… Don't hurt her.'

She shifted round, breaking his hold. He was still

asleep, his eyes squeezed tightly shut, his face a mask of pain, his body rigid with the effort to fight off the dream.

The tenderness that had felled her the night before returned. Bringing with it the deep need to save him from whatever terror was chasing him.

'Karim, it's okay…' She cupped his cheeks. The stubble abraded her palms as he shook his head, attempting to chase away the pain. 'Wake up, Karim,' she whispered fiercely, desperate to free him from the nightmare.

'No…' He gasped, and a tear leaked from his tightly closed eyes. 'Don't. She's crying… You're hurting her.' His voice was raw, deep, but beneath the man's anguish she could hear a child's fear.

This was more than a nightmare. What had happened to him? Who was he trying to protect? Was this why he had needed her so badly the night before, to keep him safe from this?

'Karim, I'm here, you're safe, she's safe, it's okay…' She raised her voice, clung onto his cheeks as his hands curled into fists and she watched him fight to escape the dream.

'No… No…' He tossed his head, the struggle so real and painful, tears rolled down Orla's cheeks too. 'I can't…'

'Yes… You can. It's okay, you can wake up now. Karim?'

His eyelids jerked open, the jagged breaths as he fought to wake making his chest lift and fall in tortured gasps. The shattered depths of his eyes were so full of anguish as he wrenched himself back to the present, a sob caught in her throat. He couldn't see her, not at first. All he could see was the painful memory.

'Karim, it's okay, it's me, Orla. I'm here.' She stroked his cheek, to soothe the hard muscles bunched there. The straining sinews in his neck softened and she saw the moment when he registered where he was, and who he was with, the terror in his gaze becoming shuttered, wary, guarded.

He clasped her wrist, to draw her hand away from his face, then ran his thumb under her eye to capture the last of her tears.

'Why are you crying?' he said, the roughened whisper raw with confusion.

'You… You had a nightmare,' she said, her throat still thick with emotion.

He blinked, and the last of the vulnerability disappeared. To be replaced by something that looked like horror.

He rolled away from her, covered his eyes with his forearm, then swore.

She laid a hand on his chest, felt the harsh tattoo of his galloping heartbeat, the spasms of his breathing still too fast and frantic.

He covered her hand with one of his, the connection arching between them. He still needed her, and she wanted to help. To be here for him.

'Karim, what…what was it about? The nightmare? Do you know?'

He shook his head, his eyes still covered, but he didn't look at her and she sensed it wasn't that he didn't know, but that he didn't want to know.

'You were begging someone not to hurt someone else, a woman, I think,' she managed, knowing she was stepping over that invisible line, again, that barrier that he had erected so deliberately the day before with his note, but refusing to let that stop her. This marriage was more than just a convenience, much more.

She'd left her father to his pain, too scared and insecure to intervene when he'd shut her out repeatedly, and it had been the wrong thing to do. Karim had asked for her help last night and she wanted to give it to him.

'Perhaps if you talked about it?' she began.

'There is nothing to talk about,' he said, his voice strained. 'I told you, I don't know what the damn nightmares are about.' She could hear the lie in his voice, just as she had with her father, when he had refused to confront the pain.

But was he lying to her, or to himself?

'Was it…? Was it your mother?' she asked.

His hand gripped hers as he lifted his arm and swung his head round to stare at her—and she could see the horrifying truth in his expression. The truth Ameera had alluded to, the reason why he had struggled so much when returning to Zafar, and why he had talked with such contempt about his father weeks ago, on the day of the ball.

'Did he hurt her?' she asked. 'More than just emotionally?'

His eyes narrowed and he let go of the hand resting on his chest. 'I don't wish to talk about it.'

He whipped the sheet off to climb out of the bed. Heat hit her cheeks at the sight of his naked buttocks, and the evidence, when he turned towards her, that he was fully aroused. The heat gathered in her sex, fast and furious and unbidden as her gaze rose from the hard evidence of his arousal to find him watching her—the answering heat in his eyes as vivid as it was compelling.

'You should go…' he said at last. 'You weren't supposed to be here,' he added, confirming what she'd already guessed, the harsh truth like a blow.

'I know,' she said.

He nodded. 'Then you need to leave now… Unless you want a repeat of last night?'

It was a taunt, plain and simple, a dare, a demand she

accept what had happened last night had never been about more than the all-consuming hunger that had blindsided them both. That she had no right to any more of him than he was willing to give her. And she had no doubt at all he expected her to be shocked, disgusted—provoked into letting him scare her away, reduce what they had shared to nothing more than desire.

But it didn't work, because she could still hear the pain in his voice, that strange echo of self-loathing. And she knew what had happened last night hadn't just been about sex, it had been so much more than that, and now she knew why he had tried so hard to diminish and disguise and control what had been happening between them ever since their first night together…

He was scared of this attraction, as much as she was. And she knew, without a shadow of a doubt, however hard it was to confront him, and however vulnerable it made her, one of them had to stop being a coward and admit what was really happening here.

So instead of denying the passion, she took the initiative he had gifted to her last night, let the emotion as well as the desire spur her on and reached for him.

She stroked a finger down the strident erection, rejoicing in the sense of power and connection when it jerked against her touch. And forced herself to say the words she had been denied during their wedding last night.

'I do… Want you.'

And so much more.

'Don't…' Karim grasped Orla's wrist, shocked not just by the fierce passion but also by the brutal tenderness, the unflinching compassion, the unguarded honesty in her gaze—and how much it made him feel.

She knew about what he'd witnessed. How did she

know? When until a few seconds ago he hadn't even known himself?

The meaning of the nightmares had eluded him—each night, though, they had become more real, more vivid… The pitiful sight of a woman's body curled into a protective ball, the hollow thud of a man's fists, the terrifying mix of shame and fear and impotent childish rage as he pressed his hands over his ears and cried and begged to make it stop.

But he had been unable to make sense of it, until now. Until Orla.

And now he knew the truth, he was terrified it would break him. The way it had when he was a boy.

'Don't say that unless you mean it,' he managed, his voice raw with need. He would give her the choice. Let her see that he could never give her more than this.

'I do…mean it,' she murmured.

Fire burned through his gut, obliterating the pain and the fear that he had carried with him since childhood. That he would never be whole, never be enough.

He climbed back on the bed, held her wrists above her head, manacling them with one hand. She was at his mercy, her body flushed, waiting, her ripe breasts thrust out, quivering with her need.

Her hair flowed around her on the white linen sheets, the delicate scent of wild flowers and arousal torturing him.

But her gaze—honest, open, unflinching—watched him without an ounce of fear. How could she look so bold, so unafraid, when he was the one in control? And why did he feel so frantic, so desperate, again…?

Once should have been enough to destroy this hunger, but the need was flowing through him like molten lava—demanding he take her again, to escape the pain.

He covered one thrusting breast with his lips, sucking the plump nipple into his mouth, until it swelled and hardened and she shuddered with need. The artless, unashamed response only fired his hunger, his desperation.

He let go of her wrists, let her bury her fingers in his hair as he skimmed his palms down her body, his lips feasting on her and devastating him as she bucked and moaned, unable to hold back. Unable to deny him anything.

He licked at her sex, found the tight nub of her clitoris, feasted on the sweet sultry moans of her surrender until she flew apart in his arms.

He rose above her, the need holding him prisoner. Her gaze—still bold, still unashamed, but soft with a tenderness that terrified him—locked on his. He angled her hips and plunged, burying the massive erection in the tight clasp of her body. He rode the storm, letting it rage around them, cocooning them both in the painful pleasure, the desperate need, and worked the spot he knew would make her fall.

She clasped his shoulders and clung on, her gaze not wavering, not faltering, letting him take his fill—so brave, so beautiful... So his.

Somehow, he held on until the last moment, until she tightened around him.

He yanked himself free with the last of his strength, just in time, to spill himself on the sheets.

Afterglow rushed through his body, but right behind it was the terrible realisation that he'd given Orla something he'd never given any other woman... A glimpse of the vulnerable child who lurked inside him—and would never deserve to be saved.

Orla held Karim, hugging him, feeling his fear and absorbing it alongside her own. She didn't know what had just happened between them, but it felt so real and significant it hurt to breathe.

She threaded her fingers through his hair, swept it back from his forehead. 'Karim? Are you okay?'

He lifted off her, but his eyes when they met hers were guarded and unyielding. 'Of course,' he said. 'Thanks,' he added, the curt acknowledgement a deliberate blow.

The mask had returned, and her heart ached. But as he threw the sheet back, to climb off the bed, his gaze landed on the sheet beneath her and his whole body stiffened.

His head jerked up and his gaze locked on hers, shocked and accusing. 'Are you on your period?' he demanded.

She could have lied. A part of her wanted to lie. Knowing she must have bled last night and he had spotted the stains on the sheet.

The truth would only make her more vulnerable.

But there were too many lies between them already. Lies and half-truths. And she was tired of trying to maintain them all.

So she shook her head.

He swore and raked his fingers through his hair. 'So you *were* a virgin last night? You lied to me?'

She nodded.

'Why? Damn it?' he demanded, his face a mask of disbelief, the same horrifying disbelief that had crossed it when he had first taken her virginity.

She clasped the sheet to her breasts and sat up, feeling so exposed now by his searing gaze—which was full of accusation, and even anger.

'Why does it matter?' she asked.

She'd given herself to him, not once, but twice. And she refused to regret it, or apologise for it. The pleasure had been immeasurable, she could still feel the last orgasm rippling through her, but there was a greater significance to what she'd done that she wouldn't hide from.

'Because it gives me a responsibility I didn't want. And you shouldn't want either.'

'What responsibility?' she asked, confused now as well as wary. Why should her sexual experience—or lack of it—have anything to do with what they'd just shared?

'You were untouched, you lied about it, but the consequences are the same. We can't just get an annulment now.' His eyes filled with suspicion and arrogance, and denial. 'If you think you can trick me into intimacy, you're wrong,' he said, his gaze flat and so cold it chilled her to the bone.

The words were like blows, the bitter rejection of what they had just shared hitting that tender part of her heart she'd opened to him. To them.

How could she have been so misguided? she wondered. Karim wasn't a highly strung horse, or a foal just out of its mother's womb. He was a man, who had a great deal more power and experience than she did and that hadn't changed. He might have been vulnerable for a moment, but he didn't want her help.

She couldn't fix his past any more than she could fix her own. And it had been naïve of her to try.

She gathered what was left of her dignity, while her sex was still throbbing from the urgency of his lovemaking, and scooted off the bed.

'Where are you going?' he demanded as she wrapped the sheet around her trembling body and headed towards the bath chamber where the maids had prepared her for his bed last night, without her even realising it. She'd been served up like a sacrificial lamb, and then participated in her own downfall.

You're such a fool, Orla, when will you ever learn? You can't fix a person who doesn't want to be fixed.

'I'm going to take a bath,' she said, planning to wash and leave as soon as was humanly possible.

His rejection hurt, she realised, but not as much as her own stupidity, because she could still feel the deep pulse of yearning threatening to shatter her heart.

She crossed the large room, desperate to escape as arousal rippled through her traitorous nerve-endings while he donned a pair of black pants. But as she walked past him, he grasped hold of her upper arm.

'We're not finished here. We need to discuss the possible fallout.'

'What fallout?' she asked, as she struggled to hold onto the tears she knew she couldn't shed in front of him without risking the loss of the last thing she had left—her pride.

'You could be pregnant,' he said. His gaze strayed to her belly beneath the sheet, the thickness in his voice something she couldn't interpret. 'The first time... I didn't take any precautions.'

She nodded, her cheeks heating at the memory of that tumultuous joining, all the things she'd imbued it with that weren't real—at least not for him—only damning her foolish heart more.

'It's... It's okay,' she said. 'I wear a contraceptive patch. There won't be any repercussions.'

He frowned, but when she went to tug her arm free, his grip tightened. 'Why do you use contraception, if I'm the only man you've ever had sex with?' he asked.

The heat in her cheeks ignited to sear her chest at the probing enquiry. The personal nature of the conversation felt far too intimate—which was no doubt as ridiculous as the pain in her heart, which refused to go away, given what they'd just shared, not once, but twice.

'I used to have very irregular periods and…' She pushed out a tortured breath. Why was it so hard to talk to him about her menstrual cycle? 'They were very painful. The doctor recommended the pill to regulate them and help with the pain. It worked but I kept forgetting to take it, so I started using a patch.'

It was probably way too much information. But still his eyes narrowed, and she realised he didn't trust her. The irony would have been funny if her heart weren't busy breaking into a million pieces at his cynical expression. How had they come to this?

'I'm not lying,' she said. 'This time.'

Something flickered in his eyes that almost looked like regret, but he let her arm go at last. As she turned to leave, though, his raw voice stopped her, tight with barely concealed fury.

'If you think you can leave me now, it's too late.'

She swung round, the shattering pain in her heart threatening to consume her. She hadn't wanted to leave him, had given herself to him freely, but he'd taken what she offered, and rejected it. And she could see on his face, that hadn't changed. He was still closed, unyielding, unwilling to bend, unwilling to accept they could have had more.

'I can't stay, surely you can see that?' she said, the battle to hold onto the tears, and keep her voice devoid of the jagged pain now clawing at her throat, making her jaw hurt.

'This is a real marriage now,' he said, his expression tense and wary and utterly uncompromising. 'You don't have a choice, and neither do I.'

CHAPTER FOURTEEN

'WHAT DO YOU MEAN, she's left? Where did she go?' Karim glared at Orla's prim, neatly dressed personal assistant, Jamilla. Unlike his other staff, she didn't flinch instinctively at the sign of his temper, something that for once he found extremely annoying.

He'd given Orla a full six hours to recover from the life-changing events of last night and this morning before having this conversation. But if she thought she was somehow going to avoid the truth by going walkabout in his palace she would soon learn that the power of the King was absolute.

'I don't know, Your Majesty,' the woman said, not even blinking now, let alone flinching…

Karim felt the slow-burning fury—and frustration—turn to something more volatile: panic. 'Isn't it your job to know where she is? You're the Queen's PA.'

'She asked me not to ask her where she was going, so I did not,' the young woman said.

'She…' His glare became catastrophic, but it was the twist of anxiety deep in his stomach that concerned him more. 'She's not in the palace grounds?' The panic rose up to strangle him, the fear more real and vivid than it had ever been in his nightmares. Where could she possibly have gone? They were in the middle of a desert. The nearest town to the palace was over forty miles away. And she had no means of transportation.

'I don't believe so, Your Majesty,' the young woman said. 'She seemed quite distressed when she returned to her rooms this morning,' she added. And he heard it then, the note of accusation, and loyalty.

His temper flared, fuelled by the panic. And the guilt. He should never have let Orla out of his sight.

He'd needed time to calm down, to deal with the turmoil of emotions that had all but gutted him, while she'd stood in front of him, her eyes full of the pain he'd caused. At the time he'd been furious, convinced her virginity had forced his hand. She couldn't leave Zafar now. Not after last night. An annulment was now out of the question. Because of the Law of Marriage of the Sheikhs, an arcane tradition that had existed in this region for hundreds of years, that stated if a king ever took a virgin to his bed, he must make her his wife. It had all been detailed in their engagement contract, something he was now convinced Orla hadn't actually read.

But once he'd calmed down enough to question his re-action, he'd begun to wonder where that trapped feeling had really come from when he'd spotted Orla's blood on the sheets and realised the truth. Was it really because of an arcane law? When had he ever abided by the laws of Zafar? When had he ever even cared about the country's customs? Or was it because she had blindsided him with her bravery and compassion and the heat that had only got worse each time they had sex?

What had he really been furious about? That he would be forced to make this marriage real, or that he had known, despite everything, he couldn't bear to let her go now?

Was this about her virginity, or was it about his need,

the need that had flared and pulsed inside him, a need he'd never even acknowledged existed until he'd met Orla? And the fear he could only ever be whole now with her in his arms?

But he had to find her first to figure out the truth.

The fear that something might happen to her before he could made the turmoil of emotion tie his guts into knots all over again. He glared at the assistant, satisfied to see her blink at last. He spoke to her in low tones, the menace in his voice a cover for the desperation. 'Where did she go?' he demanded again.

'All I know is that she headed to the stables,' the woman replied.

The stables? The panic swelled and careered into his throat, making it hard for him to breathe, let alone think. He charged past the assistant. He would have to fire her another time.

'Hakim, get to the stables now,' he shouted as he strode into the office next door to his study. 'Have a stallion saddled for me and then speak to the stablemaster… My wife has left the palace on horseback and I need to know where she went. I will meet you there in fifteen minutes.'

'But, Your Majesty—' The young man began, looking stunned.

'Now!' he shouted.

He heard Hakim racing down the palace corridor towards the stables as he took the stairs to his suite two at a time.

Why had he given her time to consider her options? To run away from him? Perhaps because he hadn't really been able to think clearly ever since he'd met her?

He arrived in his chamber and began stripping off the

ceremonial robes he'd worn that morning to say goodbye to his official guests.

Thank you for inviting us all to your wedding, Karim. It was wonderful to meet your wife. Orla seems smart and brave, both qualities she will need to adapt to the role of Queen.

Queen Catherine Nawari Khan's parting words—before she and her husband had escorted their children to Zane's waiting helicopter—echoed in Karim's head again as he yanked riding clothes out of his closet.

He'd tried to dismiss the look in Catherine's eyes at the time—full of empathy, but also concern. Had she guessed that he had been using Orla? That he needed her much more than she would ever need him?

Guilt stabbed into his gut.

If Catherine knew, a woman he'd only met a few times, did Orla know too…?

That he simply did not have the courage to let her go. He'd seen the need in her eyes, not just desire, but something more than that, something that had terrified him while also making the yearning to keep her so much worse. And he'd chosen to exploit it.

He should have guessed, though, that Orla was too stubborn and independent—too smart and brave—to settle for his demands. What he hadn't counted on was that she would do something so reckless.

After tugging on his riding clothes, he headed down to the stables.

He had to find her. The panic kicked his heart rate up another notch.

The Zafari desert was a dangerous place, especially at night. And there was less than two hours before sunset.

Orla was his wife now, and his Queen, in every way

that mattered, which made her his responsibility—and the sooner she accepted that, the better.

Maybe he could never give her his heart… But she would always have his protection.

He had failed one woman once, and it had eventually destroyed her.

He would not fail another.

Orla huffed out a breath as the beautiful white mare crested the rocky edge of the dune and she spotted the shimmer of water in the valley below.

She tugged on the mare's reins and the horse paused, waiting patiently for her next instruction despite the scent of the water making her nostrils flare.

'Good girl, Sabella,' she said, patting the horse's sweaty neck.

The oasis was stunning, just as Ameera had described it when she had given her directions to it that morning. A grove of palm trees and desert scrubs surrounded a large rocky pool, formed by a waterfall seeping from the rocks.

Clucking her tongue and pressing her heels into the mare's sides, she directed the horse down the rocky slope towards it, knowing she would have been just as relieved to see a puddle after three hours in the saddle.

She shouldn't have left the palace, shouldn't have taken the horse, or the risk that she might get lost in the desert. A desert that, she had soon discovered, was as harsh and inhospitable as Ameera had warned her. But she hadn't been able to stay, had known she needed time and space and distance before she faced Karim again.

As Sabella reached the water, Orla climbed off the mare's back and allowed the animal to stick her snout in the pool, while she tied the reins off on a rock. After taking the last sip from her water pouch, she set about removing the saddle bags filled with the gear she had packed for an overnight stay at the oasis. And then the saddle.

She took care of the horse first, preparing her feed pouch for later and brushing her coat, before tethering her to a cooler spot under the trees. Then she set about putting up the tent and making a campfire in the shade, the water still beckoning.

But with the tough ride now over, the chores failed to provide enough distraction to stop the painful thoughts that had been torturing her, ever since she had walked away from Karim that morning.

'This is a real marriage now...' His words shot through her mind again bringing with them that swift, painfully misguided burst of hope, which had been shattered less than a second later—before she'd even had a chance to acknowledge it, or the terrifying truth behind it—when he'd added, *'You don't have a choice, and neither do I.'*

Somehow she had fallen in love with this hard, intractable, emotionally unavailable man. Who she was now very much afraid could never love her back.

What had happened with his mother...and his father... had scarred him in a way that had closed him off to even the possibility of love.

She couldn't save him if he didn't want to be saved. Trying to make him want her, to make him love her, was a pointless task. All she would end up doing was hurting herself more. She'd realised as much when Ameera had told her about the Law of Marriage of the Sheikhs, and she'd finally understood why he had demanded she stay married to him.

Something to do with her virginity. Nothing whatsoever to do with her, or the connection she'd thought had begun to develop between them.

She needed this time in the desert alone to find the strength, not just to defy him, but to leave him and return to Kildare.

After finally attaching the feed pouch to Sabella's bridle so the horse could regain the calories she'd lost during the arduous—and somewhat roundabout—trek to the oasis, Orla stripped off the dusty riding robes down to her panties and T-shirt.

She stepped into the cool water, aware of the ripple of sensation as she submerged herself, wanting to wash away the feel of his touch on her skin. The feel of him, hard and possessive and hers, inside her body. And yet at the same time not wanting to.

The sun was starting to sink towards the horizon at last, the heat still shimmering in a haze, but what should have been refreshing, rejuvenating, was anything but, the heated, painful memories still bombarding her and making her skin feel achingly sensitive, and her heart shattered.

She ducked her whole head beneath the water, scrubbed her aching body, the tender flesh between her legs that still yearned to feel him thick and firm inside her.

But as her breath got trapped in her lungs she was forced to lift up through the surface. The rushing sound of the waterfall covered the hasty beat of her heart, until she realised the pounding sound was getting louder and closer.

She turned, to see a magnificent black stallion gallop to a stop at the water's edge, and the man astride it— dressed in flowing riding robes—his face marred by a thunderous frown, jump down in one fluid movement and declare in a low voice, husky with barely leashed fury: 'Get out of there. Now!'

Karim.

She shuddered at the temper on his face, but kept her chin firm and her breath even—or as even as she could manage while the emotions she'd come here to suppress raged through her again—as she walked out of the water.

At last she stood on the banks, pushed her wet hair out of her eyes, and realised how far she'd come as his gaze raked over her body, making it flare and spark.

Funny to think that the first time she'd ever seen him she had been soaking wet too. But that anxious, desperate girl was gone. She was a woman now, in so many ways, and she didn't need to be scared of how she felt about him.

'Why did you run?' he said, his voice hoarse with fury... But as her gaze met his, her knees trembled, weakened by the pain she could see shadowing his golden eyes. Pain she realised he could not disguise.

'I didn't run.' She locked her knees. If she showed him a weakness now, she would be lost. For ever. 'I just needed time to think.'

'About what?' he said, the caustic question so ludicrous she almost laughed.

'About everything, Karim. About you, about me.' She jerked her thumb between the two of them. 'About what happened between us last night. And about what has to happen now.'

He stepped closer, his gaze so dark and tortured now she could feel the emotion threatening to overwhelm her. 'I told you what is going to happen now. You'll have to stay...your virginity has a significance that you—'

'I know about the Law of Marriage of the Sheikhs,' she cut him off.

His eyes narrowed. And she thought she might be sick, her stomach turning over with dread. Did he think she had always known, and that was why she'd lied? To force his hand, to make this a real marriage? Didn't he trust her at all?

She had always, always trusted him. Did that make her a fool? Or did it simply make her a woman in love... with the wrong man?

'If you knew, why did you lie about your virginity?' He bit the words out through gritted teeth, the fury sparking in his eyes, but behind it she could hear his defensiveness, and knew this was about so much more than that foolish lie.

'I lied originally because I was scared you wouldn't want to go through with the engagement,' she said, with brutal honesty. 'And I never thought you would find out the truth.'

'You must have known I would though, once we agreed to sleep together,' he murmured.

And she realised he was still guarding his heart with a fervour she had never even attempted to guard hers.

'Did you think you could trap me into making this marriage real?'

There were a million ways she could defend herself. But all she said was: 'Apparently not, because now I want a divorce.'

She could see she had shocked him, the turmoil of emotions crossing his face easy to read for the first time since she had met him.

'What?' he said, the stunned disbelief making it very clear to her that he *knew*... He knew he had captured her heart—that last night had been about so much more than just sex for her—and he'd planned to use it against her. 'Why?'

She dragged a steadying breath into her lungs, wrapped her hands around her waist, the last of the sunlight disappearing behind the rocks to chill her skin, and gathered the last of her courage. 'Because I love you, Karim. And I don't think you can ever love me back.'

Her declaration—so open, so forthright, so vulnerable—struck him like a sucker-punch to the gut, the bravery and dignity on her face as she offered him her heart simply staggering.

A single tear ran down her cheek, joining the sheen of fresh water making her skin glow in the dusky light.

A part of him didn't want to believe her. Didn't want to accept she had offered him everything. Because then it would require him to admit why he could offer her nothing in return.

But then she swiped the tear away, the courage and determination in that single gesture almost bringing him to his knees, and the truth pierced his heart.

He needed her, he wanted her, he loved her too, body and soul.

It didn't matter that it was too soon, too fast, too terrifying. He felt the ice he'd wrapped around his heart for so long cracking and breaking open inside him, and he knew he couldn't stop it happening any more. Couldn't deny or deceive or hide or escape or fail to confront these feelings any longer. Or he would lose her.

'I'll get dressed and we can return to the palace,' she said.

But as she went to walk past him, he grasped her arm.

'No...' he said. 'Don't...' The words choked off in his throat as she turned, her eyes still so full of the compassion he'd tried so hard to reject. 'I don't want a divorce.'

The look she sent him was full of the pain already

tearing him apart. 'It's not enough, Karim,' she said softly. 'I can't stay just because you need me, or you want me, or because of some old law that says you have to keep me as your wife. I need more to make this marriage real. I need to know you are at least capable of trying to love me back.'

'You wouldn't want my love...' He pulled her round to face him, dragged her into his arms, felt her shake, her body so fragile, so slender and yet so strong, so perfect against his. 'Not if you knew.'

She looked up at him, grasped his cheeks, her hands cool against his hot flesh, the shattering tenderness in the misty green destroying the last of the ice.

'Knew what, Karim?'

The sob that had been lodged in his throat ever since he was a child, ever since that fateful night, when he had let his mother be beaten and done nothing to help, and all the days after, when he had watched her sink into herself and he had been unable to beckon her back, grew so huge it tore into his chest... And finally unlocked the words burning in his throat.

'I don't deserve you. I never could.'

Orla could see the crippling pain, the same nightmare that had haunted him that morning. And all the platitudes she could have told him died in her throat. It wasn't enough to tell him he did deserve her. What she felt for him was new and scary and untried. But she knew it was real. And she knew he could love her too, if only he would let himself be vulnerable.

It was a start, an opening, she'd thought she'd never have, and she needed to be so careful now, not to destroy that fragile seed with her own fears and inadequacy.

'Why do you think that?' she asked, the tears clogging her throat as she stroked his cheeks, the muscles rigid with tension.

He pulled away from her, thrust shaking fingers through his hair, and she knew he didn't want to tell her, from the guilt and shame in his eyes.

'I used you, Orla. All the way along the line. How does that make me any different from him?' he said, his voice breaking, his chin sinking to his chest. 'He hurt her, and I couldn't protect her.'

'But you were just a little boy,' she said, her heart shattering for that frightened child. 'How could you have protected her?'

'I know but… She never recovered,' he said. 'She was always so sad. I tried to make her happy…' She watched his throat contract as he swallowed, the burden that boy had taken on still weighing him down. 'But I never could.'

The tears ran down her cheeks now. 'That wasn't your job, Karim.'

He lifted his head, his gaze finally locked on hers. 'I can't go through that again. I'm sorry.'

And suddenly she knew why he was so scared to love her. And her heart lifted in her throat. All this time she'd thought he was protecting himself, when what he'd really been trying to do was protect her.

The words Ameera had said came back to her again— *I think he is not a man like his father—and you are nothing like his mother'*—and at last she knew what to say.

'You're not him, Karim. And you never could be.' He shook his head, but she held on. 'But more importantly, I'm not her.'

His tortured gaze intensified, until she felt it sear her skin.

'I'm not fragile,' she said, because she knew she wasn't, and she never had been. He'd shown her that, protecting her and cherishing her in ways no man ever had before him, even when he didn't want to. 'And I won't break the way she did.'

He swore softly and she saw the moment he realised the burden had been lifted. That what she was telling him was the truth.

He gripped her shoulders, then tugged her back into his arms, hugging her so hard she felt her heart soar.

'That's good,' he said. 'Because if you ever run away from me like that again, I may have to spank you.'

Even though she knew he was kidding, the threat felt somehow erotic as the laugh burst out of her mouth and she struggled out of his arms. 'Good luck with that, Your Majesty.'

His eyebrows rose up his forehead, but then he barked out a laugh of his own, the husky chuckle music to her ears.

'Goddamn it, I love you,' he said, before covering her mouth with his in a harsh, searing kiss.

I know.

She kissed him back with all the new, exciting love in her heart.

As she fisted her fingers into his sweaty hair and dragged him closer to let the soft line of her body mould to the hard, unyielding line of his, she knew this was just the beginning. That they had a long way to go yet. But she intended to enjoy every single hot, exhilarating minute, getting to know this dominant, commanding, overwhelming man—her King, her husband, her lover. While trying to figure out how the hell to be his Queen.

But as he scooped her up into his arms and carried her towards the tent she'd set up in the palm trees her core quickened, and her heart swelled—and she knew she was already Karim's Queen in the only place that really mattered.

Inside his full, open, possessive and wonderfully overprotective heart.

EPILOGUE

One year later

'KARIM, YOU HAVE to let me go, everyone is due to arrive in less than three hours and I've got a million and one things to do,' Orla demanded, going for firm and getting giggly instead when her husband's arms banded around her waist and he dragged her back into their four-poster bed. 'And so do you!' she shrieked, a shiver of excitement rippling through her body as he nuzzled the spot behind her ear he knew was guaranteed to melt every last one of her cognitive braincells.

'Explain to me again,' he murmured, nibbling kisses across her nape and sending more delicious shivers of sensation into her sex, 'why we had to invite Zane and Raif and their wives and their five thousand children to Kildare on our wedding anniversary? When I wanted you all to myself?' he added, still doing diabolical things to her neck.

'Because it's been eight months since we went to Rahim and Omari's naming ceremony,' she said, thinking of Raif and Kasia's identical twin boys. 'And four months since we saw them all in New York. And I miss them.' The families had become friends of both her and Karim, treasured friends. Orla, particularly, had relied on the help and advice of Catherine and Kasia in the last year as she had adapted to her new role as the Queen of Zafar.

These days she and Karim divided their time between the desert kingdom, his house in London and their home in Kildare—which Karim had spent a small fortune bringing back to its former glory, just for her.

She placed a hand on her belly, except it wasn't just them any more.

'Plus I promised Kaliah we'd let her see the stud,' she said breathlessly, attempting to squirm out of his arms as his focussed caresses had the shivers of excitement multiplying.

She really did have a ton of things to do.

But then he placed his hands on her breasts, plucking the nipples the way he knew she loved, and she flinched.

'Hey?' He let her go immediately, and turned her to face him, the playfulness abruptly gone. 'Did I hurt you?'

'It's okay, Karim,' she said, the concern on his face making her heart melt… As it did on a regular basis, every time he treated her as if she was the most precious thing in the world to him.

He swore under his breath and cradled her cheek. 'Are you sure? You flinched…' he said, the bone-deep concern in his eyes making her realise she was going to have to tell him her news. Sooner rather than later. 'Was I too rough? I'm sorry.'

'No, not at all… It's just…' She hesitated.

She'd wanted to prepare for this announcement. She still wasn't quite over the shock of what she'd discovered yesterday morning herself. They hadn't planned this. Had never even spoken about the possibility. Not yet anyway. Perhaps she should have paid more attention when she'd switched contraception, but she must have slipped up somehow. And so here they were.

And while she was sure he would probably be as excited as she was…*probably*…she really wasn't sure if they were ready.

The last year had been one full of tumultuous choices and decisions, a huge adjustment for both of them. They'd had to make so many big changes already, Karim deciding to remain as King, in a constitutional capacity, while Zafar clawed its way back to full democracy and prosperity. The decision to come back to Kildare during the racing season and the job she had taken in charge of the stud when Carly had been headhunted by another stud… And, of course, the commitment they'd made to each other, to do whatever it took to make their marriage work.

This was going to be another massive change, and, as excited as she was about it on one level, she didn't want it to threaten what they had worked so hard to achieve over the last year.

'It's just what?' he said, dropping his hand to rest on her shoulder, the concern in his gaze intensifying. 'What aren't you telling me?'

She covered his hand with hers, forced a tremulous smile to her lips. 'It's just, my breasts are super-sensitive at the moment.'

'Okay,' he said, still looking concerned. And totally not getting it. 'Are you unwell?' he asked, the concern turning to worry.

'No, I'm… I'm…' *Oh, for goodness' sake, just tell him.* 'I'm pregnant,' she blurted out, past the boulder of anxiety starting to strangle her.

'You're…' His gaze darted down to her belly, her very flat belly, then back to her face. The flush of colour on his cheeks only added to the shock shadowing his eyes.

'You're… You're going to have a *baby*?' he managed. '*My* baby? *Our* baby?'

She nodded, blinking back tears now, the glazed wonder on his face making hope swell right past the anxiety and burst like a firework in her chest.

He's not upset, he's not unsure, he looks absolutely overjoyed.

She laughed as he rained kisses over her face, her hair, her body telling her how excited he was, how proud he was, how he couldn't wait to meet their child…

Then he made love to her, so carefully, so tenderly, cherishing each sigh, each sob, each shiver, drawing out her pleasure until she had to beg him for release. And her heart filled with joy all over again. Everything was going to be wonderful.

Karim lay in the bed a little while later, the afterglow still echoing through his system while he stroked his wife's hair.

'It's all right, Karim,' she murmured sleepily beside him as she snuggled into his arms. 'I still won't break.'

You might not but I probably will.

'You better not.' He let out a husky chuckle, and placed a tender kiss on her forehead, swallowing down the familiar flare of panic.

He loved her so damn much, and in approximately eight months' time there would be two people whom he would have to guard with his life, because he could not afford to lose them.

He shuddered, remembering the two squalling baby boys in Raif and Kasia's arms and the two little girls by their sides at the naming ceremony he and Orla had attended eight months ago.

Dear God, possibly even three people—if Orla has more than one baby.

He wasn't remotely prepared for this, was fairly sure he did not deserve it. He placed a hand on her belly, let the well of love inside him deepen and swell... And forced himself to relax.

Perhaps he could get some tips on fatherhood from Raif and Zane, when they arrived. They seemed to have survived it.

He sucked in a breath and let it out again, then murmured, 'I hope you realise you've totally topped my surprise anniversary gift.'

Orla lifted up, propping an elbow on his chest to grin down at him, not looking remotely remorseful. 'I have? What is it?'

He grinned back at her. 'Not quite as phenomenal as a baby.'

Or possibly two babies! Damn.

She sank down to prop her chin on her folded hands. 'Really? But close?' she said, excitement and curiosity sparking in her eyes. 'So what is it?'

'That's for me to know and you to find out,' he said, kissing her nose.

He'd had the deeds to the stud put back in her name. So that she—and her sister Dervla—would own it again. He knew she'd be thrilled and humbled and overwhelmed, but not nearly as thrilled and humbled and overwhelmed as he was right now after *her* surprise gift, so it seemed only fair to tease her about it.

He lifted her off him. 'Come on, we need to get up,' he said, giving her a gentle pat on the bottom.

'But, Karim,' she cried as he managed to manoeuvre himself out of the bed. Reluctantly. 'Seriously you're not going to tell me what it is?' she finished with a definite whine in her voice.

'Nope, no time,' he said, his grin spreading when she frowned. 'We've got a million and one things to do before our guests arrive.'

By which time she'd be positively bursting with anticipation and desperation.

Welcome to my world, my darling wife.

* * * * *

To my sister Nemone.
Thanks for taking me to my first ever race horse auction—
who knew it was so grand!
H x

RETURNING TO
CLAIM HIS HEIR

AMANDA CINELLI

For those who have grieved.
May the sun always shine after the storm.

CHAPTER ONE

IT WASN'T OFTEN that a man could say he'd looked upon his own grave. Duarte Avelar stood frozen in the sleepy English village graveyard, staring at the elegant family crypt where he and his twin sister had laid their beloved parents to rest seven years before.

But now a third name had been added to the marble plaque.

His own.

Dried wreaths and bouquets lined the resting place, with small notecards and offerings of condolences from friends and business colleagues alike. He'd been told his memorial service had been a grand affair, filled with Europe's wealthy elite, come to pay their respects to one of their favourite billionaire playboys.

His mind conjured up an image of his twin sister, Dani, accepting their sympathies, standing in this very spot to watch as they lowered an empty coffin into the ground...

His stomach lurched, nausea burning as he turned away and moved swiftly through the empty cemetery grounds. A sleek black car awaited him outside the gates, the young male chauffeur studiously staring at the wet ground as he held the door open. A pair of hulking bodyguards in plain clothes stood nearby, quietly focused on monitoring the surrounding countryside.

He had once enjoyed a certain level of familiarity with his staff. Had prided himself on being considered a likeable employer, easy-going and approachable. And yet for the past two weeks, since his shock return, he had been a pariah. It seemed everyone had been forewarned of his unpredictable temperament and had decided that ignoring him was the safest option.

Still, he caught them trying not to stare at the thick crosshatched scarring that spanned his face from the centre of his left eyebrow to the tip of his ear. He saw their stricken gazes upon seeing the scars along the rest of his torso when he went for his twice-daily swim.

He had gone from being the kind of man who could command a boardroom and charm any woman in his path to being one who avoided his own staff so as not to make them nervous.

His sister had managed the media, laying down an embargo for a couple of weeks until Duarte was ready for the attention. He had walked out of their first press conference less than an hour ago, knowing he hadn't been ready, but there was nothing to be done now.

The press had called him a walking ghost, a man returned from the dead. They had jumped at the chance to paint him as some kind of hero to fit their own sensational narratives.

No one seemed to understand that his survival was not something he wished to be celebrated for. Not when he was sure that his disappearance and the suffering he had endured had been entirely his own fault.

By rights, he *should* be dead.

He sat heavily against the back seat of the car, running his hand along the length of the long scar that traced the side of his head above his ear. It turned out that the nightmarish recovery process he'd endured after a gunshot wound to the head had been child's play compared with trying to fit back into a world where Duarte Avelar had ceased to exist.

As they drove away he watched the sun shine over the picturesque countryside hamlet that his family had adopted as their home after moving from Brazil. As a young boy he had been angry and homesick, barely even ten years old, but this quiet place had soon become home. Even when he had made his fortune, owning homes in every corner of the world, nothing had compared to the feeling of this small slice of peace and paradise.

Now...nowhere felt like home.

Everything was wrong. *He* was wrong.

He saw it in the glances his sister shared with Valerio, his business partner and best friend. They had witnessed his shifting moods, his restless lack of focus and his irritation with the debilitating headaches that could hit at any moment.

Two weeks previously, when they had been informed that he had miraculously survived, they'd both rushed to where he'd been kept, at an elite private medical facility on a tiny island off the coast of Brazil. Up until that point he'd had no memory of who he was, and had been singularly focused on rebuilding the physical strength he had lost during the months he'd spent confined to a hospital bed.

Talking to them had been painful, but he had started to recover some memories with their help. Coming back to England had been Dani's idea, and he had seen her eyes fill with hope that he would somehow come back to their childhood home and magically be restored to his former self.

It had worked to a certain extent. With their help, the gaps in his memory had begun to fill, but he still felt a strange disconnection from it all. Dani was determined to think positively, but Duarte felt nothing but apathy for the strange world he had re-entered. At times he even longed for the peaceful solitude of his anonymous life on the island, then felt guilt for his own selfishness.

In his absence, so much had changed. With every passing day he continued to be reminded of how people had moved on and adapted, growing over the hole he had left behind. Growing together mostly. He scowled, thinking of the look on his best friend's face when he'd revealed that in Duarte's absence he and Dani had fallen in love and were now engaged to be married.

His best friend and his twin sister were going to be man and wife. The fact that their relationship had begun as a measure to protect Dani from the corrupt forces who had been behind his kidnapping had only angered him further.

It wasn't that he didn't want them to be happy. But they'd buried him. Mourned him. And then they had moved on— all while he had been trapped alone in a living hell.

His anger was a constant presence and it shamed him. They had done nothing wrong. No one could have known he was still alive. In fact, his father's oldest friend in Brazil had ensured that no one knew until the time was right.

But Duarte hadn't told them that part of the story yet... He hadn't told anybody. Telling the truth behind the events that had led to him and Valerio being captured and tortured at the hands of Brazilian gangsters would mean admitting his own part in what had happened. Revealing the secrets he'd kept from them both. Secrets that now had gaping holes in them, thanks to his memory loss.

Dani had been subtle, but pointed in her questions about when he might feel ready to get back to work. Velamar, their luxury yacht charter company, was just about to open new headquarters in the US and in the Caribbean. It was something that he and Valerio had been building towards for more than a decade. His answers to her repeated questioning had been hostile and he had refused to commit to attending.

After the press conference that morning he'd told them both that he was going back to Rio for a while, to assist with securing one of the Avelar Foundation's charity developments—a sizeable portfolio of prime urban development sites in Rio De Janeiro, which had been the catalyst for all the trouble he had brought into their lives.

Of course the charity was only one of the reasons he was returning to Rio, but he hadn't told them that.

Dani had been stone-faced and had walked away from him without a single word. Valerio had been torn between them both, his mouth a grim line as he'd urged Duarte to take a large security detail and be careful.

He knew his sister was hurt by his distant moods, but he felt stifled by her company, by her obvious happiness with Valerio and by her questions about his time in recovery. But he didn't want to talk—didn't want to remember the pain of learning to walk again and pushing his broken body to its limits. Not when he was so consumed with bringing down the wealthy criminals behind his ordeal and making sure they paid for their crimes.

The insistent chime of his phone grabbed his attention. The screen showed a text message from an undisclosed number.

We found her.

Duarte felt his body freeze for a moment before he tapped a few buttons on the phone to open an encrypted server. His team of private investigators and ex-law-enforcement operatives had been hard at work in the past week, since he'd set the course for his revenge. They'd already recovered and collated every photograph and video of him from the past year, trying to create a map of his move-ments. Judging by the most recent files added, they'd un-covered a wealth of photographs taken at a political event he had attended directly before his kidnapping.

He scanned through the countless images, one after the other, seeing that a trio of pictures at the end had been flagged for his attention. The photographs showed him standing away from the main podium area, towards the back of the large event hall. Something thrummed to life in his gut as he clicked through the files until finally a glimpse of long red hair made him freeze.

It *was* her. *Cristo*, he'd finally found her.

Of all his tortured dreams as he'd recovered on the is-land, those of the beautiful redhead had plagued him the most. When he'd first come out of a medically induced coma, the only clear memory he'd had was of her holding him as he bled out. He hadn't been sure if it was his imag-ination that had conjured such a vivid picture or if it was truly a memory he'd managed to retain.

She'd kept him warm with her body around his, her hand holding his own as she'd spoken his name so softly. Her bright silver eyes had been filled with tears, and the scent of lavender had cocooned him as she'd tried to stem the blood-flow.

'*Duarte…please don't die,*' she'd sobbed, before cursing in colourful Portuguese.

Her words had been like a mantra in his mind.

'*You need to stay alive for both of us.*'

That voice in his mind had kept him going throughout his intense recovery process. And now he couldn't shake off the feeling that she was…*important*, somehow. That she was real. But, despite all the people that Angelus Fiero had tracked down and arrested in the last two months, there had been no mention of a woman anywhere near that shipping yard.

But now, looking at the photo on his phone screen...

One look at her face and he knew it was her. He knew she was real, not a dream. She had been his very own angel that night. She had saved his life with her bare hands, but she had left before anyone saw her.

Why?

He ignored the countless theories his mind produced, knowing none of them painted her as having nothing to hide. He would think about that later. For now, this woman was possibly the only link to what had happened that night and he needed to find her.

He looked up, noticing that they had arrived at a small private airfield outside London. His pilot, Martha, stood on the Tarmac to greet him, along with the small crew of one of the Velamar fleet of private jets.

Duarte smoothed a hand over his jaw as he tried not to think of his sister's words, begging him to forget his ordeal, to let the police continue to handle it while he focused on getting back to his normal life. Now, after seeing the woman's face, knowing she was real, he felt as if he was finally doing something that mattered. The cogs in his brain were turning, giving him purpose.

But was he just tracking her down to find out what she knew, or was it something more?

He brushed off the thought and dialled a number on his phone, hearing the rasping voice of his chief investigator as he answered the call and began griping about the various data protection laws standing in the way of facial recognition and searching for the mystery woman. Duarte growled back that he didn't care what he had to pay or what had to be done. He added that if his team had eyes on her by the time he landed in Rio their fees would be doubled.

The other man swiftly changed his tune.

'You will wait for my arrival before you make a move. Nobody is to approach her or bring her in—understand?' Duarte felt anticipation build within him as he growled the warning. 'She's mine.'

Nora Beckett took one last look at the empty space of her tiny apartment and felt the weight of uncertainty descend, choking the air from her throat.

She wouldn't cry. She'd done enough of that in the last six and a half months to last her a lifetime. Crying was for people who could afford that weakness, she thought miserably as she opened her phone one last time and looked at the list of missed calls and unopened voicemails. The name on the screen read 'Papai'. Such an innocent word to cause such a violent reaction in her gut.

She placed the phone in one of the boxes, knowing she couldn't take it with her. As far as she was concerned she had no father. Not any more.

She'd thought she was almost free of his reach…

She'd thought she still had time…

Her powerful father had been in hiding somewhere outside of Brazil for months, and Nora had taken the time to finish her studies at university, cramming in as many repeat classes as she could to try to undo some of the damage of the last year.

She'd barely managed to scrape through her final exams when the first messages had begun to arrive. She had no idea if she would even be allowed to graduate with her patchy attendance record, but sadly, that was the least of her worries right now. She had to get out of Rio.

The open boxes on the floor overflowed with books on engineering and environmental studies. They were the only possessions she owned other than her small case of clothing, but they were too heavy to take with her. She'd already done far too much today, bending down and scrubbing the place all morning so she could get her meagre deposit back.

As though agreeing with the thought, her lower back throbbed painfully.

As she descended the five flights of stairs to the street below she cradled the enormous swell of her stomach, taking care not to go too fast for fear she might jostle the precious cargo nestled within.

She had agonised over booking the four-hour flight to Manaus at this late stage of her pregnancy, but the nurse at the clinic had assured her that spending three days crammed in a bus to travel across the country would pose far more of a risk.

Her legs and feet had already been swelling painfully in recent days. And arranging her swift escape had put her under so much stress that her head throbbed constantly and insomnia plagued her. When she did manage to sleep she had fevered dreams of walking into her mother's arms in the quiet, peaceful safety of the remote animal sanctuary where she'd grown up on the banks of the Amazon.

She just hoped that Maureen Beckett would welcome her runaway daughter's sudden, unannounced return…and forgive her for the past five years of silence…

Whenever she thought of the last words they'd spoken to one another shame burned in her gut and stopped her from calling, but she had at least sent a letter. She'd written that she was sorry. That she'd been a naïve, sheltered eighteen-year-old with a desperate hunger to see the world and her father's promises ringing in her ears.

She'd received no response.

The sanctuary was the only place she could imagine raising her baby without fear or threat. She wouldn't be alone there, amidst the bustling community of ecologists and volunteers, with her fierce Irish mother at the helm. There was a small birthing clinic in the nearby village, and she'd arranged to rent a room with the last of her savings in the event that her mother turned her away.

But deep down she hoped her mam would forgive her.

It was the beginning of May, technically the start of the dry season, and yet the torrential downpour that now descended on Rio De Janeiro was like something from a catastrophe movie.

Nora tried her best to stay dry under the narrow porch, craning her neck to do a quick scan of the street. The bells from the cathedral nearby began to chime midday and, as she'd hoped, there was no sign of the dark blue car that had been parked in the alley all week. Even criminal henchmen took predictable breaks, it seemed.

Even though Lionel Cabo hadn't set foot in Rio in months, he still made it his mission to make his only daughter's life hell. Having her watched was only one of the ways he'd been tightening the noose, showing her the power he wielded. When she'd continued to ignore his calls he'd somehow managed to get to her landlord and have her evicted.

He knew she wouldn't dare go to the police, who were mostly in his pocket. He knew she was utterly alone here.

She bit her lower lip as she rubbed small circles on her aching lower back.

A small group of teenagers in hoods moved out from their spot in a nearby doorway as a sleek black sports car prowled slowly up the narrow street and came to a stop a short distance away. The young boys crowded around it, peering into the windows through the rain which was now beginning to ease.

Nora felt her senses shift into high alert. Usually the

wealthy residents of Rio stayed far away from the more dangerous streets in this part of the city.

The teenagers moved aside as a tall figure emerged from the expensive vehicle. Rain instantly soaked his dark coat and he looked up, amber eyes glowing bright against the dark skin of a sinfully handsome face.

She was hallucinating.

Either her brain was playing tricks on her or she had fallen asleep, and was still upstairs, dreaming the same dream she'd had for more than six months.

The man closed the distance between them with a few long strides, stepping under the canopy with a strange stiffness to his movements. Nora fought to breathe as her headache intensified, her heartbeat thundering in her ears as she waited for him to speak.

'Nora Beckett?' he asked softly.

His voice contained the slightly clipped undertone of an English accent that she knew came from more than two decades living away from his homeland.

He extended a hand towards her in polite greeting. 'I hope you don't mind me coming to find you like this?'

Nora remained frozen, feeling as if she was watching herself from above, standing with this man who had Duarte's face and Duarte's voice. He dropped his hand after a moment, frowning, and looking back to where the boys were still investigating the exterior of his fancy car.

'I don't know if you remember me.' He spoke quickly. 'My name is Duarte Avelar. I was in an…an incident about six months ago—'

'Duarte Avelar is dead.'

Nora heard the hysteria in her own voice and willed herself to calm down, willed herself to find a logical solution for this madness.

'I'm quite alive, as you can see.'

His smile was forced, his movements strangely stilted as he reached for a split second to rub his hand across the slightly uneven hair growth on the left side of his head.

Nora followed the movement, noticing the thick dark brown line of puckered skin that began at his temple. What had once been soft, springy jet-black curls was now a tight crop that was barely more than skin at one side. She could clearly see the tiny marks where stitches had once sealed a wound that ended above his left ear.

The exact same place where she had tried to stem the blood flow with her own hands, had felt it spill over her dress and onto the cold ground around her feet.

She swallowed hard against the awful memories and focused on the man before her. His lips were still curved in a polite smile that was nothing like the man she had known. He seemed so real she almost felt as if she could reach out and touch him…

Frowning, she stepped forward and impulsively placed her hand on his chest. His sharp intake of breath took her by surprise, and she felt her insides quake with a strange mixture of fear and relief. She hardly dared to hope. She was unable to move, completely entranced by the blazing heat of his skin under her fingertips through the expensive material of his dove-grey shirt.

Almost of its own volition, her hand skimmed up a hard wall of muscle to where a glorious pulse thrummed at the base of his neck. *Alive*. She closed her eyes and felt a painful lump form in her throat at the cruelty of such a vision if this wasn't real. If it was just another one of her vivid dreams, after which she would awake in the middle of the night and expect to see him lying beside her.

Tears filled her eyes and she blinked them away, tipping her head up to find him staring down at her. His skin was still that rich caramel-brown, vibrant and healthy, so unlike the deathly pallor of that awful night.

She heard the tremor in her voice as she whispered, 'Duarte…this is impossible…'

'I've thought the same thing over the past months, believe me.' One side of his mouth twisted in the same sardonic way she remembered. 'But here I am.'

'You're actually here. You're alive…' Her voice was a breathless whisper as she felt a long-buried well of hopeless longing burst open within her.

Before she could stop herself, she closed the space between them and buried her face against his chest. He froze for a split second, and she feared he might push her away. She wouldn't blame him, considering she was essentially the reason he had received that scar in the first place.

She stiffened, bracing herself for rejection, only to feel his strong arms close around her. She was instantly cocooned in his warm spicy scent and the glorious thumping rhythm of his heart. His beating, perfect heart.

Emotion clogged her throat as she was consumed by the urgent need to feel him, to hold on to him as though he were an oasis of hope in the unbearable desert of her grief. Her breathing became shallow and she was overcome with the need to kiss him, to feel his lips on hers once again.

From the moment she had first laid eyes on him in that crowded Samba club almost a year ago he had affected her this way. She had never reacted to another man with such primal desire, and he had told her that she affected him just the same way.

'You bring out the animal in me, querida.'

He'd whispered that in her ear right before their very first kiss. They'd almost made love on the beach, in full view of the pier. It had been madness, and she felt that same desire humming through her veins just from being in his arms now.

She leaned back, looking up and expecting to see a reflection of the intense emotion she felt. Instead his face was utterly blank, and so confused it was like being doused with ice water.

This was wrong. Something was very, very wrong.

Suddenly she felt a tiny kick within her, wrenching her back to the present moment. She forced herself to take a step back, putting space between them as she composed herself and took in a lungful of air. The rain had died down and around them the sound of the boisterous youths filled the street.

Suddenly the weight of reality came crashing down upon her. If this wasn't a dream then it was a living nightmare. There was no question that this man was Duarte. And that meant her life had just become even more complicated.

She wrapped her bulky raincoat even tighter around herself and held her handbag in front of her stomach. If he was here, they were both in danger. This changed *everything*.

She looked around the streets once more, praying the blue car hadn't returned.

'How...?' she breathed. 'How are you alive?'

'It's a very long story.' He rubbed at his freshly shaven jawline. 'One that involves a medically induced coma and many months of painful rehabilitation. Let's just say I'm a hard man to kill.'

She heard the gasp that escaped her throat and closed her eyes against the image it created in her mind. He'd been alive all this time...in pain, broken...

She fought the urge to cling to him once again, never to let him go. But a tiny voice in her mind was screaming at her to run away as fast as she could and pretend she'd never seen him. Even if walking away from him now might be more painful than losing him the first time.

It was too much… She could hardly breathe…

'I hope you don't mind me tracking you down,' he said, and he spoke with a strange politeness to his tone that made her uneasy. 'You were there with me, the night I was shot.'

'Yes, I was there.' She frowned, watching the relief that crossed his face at her response. He smiled, and her heart seemed to pulse at the sight of it.

'Your care and kindness were the first things I remembered when I woke up.' His gaze softened for a moment before he seemed to shake himself mentally, then cleared his throat. 'I have a few things I'd like to ask you, if you wouldn't mind?'

'You don't remember me.' She spoke half to herself, processing the polite detachment in his gaze, the way he'd introduced himself to her—as though they were strangers.

It all came painfully into focus, like a movie replaying in her mind. He had no idea who she was…no idea what they'd been to one another.

'My injury has caused some slight memory loss. It's been a process—one I'm hoping you might help me with, actually.' He put his hands in his pockets and looked at her through his thick lashes. 'Is there somewhere private that we can talk?'

To any other woman his overtly calm posture would appear benign and almost welcoming. But Nora wasn't any other woman, and she knew when she was being baited. He might not have any memories of her, or their history, but that didn't mean he didn't still possess the killer instinct he was famous for.

He'd noticed her lengthy pause and the skin around his mouth had tightened with barely restrained irritation. She felt a shiver run down her spine. He wanted answers and he had managed to track her down. She suddenly felt as if he was a predator on the hunt and she a small rabbit heading straight for his trap.

She looked up the street and saw her bus, just beginning to turn the corner.

Duarte followed her gaze and narrowed his eyes.

'I'm sorry. I have to go. I have a flight to catch.' She forced the words from her lips, trying not to let him see the tears that threatened to spill from her eyes at any moment.

'Let me drive you to the airport. I just want to talk.'

Nora stared at the face of the man she had once loved. The man she'd *thought* she loved, she corrected herself.

If he said he had no memory of her, did that mean he had no recollection of what had passed between them all those months ago?

Guilt and anger joined the swirl of emotions warring within her. She had made her own mistakes, but he had ensured she was punished in return. He had shattered her trust and broken her foolish heart.

She had grieved for him and mourned the father her child would never have. But a small, terrible part of her had whispered that at least with his death she would be safe from his wrath. Her child would be safe.

She needed to get away. Fast.

If there was one thing she had inherited from her crime boss father, it was the sheer will to survive. She closed down her emotional reaction to his miraculous return and focused instead on the worst moments they'd spent together. The pain he'd put her through.

She lowered her hand to her stomach, reflexively protecting her unborn child from the threat of danger. That was what Duarte Avelar was to her, she reminded herself. Dangerous. That was what he had always been.

Nora opened her mouth to tell him she had no interest

in answering his questions, but instead let out a silent gasp as her entire lower body spasmed with pain. Her handbag fell to the ground and she gripped her stomach, feeling the dull throbbing that had been torturing her back all morning shifting around to her front and burrowing deep inside.

The twisting heat took her breath away. She could do nothing but breathe for a long moment.

'Are you okay?'

His voice came from close beside her, and his hand was warm on her elbow. She pushed him away, not able to look up into his face. She needed to get on that bus before her father's men returned. She needed to get out of Rio today. But she couldn't think straight.

'*Cristo*, you're pregnant…' Duarte breathed reflexively, slipping into heavily accented English. 'You're really, really pregnant.'

'Excellent observation.' She spoke through clenched teeth.

'Do you need to get to a hospital?'

'No… I was just lifting some heavy boxes. I'm moving out of town today.'

She breathed in through her nose and out through her mouth, praying this was just the shock of him showing up on her doorstep and her body was simply reminding her to take it easy.

In the back of her mind she heard the noise of the bus drawing closer along the street. She needed to *move*. 'I'll be fine. I need to get to the airport or I'll miss my flight.'

She moved to walk around him, throwing her arm out to hail the *ônibus*, but then she felt another wave of pain tighten inside her abdomen so swiftly she cried out.

Clutching onto the nearest object for balance—a very firm male bicep—she squeezed hard and prayed that this wasn't the moment her child would choose to be born.

As that thought entered her mind she felt a strange pop and the trickle of what felt like water between her legs.

This could not be happening.

She kept her eyes closed tight, a low growl escaping her lips through the waves of pain that seemed to crash into her body.

'I think my waters have just broken.'

CHAPTER TWO

Nora was vaguely aware of the sound of a loud engine slowing to a stop beside them and the bus driver calling out to see if she needed help.

'*Não obrigado.*' Duarte's voice boomed with authority.

She wasn't sure how many minutes passed before she opened her eyes and saw the bus had gone. She looked down to find herself clutching him like a limpet and groaned inwardly. She knew she should feel embarrassed, but she was rapidly becoming unable to think straight—or stand up, for that matter.

'Is there someone I can call for you?' he asked. 'The baby's father?'

Fighting the urge to sob, she shook her head and closed her eyes as she began to realise the gravity of her situation.

He frowned, pressing his lips together in a firm line as he looked down at her small suitcase. 'Can you walk? I'm taking you to a hospital right now.'

She allowed him to hold her arm as they moved carefully towards his car. She'd just made it to the door when another pain hit. He seemed to understand that she was unable to move, and he took off his coat and draped it over her while she breathed and tried not to curse.

'It's too early...' she breathed. 'I'm not due for four and a half more weeks. I'm not meant to be here in this city.'

He helped her into the car, bending down to carefully buckle her seatbelt around her before he looked deeply into her eyes. Warm amber filled her up with the same magnetic strength she remembered so well.

'Just try to relax.'

'Are you saying that for my benefit or for yours?' she groaned, closing her eyes against the beautiful sight of him.

She heard him chuckle low in his throat and opened her eyes once more.

'I'm going to drive now, okay?'

She nodded, staring up at this man she had once thought herself in love with, this man who now had no idea who she was.

This couldn't be happening. He couldn't be with her when she was about to give birth to her child.

Their child.

'I can't do this...' She closed her eyes once again, a sea of thoughts overwhelming her, and sent up a prayer to everyone and anyone who might be listening. To keep her safe. To keep her baby safe.

She felt a warm hand cover hers. When she opened her eyes he was looking at her, and there was nothing but kindness and concern in his warm whisky-coloured eyes.

Maybe it was the pain, or maybe she was just in shock, but she heard herself whisper, 'I've been so afraid of doing this alone...'

'You are not alone.' He squeezed her hand once more before turning and starting the engine of the powerful sports car with the push of a button. 'If my memory is correct, I'm pretty sure I owe you my life. I won't leave you.'

Duarte burst through the hospital doors carrying a wild-eyed pregnant woman in his arms. The drive to the hospital had been blessedly swift, and free of the usual Rio traffic, but he had still feared they might not make it in time. He was famous for pushing himself beyond his limits, but delivering an infant in the passenger seat of a rented Bugatti was not exactly the way he'd imagined this meeting going.

This hospital wasn't the nearest medical facility, but when she told him she'd been attending a community birth centre in one of the poorest areas of the city he'd been hit by a strange protective urge so strong it had taken his breath away.

She was important to his investigation, he told himself. He needed her safe and well if he was to find out the information she might have.

Nora seemed to be delirious with pain as the nurses performed some preliminary checks. In between each contraction she became more frantic, her eyes glazed as she repeated that she had to get to the airport.

Duarte saw the questioning looks that passed between the nurses as they looked at the reading on the blood pressure monitor. The atmosphere in the room changed immediately. A bright red call button was pressed and soon the room seemed to fill with people—doctors and specialists, anaesthetists and paediatricians.

Nora clutched his hand tightly as the team moved around her, performing more checks. Her nails bit into his skin as she cursed through another intense wave of pain, her neck and back arching and her hair tumbling around her face in a wild cloud of red curls.

He felt utterly dumbstruck by her ferocious beauty. This woman was a stranger to him, and yet he was witnessing one of the most intimate moments of her life. He felt the strangest urge to reach out and comfort her, but was keenly aware of her boundaries. In the end he settled for the simple touch of his hand on top of hers.

Her back relaxed as the pain eased off again and she looked up at him, pinning him with eyes the colour of the sky after a heavy rainstorm at sea—deep silver with a ring of midnight-blue. He was so captivated by her gaze that he hardly noticed as she looked down at his hand and frowned at the quartet of scarlet crescent moons left by her fingernails.

'Did I do that…?' she breathed, horrified.

Duarte leaned close to speak softly near her ear. 'Don't worry about me. This hand is yours for the duration. If you need to crush my fingers in the process, so be it.'

She shook her head, the ghost of a smile crossing her lips.

Duarte couldn't help it; he laughed at the crazy turn his day had taken.

She looked up at him through thick lashes, her eyes filled with surprise, and for a moment, Duarte felt the strong pull of *déjà vu*. His mind grasped at the feeling, but it was like trying to hold on to water and feeling its weight slip through his fingers.

Why did he feel as if seeing her was the key to unlocking some hidden compartment in his memory?

A young nurse chose that moment to interrupt, looking at Duarte as she explained that she needed to talk to the baby's father for a moment.

Nora's entire body froze, and a sudden lucidity that was almost akin to blind panic entered her eyes.

'No! He needs to leave.' Her voice lowered to a growl as another contraction hit her and her body began to arch forward. 'Get him *out* of this hospital.'

Duarte took a stunned step back just as another doctor entered the room and announced that they would be preparing her for immediate emergency surgery.

He was swiftly whisked away from her and taken down

the hall to fill out some paperwork. The surgeon was a kind-faced young woman who assured him that his partner and the baby would be well taken care of.

Duarte opened his mouth to correct her, only to find she was already rushing away.

Keeping his mind occupied, he strode down to the nurses' station and set about filling in more paperwork. He had no idea what her date of birth was, or even her nationality so, against all his instincts, he opened her handbag and her suitcase and began to search.

For a woman who said she was leaving town, she had packed suspiciously light. Her bags contained no identification nor any clues as to where she might have been headed. She didn't even have a mobile phone. Baffled, he listed his own details as next of kin and made sure it was known that no expense should be spared in her care.

The nurse's eyes widened, her gaze flickering between the name scrawled on the form and the long scar on the side of his face. For a moment Duarte was confused, but then he winced and cursed under his breath. In all the drama he'd forgotten that technically he was supposed to be dead. His family name was well known in this part of Brazil, thanks to their wealth of charity work.

He walked away from the stunned recognition in the woman's eyes, knowing that at some point he was going to have to contact Dani and explain how he'd come to be spotted in Rio, in hospital with a pregnant woman.

His shoulder twinged again, the pain hot and uncomfortable under his designer shirt. He had missed out on his evening swimming regime due to the long flight, and already he could feel his muscles seizing in protest. He seemed to be in a constant state of management, swimming against the tide and trying to live a normal life with his new damaged body.

After what felt like hours, he walked back down the corridor towards the operating theatre, feeling like a caged animal pacing its enclosure. Running a hand along the stubble growing on his jaw, he ignored the tension in his gut and instead puzzled over the way Nora Beckett had embraced him in the rain.

She'd thought him dead and had seemed overwhelmed at the sight of his return. She'd *known* him. He could have sworn he'd felt the echo of some fierce connection between them every time she'd looked at him. And yet she'd looked at him with fear in her eyes, and had bellowed for him to be taken from the room.

Something didn't make sense…

Unable to stay put a moment longer, he moved purposefully down the corridor to demand an update. At the same moment a nurse emerged from the double doors that led down to the operating theatres with a bundle of white linen in her arms.

'*Senhor*, I was just coming to get you.' She beamed. 'Baby boy is completely healthy. We'd like you to get settled in the suite while the team finish with Senhora Beckett.'

'Is she okay?' he asked, swallowing hard as he peered down at the small face, barely visible in the folds of material.

'The procedure required heavy anaesthesia and she is still sedated.'

The nurse ushered him down the hall to a large private suite. The small bundle was placed in a cot beside the bed and then the nurse apologised as she was suddenly called from the room by a beeping device at her hip.

Alone, and utterly out of his depth, Duarte felt his chest tighten with anxiety as the infant began to wriggle. Did they usually abandon babies to the care of clueless billionaires around here? Give him a priceless antique catamaran and he would know how to take it apart and put it back together blindfold. But children had never exactly been a part of his wild playboy lifestyle.

Duarte walked to the side of the cot and peered down at the infant, its tiny features scrunched up, its hands flailing. Without thinking, he reached into the cot towards one tiny hand. His heart seemed to thump in his ears as his index finger was instantly grasped in a tight fist and the wriggling stopped.

'There you go, *pequeno*,' he murmured, rubbing his other hand against his sternum, trying to control the frantic beating of his heart as he marvelled at the force of the boy's grip. 'You can hold on tight if that helps. Your *mamãe* will be here soon.'

Nora opened her eyes to find she was still dreaming.

Often in the past six months she had fallen asleep to dream of Duarte, his amber eyes alive and full of happiness as he cradled their newborn baby. In that perfect life there was no anger or lies between them, no danger or threat of punishment from her villainous father.

She blinked at the vision before her in the luxurious hospital room—the painfully handsome man in his perfect designer shirt, shirtsleeves rolled up as he cradled the tiny infant in his powerful arms. She closed her eyes briefly at the memory of how she'd embraced him so passionately in her shock, then clung to him as he'd rushed her to the hospital.

But he didn't remember her at all.

A small tear slid from her eyelids and down her cheek as she realised that perhaps that was a blessing to them both.

To all three of them.

'You're awake,' that gravelly voice murmured from

across the room. 'The nurse told me to tell you not to try to sit up by yourself.'

'My baby…' Nora croaked, her throat painfully dry. 'Give him to me.' She raised her voice, hearing the edge of panic creeping in but feeling too weak to hold it back.

Duarte frowned, but immediately did as she asked. The soft bundle was placed gently on her chest and Nora looked down at her son's perfect face for the first time.

'The nurse just fed him and she asked me to hold him for a moment.'

'Thank you…' Nora whispered, inwardly mourning the fact that her baby's first feed had not come from her.

She mentally shook herself, sending up a prayer of thanks that they were both safe. All those plans she had made for a natural birth had been thrown out of the window when the doctors had told her she was in an advanced stage of pre-eclampsia and they would need to sedate her immediately in order to operate.

Her headaches, the swelling… She was lucky they were both alive. She was lucky they had got to the hospital so quickly.

If she'd been alone…

Tears welled in her eyes at the thought.

'My sweet, sweet Liam,' she whispered, closing her eyes and brushing her lips against jet-black downy soft hair. He was beautiful, and so impossibly small she felt something shift within her. Something fierce and primal.

'Liam? An interesting name.' Duarte's voice seemed to float towards her from far away.

'It's short for the Irish for William,' she whispered, her eyes still fixed on examining the tiny bundle.

She almost couldn't believe that in the space of one day her life had changed so dramatically. She moved her fingertips over ten tiny fingers and toes, puffy cheeks and a tiny button nose. He was perfect.

She closed her eyes and placed her cheek against her son's small head as a wave of emotion tightened her throat once more.

'It's easier to pronounce than our version. My father always shortened his name to Gill.'

Nora refused to look up, unsure if he was baiting her somehow. But there was no way he could know she had chosen her son's name to honour the great Guilhermo Avelar.

She heard him take a step closer.

'You have Irish ancestry? You speak Portuguese like a native, but the red hair…'

Nora looked up and wondered if she imagined the shrewdness in his gaze, fearing that he was remembering… The reality of her situation came crashing down on her, dampening the euphoric pleasure of holding her child for the first time. She felt her chest tighten, but schooled her features not to show a thing, not wanting to give him any more information than needed.

'My mother is Irish, but I've lived here my whole life.'

'Here in Rio?' he asked.

'No. Not here.' She let her words sit and watched as he realised she wasn't going to play along.

He nodded once and took a few steps away, towards the window. Nora was briefly entranced by the sight of his handsome features in the glow of the afternoon sun. The blue sky formed a heavenly backdrop behind him, making him look like a fallen angel.

How could someone so beautiful cause her so much heartbreak? How could he remember nothing of the time they'd spent together? She'd told him of her Irish mother's lifelong work as an ecologist and about the remote Amazon village where she'd been born. He'd told her stories of his own idyllic childhood, and how happy they had been as a family until their move to England.

They'd bonded over a shared sense of having felt stifled and restless when growing up. She had never felt such a connection to another person, such an urge to speak the first thing that came into her mind. He had seemed like a good man then—before everything had become so twisted between them. But his anger had made him cold.

The last time they had spoken he had vowed to find her, to hunt her down and put her in prison alongside her criminal father. Even now she could clearly remember the simmering rage in his gaze as her father's men had dragged him away.

He might not remember that night, or all the events that had led to it, but he still felt that hunger for vengeance—she'd bet her life on it. Why else was he back here in Rio, digging around?

What would he do if he knew she had hard evidence that could put Lionel Cabo in prison for the rest of his life? The slim thumb drive sewn into the lining of her suitcase was the insurance she had used to secure her own freedom, but that same evidence would also serve as evidence of a damning connection. A connection that someone could use against her.

Trusting Duarte in the past had led to betrayal. Did she dare ask him for help, knowing that he might choose to use her past against her?

She closed her eyes and thought of the innocent life she had just brought into this battlefield. This should have been a moment of celebration for both of them.

For a split second she contemplated throwing caution to the wind and telling Duarte that Liam was his son. Maybe if she told him everything and explained herself he would see that she was not the same as her father after all. She had made her share of mistakes, but she was not the black-hearted criminal he had accused her of being.

But then she remembered his promise and imagined being thrown in jail for her crimes. She felt torn between silence and blind faith, but she was a mother now and she had a responsibility to raise her son. She couldn't risk it.

'I hope you don't mind me bringing you to a different hospital.' He gestured around them at the clean sleek lines of the private mother-and-baby suite. 'I know the staff here from my charity work. It's one of the best facilities in the city.'

'I will try my best to repay you.' Her voice shook slightly and he instantly waved away her offer.

The gesture held so much lazy arrogance that her hands automatically tightened at the reminder that Duarte Avelar wasn't just rich, he was powerful. More powerful than any of the people she'd met while working for her father among Rio's high society.

Even without the fact that he was descended from one of Brazil's oldest dynasties, he was rich as Croesus in his own right. He was the kind of man who didn't have to worry about anything. He probably had world-class lawyers on retainer just in case he needed matters dealt with. If his memory came back, if he remembered what she had been a part of...

'Nora...' Duarte didn't move, but his eyes held her captive with their sincerity. 'Was there a reason you were leaving the city today, alone and in such a vulnerable condition?'

'That's hardly your concern.'

She kept her tone firm, the anxiety roaring within her a reminder of her own vulnerability. She *was* alone and he knew it. That meant it was even more important for her to keep the upper hand. Keep what little power she had left.

She looked up at his dark features, feeling the weight of fear crush any of the remaining traces of hope she might have had upon seeing him alive. She had far too much knowledge of what happened to a woman when she put herself in the orbit of a powerful man's control. Her son deserved to be safe, and she would die before she allowed him to be used the same way she had been as a child.

Her eyes darted to the window. She was trying to pinpoint where they were in the city. Trying to plan a way out, just in case.

Powerful men did not often give up their children—even illegitimate ones. Her own mother had found that out the hard way. Sometimes a child served as the ultimate form of control.

'I had to search your bag for identification in order to fill out your chart.' His eyes met hers, searching. 'I noticed you were packing very light. You don't even have a mobile phone or your passport.'

'I must have forgotten them at home.'

The lie fell easily from her lips and she felt a pang of relief that he hadn't found the hidden pocket in the lining of her luggage that she'd used to hold her savings, the thumb drive and her emergency documents.

'I thought that…so I had my assistant go back to your apartment to retrieve them.'

Nora fought the urge to growl, feeling his eyes on her, watching her reaction. Apparently his injury hadn't addled the entirety of his wonderful mind; he was still sharp. He must have been told that her apartment was empty, that she'd been evicted suddenly and without notice.

'What exactly are you asking me?' She assumed her best poker face, feeling as though she was walking a tightrope and might fall into the web of her own lies at any moment.

'Your landlord seemed terrified that he might be harmed and refused to give the reason for your eviction. In fact, he seemed quite concerned for your wellbeing, despite having no knowledge of your pregnancy. According to him, before today you had barely left your apartment in months.'

Nora felt her pulse hammer against her chest. How could she tell him that hiding behind the walls of her shabby apartment and living in anonymous squalor for months on end had been preferable to anyone in her father's criminal network seeing her growing stomach and using it against her? Her father would have known instantly whose child she carried, and he would not have hesitated to use the knowledge for his own gains. He'd always got her under his control so easily—it was one of his talents.

She had been eighteen when she'd first moved to Rio, home-schooled and painfully naïve, with her father's wonderful promises ringing in her ears. She hadn't reacted when he'd told her she stood out in all the wrong ways, with her simple outdoorsy style and her wild red curls. When he'd hired stylists to dress her and soften her looks she had foolishly seen it as him taking care of her. To a girl who had grown up fatherless and isolated, any attention from him had seemed wonderful.

Then he'd started asking her to gather small pieces of information for him. Her successes had been met with affection and gifts, and she'd never felt so happy and loved. She hadn't known then, but he'd been grooming her for his organisation, teaching her the tricks she would need to become one of his network of spies.

She'd obeyed his every command and completed every mission perfectly...until Duarte.

She looked up at the object of her thoughts and wondered which of the men in her life had hurt her more…

'I get the feeling that we knew one another, Nora. Maybe we were friends?' Duarte's whisky-coloured eyes bored into hers, assessing her with a razor-sharpness. 'If you're in trouble, I might be able to help.'

'I'm not in trouble.' Shaken, she tried to keep control of the conversation, hoping he wouldn't notice the tremor in her hands. 'And you are *not* my friend.'

'Well, that makes your earlier reaction to my reappearance even more interesting.'

Something within her bristled at the superior tone in his voice and the evident suspicion in his gaze. The Duarte Avelar she had so briefly known had not had this hardness in him. But, then again, that version of him hadn't been almost murdered as part of a blackmail plot involving the woman he claimed to have loved.

Still, she was a vulnerable woman with a newborn baby in a hospital bed and, as far as he knew they were perfect strangers.

Duarte stood up straight, his eyes sweeping over her and the small infant, something strange in his gaze. 'You've been through a lot today. I still need to speak with you, but my questions will keep until you have recovered.'

'Did you come back to Rio looking for answers…or for revenge?' She asked the question, holding her breath as she waited for the answer that would determine their fate.

His brows knitted together, and when he spoke his voice held a mixture of surprise and keen interest, as though he were dissecting a puzzle. 'You fear revenge from me, Nora?'

'You haven't answered my question.'

She spoke with steel, despite the frantic thrumming of her heartbeat. She was exhausted, and likely still in shock from the events of the past few hours, but she knew she needed to have this conversation for her son's sake. For her own sake too.

She forced herself to hold his gaze, trying not to be entranced by the features that seemed like a mirror image of the tiny face on her chest.

He seemed to hesitate for a moment, his eyes shifting to take a sweeping look out over the city. When his eyes at last met hers, there was a haunted darkness to them.

'I came here to find out what truly happened in that shipping yard. For now, that is enough to satisfy me.'

For now.

Nora felt the threat of those words as clear as day. He might not know it yet, but he was on a direct path to retribution. His memories might be missing but his heart was still the same. He would never let this go. He would never forgive her for the part she'd played, unwittingly or not.

The silence stretched between them like an icy lake and she felt whatever slim hope she'd clung to begin to fade to nothing.

She looked up to see him watching her, his brow furrowed with concentration. Time seemed to stop as he opened his mouth to speak, then closed it, taking a few steps towards the window. He braced his hands on the sill, one deep inhalation emphasising the impressive width of his shoulders.

He was leaner than he had been before, his muscular frame less bulky but somehow more defined. The long, angry scar stood out like a kind of tribal marking along the side of his skull. She breathed in the sight of him, knowing that it might be the last time she could. That it *needed* to be the last time.

'I will leave you to rest for a few days.' He spoke with quiet authority. 'I am not so cruel as to interrogate you in your condition. But I *will* have my answers, Nora.'

She opened her mouth to order him to leave, fury rising within her at the barely concealed threat in his words, but she froze as she saw the unmistakable look of curiosity he sent towards the tiny baby she held in her arms.

'Seeing as you don't have a phone, would you like me to notify anyone about the birth?' Duarte asked, taking a step closer and peering into Liam's small sleeping face. 'Who is his father?'

CHAPTER THREE

NAUSEA TIGHTENED NORA'S already tender body, emotion clogging her throat as she inhaled and prepared herself for another performance. Another cruel twist, cementing her own web of lies beyond repair.

Just as she'd opened her mouth to respond, like an angel of mercy the nurse returned. Nora smiled politely as her son was lifted from her chest and put gently into his cot before the young woman began efficiently taking vitals, asking about her pain and making notes on a detailed chart.

Nora's vague realisation that she'd still been pregnant only hours ago was laughable, considering that her current sense of fear had completely overshadowed any of the strange sensations in her body from the Caesarean section.

She was painfully aware of his dark eyes watching her from the corner of the room. Her heartbeat skittered in her throat as the nurse widened her eyes at her blood pressure reading and then left the room, mumbling about getting a second opinion.

Nora fought the urge to call after the nurse and beg her to stay. *Please, stay.*

She wanted to delay the inevitable answer she had to give. The lies she needed to tell to keep her son safe. To keep them all safe.

In an ideal world she would celebrate finding out that the

father of her child was alive and had returned to find her. In an ideal world this would be a reunion… But she had long ago learned that no happy endings lay in her future—only an endless fight for survival. The world she lived in was filled with nothing but danger and dire consequences if she took a single step wrong.

She had a tiny life relying on her now; it wasn't just her own future at stake. She could not let her heart lead her—not again.

'Who is the baby's father?' Duarte repeated.

She avoided his eyes as she folded and refolded the linen blanket on her lap. She bit her lip, trying to come up with a convincing lie, but found she simply couldn't. So she just went with omission instead, forcing words from her throat. 'I'm a single mother. I have no family here in Rio.'

Silence fell between them. She wondered if he was judging her for her situation, then brushed off the thought with disgust. She had far bigger problems in her life than worrying about the opinion of a powerful man who had never known the true cruelty of life at the bottom of the pecking order. He might think her in the habit of random flings, but that seemed preferable to the embarrassing truth.

The only man she'd ever let her guard down with was standing five feet away from her.

And he didn't remember a single thing.

She reached out and laid one hand on the small cot beside the bed, reminding herself of the tiny life that now relied on her strength. She needed to convince Duarte to leave, to forget all about her and Liam. Once that part was done, she would get back to her original plan.

Her heart seemed to twinge with the pain of knowing she would never see him again, but she forced the pain away, knowing she must survive losing him all over again for the sake of her son.

She had to.

'You said you wanted details about what happened that night? I'll write down everything I can remember and send it to you.' She spoke quickly. 'I'll tell you everything you need to know.'

Strong arms folded over an even more powerful chest as he stared down at her. Nora ignored the flare of regret screaming within her. The urge to confess everything and beg him to take her and Liam away from Rio, away from the reach of her father and the memories of all the mistakes she'd made, bubbled up inside her.

But she couldn't trust him—not after everything that had happened. She couldn't put her child's future in his hands, or gamble on the hope that he might be merciful. She needed to be strong, even if it meant doing something that felt fundamentally wrong to her on every level.

'Why do you act as though you are afraid of me?' Duarte asked darkly, his jaw tight enough to cut through steel. 'I pose no danger to you. You can trust me.'

'I trust no one—especially not men like you.' The words slipped from her mouth and she saw them land, anchoring him to the spot. '*Please*…just leave.'

She closed her eyes and lay back against the pillows, willing him away along with the one million worries that had come with his reappearance in her life. She lost track of how long she lay there, eyes closed tight against the sight of him. She fought against the need to reach out and beg him to stay, to breathe in the scent of him one last time.

When she opened her eyes again he was gone.

She didn't cry, but the walls of the hospital room blurred into one wide canvas of beige and white as she stared upwards into nothingness.

If this was what shock felt like, she welcomed it—welcomed the cold that set into her fingers and the heavy exhaustion deep in her bones.

She had no idea how long she stared up at the ceiling before she drifted off to sleep, one hand still tightly clutching the railing of her son's cot at her bedside.

Duarte left the hospital in a foul mood, instructing one of his guards to remain for surveillance. Whether that was to protect Nora Beckett or to ensure she didn't try to disappear he didn't quite know yet. But one thing was for sure: his mystery woman was deeply afraid of something. And, even though it made no sense, he had the strangest feeling that that *something* might be him.

The drive out of the city and high up into the hills to his modern villa passed in a blur. He had purchased the house a few years ago, but had very few memories of staying there. It was a visual masterpiece of clean lines and open living spaces, designed by an award-winning architect. Every feature took the natural surroundings into account, so that the building seemed to slot effortlessly into the rocky mountain face that surrounded it.

As a man who had taught himself to conceptualise and build ships just by observing the masters and trusting his feeling for what was right, he had a deep appreciation of design in all its forms. Usually the sight of this home filled him with awe and appreciation for such a feat of skilled, thoughtful engineering. But today he just saw a load of concrete and glass.

Duarte parked in the underground garage and found himself staring at the wall, processing the turn his day had taken in just a few short hours. He felt the sudden urge to grab a full bottle of strong *cachaça* and switch his mind off. To another man, the lure of getting rip-roaring drunk might have been attractive after a day like he'd had. But he was not another man, he reminded himself.

Perhaps he should have gone into the city, to one of the trendy upscale night spots along the coast. The bars would be teeming with beautiful women only too happy to help a man like him forget his troubles... But he doubted he'd even remember how to chat up a woman it had been so long.

Since he'd woken in the hospital all those months ago his days had been consumed only by recovery and, more recently, revenge. But maybe it was exactly what he needed. To indulge himself, to shake off the edge that had refused to pass since his dreams of the redhead began. Dreams of the woman who had saved him.

Nora.

He shook off the thought of her and made his way into the spacious entrance hall just as his phone began to ring. He looked at the name on the screen and answered the call from his father's oldest friend with a weary smile.

'Angelus—*tudo bem*?'

The old man was eager to hear about his meeting with the mystery redhead and apologised for believing Duarte had simply imagined the woman.

'She must have been the one to alert me that night,' Fiero mused, not needing to elaborate any further. They both knew what night he referred to. 'I got a text from your personal phone number simply stating the address of that shipping yard and the fact that you were in danger. You and Valerio had been missing for seven days at that point.'

Duarte swallowed his frustration at his lack of memories of his captivity. He had no clue as to what had occurred other than the scars that covered his body and the haunted look in Valerio's eyes. His best friend had refused to go into detail about whatever had befallen them during their long days and nights of captivity, stating that he was better off not knowing.

Nora had saved him—but why had she disappeared?

The thought suddenly occurred to him that perhaps they had been together. Perhaps she had been taken captive too? But surely Valerio would have mentioned a woman.

Angelus interrupted his musings, launching into a detailed briefing on the latest developments in their joint sting operation.

The corrupt politician who had paid for the kidnap had already been brought to justice, shot by Angelus himself in self-defence. But they had evidence to prove the man hadn't been working alone. That there was a criminal kingpin behind the operation and he was hell-bent on taking control of the large area of land that the Avelar family owned and used for their charitable operations in Rio and Sao Paolo. Tens of thousands of tenants stood to be displaced and abandoned.

Thankfully, Angelus had arranged for the land to become untouchable, locked it into use by the Avelar Foundation, securing the homes and livelihoods of the families they assisted.

Duarte hadn't yet told Angelus that he remembered having lunch with that same politician just over a year before his kidnapping. Considering that Angelus was currently still recovering from near death because of his efforts to help Duarte, he didn't think his revelation would be well received.

It plagued him—why would he choose to meet with a man who so vehemently opposed the Avelar family's work in Rio? Their refusal to sell or redevelop prime land in what was considered an upper class area of the city had been the cause of a decades-long argument, dating back to his father's inception of the foundation. His parents had taken on the cause of the most vulnerable in society by building quality, sustainable housing projects. They had directly opposed and ignored the handful of corrupt developers that wanted to earmark the area for a luxury tourism development.

Duarte vaguely remembered the months before his kidnapping. He had been tired from spreading himself too thinly between Velamar and his own fledgling nautical design firm, Nettuno. When the Avelar Foundation had needed his immediate presence in Rio due to a large and embarrassing fire safety scandal, he'd been furious and resentful.

He'd had a few drinks with the politician and somehow they'd got into talks about what might happen if he sold the land with their family name kept solely as a front. He'd had plenty of his own charitable projects going on. He simply hadn't had the time required to pursue such a demanding cause.

Shame burned in his gut at the memory of that conversation.

But he would never have acted on it…he was almost sure. He vaguely remembered flying out of Rio determined to find another way to carry on his parents' legacy and uphold his duty to the people relying on the foundation.

His memories were non-existent from that point, but his passport showed that he'd returned to Rio three times after that trip. Whatever he'd come back for, he'd kept secret and eventually he was going to be forced to admit his suspicions to Angelus… That the person who had started this hell was possibly himself.

The infinity pool on the boundary of the villa had been serviced and readied for his arrival, as per his instructions. He had never been more grateful as he tore off his clothes and dived under the water in his boxer shorts. The fresh salt water engulfed him, cutting off the frantic hum of his mind and replacing it with a calming nothingness that soothed the anxious roar within him. Even if the relief was only temporary.

Anger and frustration had him doing more laps than usual, pushing his body to its physical limits as though reminding himself of his strength.

Teaching his damaged body how to walk and move again had been a nightmare, but he had done it. He had shocked his team of physiotherapists and smashed all their expectations. So much so that soon the staff and other patients would gather to watch him slice through the water at incredible speeds.

He'd thought that was the reason he'd become a minor celebrity in the small community, never realising that many of the staff had already been aware of his identity and had been paid heavily by Angelus for their silence.

Even without his memories he had felt the same connection to water, the same need that he'd had his whole life to swim or be out on the open sea.

It had been on that same beach that a strange man and woman had arrived and introduced themselves as his sister and his best friend. He'd remained silent as they tried to gauge how little he remembered. He soon found out that not only had he been a competitive swimmer and sailor throughout his teenage years and into his twenties, but he had apparently turned that passion into a career and was the co-founder of one of the biggest luxury yacht charter firms in the world.

Going from being an abandoned John Doe with no knowledge of his past to having his dream life presented to him should have been enough, he thought darkly. And yet he had been plagued by the thought that there was something vital he was missing—something he needed to do before his spirit would rest and accept his survival for what it was.

A second chance.

He lifted himself from the water with only minimal pain and stepped under the blistering hot spray of the outdoor waterfall shower. The heat loosened his muscles the rest of the way, ensuring that he would sleep without medication.

The heavy painkillers he'd been given on the island had become a dangerous crutch in the weeks after he'd awoken. His pain had been a relentless presence, along with the anxiety that stopped him sleeping or eating. Soon he'd begun to crave the oblivion those pills offered, and he had progressed to hoarding his dosages to achieve the maximum effect. Luckily, the nurses had recognised the signs and had made it impossible for him to continue down that path.

When a man was in constant pain, anything could become a vice, so he had adopted a strict, clean lifestyle and focused on healing his body naturally. But even now that he had his physical regimen under control, he still felt that restless hunger within him at times. It was as if he had come back to life with a great big chunk of himself missing, and no matter what he did…nothing filled the space.

His thoughts wandered back to the first moment he'd laid eyes on the woman from his dreams. Nora. How she had looked at him in that rain-soaked street, the shock and relief on her delicate features right before she'd embraced him. He'd felt something shift within him, as if something in his broken mind had awoken and growled *mine*.

Perhaps they had been lovers before his accident? She was certainly eye-catching, with her vibrant red waves of hair and large silver eyes. The thought of the two of them together filled him with a rush of sensual heat—until he remembered that she had been heavily pregnant with another man's child when he'd found her.

If they had been lovers, she had clearly moved on quickly.

Shrugging off the dark turn his thoughts had taken, he reminded himself of the more pressing matter that she was clearly in need of help and fearful of some unknown force. Afraid enough to pack up her life and move cities in an advanced stage of pregnancy.

He winced, remembering how he had told her he *would* get his answers. Suddenly the idea of getting answers seemed overshadowed by the idea that she might fear *him*. She was made of steel, that much was clear, and yet he'd seen flashes of vulnerability on her face that had made him tense with the primal need to protect.

His fists clenched tight and he shut off the water with an impatient growl. From the villa's hilltop vantage point he could see the last rays of the late evening sun glittering on the waves of the Atlantic below. He took a deep breath and wrapped a towel low on his hips, inhaling and exhaling the salty spray until he felt a sense of calm logic return.

If he had any chance of getting information from Nora he would first need to gain her trust. She was a new mother, in dire need of help, but he got the feeling that she would not accept help from him easily. Luckily for him, patience had always been something he had in abundance.

He let out a deep exhalation, a plan already taking shape in his mind.

He would get what he needed from Nora Beckett—one way or another.

'This can't be legal.' Nora stood by the edge of her hospital bed, her suitcase packed at her feet and the small bundle of her son in his baby carrier. 'It's been a full week and you've said yourself I am well enough to leave.'

'You're well enough to go home—not to fly across the country.' The doctor spoke in a firm tone. 'Miss Beckett.

You will not be cleared to fly in your condition. I won't allow it. Recovery from pre-eclampsia needs to be closely monitored, and you will both need regular check-ups here in Rio for at least another five weeks.'

'I can't stay here,' she said weakly. 'I have nowhere to go.'

'You have a home address listed, right here in Rio.'

Nora looked down at the form on the doctor's clipboard, seeing Duarte's name at the top and noting that the address listed was for his palatial villa up in the hills. A place where she had stayed before, numerous times.

'That's *not* my home.'

'We have been advised to stop you leaving.'

'Advised by who?' She raised her voice, looking around at the burly security man who had suddenly appeared outside her door and the slightly uncomfortable look in the doctor's eyes. 'Has someone asked you to keep me here?'

'I asked them.'

Duarte Avelar appeared in the doorway, impeccably dressed in a sleek navy suit and light blue shirt. How unlucky could she get? He had become even more gorgeous, while she had been in a haze of sleepless nights with a newborn and had barely mustered the energy to brush her hair in the week since she'd last seen him.

'I told you I didn't need your help.' Nora squared her shoulders.

He gestured to the doctors and the guard to leave, closing the door behind them. His eyes drifted down, narrowing as he took in the small suitcase at her feet and the baby bundled up in the infant carrier she'd asked one of the nurses to order for her. Thankfully she'd set aside a small provision of cash for clothing and supplies for her son, but she hadn't expected to need everything so soon.

'You have no right to intrude on my privacy this way.' She shook her head in disbelief. 'I told you I didn't need your help.'

'I'm listed as your next of kin. The doctors called and filled me in on your plans to leave because they have concerns. I'll admit that I do too.'

His eyes met hers with an intensity that took her breath away.

'Packing a bag and then asking for internet access to book a flight?'

Nora swallowed hard, looking away from him and crossing her arms, ignoring the tender pain that still lingered in her chest from repeated failed attempts to nurse her son. She felt raw inside and out, and having Duarte reappear was just another thing sending her closer to the edge of her control.

'I am not doing anything wrong.' She forced a tight smile and deliberately slowed and calmed her voice. 'The doctor has said herself that both Liam and I are ready to be discharged. Not being allowed to fly has put a snag in my plans, but I will find a way.'

His frown deepened even more. 'Planning to leave the city?'

She looked down at her hands, feeling the heavy weight of her situation take hold. Without a flight, Manaus was almost three days away—at the other end of the country by the mouth of the Amazon. It was utterly ridiculous even to try to plan that kind of journey with a newborn and in her condition, putting them both at the mercy of public transport and cheap motels. She'd spent almost every last *real* she had paying to rebook her flight.

'I need to get out of Rio.'

She heard the desperation in her voice but didn't care. For all she knew, her father's men were waiting outside at this very moment. She had never felt so helpless and she hated it.

'Tell me why,' he said softly. 'Are you in danger?'

She bit her lower lip, looking away from him as she felt her eyes fill with panicked tears. She was losing every ounce of control she'd gained for herself, for her son. It infuriated her, feeling so utterly powerless.

Beside her, Duarte cursed softly under his breath and looked away for a moment. 'Nora, you must know you can't travel right now. If you need protection...' He seemed to measure his words for a moment. 'We've got about three minutes before the doctor returns, most likely in the company of someone from social services, who is going to ask some pertinent questions about the welfare of your child.'

Nora clutched at her throat, feeling it clamp tight with fear and realisation. She couldn't afford for anyone to go digging into her background right now. She needed to keep herself and her son out of her father's reach.

Closing her eyes, she inhaled deeply, completely aghast at the severity of her situation. Was this how she was starting her journey as a mother? Every single plan she'd made had gone wrong and now she was going to be investigated for child endangerment barely a week into her son's life!

'My home is nearby.' His eyes were steady on hers. 'You can stay there as my guest until they say you can fly. You'd have almost an entire wing of the house to yourself, along with anything you might need.'

'I can't fly for five weeks...' She half whispered the words.

'There is no time limit on my assistance,' he said softly. 'I believe that you played a vital role in saving my life and I would like to help.'

'Does this assistance come with a catch?'

She forced herself to look at him, to analyse his face so

she could see if he was sincere. He seemed genuine as he spread his hands wide and shrugged one powerful shoulder.

'I believe you have valuable information that will help me to bring a very dangerous man to justice. I understand why that must seem overwhelming in your current position, so I won't press you for answers yet. Right now, it's my job to prove to you that I am trustworthy, and I am willing to wait and work for your trust.'

Nora bit her lower lip, focusing on calming her thoughts and laying out all her options in her mind. The way things stood, she was trapped between two utterly terrible outcomes. If she tried to leave alone she risked the attention of the authorities, and thus her father, who had webs in every area of the city. But the alternative was accepting an offer from a man who at any moment might remember who she was and what had happened and bring her whole world crashing down. A man she had spent six months mourning and dreaming of.

Could she hold herself together for five weeks?

'I want my flight changed to a later date, when I'm cleared to travel,' she said quietly, standing up straight in an effort to project an air of confidence. As though any of this was actually *her* choice…

'I will have it taken care of immediately.'

The door of the room opened suddenly and the doctor appeared, introducing a stern-faced woman in a pale grey suit as a representative from social services.

As Nora felt her body go slack, Duarte's hand reached out to her elbow and held her upright. She looked up at him, seeing the question in his eyes. Like a woman about to sign her own death sentence, she nodded once. She watched his pupils dilate, the briefest flash of triumph glowing in his amber eyes before he turned away, using his body as a shield between her and the others.

Nora felt as though she had entered a twilight zone version of her life as Duarte easily commanded the situation in a way that somehow managed to be both dazzlingly charming and authoritative.

As she watched his bodyguard gather her things, she tried to shake off the feeling that, after spending months ensuring she escaped her father's control, she had just volunteered to step into another shiny cage.

CHAPTER FOUR

DUARTE TRIED TO ignore his strange feeling of relief at having Nora agree to come under his protection.

Once they were safely within the gates of his home he allowed her some privacy to settle in, instructing his housekeeper to give her a tour of the rooms he'd had set up for her and to serve her lunch in private while she rested. He was painfully aware of the fact that he had no idea what a newborn needed, so he'd enlisted the help of his assistant at the Avelar Foundation, a young mother herself, and had instructed her to spare no expense.

Not wanting to crowd his guest, he spent the afternoon in various meetings at his city offices. With Angelus Fiero still recovering from his injury, it fell on Duarte to step in and oversee the final stages of locking down their lands for future renovation projects.

He returned to the house much later than he'd expected, his back and shoulder aching from exertion. The house was strangely silent as he slipped into the kitchen and grabbed a premade salad from the refrigerator. Usually he took pleasure in cooking his own meals, but tonight he just wanted to eat quickly and get some sleep. He was not used to being back in the world of boardrooms and business deals, surrounded by the hum of conversation. It made him restless and edgy, as if he wanted to crawl out of his own skin.

He knew he needed to get back into practice if he had any hope of returning to his full workload as CEO of Velamar. His sister had sent him an email with details of the launch of their new headquarters in Florida the following month—a week of grand events in Fort Lauderdale to celebrate their new US and Caribbean charter routes.

A noise jolted him upright and he looked up to see Nora, standing frozen in the doorway of the kitchen. She held an empty baby's bottle in one hand and her small son in the other.

'Can I help?' he asked, standing up.

'No, thank you.'

She moved with impressive agility, balancing the infant in one arm as she prepared his milk with the other. Duarte frowned, making a mental note to call in a nurse tomorrow. If she wouldn't accept help from him, he'd ensure she got it elsewhere.

'I hope you have everything you need?' he said.

'You ordered a lot of things…' She met his eyes for a brief moment. 'I can't repay you for any of this.'

'I'm happy to help you any way I can.'

'In return for information?'

She spoke with a practised lightness to her tone, but he could see shrewd assessment in her gaze.

He placed both of his hands on the marble counter between them. 'I meant what I said at the hospital. Five weeks. I am a patient man, Nora. Right now my priority is keeping you safe while you rest and recover. Nothing more.'

She hovered in the doorway for a long moment, her red hair seeming to glow under the lamps of the corridor behind her. 'What if in five weeks… I still can't tell you anything?'

He heard the fear in her words, noting her use of the word *can't* rather than *won't*. He measured his words carefully. 'I think you should think about the kind of power

I might hold over whatever it is that you fear. I might be able to help.'

She shook her head once, a sad smile on her lips. 'I wish it were that simple.'

She turned and disappeared back up the corridor, leaving Duarte alone with his thoughts.

Nora practically tiptoed around the palatial villa, in an effort not to run into Duarte. For the most part she was successful. She spent her days adjusting to Liam's needs, and was grateful for the help of the kind young nurse Duarte had provided to keep on top of her own aftercare.

Breastfeeding had turned out to be impossible with her terrible supply of milk, and she'd sobbed with guilt when her nurse recommended she stop before Liam had even reached his two-week milestone. Without the pressure of her own failure hanging over her, she found she became slightly more relaxed. In a matter of days, her blood pressure readings returned to normal range and she began to smile again.

She was slowly beginning to feel a little more human, but still she found herself scanning the exterior grounds and refused to walk outside the house.

In the early hours of the morning that marked the start of her third week as Duarte's guest Nora awoke in a blind panic, her skin prickling with awareness as she jolted upwards in the gigantic four-poster bed. Blinking in the darkness, she placed a hand over her heart as though trying to calm her erratic breath. Her skin felt flushed, and the sheets were twisted around her legs as though she'd been thrashing in her sleep.

It wasn't the first time her dreams had been invaded in such a fashion, but this one had been by far the most X-rated. In it, Duarte had touched her with such gentle reverence, his eyes drinking her in as though she were the most beautiful thing he had ever seen. She had heard herself moan that she never wanted him to stop, her voice husky in a way she'd never heard before. She had felt every touch of his mouth as he kissed a path of sensual heat down her neck...

Shaking off the shiver of awareness that still coursed down her spine, she took a deep breath and peered over into the small cot beside her bed to ensure that Liam still slept peacefully. She adjusted his blanket and tried not to think of her handsome host or his frequent appearances in her subconscious.

If she'd expected Duarte to break his vow and demand answers, she'd been completely wrong. If anything, he'd gone out of his way to give her space. He spent much of the day out of the house, likely working somewhere in the city. Some nights he didn't return at all, like tonight.

She hated it that she was so hyper-aware of his movements, his presence. She'd tried her best to train herself to think of him as a benign stranger, but it was hopeless—especially while she was staying in this villa where memories of their time together assailed her.

Every time she walked into the living room she remembered the first night he'd taken her there...his mouth on hers as they failed even to make it to a bed. He'd been shocked to discover she was a virgin, and he'd insisted on bathing her afterwards. He'd sat behind her in a large claw-foot tub, overlooking the mountain view, and his hands had stroked over her body so reverently...

After that, she'd come to the villa countless times, always after the staff had been excused for the night. She'd been living in her own fantasy, imagining that she would build up to telling Duarte the truth of her identity and never incur his wrath or suspicion.

And all the while her father had been completely aware of her movements, plotting his revenge for her lies and deception. She'd been nothing but a pawn. A disposable entity to both powerful men in her life.

Now, lying back on the pillows in the silent house, she felt on edge. Earlier that day she'd tried to take a walk outside, for the first time since arriving. But while wandering around the courtyard, with Liam tucked tight against her chest, she'd thought she'd seen a familiar dark blue car parked at the end of the driveway. Her heart had stopped and she'd moved quickly back into the house, peering out of the window to see the car remain in place for another half-hour before slowly moving further down the road.

She'd had such a broken sleep tonight that it was possible she was being overly sensitive. It was only natural that she would be feeling the effects of her captivity. She wasn't technically a prisoner here, but she knew she couldn't leave. Not yet.

Frustrated, she gave up on trying to go back to sleep, wrapped herself in a thin cotton robe and clipped the portable baby monitor to the pocket. The clever gadget had been delivered the day after her arrival, along with a whole host of other items, including boxes and boxes of clothing for both her and Liam. In the haze of her sleep deprivation at the time she hadn't had the energy to insist she would pay for the items. But she knew she must repay Duarte somehow. She refused to fall under the spell of a rich man and then begin to feel like she owed him something.

Lost in thought, she almost missed the faint sound outside the house, but her heightened senses alerted her to the fact that something wasn't right. Frozen in place, she hardly breathed as the sound came closer to the large plate-glass windows that lined the back of the house. In the absence of the moon, she could see nothing but shadows and the crash of the waves in the distance below the cliffs made it hard to distinguish what exactly was out of place.

But then she heard it again. Footsteps on gravel, slow and deliberate. Heavy steps—much too heavy for the delicate, swanlike nurse or the housekeeper, neither of whom would be outside in the dark in the middle of the night.

Her brain made quick calculations as she moved instinctively to the side of the doors, out of sight. A tall shadow moved along the glass in her peripheral vision and Nora felt panic climb in her throat. All too quickly the quiet sound of the catch sliding sideways in the doorframe became apparent. To her horror, it seemed to have been left unlocked.

She watched as the door slid slowly open and the intruder pushed their tall, hulking frame inside.

Duarte felt his breath rushing in his lungs, hardly believing the events of this night. He'd been less than ten minutes from the villa when one of his security guards had informed him there was a break-in in progress. Two large men in a dark blue car had arrived shortly after midnight and managed to scale the gates.

Duarte and the guard had arrived just as the intruders had overpowered the second guard he'd left in charge of the surveillance of his home and its occupants.

Fury such as he had never known had possessed him as he had attacked the men and subdued them, using perhaps a little more force than necessary. His knuckles had become bloody, marking his white shirt and dark trousers, and he'd growled into his phone for his investigation team to send a van to pick the intruders up and take them for questioning. He'd left his security team to handle the rest, needing to get inside and ensure that Nora and the baby were unharmed.

Something about the two burly intruders snagged on his memory. He stepped into the darkened kitchen, feeling a memory surface like a television screen coming into focus. He froze with one hand still on the door handle, his mind conjuring an image of himself being thrown into a dark room, the smell of damp earth mingling with the scent of the sea in his nose. And then there had been Valerio's furious voice, asking him if the woman had been behind everything.

The woman?

He pulled at the details, hoping for more, cursing as he felt them slip away.

He heard the movement behind him too late. Something hit him with sharp force behind his knees, jolting his equilibrium and sending him down onto the porcelain tiles. He landed on his left shoulder. The pain lanced through him like fire, a primal roar ripping from his throat.

A blur of white moved in his peripheral vision—someone trying to step over him in the narrow space. On autopilot, after months of running on his survival instinct he reached out, grasping bare flesh. The skin was butter-soft, his brain registered, and his thoughts were confused between defence and attack. He tightened his grip but did not pull, straining his eyes upwards in the darkness.

His hesitation was all his opponent needed to turn the tables.

Within seconds he found himself pinned to the floor, with something cold and metal pressed tight against his sternum. A familiar lavender scent drifted to his nostrils and his eyes finally adjusted enough for him to make out a cloud of familiar red curls.

'Nora…' he breathed, shocked to feel his body instantly react to the sight of the wide-open split of the white nightgown she wore. 'It's okay. I'm—'

'I've got a high-voltage electronic Taser here, so I wouldn't try to move.' She cut him off, pressing her knee down harder onto his shoulder to prove her point. 'I've already pressed the panic button, so don't try anything.'

'Listen, I'm not—'

'How did he find out I was here?' she gritted out, and there was a slight tremor in her voice even as she kept her aim firmly at the base of his throat.

Duarte froze, taking in the confidence in her pose, the steel in her voice. He had to admit he was both impressed by such obvious skill and worried about where she'd honed it. Why it might have been a necessity.

Suddenly, her hurry to leave the hospital took on a much darker tone…

'I don't know who *he* is.' He spoke slowly, trying not to wince at the pressure of her knee on his injured shoulder. 'I'm here because I own this house.'

She froze, easing up on her pressure with a single jerky movement. Her voice was a shocked whisper. 'Duarte…?'

'In the flesh.'

She scrambled to her feet and Duarte tried but failed to avert his gaze from another tantalising glimpse of those long bare legs. The lights were turned on suddenly, momentarily blinding him as he pulled himself up to a seated position. His left arm hung limply at his side, and a familiar burning pain was travelling from his neck to the top of his shoulder blade before disappearing into numbness.

Partially dislocated, he'd bet. After months of gruelling physiotherapy sessions, he recognised the symptoms of his recurring injury.

'I'm so sorry… I thought you were someone else.' She stood on the opposite side of the kitchen, arms folded across her chest. 'A burglar.'

'Do you routinely confront dangerous intruders and pin them down for questioning?' he drawled, moving to stand up.

The pain in his shoulder intensified, taking his breath for a moment and putting stars in his vision. He sat back against the glass door with a growl.

'You're covered in blood!' She moved towards him, her face a mask of shock and concern. 'What on earth…?'

'Not from you.' He breathed deeply against the lancing pain. 'I was in a fight.'

His first instinct was to brush off her concerns—male pride winning out over his need for assistance. His shoulder was the last stubborn remnant of his injuries, along with the memory loss. There was an angry, bitter part of him that would rather languish in agony than admit any further weakness. But then Nora leaned down, gently placing one hand on his arm, and his mind seemed to go blank.

'But this is from me.' She spoke softly, the flash of her silver eyes briefly meeting his own. 'Is it your shoulder or your arm?'

'Shoulder. It wasn't entirely your fault.'

He felt the warmth of her skin through the material of his shirt as she lifted the sleeve. The scent of lavender grew stronger.

Duarte closed his eyes, clearing his throat. 'It's fine. It's an old injury.'

She snatched her hand back as though burned and he tried not to mourn the loss of contact.

With a deep inward breath, he pinned his arm to his chest as he slowly moved to stand up. 'Besides, I was lucky you were far too busy threatening me and asking questions to do any real damage.'

The slim black device in her hand caught his eye; he could now see it was not a Taser at all but a digital monitor. The small screen showed an image of a sleeping infant. A hollow laugh escaped his lips.

Nora frowned, realising he'd noticed her deception. 'I… I had to think on my feet.'

'You're quite practised in that, it would seem.'

Her posture changed at his comment, her shoulders straightening and her lips pressing into a thin line. But still she offered no explanation for her belief that she had been found by someone. Nor did she explain who that someone was.

Duarte had always been good at reading people, and right now he could see distrust settle into her eyes. She was the very definition of a flight risk, and if he had any hope of keeping her safe and finding out what her connection to his kidnapping was he needed to keep her here.

Almost as though she could hear his mind working, she took a step away, towards the living room. 'I should be getting back to bed…'

'Not so fast.'

She turned back and placed both hands defensively on her hips.

'I need your help with this,' he said. 'I don't think your nurse would be happy to be awoken at this hour.'

'I… I'm not a medical professional. Could you take something for the pain?'

'I know what I'm doing. I just need your hands.'

'My hands?' she repeated, eyeing the space between them with a strange expression.

Duarte tried not to feel affronted by her obvious reluctance to touch him. 'It's the least you can do, really, after you knocked me to the ground without effort.' He raised a brow in challenge.

When the barest smile touched her lips Duarte felt something inside him ease. She had clearly known fear in her life, and to think she had been afraid of him had made something dark and heavy settle right in the centre of his chest.

When she moved to stop beside him he deliberately avoided her gaze, needing a moment to clear his thoughts and ready himself for the manoeuvre.

'Will it hurt?' she asked quietly, her teeth worrying her lower lip.

'It's not without pain, but it's quick and then I'll be able to sleep. If you let me guide your hands, I'll show you.'

She placed both her hands into his much larger ones and Duarte felt again that strange echo of memory in the back of his mind as he took in the contrast of her porcelain skin against his dark brown tones. Brushing off the sensation, he placed her palms on the front of his shoulder, right where the pain burned most. As expected, her touch intensified the discomfort, but he instructed her to hold her grip. Her eyes were wide with fear and yet she did as she was told, keeping her hands steadfastly in position.

He told her how and when to apply counter-pressure and then did a quick countdown, biting down on his lower lip as he quickly guided his joint to where it needed to go with a swift jerk. The muffled roar that escaped his lips was quite mild in comparison to other times, when he'd been forced to do this alone.

He took a few deep breaths as the pain ebbed, and when he opened his eyes she was in front of him with a glass of water and two aspirin, which he accepted.

'That's not the first time you've done that...' Nora frowned at him, her expression troubled as she watched him drink the water, leaving the medication untouched.

'My memory is not the only part of my body that has been injured. I have a whole collection of scars owed to my time in captivity and the men behind it all. They were an energetic bunch of guys.'

Duarte thought of the memory he'd recovered earlier and felt a shiver run down his spine.

She stood close enough for him to see her eyes move to the long thin scar that moved from his temple down behind his ear. 'Duarte, I'm so sorry.'

He hadn't heard her speak his name since that first day in the rain. The sound of it on her lips, the way it rolled smoothly off her tongue…something about it called to him.

'Why should you be sorry? It's not your fault.'

At that she looked away, clearing the glass into the sink. With her back turned, Duarte took a moment to sweep his gaze along the length of her body, noticing her narrow waist and lush curves. It had only been a month since she'd given birth and the woman looked like she could step onto a catwalk.

His initial attraction to her had deeply perplexed him, considering her delicate condition, as had the depth to which she had become engrained in his thoughts in the weeks since. He'd deliberately been staying late at work in the city so he could get past whatever madness had taken over his mind since finding Miss Nora Beckett and becoming her unwitting protector.

He was not usually the kind of man who got off on rescuing damsels in distress; he didn't feel the need to bolster his own masculinity. She was a beautiful woman and his libido responded to her as such—nothing more. The fact that he had not felt a similar attraction to any other equally attractive woman was just circumstantial.

Although truthfully, he hadn't been looking at women very hard, preferring to dive deeply into his work and avoid distraction as he fought to make up for the time he'd lost.

He had promised her five weeks before he would question her again, but tonight had changed everything. The suspicions he'd had that she was in danger had just been confirmed with that break-in—as well as her words as she'd pinned him down—and he needed answers.

* * *

Nora took deep breaths to push down the wave of sorrow that threatened to overtake her at seeing the extent of the pain Duarte had suffered up close. She had felt the strange effects of her hormones shifting since Liam's birth, but this was so much more. This was an echo of grief. The tears fell fast and heavy down her cheeks as she tried in earnest to turn her face away from Duarte's perceptive gaze.

'Are you crying?'

She heard him move from his seat and his hand was suddenly on her shoulder, turning her to face him before she could wipe her face or move away. His feather-light touch gently guided her chin so she was forced to look up at him.

'You didn't hurt me, honestly.' He spoke quickly, one hand covering hers and gently stroking across her knuckles with the pad of his thumb.

She shivered, remembering him doing that before, what felt like a lifetime ago. She felt an insane urge to ask him if he remembered that night. If he remembered that he had told her how breathtaking she looked right before he'd kissed her senseless.

It had been their first kiss—the first of many over the long month of their whirlwind romance.

With his golden eyes on hers, Nora experienced a mad desire to lean in and feel his lips under hers again. Just one more time. She felt her tongue trace the edge of her own bottom lip, saw him follow the movement. His fingers flexed on her wrist and she could see a muscle in his jaw tick ever so subtly.

'Why can't I stop thinking about doing this?' he murmured, his eyes dark as he leaned forward slightly and brushed his lips across hers.

Nora inhaled sharply at the contact, hardly believing it.

Judging by the sudden widening of his eyes, he was just as shocked at himself. But the shock was short lived and Nora reached up on tiptoe and wound her arms around his neck, touching her lips to his again, seeking the heat of him.

Without warning, he took a step forward and spanned her waist with his big hands, holding her in place as she was pressed back against the kitchen units. The sleek wood was cool against her back and the hard, blazing heat of him engulfed her front. There was no softness in his kiss now…only fire and need. He somehow managed to be delicate even as his lips took hers in an almost brutal sensuous rhythm.

She heard herself moan against his mouth and felt him move even closer, one hand cupping her jaw as he deepened the kiss.

In the months after she'd lost him she'd lain in bed and tried to conjure up the memory of his kisses. They'd only spent a month together—a month of scattered secret moments in between his travelling and her own duties to her father's organisation. They'd spent most of their time in bed…and yet it had felt like so much more.

She'd thought her memory vivid, but right now she knew nothing had done justice to what it actually felt like to be in his arms, his sinful mouth demanding and coaxing… And she also knew exactly what it would feel like to guide him up to the master bedroom and re-enact every detail of her dreams…

She froze, pressing her hands against Duarte's chest and putting a few inches of space between their lips. He frowned, his amber eyes black with desire. And then that frown deepened and she felt the atmosphere suddenly shift.

Duarte took a few steps away, bracing his hands on the marble counter of the kitchen island as he continued to breathe heavily.

'You have been lying to me, Nora.'

Duarte's voice was a sharp boom in the stillness. He turned back to face her, amber eyes narrowed with suspicion.

'That was not the first time we've kissed, was it?'

CHAPTER FIVE

NORA CLOSED HER EYES, knowing she had made a fatal error.

'Answer me,' he demanded.

All trace of passion from their kiss had gone from his face.

'No. It wasn't the first time.' Nora whispered, closing her eyes tightly as if to block out the weight of her words as she spoke them.

'We were together.' He said quietly.

It took her a moment to process the fact that his words were a statement rather than a question.

A strange look transformed his dark features. 'We were…lovers.'

His words were like a whip against her frayed nerves and for a moment she feared that he had got his memories back—that he would figure out that he was Liam's father and she would be completely at the mercy of his anger. But then she looked up into his eyes and saw a brief flash of uncertainty as he waited for her to speak.

She had always been a terrible con-artist. Her father had tried and tried to toughen her up and mould her to fit in with the other female operatives in his criminal empire, Novos Lideres. She was too innocent, he'd said. But that innocence had long ago been taken from her in so many ways.

She straightened her shoulders and met Duarte's eyes.

'We went on a couple of dates, Duarte. I saw no reason to further complicate things for you over a minor detail.'

'You are still lying.'

His words were a menacing growl. He took a step forward, closing the gap between them.

'My mind may not remember you but my body does. I know that if I kiss a certain spot on your neck you will lose control and your legs will begin to shake.'

Nora gasped, shaking her head in an effort to stop him. 'You're mistaken.'

'Stop! No more lies between us.' His voice was a seductive whisper. 'I remember touching you, Nora. I remember your beautiful face as you climaxed with the most delicious whisper of a scream.'

He looked into her eyes and Nora was utterly helpless, unable to move under the sensual weight of his amber gaze.

'I suddenly know all of these things and yet everything else is still in shadow. How can that be?'

Nora wasn't sure whether he was asking her or himself, but she inhaled a deep shuddering breath and found that the few distraction tactics and acting skills she was able to draw upon had thoroughly escaped her. She felt a mixture of arousal and fear creep up her spine, holding her paralysed and powerless to do anything more than stare at him in damning silence.

'Am I still mistaken?'

Nora closed her eyes and felt the echo of their passionate whirlwind affair rush through her like a hurricane, destroying all the hopes she'd had of talking herself out of this.

'It was a casual thing. Barely more than a few weeks until it was over.' She forced the words out and watched as Duarte's eyes blazed with triumph, then narrowed on her once again.

'When?' The word was a harsh demand.

'A year ago. Five months before your kidnapping,' she said, wondering if he was mentally doing calculations.

The idea that he was suspicious enough to ask for that confirmation was more fuel heaped onto the fire of anxiety within her. She had told him the truth. Their short-lived fling had ended the day he'd walked out of her father's home. But of course there had been that crazy day when he had appeared in the rain outside her university a couple of months later…

An involuntary shiver went down her spine as she remembered the anger and frustration of their conversation erupting into a single desperate explosion of passionate kissing in his low-slung sports car. They'd been parked near the beach in broad daylight, and she had shocked herself when she had moved to spread herself over him and felt Duarte enter her unsheathed.

The madness had only taken them briefly, before they had realised what they were doing and stopped, but apparently that was all it had taken for her to fall pregnant.

She wouldn't regret it—not when it had given her the greatest gift of her life. Her son.

Duarte took a deep breath, opening his mouth to speak, but just then they were interrupted by the arrival of one of his bodyguards in the doorway. Nora was shocked to see that the man was covered in blood and had a split lip. It suddenly dawned on her that Duarte had told her he'd been in a fight. What had happened?

'The intruders have been removed, sir.' The guard spoke quietly but his rasping voice carried on the wind. 'Senhor Fiero has confirmed that they are members of Novos Lideres.'

Nora felt the ground shift beneath her.

'There's been a break-in and you didn't tell me?' She gasped, feeling her body begin to shake as she desperately grasped for the baby monitor, half expecting to see her father's face there instead of her peaceful, sleeping child.

'Thank you—you can take the rest of the night off.' Duarte's mouth was a grim line.

'That's not all, boss.' The guard flashed a glance towards where Nora stood. 'I don't think they were here for you. There were months' worth of surveillance pictures and notes all over their car…photos of her.'

Duarte's face turned to pure thunder as he instructed the guard to gather the evidence and bring it to his office.

Once the man was gone, he advanced on Nora. He was dangerously still, his arms crossed as he looked down at her like an angry god. 'Have they approached you since that night in the shipping yard?'

'I knew I was being watched,' she answered truthfully.

He closed his eyes, torment in every inch of his face. 'This is why you fear me. Why you have been so mistrustful of my help. I'll bet even now you are making plans to run. To disappear from here.'

'Running is the only defence I have to keep my son safe. Away from the crossfire. From all of you.'

'All of us?' His brow darkened with sudden ferocity. 'You consider me the same as *them*?'

Nora turned to walk away, but her progress was hampered by a strong, muscular arm against the doorframe. She looked up to find him dangerously close, his eyes twin fires of fury.

'Don't *ever* compare me to that lowlife gangster and his cronies again.'

'You say you're trying to help me, but we both know why you've really taken me under your protection.' She steeled herself, determined not to back down in the face of his anger. 'You're keeping me here to get information against your enemies. What makes you any different?'

'I don't take people against their will.'

'Well, that's good news for me.' She felt her breath expand painfully in her chest. 'Because I won't be staying here a moment longer to be used as a pawn in your game.'

'I have been up-front with you from the start. I do not use women.' He moved forward, pressing his hand to her cheek and forcing her to look into his eyes. 'Whatever this connection is between us, it is not some kind of ploy. I didn't plan that kiss.'

Nora blushed, remembering the heat of his mouth on hers, but she pushed the feeling away. 'That is another reason I can't stay here.'

'You can,' he said softly. 'You can choose to be a witness in my case and help bring a criminal to justice. You can choose to trust me to protect you.'

She shook her head, hardly believing the words coming out of his mouth. He spoke of trust. What would he do if he knew the truth of her terrible past. Right now, he was assuming that she was an innocent victim, caught in the crossfire of his war. That she could simply go on the witness stand and give evidence without repercussions.

She closed her eyes, thinking of her father and his clever net of spies and his unending power. He would likely pay the judge to throw her in jail while he walked away with a smile on his face. She was simply circling under his net and he was waiting to make his move and catch her. She knew how he operated. She knew that even if he didn't know about Liam yet, the very thought of his daughter reunited with Duarte Avelar would be enough to tip him over the edge into one of his rages. He would want Duarte dead for sure this time. And he would make sure she watched it happen.

And her son? She shuddered to think of Lionel Cabo using Liam in his games.

Panic edged her voice and she didn't try to hide it. 'I can't be a witness for your case, Duarte. I can't willingly put myself in danger like that just so you can have your revenge. I have to protect my son. I just want to get away from all of this and raise my child in peace.'

'Nora, this isn't about me getting revenge for myself.' He walked to the window, turning his back to her. 'Those people almost burnt down a tower block full of apartments with living occupants inside. *My* tower, that *I'd* refused to sell to them. They have no morals, no limits when it comes to getting what they want. Those apartments were filled with hundreds of the most vulnerable people in society: elderly couples, people with disabilities and single mothers with their children.'

'The fire safety scandal…' She froze, remembering him telling her the reason he'd been in Rio, trying to save his parents' housing foundation. 'That was Novos Lideres?'

Duarte nodded. 'There is proof of a politician's involvement. A politician who was in Lionel Cabo's pocket. A friend of mine pursued the evidence and was almost killed as a result. But that politician was our only hope of pinning the crime on Novos Lideres and now he's dead. Cabo thinks he's untouchable. One of the things my business partner Valerio told me about the beatings we endured was that they threatened to kill my sister. They have no respect for human life, Nora.'

His fists pulled tight as he spoke the words and Nora was quiet for a long moment. Up until now her decisions had been solely focused on how to keep herself and her son as far away from this mess as possible. To keep them safe and out of her father's nefarious clutches. But in walking away would she actually give her father more power? She had evidence that could put him away; she was an eye witness to many of his crimes.

Wrapping her arms around herself, she shuddered out a long breath and stared at the ground. Perhaps if she helped Duarte he might forgive her. More importantly, she might undo some of her own poor choices and finally be able to forgive herself.

Until Duarte, she'd told herself that the effects of her father's business dealings had only been on the money and power of wealthy men. She had fooled herself into thinking that she wasn't a true criminal if she wasn't hurting people. The truth was, every time she'd stolen information before feeding it back to her father it had hurt someone in one way or another. There had been political coups, corporate espionage... But she had never considered that perhaps her father had only ever let her see areas of his business that wouldn't scare or upset her. She had been unbearably naïve not to realise that her actions had hurt vulnerable people through cause and effect.

Her silence was part of the problem.

When she looked back up Duarte was assessing her with his shrewd gaze. She shivered to think what might be going on in his mind. She was fast realising that keeping her son away from all this was impossible. Perhaps she'd be better off choosing the lesser of two evils and putting her faith in the man in front of her.

'I don't want to let them get away with it,' she said quietly. 'I don't want to be afraid any more.'

'Such a fierce little angel you are.' His eyes blazed with triumph.

'I'm far from an angel...'

She heard the hitch in her own voice and felt an urge to tell him everything. Every terrible detail of her sins. She craved his forgiveness. She craved the bond they had once shared—before the reality of her awful family connections had torn it all apart.

'I have a house a short helicopter ride down the coast. I'll help you pack now and we can have your nurse flown in for check-ups each day.'

'Now…?' she breathed, looking out at the inky blackness of the sky.

'It's best if we leave before dawn.' Duarte's voice was quiet and filled with sincerity. 'Let me keep you and your son safe.'

Our son. Something inside her shouted.

She felt a heaviness in her chest in the region of her heart. *Tell him*, it said. *Tell him everything.*

But she couldn't. Not until she was sure of him and of the man he now claimed to be.

An uncomfortable thought flickered in her mind. If he was truly a good man and she had kept his son from him… did that make her a villain all over again?

'I'm not ready to make any statements yet, Duarte…' She steeled her voice, trying to muster some strength. 'But I'll come with you because I can't stay here. I want to help you, but I need some time to think about all of this, to make sure my son and I will be safe.'

'I'm a patient man, *meu anjo.*'

They both froze at his use of the endearment. Nora's heartbeat seemed to thump in the region of her ears.

After a prolonged silence she mumbled that she would go and get packed before quickly turning away from the haunting amber gaze that saw far too much.

Duarte walked out onto the terrace and made a quick call to order a helicopter from one of his trusted private firms. Paranoia had his head snapping up at every small sound.

He sat down heavily in the nearest deckchair and rubbed a hand down his face, feeling the dull pain still throbbing in his shoulder. His skin seemed to be on fire after that surprising embrace and the revelations that had followed.

He closed his eyes, remembering the softness of Nora's hands on his skin.

They had been lovers.

The faint memory of their connection had come to him the moment her lips had first touched his. He'd seen her underneath him...over him... Everything else was still in the shadows, as though the way his body had responded to her wouldn't let him remember anything else.

The moment she'd admitted the truth he'd immediately thought of the child. But unless she'd had a year-long pregnancy, the dates didn't match. The boy had even been born early, he reminded himself. He should have been relieved, but something within him had been quietly furious at the thought of her finding pleasure with another faceless man and conceiving a child.

The image of her fiery passion being given to someone other than him made his fists clench painfully. He briefly considered asking his team to find out who the man was, simply so he could land a punch on the bastard's face for abandoning his pregnant lover...

Duarte might have spent most of his twenties enjoying women in all their forms and wonders, but he had always used protection. And if by chance one of his lovers had ever become pregnant he would have done his duty and cared for his own flesh and blood.

Nora was a mystery to him in so many ways still, but this new knowledge of their intimate history together had changed something within him. He no longer felt adrift and lost in his own body. That single kiss seemed to have created a tether between them, from his solar plexus to hers, reaching out across the house and pulling her towards him.

He could feel her presence like a moth being drawn repeatedly to the warmth of a burning flame.

He knew it was a bad idea to want her. He knew there was a chance she would refuse to tell him the truth of how she'd ended up in the shipping yard with him. And yet still he imagined having those soft curves underneath him once more. He imagined hearing her cry out her pleasure in real time and seeing if the vague memory he had did it any justice.

He didn't know how long he sat, staring out at the blackness of the night sky, but by the time the distant sound of rotor blades sounded around him he had made his decision.

He would have her in his bed again.

As the helicopter began to descend over the small coastal town of Paraty, Nora tried to quell the roiling anxiety in her stomach. In her arms, her son slept peacefully, completely unaware of the upheaval taking place around him.

When they touched down on a sprawling property on the beachfront outside of town, she watched as Duarte set about ordering his guards to secure the perimeter while he escorted her inside. This reminder of the danger she had been in back at his villa made her begin to tremble all over again.

She knew that Duarte's protection was the safest thing for her and Liam right now, but it was only a matter of time before he figured out that she was hiding far more than just her brief relationship with him.

Nora barely registered her surroundings as he showed her to the large master suite of the house, explaining that his cousin and her husband lived on this historically preserved property year-round, in a separate groundskeeper's cottage, and sometimes gave guided tours to tourists. He quickly added that the house would be secured and closed for their use for the duration of their stay.

Nora eyed the sumptuously inviting pillows on the large four-poster bed and felt all the tiredness and exhaustion of a sleepless night hit her.

'Get some sleep.' Duarte followed her gaze to the bed, his eyes darkening for a moment before he exited the double doors of the suite and left her alone.

Nora felt raw inside, as though all her emotions had been swept up into a swirling storm within her. Liam still slept soundlessly, his cherubic face so serene and innocent she felt her throat tighten with emotion.

She was fast beginning to entertain the idea that Duarte wasn't as cruel and ruthless as he'd shown himself to be all those months ago. She thought back to that night in her father's home, when she had arrived to overhear them together, using her as a pawn in the game they'd played.

Her father had told her that Duarte had been playing her all along. That his interest in her had been an attempt at getting inside information on the organisation.

Nora had refused to believe it. She'd fallen in love with a kind-hearted, creative soul. They'd talked about her dreams of travelling as a freelance architect, once she graduated. They shared a passion for design and he'd promised to take her to Europe, to show her some of the beautiful buildings she'd only ever seen in books. It had been real…or at least she'd thought it had been real.

She'd felt sick as she stood there outside the dining room, listening to her father threatening to have her punished for the affair unless Duarte agreed to marry her. And telling him that a stipulation of the marriage contract would be that the Avelar Foundation signed a certain piece of land over to Novos Lideres.

When Duarte had flatly refused the contract, her father had been furious. He'd revealed his ace in the hole, threatening to have Duarte's jet-setting playboy image ruined by bringing him up on charges of sexual assault. Her own father had told him that he had friends who would enjoy giving Nora some nice big bruises to create photographic evidence, saying that hopefully they wouldn't get too carried away with their task now that they knew their princess had been deflowered.

Nora had almost fainted with terror and disgust.

She had waited for Duarte's outrage, waited for him to swear to defend her from such violence, but the silence had been deafening. Then Duarte had dialled a number on his phone and three police officers had entered. The men had been listening to the entire conversation. He'd smiled and spat that *nothing* would make him marry a mobster's daughter or hand over his land to such a crook.

His parting words had cut through her like a knife.

'If you think your daughter is worth anything to me, you're a bigger fool than she is.'

She lay down in the bed, turning her face into the covers to try to stop the tears that threatened to fall from her eyes. She had always known that her father was a dangerous man, but she'd naively believed herself out of the bounds of his cruelty. Hearing him threaten to use violence against her had been the catalyst she'd needed to begin her plan to escape.

Realising how she had been duped—how she had let herself be duped because she had craved love and attention from her father—had meant she no longer trusted her own judgement when it came to anyone. Especially not men who had a motive to use her for their own gains.

But she was no longer sure about her decision to leave Brazil and hide her son's existence. She wasn't sure about anything. She needed to be sure Duarte was telling the truth before she made herself—and her son—vulnerable.

She fell asleep with the memory of Duarte's lips devouring hers and dreamed of him watching her from the shadows of the bedroom, his amber eyes filled with longing and unrest.

CHAPTER SIX

Nᴏʀᴀ ᴀᴡᴏᴋᴇ ᴀFᴛᴇʀ a few hours of restless sleep with her body still taut with anxiety from the night before. She contemplated a shower, but no sooner had she stood up from the bed and stretched than Liam began to wake and fuss for his morning feed.

She dressed in the first thing she pulled out of her case that wasn't wrinkled—a simple coral sundress that was loose and flowing around her legs. She still hadn't quite figured out how to dress for her new body shape, but there was a more pressing matter at hand: feeding the fussing infant who had begun to let out intermittent squeaks, demanding her attention.

Scraping her hair up into a messy bun, she set out for the kitchen. It had been too dark to see much the night before, so she didn't know what to expect.

A long narrow corridor led from her bedroom to a sweeping mahogany staircase. She paused halfway down and looked up, transfixed by the breathtaking original stonework on the walls and ceilings. She could see where the historic features had been lovingly preserved, creating a perfect balance with modern touches.

The large living area had been extended at some point, with a clever stone pillar holding a modern glass fireplace acting as a transitional centrepiece that reached from floor to ceiling. She shook her head, hardly able to take in every wonderful detail at once.

From her vantage point at one of the full-length windows she could see that the rear of the house was surrounded by a stone terrace. Marble steps led down to an ornamental garden that looked perfectly maintained.

The property was cocooned by tall trees on either side, with just enough space at the front to see the South Atlantic Ocean spread out before them.

It was a home fit for a king—or at least some form of nobility—and sure enough, when the housekeeper, who introduced herself as Inés, spied her and showed her to the long galley kitchen, she was only too happy to give her a brief history lesson, outlining the passage of Casa Jardim from being the home of eighteenth-century Portuguese colonials to its present incarnation, housing three generations of the wealthy Avelar family.

Nora bit her lip, looking down at her infant son in her arms. This was what she was denying him. Not just wealth, but history and heritage.

But that life would mean nothing without safety. She couldn't remember ever being carefree as a child. The shadow of her father and his power had always hung over her and her mother, even when they'd tried to live peacefully in Manaus.

On that long weekend when they'd first met, Duarte had told her of the dangers that came with being an Avelar. He was regularly subjected to threats and scrutiny, requiring security wherever he went. She didn't want that for her son. He deserved to grow up free from fear, free from threat.

Steeling herself, she fed Liam and then settled him to kick his legs in his pram before tucking into the delicious spread of fresh fruit and pastries Inés had laid out on the open terrace.

The gentle clearing of a throat caught her attention, and she turned to find the subject of her dreams standing at the end of the stone steps, his body only partially covered by the white towel slung low on his hips.

Nora felt her mouth go dry and a groan of pure disbelief threatening to escape her throat. Of course he would be in a towel…

'I hope you both slept well?' he asked as he took a seat opposite her and sent a single fleeting look down to where the baby now slept in the shade.

'He doesn't sleep longer than a few hours yet,' Nora answered truthfully. 'The bed was very comfortable though.'

'That must be difficult…losing so much sleep.' Duarte frowned, thanking Inés as she brought him out a fresh cup of steaming hot coffee.

'I have many tricks to make *o menino* sleep.' Inés leaned down to coo at Liam, who had woken and begun to fuss and pull up his legs as if with discomfort. 'May I hold him?'

Nora nodded and bit her lip as the dark-haired woman gathered the baby into her arms and expertly placed him over her arm. 'I call this *macaco em uma árvore*. Monkey in a tree.' She smiled and began to sway from side to side, as though dancing. Liam immediately let out a loud burp and relaxed onto her arm with a dreamy little gurgle.

Once Inés and the baby had moved slightly out of earshot, Nora looked up to see Duarte watching her intensely.

'You are exhausted,' he said.

'I'm a new mother.' She frowned, touching a hand to the hair she'd so carelessly thrown up earlier. 'I don't have time to hide my exhaustion under make-up and smiles just to look presentable for your comfort.'

'*Deus*, I'm not criticising your appearance, Nora.' He shook his head with a mixture of anger and surprise.

'Things must have ended badly between us if you think me such a shallow, callous bastard.'

'I don't want to talk about that right now.' She stiffened.

'I know. You asked for some time and I will give you that.' His eyes were sincere, his mouth a firm unyielding line. 'But, for the record, I don't think you need to *try* to look presentable. You have the kind of natural beauty that most women would kill for.'

He leaned back in his chair, showcasing the impressive deep brown expanse of his bare torso. Nora felt her gaze linger for longer than necessary, her eyes drinking in the smooth muscles that were so tautly defined in the morning sunlight. It had been so long since she'd felt the heat of his body on hers...

She bit her lip, turning to look out at the ocean in the distance.

'I do have one small stipulation,' he said gently, drawing her attention back to his amber gaze.

Nora felt trepidation shiver deep inside her at the predatory gleam she saw for a brief second before he disguised it.

'For the duration of our stay here I wish for us to have dinner together.' He steepled his hands over that magnificent stomach, his eyes never leaving hers. 'Just good food and conversation—no tricks or forcing the issue of the past or the future.'

Nora narrowed her eyes at him, processing his words slowly and trying to figure out his angle. 'What's in it for you?'

Duarte fought the urge to smile at the obvious suspicion in her gaze. 'Perhaps I just don't like to eat alone,' he said simply.

'You are a terrible liar.' She pressed her lips together, the faintest glimmer of a smile appearing on her lips before she stopped herself. 'Let me guess—you plan to play the gracious host and wear me down until I agree to give you what you want?'

'I don't need to wear you down.' He took another sip of his coffee. 'I have faith that you are going to do the right thing, and I am determined to make sure you are kept safe.'

'You don't need to be nice to me,' she said uncomfortably. 'You are a busy man and I'm sure you have things to do back in Rio.'

'Of course I do. But those things can be managed from afar. You cannot.'

'You wish to *manage* me?' She narrowed her eyes.

'I wish to get to know you, Nora.'

He heard in his own words a bare honesty that shocked him. He saw her eyes shift away from him uncomfortably, her hands twisting the napkin in her lap as she watched Inés pace with the baby, singing softly.

'Trust me—you don't.'

Her words were barely audible but he caught them. He heard the weight of sadness and hopelessness woven through each syllable and was consumed by the urge to stand up and gather her into his arms. To figure out what on earth had happened between them that could put such a miserable look on her face.

'Will you agree to my terms?' he repeated, knowing she had every right to say no and knowing that he wouldn't push the issue.

Inés walked back towards them and revealed the peacefully sleeping baby in her arms. Nora's face lit up with surprise and gratitude as the older woman settled Liam into his pram.

Duarte peered down at the small bundle wrapped in blankets. The child had grown significantly in the month since leaving the hospital, and yet he was still tiny. He took in the boy's dark colouring and once again thought of the man who had walked away from fatherhood. Anger coiled within him.

Inés's voice penetrated his thoughts, asking Nora if she would like to take a moment to rest or freshen up and offering to sit with the baby in the fresh air of the upstairs balcony.

Nora hesitated, looking towards Duarte for a moment. 'I don't mean to leave you alone in the middle of your breakfast…'

Duarte assured her that he would be working all day and instructed Inés not to take no for an answer. No one should be expected to do everything for an infant without a little help.

She smiled, and the two women began to make their way back into the house. A few footsteps from the door Nora stopped and turned around to face him.

'I'll see you at dinner, then.' Her voice was a little uncertain as she waited for him to nod before she disappeared through the doors.

Duarte tried not to roar at the small victory. He watched her walk away, his gaze lingering for far longer than was proper. He mentally shook himself and tucked into the spread of freshly cut papaya slices and warm bread rolls that had been filled with cheese and pan-fried.

This traditional dish of *pão de queijo* that Inés had prepared was one of his favourites, reminding him of long weekends and summers spent here as a child, when he and his sister would fight over the last piece while their father laughed and their mother scolded.

Every time he thought of his parents he wondered why his memory loss had not wiped away the grief he still felt from their death seven years ago. From the moment he'd set foot inside this, their special family vacation spot, he'd been instantly overcome with memories of when he was a child. Yet for some reason he had no memory of the past year of his life beyond blurred snatches here and there. It made no sense.

Shaking off the frustration, he opened his phone and dialled Angelus Fiero's number for an update. Upon hearing that the two criminal henchmen had escaped and gone straight back to Novos Lideres and Cabo, he clenched his fists on the table.

'Filho da mãe!' he cursed, banging his fists hard against the wood.

He quickly recovered and forced himself to think logically. Those men would never have testified against him anyway; it was a part of the sick code of the Novos Lideres. Men quite literally pledged their life to their *patrao*—their boss. And Lionel Cabo got to sit at the top of the pecking order, watching them all fall like good soldiers.

He wasn't prepared to tell Angelus any details about the woman staying under his protection. He simply said that he was working with a witness who was possibly willing to assist in their case. The older man's voice brightened substantially, and he assured Duarte that witness testimony would be enough to get an arrest warrant at least, but they still needed solid evidence to make the charges stick.

The idea of finally putting Lionel Cabo behind bars for his crimes was immensely satisfying. But what would he do if Nora decided not to do the right thing? What if fear won out over that tiny spark of fury he'd seen in her eyes when he'd told her the depth of the mobster's crimes?

Once she could leave, he wouldn't be able to stop her.

In an ideal world, he'd simply offer her a large sum of money in return for information—but he had a feeling that bribery would only send her running faster. She had seemed uncomfortable with his purchases for her and the baby, continuously offering to repay him.

His father had taught him to follow his instincts in business and he'd honed that skill to a fine art, using it to his advantage in all areas of his life. He needed to stay, to get under her skin and find out what she was holding back and why.

Nora Beckett was proving to be quite a perplexing distraction, but if there was one thing Duarte Avelar relished above all else, it was a challenge.

Nora waited patiently for her distractingly handsome host to disappear back to his busy life, as he had done while they'd been in Rio, but he surprised her by staying put at the villa. Shockingly, he didn't attempt to question her further about her revelations. Nor did he mention their kiss.

He spent most mornings doing laps of the pool at a punishing pace, while she tried to focus on tending to Liam, trying not to catch glimpses of his powerful body slicing through the water, or heading off bare-chested for a jog along the beach. The middle hours of the day were spent working, but she soon found that he was not the kind of man who holed himself up in an office all day in front of a screen. Instead, he took conference calls out on the terrace, as he paced back and forth like a lion in his den, issuing orders and asking questions in more languages than she could count.

He'd taken over the large dining table that overlooked the sea, filling it with complicated blueprints and large heavy books filled with technical information. Sometimes when she woke at night, to pad to the kitchen for milk for Liam, he would still be there, frowning as he fitted together odd-shaped plastic pieces and transferred calculations to technical-looking documents.

His yacht designs, she presumed, remembering how passionately he'd once spoken of his creative projects.

They had eaten dinner together for four nights in a row, and the conversation had been far from boring. He was a deeply intelligent, well-travelled man, and yet he didn't try to make her feel inferior because she didn't know about worldly things due to her sheltered life.

At their first dinner she had briefly mentioned she loved to swim, and the next day she'd found a brand-new powder-blue swimsuit in a package outside her bedroom door.

The next night Duarte had surprised her by showcasing his cooking skills, and had prepared a delicious platter of barbecued *picanha*, the meat so tender it had made her moan with delight. Afterwards, Inés had offered to rock Liam to sleep, and Nora had accepted Duarte's offer of a short walk down to the beach.

As she'd stared out at the wide expanse of the ocean, spread out ahead of them, she had found herself confessing to him her dream of travelling, of seeing in real life all the amazing places in her architecture textbooks.

He'd seemed genuinely interested, and impressed that she'd completed a degree during such a turbulent time in her life, and he had frowned when she'd revealed that she'd had to abandon all her books back in Rio.

The next day there had been an entire shelf of thick hardbacks installed in the formal study at the back of the house, along with a note from him instructing her not to give up on her dream.

He somehow managed to make her feel on edge and completely at ease all at the same time.

On the sixth day after their arrival, she found herself sitting outside in the sunshine with Liam peacefully asleep in his pram by her side. When she felt a strange prickle on her neck she turned to see a familiar pair of golden eyes watching her. Quickly he turned away, going back to his work, as though chagrined at being caught looking her way.

Nora bit her bottom lip, wondering if he felt the unbearable chemistry simmering between them just as much as she did.

That evening, Duarte passed a message through Inés that he had to leave for the city. Nora tried not to be hurt by his lack of a goodbye, reminding herself that she was a guest in his home and nothing more. But she had got used to their evenings together and felt silly for being disappointed.

The next morning she awoke, ready for the nurse's daily check-up, and was shocked when the woman reminded her that it was the day of Liam's six-week check-up.

She waited with bated breath until the nurse announced that her son had grown and developed at a typical rate over the past six weeks and congratulated her on a job well done.

Her own check-up was just as detailed, and ended with another smiling declaration that she had healed perfectly and the pre-eclampsia would have no lasting effects. She watched in silence as they were both officially declared fit for travel, and then gave the nurse a long hug as she bade the woman goodbye for the last time.

Duarte had kept his word and booked her flight, the details for which were printed out and safely stashed in the hidden compartment of her case.

There was nothing to stop her from leaving, she thought sombrely as she stood on the balcony and watched the helicopter recede into the clouds above. And yet she had already decided she would stay.

Her complicated feelings for her son's father had clouded her mind, making it impossible for her to come to a decision about trusting him. But really she knew she had to tell him. Even if he had treated her terribly all those months ago and broken her heart, was that enough of a reason for her to deny him the right to see his own son?

Her body was on edge with tension as she tried over and over to think of the best way to tell him that he was a father. She hadn't outright lied to him about Liam, she told herself as she worried at her lower lip. He had made assumptions which she hadn't corrected, but she hadn't directly fabricated the lie, had she?

As if sensing her turmoil, Inés insisted she take an hour for herself to unwind in the pool. The older woman refused to take no for an answer, so Nora changed into the powder-blue swimsuit, covered her pale skin with sun lotion and spent a delightful half-hour wading from one side of the huge pool to the other, floating on her back and staring up at the cloudless sky.

Taking a moment to lie back on a sun lounger and dry off, she found herself able to take in the details of her surroundings. She was awed by the solitude of this cliffside villa. The nearest neighbour was a five-minute drive away, leaving no man-made sound to disturb her peace, only the wind in the trees and distant rush of the waves on the rocks below.

Inés had been right; she'd needed some time to reconnect with herself. She had almost forgotten she could function outside of the tiny bubble of motherhood.

When she got back to her room she found Inés had already fed Liam and put him down to sleep. Her son was starting to slumber for longer stretches at night now, and it was all down to Inés's magic touch. In the absence of her own mother, Nora felt enormously grateful to have such a caring maternal influence. And Inés had developed quite a bond with her son too—although she often threw strange glances Nora's way and commented that the boy could almost pass for an Avelar, with his defined dimple and dark skin.

Nora only blushed and looked away.

The older woman told her that dinner would be at seven and gave her a stern look, instructing her not to be late. It was already getting dark outside, so she forced her tired body to shower and dress in a simple emerald-green shift dress and flat sandals, not wanting to be rude if Inés had prepared a meal.

Putting the baby monitor into the pocket of her dress, she padded downstairs.

In the short time she'd been gone the net of lights above the terrace had been switched on, and underneath was a small dining table, neatly set up for two. In the distance she could see two bodyguards, doing their nightly sweep of the property. She frowned. If there were two bodyguards, that meant Duarte had returned.

'Welcome, *senhorita*.' A slim waiter appeared, motioning for her to take a seat.

'I don't think this is for me…'

She looked around, half expecting a parade of wealthy socialites to come marching through the house. Instead, she saw Duarte emerge from the dining room, striding towards her as if he'd just stepped off the cover of a fashion magazine. He wore a crisp white shirt, unbuttoned at the neck. His short crop of hair was still damp and glistened in the twinkling lights, as did his eyes as he pinned her with an intense gaze.

'I decided I needed to make up for missing last night.' He smirked.

'You've done all this for me?' She frowned, a knot of anxiety twisting in her stomach as she looked around, seeing a man in full chef's uniform hard at work in the kitchen.

'Not exactly.' Duarte let out a low hum of laughter. 'Chef

Nico and his team have applied for the catering contract on the new superyacht I'm designing. I'm seeing if he lives up to the hype.'

'Oh.' She felt her arms relax slightly with relief. The name sounded vaguely familiar—she thought he was a minor Brazilian celebrity. 'They're cooking for you as an audition, then?'

'They are cooking for *us*.' He raised a brow. 'You need to eat, no?'

'Well, yes, but…'

'Inés made me promise to feed you. Besides, I found I rather missed your company last night,' he said softly, guiding her over to a chair. 'Do with that what you will.'

Her eyes widened at his admission and Duarte had to fight himself to look away, to ignore how his heartbeat sped up in his chest and pay attention to the dishes that began arriving in front of him for his judgement.

It turned out that Chef Nico's hype was more than justified. By the time the last of the dishes had been cleared away he had already decided to hire the man.

Nora glanced down at the slim monitor in her pocket every so often, but otherwise seemed to be genuinely enjoying herself, and kept up with his deliberately light tales of the day of manual work he'd completed at one of the Avelar Foundation's newest housing projects. He'd spackled walls and lifted furniture up and down steps all day, thanking his good luck that his body was strong despite his injuries.

It dawned on him that he hadn't had a headache in weeks, and that his mood had become more balanced and predictable—almost like his old self.

They took a small break before dessert, and Nora slipped up to her room to check on her son. When she returned,

Duarte suggested they take their drinks to the viewing deck and allow the serving staff to clear away the dishes.

She walked ahead of him, the gentle sway of her hips a naturally sensual sight. He shook off his errant thoughts, realising that while he should be planning his approach to secure her agreement to be a witness against Lionel Cabo, all he could think about was kissing her again.

'I love the view from up here. I can't remember the last time I left the city.' She sighed, taking a long sip of her drink.

'You said you didn't always live in Rio…?' Duarte said, keeping his gaze straight ahead. Still, he couldn't miss the way she visibly stiffened by his side, then forced herself to relax.

'Not always, no. My mother and I moved around a bit.'

'You said she's Irish?'

Nora nodded her head, her fingers twirling around the stem of her glass for a moment.

'Ireland's a beautiful place to live,' Duarte said. 'She moved all the way across the world for her work?'

'Something like that.' Nora cleared her throat. 'You know what that's like, though, I suppose?'

He nodded. 'We moved to England when I was just a boy and I started boarding school not long after. My parents wished for me to be a great scholar.' He laughed, seeing the ice in her gaze shift a little, and congratulated himself on his efforts.

'I wouldn't say their efforts were wasted, considering your success.'

He shrugged, tugging at his collar, which suddenly felt too constricting. He disliked it when others commented on his success—an old habit after the years of torment that had come with being the smartest kid in class. He always tried to be modest, to downplay the ease with which he seemed to accomplish certain tasks.

She seemed to sense his shift in mood and changed the topic to the yacht she'd seen him working on, asking if he was enjoying his work. To his own surprise he answered honestly—perhaps too honestly. He told her of the large-scale launch for their US operation, and the pressures his sister and his business partner had been under with Duarte's sudden reappearance and subsequent return to the company.

He didn't go into the guilt he felt about the pain his twin had endured when she'd thought him dead, or how his best friend had blamed himself for the events leading to their kidnapping.

'It sounds like you're feeling the need to prove yourself and your health by going above and beyond all your previous achievements,' she said quietly, turning to look up at him.

Duarte paused and smiled, shaking his head and sitting back in his chair to survey her.

'Did I say something wrong?' She frowned.

'It's more what you didn't say.' He raised one brow. 'I could have sworn I set out to learn more about *you*, and somehow I end up talking non-stop about myself for ten minutes.'

She moved to take a step away from him, and to his own surprise he found himself circling his hand gently around her wrist. Her eyes widened with surprise, but she made no move to pull away.

'You said you've missed my company...but you don't know me. Not really,' she said softly, barely audible above the rush of the breeze and the waves around them. 'If you knew all the things that had passed between us...'

He watched as she swallowed hard and moved further away from him. If she was hiding things from him, it was likely she had her reasons. But still, looking down at the small handful of steps that separated them, he found he didn't care about the circumstances. He looked at her and he wanted her as he had never wanted another woman. And if she were to give him the barest hint that she wanted him too he knew all bets would be off. He'd have them both naked and in his bed before they could take another breath, gourmet chef and their dessert be damned.

As if she sensed the intensity of his thoughts, she took a deep breath that seemed to shudder a little on the exhale. 'When you look at me like that I can't think straight.' She shook her head softly. 'Liam turned six weeks old today. The nurse declared us both fit for travel.'

Duarte froze, the news hitting him like a bucket of ice water. He leaned against the handrail, looking out at the ocean. 'Have you made your decision?' he asked.

She closed her eyes, as if some unknown emotion was threatening her composure. It dawned on him that he'd never seen her so undone, so close to tears. She was always so strong.

'Hey…hey…' He wrapped an arm around her. 'Look, I understand that you're afraid.'

'I'm not afraid of being your witness, Duarte.' She pulled away from him. 'But I can't tell you about what happened that night without revealing my part in all of it. Without revealing that *I'm* part of the reason you were there in the first place.'

She reached one hand into her pocket and pulled out a slim black thumb drive, placing it into his hand. 'This contains everything. It's encrypted with some kind of code, but I know it's more than enough to blow Novos Lideres apart for good.'

Duarte felt shock pulse through him as he absorbed her words. 'Explain.'

Her words were dull and emotionless. 'The reason Cabo's men were looking for me is because I was a part of his organisation. I... I worked for him for a while.'

She looked away from him, her lips pressing together in that tell-tale way he could now recognise.

'I was initially tasked with getting information from you that they could use to force you to sign over your land.'

She went quiet again for a moment, her eyes flickering between him and the horizon in the distance.

'But it all went wrong.'

'Clearly.'

He frowned, shocked and horrified at her words, and stared down at the black rectangle that supposedly held all the things he'd been working to find. Could it be true?

'I was already trying to get away by the time you were kidnapped. They held me captive in a different location, to ensure that I didn't go to the police. I got free and I got word to your friend, Angelus Fiero, but by the time I got to where they had you...you had already been shot.'

'Why save me?' he asked, watching her reaction closely. 'Why risk being arrested yourself or punished for your actions?'

'I may have done things I'm not proud of, Duarte, but I'm still human.' She shook her head. 'There was so much blood... But I couldn't risk being seen. I had to leave you there. The next thing I heard was your death announced on the news. And then your poor friend was found alive. I didn't even know he was still in there...'

'He suffered greatly but he is okay now. Physically at least.'

Duarte was silent for a long time, his mind working double-time to process the new information. He'd known she was hiding something, but this was unbelievable.

'Look, I'll get my things packed first thing in the morning and I'll be gone, okay?' She moved towards the door. 'I just want you to know that I am sorry for the part I played. I never meant for any of that to happen.'

'You saved my life. You risked your own life to save me,' he said softly. 'Did you love me, Nora?'

She shook her head, anger in her eyes. 'Don't make me out to be something I'm not. I'm not the worst of them, but I was still one of them. I still conspired to hurt you. To hurt other people through you.'

'Did you love me?'

He asked the question again, more harshly this time, and watched as her eyes drifted closed. She was consumed with guilt—that much was clear. And he should be furious at her deceit. So why did he have the urge to offer her comfort instead?

He closed the space between them, forcing her chin up so she met his eyes. Twin stormy grey pools of torment reached out to him and pierced him somewhere in the region of his heart.

'Yes...' she whispered, a choked sob escaping her lips. 'Despite everything, I loved you...so much.'

Duarte claimed her lips, swallowing her sadness and her guilt and wishing he could take the burden from her. She had been in a purgatory of her own making for months, believing him dead and believing she had been responsible.

Her hands clutched at his shoulders, pushing slightly, and Duarte froze, fully prepared to stop. He was not the kind of man who needed to force a woman to get his way, no matter how strongly his body had reacted to her touch. But before he could pull back she seemed to make a decision of her own, moving up on her toes and pressing her soft, full lips against his.

CHAPTER SEVEN

SHE HAD KNOWN it would come to this from the moment she'd taken a seat across from him at dinner and looked into his warm, whisky-coloured eyes. It was too much—having him this way but not having him at all. If there had ever been a more perfect torture, she'd like to see it. This man who had stolen her heart and then broken it into a million pieces…he was everything she remembered and more.

His strong muscular arms locked her in place as their mouths moulded together like twin suns re-joined. He was a skilled kisser, and the heat of his mouth on hers was sending delicious shivers down her spine. Nora felt her body sing out the 'Hallelujah Chorus' even as her mind screamed at her to stop. To think of the consequences of her actions.

She was sick of thinking.

She felt brazen and rebellious as she moved her body even closer into the cocoon of his arms, letting her tongue move against his in the sensuous rhythm he had once taught her on a darkened beach.

If she kept her eyes closed she could almost imagine that this moment was entwined with that one. That their lives had never been torn apart by the awful events in between. No. She couldn't think of that. It was just him and her and this glorious fire they created between them when they touched.

'I'd be lying if I said I wasn't hoping for this, but I'm not apologising,' he whispered, his head dipping to kiss a path along her neck.

She gasped as his teeth grazed along the sensitive skin below her ear. His hands slid down her back to cup her behind, holding her against him. She could feel the evidence of his arousal pressing against the fabric of her dress. It would be so easy to lift the fabric and feel him properly...

A long-ago memory of him lifting her legs around his hips and taking her in a public elevator rose to her mind unbidden, heightening her arousal. She had always been like this with him—like a moth to a flame. She'd never reacted at all to any of the men her father had allowed her to date...

The single errant thought of her father was enough for her to get a hold on her rapidly deteriorating rational mind and detangle herself from Duarte, moving a single step away.

'Why do you want me, Duarte?' she asked. 'Even after the things I've revealed, you still kiss me like that and it ties me up in knots.'

He shoved a hand through the short crop of his hair, golden eyes seeming luminous against his dark skin. 'I've tried to ignore my attraction to you, because you have made it more than clear that whatever we had before is over. But every time we're together I'm more drawn to you. You're intelligent, and beautiful, and I find myself thinking of you far more often than I should probably admit. I think you still want me too.'

Nora felt heat and desire prickle across her skin at his words. She didn't know what to say to that.

One half of her was crying out to kiss him again and throw caution to the wind—to take one selfish night of pleasure and deal with the consequences of her lies of omission tomorrow. The other half told her she needed to tell him everything, not just a half-truth. She was stalling and drip-feeding him all the terrible things in the hope that she might somehow manage to keep him. That they might make it through all her painful revelations with this fragile new beginning still intact.

The idea of tipping him over the edge into the kind of hatred she'd seen on his face once before was more than she could bear.

She closed her eyes, hardly believing the selfishness of her own thoughts. This wasn't just about her. Liam deserved to have his father in his life; he deserved the chance to know him. She had to tell him. She had to rip the sticking plaster off.

She opened her mouth to speak, but a small cry came from the monitor in her pocket. She looked at the screen, then up to Duarte.

'Go,' he said simply.

The cry sounded out again—faint, but enough to tell her she needed to go. It was a divine intervention, of sorts, saving her from her own uncontrollable libido. *Stupid, stupid girl.*

'Nora.'

She turned around and saw he was still standing where she'd left him. The night sky formed an impressive backdrop, making him look even more otherworldly than he already did.

'I have to leave again shortly for the city.' He cleared his throat and adjusted the collar of his shirt, looking up at her. 'Have dinner with me again tomorrow?'

She swallowed hard at the knowledge that she had a twenty-four-hour reprieve. She would figure out how to tell him about Liam. She had to. Nodding and throwing him a tight smile, she practically ran the rest of the way up to her room, her heart hammering in her chest.

* * *

Duarte stepped inside the entrance hall of the house and was struck by the utter silence. He'd spent the morning with Angelus, and they'd agreed to send the thumb drive for immediate decoding, finding a source they trusted so the information wouldn't be lost. The rest of his day in Rio had been spent in meetings with the future tenants of his new developments, figuring out what they needed and ensuring he was offering the best fresh start possible for them.

He'd eventually cut his day short and decided to return to the coast early, knowing he wanted to ask Nora more questions but also just wanting to be with her.

Upstairs, he passed the door to Nora's room. It was open. He saw the bed freshly made and the small cot. He entered the room, his gut tightening at how empty it looked. He felt his body poised to run downstairs, to investigate further, when a splashing noise outside caught his attention.

He reached the balcony in a few quick steps, peering down to see a blur of action in the pool. Nora sat at the edge, dipping her tiny infant's toes into the water. As though she felt his presence, she looked up and spotted him. A shy smile crossed her lips and she waved.

Duarte pressed his lips together, hardly able to manage the riot of emotions coursing through him. For that split second he'd believed she'd gone, he'd been ready to rip through the country in search of her. It was madness. He felt as if he was losing what little control he'd gained over himself in the past months. How was it possible to feel calmed by this woman's presence and yet so completely undone?

She had essentially admitted to being part of the syndicate that had tried to kill him. She was a criminal by her own admission. And yet something in him refused to believe that was all she was. He had witnessed her care for her son, her intelligence and heard of her determination to finish her studies.

She was a contradiction. He usually despised things that didn't make sense, and yet he kept moving back to her, time and time again, as if he was a magnet and she was his true north.

Even as he told himself he needed to keep his distance, and regain the upper hand in order to move forward with his investigation, he found himself moving down the stairs and through the house towards the sound of her gentle laughter.

Nora had felt as though she were breaking apart all day as she'd wrestled with her decision and her fear of staying too long here in this wonderful place. She didn't quite know how to accept the calm happiness of being so secure and cared for... Deep down, she knew this kind of life was never meant for someone like her. She knew she couldn't stay for ever. Especially once Duarte knew everything. She wished that everything could just stay the same in their little bubble, but it couldn't.

And then Duarte had come back early from the city, and he had looked down at her in his intense way and she'd felt her heart sing in response.

He'd stayed outside with them for much longer than he ever had before, even offering to hold Liam while she took a short swim. She'd felt her hands shake as she'd passed her precious child into Duarte's arms, trying not to stare at their identical colouring and the same little frown between their brows.

The urge to tell him in that moment that he held his son in his arms had been overwhelming, but Inés had been watching them, and Nora hadn't been prepared to do it in the middle of the day.

Coward, she'd told herself as she'd dived under the water to disguise the tears that had flooded her eyes.

And even now, as she showered and dressed for dinner, her stomach flipped as her mind replayed the image of the two of them together in her mind. Father and son…

She knew she couldn't stay there another moment, knowing she was keeping such a huge thing from him. Duarte was not the man she'd thought he was. He was not like her father. Yes, he would be angry at her deceit, but she didn't believe he would be cruel.

She no longer feared that he would want to take her son from her and she now knew she couldn't keep his son from him. Liam was an Avelar by birth, and no matter how much she wished it to be different she had no hope of competing with the kind of life such a birthright would offer him.

She needed to tell Duarte and hope that they could find a way through this together.

Duarte had taken his time showering and dressing for dinner, his senses heightened. Now he waited in the dining room, listening to the sounds above of Inés and Nora talking as they readied the infant for bed.

He had surprised himself with his interest in the boy, offering to hold him that afternoon out of pure curiosity. And something had tightened in his chest as he'd looked into the small silvery blue eyes so like Nora's. He'd felt something protective and primal that he'd feared examining too closely.

He didn't want to come on too strong, he reminded himself. This was just dinner between two people with a mutual attraction.

When Nora appeared, the sight of her curves encased in jade-green silk stole his breath. She always looked beautiful, but tonight she looked radiant. Her eyes looked wider, outlined with the barest sweep of shadow, and the apples of her cheeks glowed with vitality. Her soft full lips were painted a rose-pink that made his own mouth water at the memory of how she tasted.

'You're really dressed up.' She smiled nervously. 'Have you ordered another chef audition?'

'Not exactly.' His voice sounded a little rough even to his own ears, and he could see the way she looked at him a little uncertainly. He cleared his throat, running a hand along his freshly shaved jaw. 'I thought we could go out tonight—if that's okay? The old town is really not to be missed, and I know a place that makes the best *moqueca de peixe* in the whole of Brazil.'

She smiled, and Duarte felt his chest ease.

Nora felt slightly nervous at leaving the house for the first time, but Inés had practically pushed her out through the door, assuring her that Liam would be fine for a couple of hours.

He had begun sleeping for longer stretches of the night now, she reassured herself, trying to ignore the almost painful tug of anxiety as Duarte's car moved away from the house and along the dirt road.

As though he sensed her anxiety, Duarte began filling the silence with commentary, telling her about the small town of Paraty and its rich history dating back to the time of the gold rush.

The historic centre of town was a bustling labyrinth of pedestrianised cobbled streets, with pretty whitewashed buildings and a surprisingly cosmopolitan array of restaurants. Duarte had booked a table in a small modern-looking eatery near the pier, where the ambience was like stepping into a warm golden cavern.

True to his word, the *moqueca* was the best she'd ever

tasted. The traditional fish stew melted in her mouth and was washed down by a local wine. For a dinner with a billionaire, it was surprisingly low-key and cosy. She found herself slowly relaxing as she tried not to think of the words she had rehearsed all day.

All day she had been tortured with anxiety. She didn't want to lose him all over again. She'd made bad choices in her life and allowed herself to be controlled by her father, but she did not believe she was truly bad.

After the last of their food had been cleared, Duarte suggested they take a walk down the stone-walled pier to where he had something he wanted to show her. Nora walked alongside him, keeping her eyes ahead and trying to control the swirl of butterflies flapping around her stomach.

The way he looked at her and listened to her, his curiosity unmarred by the hatred she'd once seen... It was as if she'd been given a true second chance with him—with the Duarte she'd known before his betrayal and all the ugliness with her father.

'It's just down here.' Duarte smiled as he took her hand and led her down one of the narrow wooden walkways of the marina. Small fishing boats bobbed gently on either side, gradually getting bigger and more expensive-looking as they walked further on.

Duarte came to a stop at the end, gesturing to a gigantic dark-painted ship that looked completely out of place amongst the more modern white and grey giants that surrounded it. It had several tall sails and an elegant golden trim. A large painted sign along the side read *O Dançarina. The Dancer.*

'This was the first ship I ever set foot on. My father's pride and joy.' Duarte spoke quietly beside her. 'It's been in storage for seven years...ever since their accident.'

Seven years. Nora closed her eyes briefly. She knew

exactly when his parents had died, and felt sadness on his behalf.

Duarte pulled down the gangplank and gestured for her to follow him on board. She'd bet the deck alone was longer than her entire apartment back in Rio. It was polished teak and spotlessly clean, as though it had just come back from a week at sea with its wealthy owners. She half expected staff to be teeming below-deck, ready to offer refreshments and hors d'oeuvres.

'I had it cleaned. It still looks exactly the same.'

Duarte smiled, taking his time as he ran his hands along the wooden handrail that lined the sides. He reached down to a small panel and with one flick of a switch the entire ship was lit up with golden light.

'It's…beautiful…' Nora breathed. 'I always knew that you own a yacht empire, and that you design your own ships, but this is the first time I've seen you on one.'

He laughed, a glorious smile touching his full lips. 'I was thinking I might take her out on the water tomorrow, but for tonight we'll have to make do with a champagne picnic right here in port.'

He poured her a glass from the bottle waiting for them.

'This is…magical…' Nora mused, feeling the bubbles warm her throat as she swallowed. 'Thank you for tonight. For being such a kind host.'

He raised a brow in her direction, leaning forward to sweep a lock of hair from her face. 'I'm not here as your host tonight, Nora. I thought that was pretty clear.'

She blushed, turning her face away from him and feeling warmth spread down her body. When she looked up, she saw the twinkling lights of the marina reflected in his golden eyes. His arms circled her waist, pulling her closer so they stood barely an inch apart.

'I've thought about nothing but kissing you all day,' he

purred, his fingers softly sweeping along her cheek and down to cup either side of her neck. 'You almost made me sign half my paperwork with your name.'

'I'm sorry.' She smiled, shivering at the sensation of his touch branding her skin. She felt caged in by his large body and his leonine eyes. Trapped in the most sensual meaning of the word. She'd never felt happier.

'You don't sound sorry,' he growled. 'You sound quite delighted at the thought of me in my office, half mad with lust, hardly able to wait to get back to you.'

'I thought of you too,' she whispered. 'I... I missed you.'

Her voice broke on the words, on their heartbreaking truth. She had missed him so much. She needed to tell him everything—needed to take a leap of faith and believe that he wouldn't punish her—or their son—for her hesitation.

But then his lips were on hers, his hands sweeping down to caress her hips and the small of her back. As she sighed into the kiss, sliding her tongue against his, she felt her control begin to unravel. He pressed himself and his hard length against her and she had to fight not to groan against his mouth. Her body remembered his hands and seemed to heat up on command, until the fire within her threatened to consume her entirely.

As though he suddenly realised he was grinding himself against her, he broke the kiss and pressed his forehead against hers. 'I'm sorry... It's been a while for me. I swear I've never felt so out of control.'

'I know the feeling...' she breathed, her mind a tangle of desire.

He framed her face with his hands and kissed her again, slower and deeper this time. His tongue was her undoing, its slow seductive teasing sending her completely over the edge of reason. She groaned softly, sliding her hand under the edge of his shirt to touch his skin. Having him like this, feeling him under her palms…she was half afraid he would disappear if she blinked.

The truth was like an invisible barrier between them, and here in the golden light, with his eyes on hers, she felt as if she'd been given the cruellest gift. She thought back to all the times she'd wished for just one more night with him. She wanted to take this moment and live in it. To have him, even if it was selfish.

The thought jarred her. Of course it was selfish.

She bit her lower lip, feeling the weight of the moment press down on her like a ten-ton truck. She took a step back from him and the words she knew she needed to say seemed to stick in her throat, choking her.

'We need to stop.' She closed her eyes. 'There are things I promised myself I would tell you tonight, even though I know it could ruin everything between us. But now I'm standing here I have no idea how to begin.'

'Then don't,' he whispered. 'I promised you a night out and that means no serious business. Right now, all I want to do is keep kissing you.'

'You don't mean that,' she breathed. 'You're not thinking with your head.'

'I'm trusting my gut, and my gut is never wrong.' He met her eyes. 'Will these things still be exactly the same tomorrow? Are they time-sensitive?'

Nora breathed in a shaky breath, looking up into his gold-flecked eyes. 'It will still be the same.'

He leaned down, gently pressing his lips to her temple and pulling her close. 'Being here…being with you…it's the closest I've felt to happiness in a long time. Even long before what happened to me. I was always seeking new thrills, always on the move. I was never actually calm enough to just…*be*. But when I'm with you, I'm actually here. I feel present in a way I've never been able to tolerate or enjoy before. I think we owe it to each other to allow ourselves a moment of happiness, don't you?'

'Just a moment?' Nora breathed, half hoping he would draw the line at tonight.

If he ended it—if he showed her he was the careless billionaire she'd once believed him to be—maybe this would be easier. Because this version of Duarte—the one who spoke of happiness and called her beautiful… It broke her heart to imagine a life without him.

She had never stood a chance of resisting him from the moment he'd swept her off that dance floor all those months ago, she realised. She was hopelessly in love with this man and helplessly careening towards full-on heartbreak once she revealed everything to him. Her heart seemed to ache at the thought, as she imagined him looking at her and seeing the lying, deceitful criminal that she was.

Closing her eyes, she sank against him and kissed him with every ounce of love she possessed in her foolish, foolish heart.

When they were both finally out of breath, and in danger of committing a public indecency offence, Nora took a step back, meeting his eyes steadily, without a single doubt. 'Does this ship have a bed?'

Duarte fought the urge to throw her over his shoulder like a caveman and kick open the doors to the cabins below. He'd never been more grateful for the top-to-toe valet service he'd ordered before he'd arranged for *O Dançarina* to be skippered to Paraty. The ship was freshly cleaned and gleaming, ready to sail and with the cabins made up.

Taking Nora's hand in his, he led her down towards the master cabin, briefly giving her a lightning-fast tour as they passed through the ship. Her eyes sparkled with mirth as he pulled her into the large cabin and laid her down on the giant bed before she even had a moment to take in the sumptuous décor.

He adored *O Dançarina*. The ship was beautiful—one of the most exquisitely restored sailing yachts he'd ever known in his two decades of sailing. But right now nothing compared to the view of Nora spread out on the bed below him, her lips slightly parted and swollen from his kisses.

She reached up, looping her arms around his neck and pulling him down for another deep, languorous kiss. Her hands tangled in his hair, pulling roughly against his scalp and sending shivers down his spine.

'I don't think I can wait another minute,' she breathed, her hands exploring his ribcage, and lower, pulling at his belt.

He allowed her free rein for a moment, before taking hold of both her wrists and clasping them above her head. She gasped, her hips flexing against him with surprise and definite appreciation. His little lioness liked being commanded—he could see it in the darkness of her eyes and feel it in the way her heartbeat pounded.

'I didn't come prepared,' he said, groaning with sudden realisation of his lack of contraception. 'I wasn't expecting us to…'

Nora bit her lower lip, desire warming her cheeks. 'The nurse has already got me covered in that regard.'

Duarte fought the urge to sink into her then and there with relief. 'Remind me to send that woman a gift basket,' he said, and smiled against her skin. 'I know I'm clean.'

'Thank God,' she breathed.

Her nervous chuckle fast turned into a groan of pleasure as he licked the sensitive skin below her ear and gently bit down.

'I don't know where I want to kiss most,' he murmured, trailing a torturously slow path of kisses along her collarbone. 'The glimpses of you in that bathing suit have played in my memory for so long I could hardly imagine having you in the flesh.'

'You have me,' she breathed. 'I'm not going anywhere.'

Something blazed in her eyes and made his chest feel so tight he had to look away, his mouth seeking out her hardened nipples through the silk material of her dress. He focused on teasing the peak, feeling her gasp and thrust against him, following the delicious friction.

Heat, passion, desire. This he could deal with. Two people using one another for pleasure and release. His sex-starved body seemed to have gone into overdrive, wanting all of her at once. That was the only explanation for the overwhelming feelings coursing through him with each touch.

If he wasn't careful this would all be over before he'd even begun, and he wanted to make this good for her. For both of them. She wanted him just as badly as he wanted her—he could feel it in the gentle flex of her thigh muscles around his shoulders as he moved lower.

Letting go of her wrists, he looked up at her from the valley of her thighs. 'Take off your dress.'

She slid the material over one shoulder, then the other, drawing it down to her waist. Duarte pulled it the rest of the way, biting down on his lower lip as her perfect porcelain skin was revealed to him inch by inch. Her small firm breasts were tipped with rose, the skin leading down to the lush curves of her waist and hips flawless, with only the lightest silver streaks on her hips to give any hint that she'd been swollen with a child six weeks before.

His eyes fell to the thin pink scar at the bottom of her stomach, his fingers reaching out to caress it. She froze, her hands covering her stomach with a grimace. Duarte frowned, lowering his lips to kiss her navel through her fingers, distracting her and easing the tension away until she was molten beneath him once more.

The idea that she might want her to hide her body from him was ridiculous. Did she not see what he saw? She was beautiful. More than beautiful—she was intoxicating.

He remembered that once, a long time ago, he had believed himself to be an accomplished lover, but right now he felt as if he was drunk on her beauty, his senses overwhelmed and uncoordinated.

Using her responses as his map, he slowly found his rhythm again, leaning down to kiss the inside of one knee and moving slowly upwards. His hands held her hips in place and she gyrated against his grip, begging him to move faster. To take her where she wanted to go.

'Please, Duarte,' she breathed, her hands moving down to tangle in his hair once more.

Her words seemed to echo in his mind, and there was something so familiar in them, something so right. He felt as if he had been waiting a lifetime to claim her this way, as if something deep within him craved having her body under his command.

He focused on the slow torture of removing the delicate white silk that was the only barrier left between them. His lips moved slowly along her soft flesh to where a silken thatch of red curls was the last barrier to the heart of her. He knew exactly what she wanted, what she needed, as he set about stroking and kissing her exactly where she needed him most.

Her low, drawn-out moan of pleasure was almost enough to send him over the edge himself. He focused on her, on the erotic breathless sounds she made as she crested towards the release she needed, and prayed that he wouldn't lose himself in such torture.

She looked down at him, meeting his eyes just as she neared the peak.

'Come for me, Nora,' he growled against her, feeling heat pulse in his groin as she followed his command with a brutal arching of her back and a sound that sent him wild.

He was over her in seconds, readying himself at her entrance.

Nora took him into the cradle of her thighs, her heart on the verge of bursting open with pleasure and emotion sweeping through her body. The way he looked down at her as he braced his powerful arms either side of her head... She almost came all over again.

Neither of them spoke as he pressed the tip of himself against her, but his eyes remained focused on her face as he slowly joined them, inch by glorious inch.

She felt a delicious stretch that almost bordered on pain at his more than sizeable girth. She looked away, embarrassed that she was not used to the sensation, and her body seemed to clench momentarily against the invasion.

He frowned, one hand cupping her cheek, forcing her to look up and see the silent question in his golden eyes. She covered his hand with her own, moving slowly against him, testing the sensation and feeling her inner muscles relax and pulse against the heat of him. He followed her lead, withdrawing slowly, then angling himself to move back inside in a slow stroke.

The sudden pulse of electricity that tightened inside her made her gasp, then smile up at him. That was all the encouragement he needed and he slowly moved against her, closing his eyes and letting out a low growl of pure animal pleasure. She moved too, her nails digging into his shoulders as he kept his rhythm slow but firm.

Her body remembered what to do, her hips seeming to

arch against him of their own volition, her legs winding around him and pulling him closer. His thrusts became a delicious brutal force against her core, sending her towards a second release.

She didn't think her body could withstand any more pleasure, but she was wrong. This climax felt completely different from the first, so intense she felt a knot in her throat as he looked down at her and twined his fingers through hers. She had the strongest urge to close her eyes against the intimacy of the moment, fearing she might ruin everything by crying. But if this was the last time he would look at her this way, she didn't want to hide.

She watched him move, feeling him grind the pleasure between them higher than she'd even thought possible. Just as her pleasure broke, and she heard an earth-shattering moan escape her own lips, he kissed her. His mouth captured the sound as he shuddered, growling into the kiss as he finally gave in and found his own release.

Nora wished they could have stayed lying side by side on the beautiful antique yacht for hours. The gentle sway of the water beneath them made it feel even more like a dream, but like all fairy-tales the magic had a time limit.

When she reluctantly announced that it was time to get back to the house and relieve Inés of her duties, Duarte agreed, helping her to dress. But his attempts at help quickly turned into another frantic lovemaking session, with her pressed against the stern of the ship, looking out at the lights of the town glittering across the black glass of the Atlantic.

Breathless, and drunk on passion, she smiled for the entire drive back to the house.

Inés was waiting in the kitchen and chuckled knowingly

at Nora's rumpled dress, before quickly updating her on Liam's thoroughly uneventful sleep and leaving them alone.

Nora went upstairs, checking on her son and tucking his covers around him. When she turned around, Duarte was in the doorway of the balcony watching her.

She bit her lower lip, feeling the weight of the moment pressing down on her. She walked towards him, and once more the words she knew she needed to say stuck in her throat, choking her. When she finally reached his side, his fingers came up to her lips.

'I see that serious look creeping back in,' he whispered. 'But the night isn't over yet.'

He gathered her up against him, taking her across the balcony and through the doors to his bedroom.

Nora shut off her mind, focusing on showing him the love she felt with every touch of her lips and her body against his.

CHAPTER EIGHT

DUARTE AWOKE TO an empty bed.

Sunlight streamed in through the balcony doors and a single look at the time on his watch had his brows raising. He hadn't slept for this long or this peacefully... *ever*. Not a single nightmare had plagued his sleep and his dreams had been filled with Nora. Vivid depictions of them together that had been so realistic they'd almost seemed real.

He ignored the strain of his own desire against the sheets, showering and dressing in clothing fit for sailing. He had a mountain of emails that needed his attention before the Florida opening, but he felt a deep longing to get out on the waves. He felt an urge to grab his sketchbooks and disappear into his ideas—but, strangely, he didn't want to be alone.

His mind conjured up an image of red curls flowing in the sea breeze and sultry silver eyes watching him as he commanded the ship to move over the waves. No, he didn't want to be alone today. He'd take them all out on *O Dançarina* for the afternoon.

His light mood followed him downstairs, where he stopped in the doorway that led out onto the terrace and took in the simple sight of Nora below, dangling her legs in the water of the swimming pool, Liam in her arms. She looked beautiful, her glossy red waves seeming to glow around her face in the mid-morning sunlight.

He was hit with a sudden erotic image of wrapping her hair around his fist as he made love to her from behind—one of the moments in his strange dreams the night before. She'd been different in the dream…her hair shorter. They'd been in the back seat of a car, with mountains all around them. The image had been intense…

As though she sensed him, she turned—and the look on her face was not what he'd expected. She looked miserable.

Something heavy twisted within him as he moved to walk towards her, but the gentle clearing of a throat behind him stopped him in his tracks.

Angelus Fiero stood just inside the archway of the dining room, his expression sombre and agitated.

'Angelus. It's good to see you.'

Duarte tried and failed to keep the annoyance from his voice. For once he hadn't been thinking of his investigation. He hadn't been consumed with revenge. But Duarte shook his hand, dropping the customary two kisses on his cheeks.

His father's oldest friend was a thin man, but today he looked even thinner since the last time Duarte had seen him, a few weeks previously. He leaned heavily on his cane—a recent addition after the gunshot wound that had almost ended him.

'You've always been a terrible liar.' Angelus chuckled, a strange tightness in his gaze. 'I'm sorry to bother you here, with your lovely guest…'

In his peripheral vision Duarte saw Nora stand up next to the pool, Inés at her side, the two women chatting animatedly.

He guided Angelus away from the windows and down the long hall to his barely used study at the back of the house. It was a dark room, lined with dusty bookcases, and it had an air of bleakness about it. He'd always hated the room, even when his father had used it as his study during their long summers here.

He sat on one of the high-backed armchairs and motioned for Angelus to take the other, frowning when the man refused his offer of coffee or any other refreshment.

A tightness settled into his gut.

'I have news.' Angelus snapped open the slim file he carried, a look of mild discomfort on his face. 'The evidence on the thumb drive was…fruitful.'

'Excellent.' Duarte reached for the file, only to have Angelus pull it back, a look of warning in his eyes.

'It involves your parents.'

The older man's eyes shone suspiciously as he glanced away, out of the window, towards the view of the front courtyard beyond. When he finally met his eyes again, they were suspiciously misty.

'Their deaths were not an accident, Duarte.'

The world stopped for a moment.

Duarte felt himself stand up, felt his hand snatch the file from Angelus's fingers. He saw the old man's pained look as though through a fog.

His heartbeat pounded in his ears as he read the detailed report outlining the various anonymous hitmen on Lionel Cabo's payroll and the jobs they'd been paid to complete. One item had been highlighted, dated seven years previously in London, England. Targets: Guilhermo and Rose Avelar.

He closed his eyes against the awful truth, willing it to disappear.

His parents had been good people. His father had been sole heir to his family fortune and had made the difficult decision to risk it all on a better future for his home city. The Avelar Foundation's development projects and charity efforts in Rio were world-famous. To think that their vision and refusal to bow to corruption had led to their deaths, just as it had almost led to his own…

'This was on the thumb drive Nora gave me?' He heard himself speak.

Fiero let out a heaving sigh. 'That's the next thing.' He stood up, his mouth tightening into a line. 'We pulled in a few of Cabo's associates for questioning. It didn't take much for them to start talking once they saw how much evidence we had against them. And they seemed to know exactly who our informant was: the only person Lionel Cabo had ever allowed to leave his organisation alive—the only person who had access to such secure information because she lived under the same roof. Duarte, she's his daughter. He had her identity kept secret, but we found it all.'

Another file was shoved into his hands. Images of countless passports and identities on each page. A couple of arrests under fake names. But there was a name at the top, on an original birth certificate that had been hidden from public record: Eleanora Cabo.

Duarte felt the world tilt on its axis for a moment.

Eleanora Cabo.

That name…

He stared from his old friend to the serious, frowning photograph of the woman he'd just made love to for half the night, feeling shock turn him to stone. 'How can this be?'

'Her mother is an Irish ecologist, currently running a wildlife sanctuary in Manaus. She divorced Lionel Cabo after less than a year of marriage, a divorce most likely linked to severe injuries sustained by her at the hands of a male she refused to name. Her anonymity was part of a legal agreement. As was changing her daughter's name and barring him from all access to her until she was an adult.

It seems she reconnected with her father the moment she turned eighteen.'

Duarte felt nausea burn his gut.

Lionel Cabo's daughter.

Cabo. The man who had killed his parents. Who had tried to have him killed.

Disbelief and rage fought within him. His temples throbbed and he rubbed circles against his skin, trying to calm the rising sensation.

A flash of memory struck, the picture in his mind so clear it made him dizzy. He saw himself standing in the grand entrance hall of a house he'd only ever seen before in pictures from his investigations: the Cabo mansion. He was looking down at the woman in front of him, cruel words spilling from his lips.

Nora's hair was shorter, blow-dried into a perfect style. She grabbed his wrist as he walked past her. *'Duarte. Please...don't leave me with him.'*

It was definitely a memory... Dear God!

Suddenly all his vivid dreams made sense. They were *memories*. Memories of the weeks he'd spent falling for a mysterious redhead in Rio, only to have his life become a living nightmare.

He turned away from Angelus's worried face, striding to the window and bracing his hands on the cold marble ledge for support. He crushed his fist against his forehead as more memories came rushing back.

The first time he'd seen her...the way he'd been drawn to her like a moth to a flame across the dance floor in a crowded samba club.

He'd been taken from that first glance. She'd been sexy, yet shy, fiercely intelligent and adventurous. Only having her for stolen hours at a time had been a thrill. She'd been shockingly inexperienced, but eager and honest in her pleasure, and of course he'd risen to the delicious challenge of initiating her into the world of lovemaking in every way he'd been able to think of.

She'd become an obsession. He'd even thought himself halfway in love with her until Cabo had approached him and revealed everything.

It had all made terrible sense. He'd been her mark. She'd been playing the part of his perfect woman.

And when the opportunity had come to play her at her own game he'd taken it—meeting with Lionel Cabo right under her nose and letting him offer his own daughter as a reward, only to throw it back in the man's face.

Angelus's words rang in his ears. *A secret.*

On their last night together they'd fallen asleep and she'd awoken in a panic. He'd had to run after her and convince her to let him drive her home. She'd refused, saying her father was overprotective. Their hours together were stolen because she had to sneak out. She wasn't allowed to leave the house alone.

He'd thought perhaps it was a religious thing, but then he'd found out the truth.

To know that her mother had gone so far as to get a court order against her child's father suggested something more than normal marital discord.

That haunting image of Nora's face in her father's entrance hall replayed in his mind again.

'Please, don't leave me with him.'

The Nora he knew would never beg. Not unless she was desperate. She'd been a prisoner in her own home and he'd left her there. He'd used her just as badly as her own father had done.

The memory of it made him tense with guilt.

No, not guilt.

He stood up, fisting his hands through his hair. She'd

made a fool of him. She'd had the evidence that could prove her father's guilt all this time. She'd been a guest in his home, eaten meals with him, made love to him, and never once thought to reveal all this. She'd said she'd had that thumb drive for months, that it had been her insurance. Surely that meant she had read it? Had seen his parents' names on that hit list?

He closed his eyes against the thought, the pain in his temples almost unbearable. The resurgence of his buried memories was like being hit in the head with that bullet all over again. He felt unbalanced and nauseated.

'I understand that this is a lot to take in,' said Angelus, sighing and shaking his head solemnly. 'What do you plan to do with her?'

'What do you mean?' Duarte frowned.

'Well, I came here to talk to you first. To warn you that the police want to move to arrest both Cabo and his daughter immediately.'

'No.' The word emerged as little more than a growl from his lips.

Angelus pursed his lips, eyeing him speculatively. 'She was part of Cabo's mobster family, Duarte. Possibly she knew that your parents were murdered and kept it to herself.'

'She gave me that evidence willingly. Surely that is in her favour?'

'Are you involved with her?'

When Duarte merely scowled, the old man let out a harsh frustrated sigh.

'This could be another part of Cabo's plan. Slithering her in here unnoticed and getting her under your skin. As the saying goes, "The apple doesn't fall far from the tree."'

'Don't talk about her like that.' Duarte bared his teeth, shocking himself.

'She has been lying to you this whole time!'

'When I found her she was just about to give birth, and she is being hunted by men she fears,' Duarte gritted. 'I quickly figured out that she was part of the organisation. Her personal relationship to Cabo is her own business. She's done nothing to me.'

Except lie to me. Such convincing lies.

'She has a child?' Fiero frowned. 'There's nothing about that in there.'

'He was born the day I arrived in Rio.' Duarte stood, running a hand over his scar as his mind processed the information he'd recovered with his memory. 'That's why I've had her under my protection.'

He didn't mention the fact that he'd also kept her here longer because he'd been enjoying her company, slowly courting her. He felt the older man's eyes on him, could practically hear him silently screaming at him not to be such a fool.

'I'm going to need time to process this.'

Angelus nodded and left just as stealthily as he'd arrived, his cane clicking as he departed from the house.

Even when the sound of his car's wheels had long disappeared up the driveway Duarte stood frozen at his desk, his mind going over and over all the information and wondering what it was about it that felt so wrong.

Nora had just finished settling Liam for his morning nap and now stood frozen on the staircase as she watched Angelus Fiero emerge into the entrance hall at the front of the house. She froze, anxiety stealing her voice.

She'd already been on tenterhooks since slipping back into her own bed in the early hours of that morning. She'd wanted to wake Duarte before she left and just get it over with. Tell him everything. But he'd been sleeping so peacefully, and she'd known her son would wake for his usual feed at dawn, so she'd left.

No matter how hard she'd tried to hold on to the afterglow of their night together, she'd spent the morning with a steadily increasing sense of dread in her gut. And when Inés had told her that Angelus Fiero had arrived, and he and Duarte had disappeared to speak in private, she'd prayed she wasn't too late.

The older man paused for a split second when he saw her, and then looked back towards the open door of Duarte's study down the hall. When he spoke, his voice was low.

'Finally I get to meet our selfless informant.' He narrowed his eyes at her, not with cruelty but not entirely kindly either. 'Surely you must have known that giving us that information would reveal your identity... Eleanora?'

She heard her birth name and something within her shattered. He knew. That meant Duarte knew. She'd waited too long to tell him and now...

The older man must have seen something in her face because he shook his head sadly. 'Just so you know, I came here expecting to leave with you in a police car.'

Nora felt cold fear sink into her bones, freezing her where she stood on the last step of the marble staircase.

'But you can relax. Apparently you planned your seduction well. Clever girl.' Angelus Fiero tutted, brushing invisible dust from his lapel. 'He's a better man than most.'

'I did not plan for any of this,' she said. She heard the steel in her voice and wondered how on earth she'd managed it when her legs felt like jelly beneath her.

The older man raised one brow, surprised. 'It doesn't matter. The situation remains the same. Goodbye, Senhorita Cabo.'

Angelus Fiero's voice had been a thin rasp in the echoing entrance hall, and the weight of his words remained in the air long after his car had disappeared down the driveway. She wanted to scream after him that it was not her name. It had not been her name for eighteen years of her life. She might have been a naïve teenager when she had been drawn into her father's world, but she had never taken his name.

She took a few shaky steps towards the study, where her reckoning awaited her. She hesitated, and braced her hand on the wall for support as she fought to compose herself. She was angry at herself—at her own cowardice and selfishness. And angry at the history she and Duarte had shared and how they seemed destined to hurt one another over and over again.

She stood in the doorway of the study and took in the silhouette of Duarte's powerful frame against the light from the window. He faced away from her, both hands braced on the ledge as he stared out into nothingness.

She wasn't sure how long she stood in silence, just listening to the sound of her own heartbeat in her ears. But eventually she must have made some barely perceptible sound because he spoke, still with his back turned to her.

'I assume you met Angelus Fiero on your way here?'

His words were a slash of sound in the painful silence, devoid of any emotion or the kindness she'd come to know from him.

'Yes.'

Nora fought not to launch into her own defence—fought to give him time to speak. She let her eyes roam over him, already mourning the feeling of being in his arms. He wore sand-coloured chinos and a navy polo shirt—sailing clothes, she thought with a pang of remorse. He'd told her he planned to take them all out on *O Dançerina*...

Without warning, Duarte turned to face her, then leaned back against the window ledge and folded his arms over the wide muscled expanse of his chest as he surveyed her.

Nora felt as if all the air had been sucked from her chest. The look in his eyes was a mirror image of that day in Rio, when he had walked past her in her father's entrance hall. It was like a cruel joke, having to relive one of the most painful moments of her life.

'Nothing to say?' he prompted, his voice cold as ice.

'I wanted to tell you. Once I was sure you wouldn't turn me in to the police…' She inhaled deeply, biting her bottom lip hard to stop her voice from shaking. 'I promised myself I would tell you yesterday, but then you were so wonderful. I couldn't find the right words…the right moment. I was a coward.'

'Yes. You were.' He met her eyes for the first time, assessing her. 'Did you know about your father's connection to my parents' death?'

She felt her blood run cold. 'What do you mean?'

'He ordered their murder. Staged it to look like an accident.'

He slid a file across the desk between them and she saw the brief flash of pain on his face as he spoke the words. She felt them hit her somewhere squarely in her solar plexus. She picked up the file with shaking hands, noticing the highlighted dates and names, reading that further investigations by the police detective in charge of the case had shown the report to be true.

Each line brought to her a sense of horror she'd never felt, and her stomach seemed to join in, lurching painfully. 'I think I'm going to be sick,' she breathed, dropping the file to the floor and seeing the pages scatter in a blur of motion.

She heard Duarte move around the desk to her side, touching her elbow briefly to guide her into one of the armchairs beside the tall bookcases that lined the room. Nora took a deep breath, then another, until finally the nausea and dizziness passed.

When she looked up again he stood at the bookcase, watching her intently. 'I swear I didn't know.' She shook her head, fresh hatred burning within her for the man who had caused so many people pain. 'I hope he rots in hell.'

Duarte looked away from her. 'I plan to ensure he never sees another day of freedom for the rest of his miserable life.'

'Prison is too good for him.'

'And what about you?' He looked down at her. 'You handed me that thumb drive, knowing it held evidence that could put you away too.'

'I hoped you would understand. I chose to...to trust you.'

'Listen to yourself.' He raised his voice. '*You* chose to trust *me*? I have never lied to you once. I have given you nothing but time and patience.'

Nora felt his eyes on her, felt the question in his words, but her shame and regret was too much. She closed her eyes and pressed a hand across the frantic beating of her own heart, trying to gather her remaining strength and get through this.

When she opened her eyes, he had moved closer. She bit her lower lip, seeing the distaste in his gaze. Then took a deep breath, knowing the moment had come for her to give him the truth he deserved. She only prayed she would be able to take his reaction.

'Your parents were being honoured posthumously in the Dia da Patria festivities. You came to Rio to accept their honour. I was sent to find you—to get information from you that my father could use against you for blackmail, to make you sign over that land.'

She placed her hands on her knees, avoiding his face, but she heard his swift intake of breath.

'We danced, flirted, then we walked along the beach and talked. You told me many things I could have used against you. About your sister, about your plans for the future. You were as shocked as I was that you'd given so much away. After our first kiss, I decided to defy my father and pretend my recording equipment had failed. I liked you. I said I was going to the bathroom and disappeared. But the next day you found me at school. I'd mentioned where I went to college and you wanted to return my coat…'

She shivered, remembering the sheepish look on his face when she'd emerged from her lecture to see him leaning against the bonnet of his sportscar, her classmates gawking at such a beautiful specimen of a man.

'But that's not the end of it,' he prompted. 'I remember…more.'

'There was more. You stayed in town for a week and we became…intimate. You returned a few days later and we continued our affair. It carried on like that for a month—until my father found out what was going on.'

'He threatened to hurt you…' Duarte spoke slowly.

'He threatened me in order to force your hand but you walked away. He was bluffing.'

'But my passport records show I took one more trip to Brazil, two months after that.'

'You tracked me down again, all anger and imperiousness. Still, we never could keep our hands off each other for long. I walked away from you that time. Only…we didn't use protection.'

Nora watched the realisation enter his eyes, moving into shock and narrowing to a deathly glimmer. He swallowed a few times, his voice seeming to fail him before he spoke.

'Are you telling me… Liam…?' His voice was a rasped whisper.

'I didn't want to lie to you,' she breathed, feeling her throat catch.

She had no idea how to make him see why she'd waited.

To tell him if she could have gone back in time she'd have told him the moment he'd appeared on that street in the rain. But now it was such a mess…

The space between them seemed to shorten and the room felt too small. It felt as if minutes of silence passed as they simply looked at one another, Nora still frantically trying to voice the truth she waited to give him.

'You are sure I am his father?' Duarte's question was like a gunshot in the silence.

She closed her eyes against the tears that threatened to fall. She would not cry in front of him. She had done enough crying over Duarte Avelar and all the strange, dangerous turns her life had taken since she'd met him.

She had often wondered how an intelligent woman like her mother had ever allowed herself to be controlled by a wealthy man. Why she had feared him. But now, looking up at the cold golden glint of Duarte's eyes on hers, knowing the sheer power he had at his fingertips, she was afraid.

She felt utterly powerless as she spoke, as if she was putting herself entirely at his mercy. She silently prayed that she wouldn't regret it.

'Yes,' she whispered. 'Liam is your son.'

CHAPTER NINE

DUARTE DIDN'T KNOW how long he remained silent, her words repeating themselves over and over in his mind as he fought to process them.

His son. He had a son.

An infant he had protected from the moment he was born...

He closed his eyes and swallowed hard. When he opened them Nora was staring at him, her large eyes so innocent and filled with sadness. He felt anger burn in his gut.

'Were you ever going to tell me?'

He heard the coldness of his voice and saw the way she flinched as he took a step towards her, but he was past caring. His logical side had been overtaken by pure outrage in the wake of her deceit.

'You don't understand...' She frowned, standing and taking a few steps away from him.

Duarte closed the space between them easily. 'Explain it to me, then.' He loomed over her, seeing her shoulders curve and her face turn a little paler. He heard his voice explode from him in a guttural growl. 'Explain why—even after seeing I was still alive, even after I offered you my protection and proved I was not a danger to you—you still decided to keep the knowledge that Liam was my own child from me?'

'I wanted to tell you from the first moment, but I didn't trust you. I needed to be sure you weren't a danger. You know who my father is—you know what he would do if he knew that not only are you alive but I had also given birth to your *son*. I was protecting us both. Protecting Liam.'

Her voice cracked on the last word—the first genuine loss of control he'd seen in her. She bit down hard on her lower lip, holding back the obvious emotion welling in her eyes.

'My son is my first priority. He didn't ask to be born into a world of danger and constant threat. It's my duty to keep him safe.'

'You think I would allow any harm to come to my own child?' The words felt both strange and right as he spoke them aloud. *His* child. *His* son. 'I deserved to know. All this time we've spent together...'

She looked up at him, her face a mask of barely controlled pain. 'I'm so sorry. I never wanted to hurt you. I think that's why I was delaying the inevitable.'

'That was not your choice to make.'

'It was better than having no choice at all.'

She spoke quietly, but he heard a thin thread of steel as it wound into her voice.

'Duarte, I've handled this poorly, but you need to understand that I was the child of a wealthy man who believed he knew what was best. My mother almost died trying to protect me from my father's enemies. Trying to keep him from taking me away once she decided to leave him. I know all too well what it means to be beholden to a man with power.'

'Don't you *dare* compare me to him.' He breathed hard.

'I'm not.' She shook her head, briefly touching his sleeve. 'You are nothing like my father, and I know that now. But when you came back...' She shook her head and walked away a few steps. 'At the end of our month together, after my father found out about us, and he went to find you. You know he put my safety on the table. Threatened to punish me for defying him with you.'

'He offered you to me like a prize,' Duarte said, the memory as clear as day.

'And you made it quite clear you didn't feel anything for me. You said I was nothing to you.'

Duarte froze, watching her closely. 'Did he hurt you?'

She looked away. 'Not physically. He always preferred emotional torture. I had to watch them take you, Duarte. My father forced me to go to that Avelar Foundation dinner the night of your kidnapping. He made sure I saw them take you. I screamed and I fought, but I was restrained and taken back to my father's house. He locked me up so I couldn't get help.' She wrapped her arms around herself, looking away from him. 'It was there, during that week, that I felt so sick...so tired and so faint. I calculated my dates and realised that I was carrying your child.'

'Did he know?'

'He called a doctor, who confirmed it. He was furious, but then...' Nora shivered, her eyes haunted. 'Then he smiled. He said now he had another thing over you... That night, I knew my father was at an event with his politician friends. I knew my time was limited, so I demanded to be taken to hospital for fluids, because I couldn't keep anything down. At the hospital I managed to slip away from my guards, borrowed a phone and found out where they were keeping you and Valerio. I sent a message to Angelus Fiero, praying he would get there in time. But when I got there you had already been shot.'

'You told me...' Duarte heard himself speak as the dreams he'd had all those months during his recovery finally made sense. 'You told me to live for you both.'

She nodded.

Duarte felt emotion tighten his throat but he pushed it away, turning from her and trying to get a grip on his thoughts, on the memories that swirled around like loose waves, intensifying his aching temples. She sounded as if she was telling the truth, but something within him re-sisted her words—resisted the belief that she was a victim just like he was.

How could he believe what she said? She had planned to keep this from him; she had lied.

He steeled his voice. 'Does your father know about Liam?'

'When I believed you were dead, I told him I'd lost the baby. I think his guilt over that was the only reason he let me go, let me leave the organisation. I was afraid he would try to use an heir as leverage against your estate, somehow. I kept my pregnancy hidden while I tried my best to finish my final semester, and then I made my plan to leave Rio. You know the rest.'

'I'll need a paternity test.'

He heard himself speak and saw her flinch at the words before she nodded silently, but he didn't care. Not when the memory of how they'd conceived their child was playing in his mind and tying him up in knots.

She had lied to him. She'd had all these memories that he was only now getting back, and still she had been able to pretend they were strangers.

She had believed him to be cruel and controlling—perhaps it was time he showed her just how heartless he could be.

'If he's my son…' Duarte felt his jaw tighten at the words, at the emotions they evoked within him. 'I won't be kept from him, Nora.'

'I know.'

'Your actions say differently. How do I know this isn't

some kind of new play from Cabo's organisation? His blood runs in your veins.'

She flinched as though he'd struck her with his words. 'You could trust me.'

He laughed—a harsh, low sound in his throat. 'Like you have trusted *me* so far?'

'Liam has Cabo blood too. Will you hold that over him? Blood is not the making of a person.' Her eyes met his, fire burning in their grey depths.

'How do I know you won't disappear the moment I leave this house? Where did you plan to go?'

'I grew up in Manaus on a small wildlife sanctuary.' She shrugged. 'I didn't like being so secluded then. But I wanted to make a fresh start for Liam somewhere safe, far away from the reach of my father.'

'If I hadn't brought you here…if we hadn't got close… would you ever have told me?'

She pressed her lips together. 'I don't know.'

She met his eyes without hesitation, but he couldn't hold her gaze. He couldn't look at her without thinking of what she'd planned to do, without imagining her choosing to keep something so important from him.

The thought that she might even have left Brazil with his son made something roar within him. The anger he felt was too much; he needed to get away from here—from her. He felt as if he was walking a razor-thin edge between control and madness.

A small cry sounded from the monitor at her hip and Duarte felt his chest tighten as Nora met his eyes again. He gestured for her to go, turning away from her to pinch the bridge of his nose.

He hesitated for a moment, then found himself following her, unable to stop his feet from moving in the direction of the infant's cries.

The windows of the room were closed, the shutters keeping the heat of the day out. Nora stood there in the dim light, holding the child to her chest as his cries softened. Duarte took a step closer, looking at the tiny face and wondering how he had ever missed it. The child had Nora's wide eyes, but that was where the resemblance ended. Everything else, from the colour of his skin to the dimple in the centre of his chin…

He reached out, touching his pinkie finger to that miniature dimple, and remembered that first moment in the hospital room, when a tiny hand had reached out to grip his finger. He wondered if Liam had sensed that he was safe with his *papai*? Would he have any memory of his first couple of months of uncertainty?

Duarte knew there and then that he didn't need a paternity test to tell him what he felt.

This was his son.

He looked up to see Nora watching him, a suspicious sheen in her silver eyes.

Clearing his throat, he stepped back from the intimacy of the moment. 'The Fort Lauderdale opening is in a few days. I see no reason to delay travelling.' Duarte kept his voice low. 'Be ready to fly in the morning.'

'You want to take us with you?' Nora's voice was calm, but he saw the sudden flash of defiance in her eyes, a bristling at the authority in his tone.

'I don't want to leave either of you anywhere in Brazil while your father is being taken into custody.'

He fought the urge to reach out and touch the child again, to memorise each tiny detail of his face. Something within his chest tightened again, almost painfully.

'I said I would protect you and that has not changed.'

'Okay.' She breathed. 'Duarte, I'm so sorry.'

He pressed his lips together, unable to look at her without feeling that roar within him starting up all over again.

'I have phone calls to make.'

He ignored the pain in her eyes and forced himself to leave the room. To leave behind the sudden need within him for the child who was such an integral part of him. To leave the woman who had made him feel as if he was finally glued back together only to tear him apart all over again.

He kept walking even after he reached the ground floor and went outside, passing the pool and moving down the length of the garden towards the sea. When his feet hit the sand, he left his shoes and shirt by the trees and broke into a run, taking out all his anger and pain on his body and pushing himself to his limits.

Nora had barely slept all night, and spent the eight-hour flight to Fort Lauderdale on tenterhooks because of the complete silence of the man by her side.

He seemed flat, somehow, as if all the colour had faded from him. He was helpful, checking if there was anything he could do to help with Liam, but there was a tightness to his eyes when he held him.

Eventually she stopped trying to talk at all and quietly watched a movie on her screen while he worked on his computer. The result was that she was practically delirious with tiredness by the time the warm Florida sun kissed her face.

When she saw a private SUV awaiting them on the Tarmac, she inwardly groaned with relief. She had never been more grateful for Duarte's ridiculous wealth, even if every other passenger on their flight did gawk at them as they were guided off the aircraft first.

When their driver finally came to a stop at the marina, she stepped out into the warm, humid air with shaky legs. Fort Lauderdale was very different from Brazil. The air was almost as heavy as the Amazonian climate in Manaus, but without the sounds of nature, and there were people everywhere. Well-dressed, wealthy people, who drove expensive cars and dripped with luxury brands.

She fought the urge to look down at her own three-year-old sandals and well-worn blue jeans.

Duarte pushed the pram across the wooden promenade, oblivious to the hordes of women who followed him with their eyes. He looked effortlessly gorgeous, in simple charcoal-coloured chinos and a silver-grey polo shirt. Even without the expensive watch on his wrist and the designer labels of his clothes, his entire being just screamed wealth.

Now he was turning that devastating smile on a well-dressed woman who introduced herself as one of his employees, and instructing a young man to bring the rest of their things as he confidently strode ahead towards the gigantic ship at the end of the pier.

Onboard the *Sirinetta II* superyacht, the staff jumped to attention around him, greeting Nora with wide smiles and curiosity. She knew that the Avelar family were practically royalty in Brazil, because of all their charity work, but clearly he was adored among his staff here too.

She avoided their gazes, wondering what they thought of the shabbily dressed woman walking onboard with a man like him.

Duarte took the lead, placing Liam down in a crib that had been set up in one of the cabins and ordering dinner to be served in the spacious dining area. He told her he would go for a swim first—the daily physiotherapy that he needed to keep his injuries at bay.

Nora debated going to lie down in bed herself, exhaustion warring with her need to speak with him alone. But in the end, she poured herself a glass of wine and waited.

He walked into the dining room still wet from his

shower, his chest bare and wearing only a low-slung pair of jeans. Nora groaned under her breath.

Over dinner she made an effort to ask him about his company's expansion and how it had come to pass, but his answers were short and clipped, and eventually she let the silence sit between them, the food having lost its flavour.

'Are we done?' he asked roughly, once he'd finished his meal and excused the staff for the night.

'I thought we might talk,' she said.

'I have no interest in talking with you tonight.' He rubbed a hand over the growth on his face, and there was a coldness in his eyes that made her cringe inwardly.

'Duarte, I know I have made mistakes…' She steeled herself against the flash of anger on his face. 'But I won't be kept on this yacht alone and punished with your silence. I came with you to see if we could try to find common ground.'

'There is only one piece of common ground between us that we've shared without dishonesty.' He sat back in his seat, a cruel twist to his lips as he surveyed her with obvious interest. 'If you're interested in communicating again in that way, I won't protest.'

'Is this your plan?' Nora stood up from the table. 'You're going to toy with me and keep me on edge with every conversation?'

'Only if you beg me to, *querida*.'

Duarte felt himself reacting to the fire in her more than he'd have liked. She was furious, her cheeks turning pink once she'd gathered his meaning.

He could have groaned as she braced her hands on the table and glared down at him.

'Hell would freeze over before I beg you for anything.' She spoke with deliberate sweetness. 'But, please, feel free to continue using my mistakes to avoid admitting your own part in this.'

'What part is that, exactly.'

'You told me you had never felt anything like what we shared in Rio. I was a virgin, and you didn't treat it like something to shy away from. You made me feel like I owned my body and my choices for the first time in my life. And yet when you discovered the truth you discarded me like old trash and discussed my worth over *cachaça* at Lionel Cabo's dining table.'

'You might have been inexperienced, but you were not innocent,' he drawled, leaning back in his chair. 'You are just as wicked as I am—in every way.'

She licked her lower lip, her eyes darkening. He waited for her response, knowing it was cruel to spar with her this way, but helpless to stop.

But she only frowned, turning away from him with a sigh. 'Stop trying to punish me, Duarte.'

He was behind her in a moment, gripping her wrist and pulling her towards him. He waited for her to move, to bridge the gap between them. Sure enough, her lips sought his without hesitation, giving him permission. He growled low in his throat at the heat of her mouth on his, as if he'd been starving for it. As if it had been months rather than a mere day since he'd last held her.

They both felt it—the current between them that pulsed and demanded attention. He'd hardly been able to concentrate during his swim, with images of the night they'd spent together playing in his mind, torturing him. It infuriated him how much he thought of her, of how she'd felt in his arms. Despite the revelations of the past twenty-four hours, he could concentrate on little else.

He turned her around, pushing her against the wall of the dining room and removing her worn jeans with one ferocious swipe of his hands. He hiked one of her thighs up over his hip, so he could angle himself against her through her underwear. She shivered, her hand reaching up to cup his jaw, a sudden tenderness in her eyes.

He pushed her hand away, grasping her wrist as he deepened the kiss for a long moment and then pulled back. 'If I wanted to punish you I know exactly where I'd start.' He moved his mouth to her neck, nipping softly as his hand moved down to pull the hem of her T-shirt up with a sharp tug. 'And believe me, Nora, you'd beg.'

She froze, placing her hands on his shoulders. 'What are we doing,' she whispered.

'I'm about to take you, hard and fast, against this wall.' He nuzzled her neck.

'I can't do this.' She pushed against him and he pulled away from her instantly. He watched as she pulled at the hem of her T-shirt, studiously avoiding his eyes. 'I can't be this for you...for whatever anger you're feeling. I won't be used.'

'I'm not...'

He struggled to find words, knowing she wasn't wrong. He *was* angry. He was using her body because it was easier to lose himself in his physical attraction to her than it was to look at all the rest of the things he felt when he thought of her betrayal. When he tried to align the Nora he'd come to know in Paraty with the one he'd met all those months ago as part of her father's schemes.

She moved away from him, her eyes filled with sadness, and he let her go, knowing he needed to put some space between them.

He needed to get a handle on himself.

CHAPTER TEN

NORA AWOKE WITH a start, the light streaming through the open curtains showing it was well past dawn. She reached out to the crib by the side of her bed only to find it empty. In a blind panic, she rushed out into the main saloon, only to find it silent.

She looked around, eventually hearing a low snore coming from one of the larger cabins at the end of the corridor. What she found there made her freeze, rooted to the spot, afraid to breathe lest she disturb the unbelievable scene before her.

Duarte lay on his back, one arm flung over his head as he slept on the large bed of the master cabin. Liam lay asleep by his side, in an almost identical pose, safely guarded by a nest of pillows. Nora placed a hand on her chest, feeling as though her heart might break at the beauty and pain of what she was looking at.

She wasn't sure how long she watched, how long her mind fought between happiness and despair over their uncertain future, but when she looked back to the bed Duarte's eyes were open, watching her. She waited for another flash of anger or reproach, but his face was utterly unreadable.

He rose gently, pressing a finger to his lips and motioning for her to follow him from the cabin.

'I never even heard him cry during the night,' she spoke

quickly, once the door was closed between them and the sleeping infant.

'I was still awake when I heard him get restless and I wanted to let you sleep.'

He stretched both arms above his head, unintentionally showcasing his impressively naked torso. The jeans he wore were slung dangerously low on his hips and Nora felt a sudden swift kick of desire so hard she was forced to avert her eyes.

'I didn't expect you to be comfortable with him so soon,' she said without thinking, her rational mind seeming to have gone out of the window at the sight of this gorgeous half-naked man being so caring for a small child.

'I'm full of surprises.' There was no humour in his gaze.

Nora swallowed the lump in her throat, wishing she had a cup of coffee to busy her suddenly trembling hands. Suddenly she was painfully aware of the fact that she wore her comfortable old pyjamas and her hair was likely a tangled mess.

'He'll sleep for a while more, I think.' Duarte handed her the small digital baby monitor. 'I'll order breakfast to be served up on the top deck. I'd like to discuss some things with you.'

She felt her chest tighten at his words and tried not to conjure up every terrible scenario she'd already thought of. Instead, she nodded once. 'I just need to freshen up first. I don't think your fancy staff would appreciate being made to serve me looking like *this*.'

'On the contrary. I find this look to be one of my favourites.'

His eyes swept briefly downwards to take in her worn flannel pyjama bottoms and white tank top before he shrugged one bare shoulder and leaned lazily against the panelled wall of the narrow corridor.

'However, if you need some help showering I will gladly play the kind host.'

Nora's mind showed her an image of him helping her to shower, his hands sliding slowly over her body...

They both seemed frozen in time for a moment, and she wondered if he could hear her heartbeat thundering against her ribs. He waited a breath, then let out a low whistle of amused laughter as he walked away.

'Don't say I didn't offer.'

She went into the cabin she'd claimed for herself and leaned back heavily against the door, exhaling long and hard with frustration. Was this how it would be between them now? Barely veiled anger followed by meaningless flirtation? Would she ever be able to have a conversation with him without remembering everything they'd shared?

They hadn't spoken yet about any plans for the future, but she knew it was coming. She knew Duarte was already analysing every angle and coming up with a plan.

She pulled a crinkled shirt over her head and looked at herself in the mirror. Even with the sleep she'd had, her eyes were still bruised underneath. She looked as exhausted and weak as she felt inside. She knew that if she had any chance of standing her ground with Duarte Avelar and his powerful world, she had to get back in control of herself. The idea that she'd need to dress to fit in with her surroundings chafed, but she knew how these circles worked.

She looked at herself in the mirror, closing her eyes against the dream she'd harboured of a simple life in the quiet peace of her mother's animal sanctuary. A life free of ridiculous rules and unwanted attention. A life free of deception and threats.

The more she thought of her mother's choices, the more she understood. But she was not her mother. She knew what came from hiding your child away from the world. She would not make that same mistake.

Duarte was not going to allow his son to be raised away from the privileged life he led. So she would do well to stop fighting him. She would have to overcome her emotions and put them behind her so that they could find a way to co-exist.

They had to.

She would not fight, but she would still remind him that she was not weak. She was not going to be ordered around, held to ransom under the weight of his unending anger towards her. She would hold her head high and stand her ground. If there was one good thing she'd learned from living under the tyrannical rule of her despicable father it was how to put on a show of strength even when she felt like crumbling inside.

She would not crumble—not for anyone.

Duarte had just sat down at a table on the open-air deck to pour himself a cup of coffee when he heard heels on the steps. His hand froze on its way to his mouth as Nora emerged into the morning sunshine. She carried Liam in one arm and in the other one of the colourful cushioned mats Duarte had ordered. She unrolled the mat in a shaded corner near the seating area and laid the infant down gently. He immediately began kicking his legs.

She looked up and met Duarte's gaze, a polite smile on her lips as she stood to her full height and walked over to the breakfast table.

His eyes devoured the jade-green dress she wore. Her long red hair was twisted into a neat coil at the base of her neck and he spotted the glint of delicate pearl earrings in her ears as she moved towards a seat and glanced back at Liam.

The serving staff arrived just as he moved to pull out her seat and he felt himself annoyed by their presence, by the pomp and glamour of the entire set-up in comparison with the simple days they'd spent at the beach house. Ornate dishes were being set out between them: fresh fruit platters and warm bread rolls, along with perfectly poached eggs in a creamy hollandaise sauce.

He tried not to watch her as she ate, his thoughts going over and over the events of the past few days.

'You wanted to talk.' She interrupted his thoughts, sitting back to dab her mouth delicately with her napkin once they'd both finished.

'My sister and Valerio will be arriving today.' Duarte sat back too, folding his hands on the table in front of him. 'I haven't told them about Liam yet.'

'You want to keep us hidden?' She clasped her hands together, pursing her lips slightly. 'Until your paternity test comes back?'

'There won't be a test, Nora.' He sat forward, running a hand along the length of his scar. 'I was angry when I said I wanted proof. Anyone with eyes can see that he is my son.'

'Well, that's good, I suppose…' She shrugged.

Duarte felt a flare of annoyance at this change in her. 'You *suppose*?'

'I told you that you are his father, that there is no doubt. But I understand why you wouldn't accept my explanation.' She took the napkin from her lap and folded it delicately beside her plate. 'So—your sister and her fiancé…will they want to meet him today?'

'They will want to meet both of you, I would imagine.'

'Surely there is no need for them to meet *me*.'

Her shoulders immediately became tense, and Duarte fought the urge to stand up and knead her unease away with his hands.

'I disagree. You are my son's mother.' He sat back, pushing away his errant thoughts. 'I had a lot of time to think last night. And I realised a few things. The first one is that I do not want to miss a single moment of my son's life.'

'Duarte, you know that's unreasonable, considering our situation.'

'Is it unreasonable to want to give him the kind of upbringing he's entitled to?' He measured his words, keeping his tone light. 'I have a large empty house in a quiet English village. It's safe, and the area is filled with young families. He would have access to a great education and the freedom to become…whatever he wishes.'

'That sounds wonderful.' She swallowed hard. 'Of course I want all those things for him. But I can't be expected to drop everything and follow your demands.'

'I'm not demanding anything, Nora. I'm offering a solution that I think will suit us both. I'm making a proposal.' He leaned forward, looking at her until she finally met his eyes. 'I realised last night that we don't need to make this difficult. Despite my anger towards you, I still find you intensely attractive. The idea of marriage to you is not unpleasant.'

Her face was a cool unflinching mask. Her words were deathly calm. 'Am I supposed to be flattered by that romantic statement?'

'I don't believe in perfect fairy-tales, and I'm pretty sure you don't either. That doesn't mean we can't try to be a family together. It's the most logical path.'

'First of all, you have no idea what I believe in or what I want for myself.' She leaned forward slightly, taking a deep breath before her eyes met his. 'And, secondly, are you telling me that you now trust me? That you suddenly forgive me for the things I've done and who my father is?'

Duarte felt her words hit him square in the chest. He

hesitated, looking away from her for a moment to try to school his features, and apparently that was all the confirmation she needed.

Her harsh exhalation of breath held the smallest hint of sadness. But he wouldn't lie to her to make her accept his proposal. He wouldn't make promises and say things he didn't mean. He believed she would put their son first and come to realise that this was the best way forward for the three of them. Surely his honesty was better than empty words?

She turned herself away from his gaze. 'Don't do it, Duarte, whatever it is you're about to ask of me...'

'You know exactly what I'm asking.' He reached across the table for her hand.

She pulled it away, closing her eyes. 'And if I say no?'

Her voice was barely a whisper and he heard the fear in it. 'I won't force you, if that's what you're asking me.'

He sat back in his chair, furious at her and at the way she viewed him. He took a moment to compose himself, feeling the urge to reach across the table and haul her into his arms to dispel those shadows from her eyes. He knew he needed to go into this with a cool head, but his logic seemed to go out of the window when it came to this woman, time and time again.

'I cannot abide the idea of splitting my son's life across two countries on opposite sides of the world, Nora.'

'That is not fair...' Her voice broke slightly on the last word.

'I never promised to play fair.'

'Why marriage?'

Nora could feel hurt and anger warring within her at the knowledge that he could be so cold and calculating.

'Do you trust me so little that you think I won't agree to any reasonable terms for co-parenting?'

'Marriage makes sense.'

Duarte took a sip from his coffee mug, as though they were discussing the weather and not the future entwining of their lives.

'From a practical viewpoint, we live on different continents with very different legal systems. It would make my legal rights regarding my son unclear.'

'That's not an answer,' she challenged him. 'Nor was there an actual marriage proposal anywhere in that ridiculous statement.'

He stood up and took a step towards her. 'I grew up with two loving parents and had a very happy childhood. I'm not some eternal bachelor; I always planned to settle down and start my own family someday.'

'What about *my* plans?' she asked, trying to ignore the warm, needy feeling his words stirred up. That yearning she had always harboured to truly belong somewhere, to be a part of a steady, happy home.

To give that kind of life to her son...

It would be so easy to say yes—to become his wife and commit to live with him, raising their son together. She had a feeling he wasn't suggesting a cold marriage of convenience—he would want her back in his bed—but that was where it would end for him. She would always be the woman who had lied to him. She would always be the daughter of the man who had killed his parents.

She closed her eyes against that painful truth, preparing herself to reason with him as to why marriage was never going to work between them...

The noise of a loud whistling from the marina below jarred them both.

'Duarte Avelar—you'd better not be hiding from me on my own ship.'

The female voice was calling from a distance and Nora felt her brows rise into her hairline.

Duarte cursed under his breath, and a thoroughly apologetic look crossed his features as he raised a hand and motioned for her to stay where she was while he strode across to the top of the steps.

Nora waited a few minutes, trying and failing to hear more than the slight murmur of voices as Duarte stood halfway down the stairs and greeted whoever it was. She moved to check on Liam, scooping him up into her arms and breathing in his comforting baby smell.

When the voices came closer, she turned to see a woman emerging onto the deck. Her hair was a cloud of thick ebony curls, her skin the same dark caramel as Duarte's. Even her golden eyes were a mirror image of the man who stood by her side. Another man followed them, sallow-skinned and blue-eyed.

Nora recognised him from the night of the Avelar Foundation dinner. The night of the kidnapping.

She felt a slight wobble in her legs as Valerio Marchesi looked up at her and narrowed his eyes in a manner that suggested she wasn't the only one who remembered that painful day.

What followed was perhaps the most intense hour of Nora's life, with Daniela Avelar sobbing as she held her nephew for the first time while Valerio and Duarte watched in shock. Apparently the elegant businesswoman had never been a baby person, and nor was she prone to such displays of emotion.

At one point Nora was very aware of the two men speaking in low tones in a corner of the deck. Duarte's friend and business partner seemed to have some things he wanted to say out of earshot. She saw the man's eyes dart to her, filled with evident mistrust, but she tried to pretend it didn't bother her.

When Dani insisted that Nora and baby Liam come to the launch of the new headquarters that evening, she politely declined.

So far Duarte had managed to navigate their entire interaction without once mentioning their relationship status or any details of their history together. She was grateful, but one look in his eyes as he was leaving told her he wasn't finished with their conversation from earlier.

She found herself suddenly intensely grateful that he was a hotshot CEO and his presence at the event was necessary.

When she was finally alone in her luxurious cabin, she lay down on the bed with her son by her side and blew out a long, frustrated breath.

The look on Duarte's face when she had asked him whether he had considered her own plans had spoken volumes. He hadn't even thought of her career dreams, her aspirations. No, he'd weighed up the situation and how it affected him and come up with the perfect solution to fulfil his duty to his son and keep her around as a handy bonus.

Was this what life would be like if she accepted Duarte's proposal? Trailing after him from city to city and waiting around while he attended events? Or, worse, would she be forced to play the dutiful wife on his arm?

He'd said he had a home in the English countryside and he'd made it sound idyllic. But the reality was he was a global businessman; his success took him to every corner of the world and she didn't expect that would change.

The last time Duarte had seen the Fort Lauderdale headquarters of Velamar International, the entire building had been mid-construction. Now he stepped into the glass-walled lobby and was awestruck at the level of detail everywhere he looked.

One detail caught him by surprise. The wall of the corridor that led to the common areas, where the drinks were to be served, was lined with picture frames. Upon first glance, he almost just walked by them, but something caught his eye.

He stopped and took a step back, frozen at the sight of his own blueprints and sketches for the original *Sirinetta* superyacht. For a moment Duarte wondered if they had been framed and put on show in memoriam—if perhaps he should avoid looking too close lest he should be met with an epithet of some sort about his tragic demise. But there was no mention of his death, only a succinct note on each frame, giving the date of his first concept and each stage on the road to production.

'We wouldn't be here without your brilliant mind.' Valerio appeared by his side, sliding a glass of champagne into his hands. 'You have always been the brains.'

'The creative brains, perhaps.' Duarte raised his glass in toast and gestured to the amazing building around them. 'But you were the one to come up with this crazy venture and build it into the powerhouse it is today.'

'I can't take the credit for any of this particular venture. Your sister did most of the legwork.'

Valerio smiled and raised his glass to where Dani now stood, welcoming their guests into the large conference area at the end of the corridor. She walked towards them, beaming.

'I still can't get used to seeing you together,' she said, and smiled as Valerio wrapped his arm around her waist and looked down at her with obvious adoration.

'I could say the same.' Duarte smiled too, noting their

mild shock at his light words as they all began making their way towards the party.

Dani moved away to talk with some of their investors, and Duarte saw his best friend staring at him in silent question.

'What I mean is, it's strangely normal to see you this way. It's like it was always going to come to this.' He placed a hand on his friend's shoulder. 'You make her happy.'

'She is everything to me.' Valerio spoke with gruff sincerity. 'Once I accepted that, everything else just followed. I knew it might cause a strain between us, but I hoped you would understand eventually.'

'I was a bastard when I first came home.' Duarte shook his head. 'I'm sorry.'

'You're not a bastard.' Valerio laughed as they entered the fray. 'You're just brutally stubborn and despise change in all its forms.'

Valerio's words were repeated in his mind long after they had finished their private conversation and separated to move through the crowd. He *did* despise change; he always had. It made him irritable and hostile. And when he looked at the past few months of his life he realised it had been one brutal change after another. He'd felt completely drained of mental energy.

Except at the beach house in Paraty he hadn't felt drained. He'd felt calmer and more at ease than he had in years. Now, surrounded by a mix of elite international business associates and clientele, he felt wound up and stifled. But he knew his role—knew what was expected of him.

He smiled and shook hands and tried to pretend he cared, when really he wasn't sure why he'd ever cared for this world at all.

The ship was quiet when Duarte arrived back from the event. Most of the staff had finished for the day, in anticipation of an early start preparing for the glamorous party on board the next afternoon to mark the opening of their new routes.

He wandered along the rows of empty tables on the entertaining deck, surrounded by stacks of chairs and boxes of decorations. In his old life he would have stayed to the end of the party at the new headquarters and ensured there was an after party in a fancy hotel penthouse, where everyone would have gone wild and he'd have ended the night with a beautiful woman in his bed.

The thought of it now made his blood run cold. He'd barely managed to stay for a full two hours tonight—only until his disaster of a speech had been given and he'd been able to slip away.

He was so distracted as he made his way down to the private saloon that separated the guest cabins that he almost missed the subtle clearing of a throat. Nora sat cross-legged on a sofa, her hair once again loose and flowing over one shoulder. She wore her ridiculous pyjama pants and tiny tank top, and one of her giant architecture books was splayed across her lap.

She looked like *heaven*…

He would be content to just lie down alongside her and sink into her warmth while she continued to read and ignored him.

He shook his head to clear the ridiculous thought. If she evoked such intense feelings in him it was just because he was stressed and irritated after his first evening of being 'on' as CEO of Velamar for the first time in months.

'You're still awake,' he said, trying to mask his inner turmoil with a light tone.

'I was waiting for you.' She stood up, folding her arms across her chest. 'I assume you got the message from Angelus Fiero?'

Duarte shook his head. 'I haven't received anything.'

She frowned, picking up an unsealed brown envelope from the coffee table and extending it towards him. 'It arrived an hour ago by courier. It was addressed to both of us. I assumed he must have already spoken with you.'

Duarte shook out the contents and read through the police reports quickly. Angelus had worked quickly, and a warrant for Cabo's arrest had been issued within hours of his leaving Duarte's study. The police had hauled the crime boss out of his Rio mansion in broad daylight and questioned him for hours until he cracked.

He'd confessed to everything, including the false imprisonment of his own daughter and his coercion of her to blackmail and work on his behalf. Nora would be given immunity for supplying evidence.

He looked up at the woman before him, her eyes tight with strain.

'He's going away for this, Nora,' Duarte said gruffly. 'The trial may not happen for a few months, but thanks to your evidence he won't get bail.'

'He's confessed to what he did to me…' She pressed her lips firmly together. 'He didn't have to…there was never any hard evidence.'

Duarte took a step towards her, seeing the way her lips trembled as she shook her head in disbelief. 'It's over, *querida*. He has no power over you any more.'

Nora had dreamt of the day that her father would get the punishment he deserved for all his wrongdoings, but a part of her had always believed him when he said he was untouchable. Now, seeing the cold, hard evidence of his sorry end in black and white, she came undone.

She let herself break, unable to stop the tears falling or the messy sobs racking her chest. She sobbed with relief for herself and the terror she'd endured under his tyranny, but she also sobbed for Duarte's mother and father, who had never got to see their children's wonderful achievements or to meet their grandson.

Eventually she closed her eyes and felt warm arms envelop her. She didn't pull away and stiffen, even though she knew she should. She accepted his comfort and sank into his chest until she could breathe again, which wasn't for a long while.

He didn't complain. He simply held her, his face on the top of her head so she could feel his breath against her hair. When she had finally quietened down, he pulled back just enough to look down at her.

'You are more than just his daughter, Nora,' he said gruffly. 'I was wrong to say that to you…to compare you to him. I'm sorry.'

She nodded, taking a step backwards out of his arms. 'It's okay.'

He seemed almost to extend an arm towards her, as though he wished to pull her back, before thinking better of the movement. 'It's not okay. I know I can be harsh and judgemental. I've done it before to my sister and my best friend and now to you.'

Nora looked down as his index finger and thumb circled her wrist and his hand slid down to entwine with hers. She shivered at the contact, tightening her hold on him and feeling her body sway towards his.

CHAPTER ELEVEN

'I'VE WANTED TO kiss you all day,' he said quietly.

His golden eyes were filled with such sombre sincerity that she felt her throat catch as his lips gently brushed hers.

'I've thought of nothing else…'

She felt herself fight against the intimacy of the moment, taking into account her own vulnerable state and the memory of his earlier proposal. But she wanted to kiss him too. She wanted to sink into the comfort of his heat and his strength and harness it, to chase away the shadows that haunted her.

A small part of her cried out to stop, to keep talking about the deep, dark cavern of mistrust that still lay between them. But she shook it off, losing herself in the glorious sensation of his lips devouring hers and his arms holding her so tightly.

When he lifted her up and walked them over to one of the plush sofas, she lay back and offered herself to him. His eyes darkened with arousal and he wasted no time in removing her pyjama bottoms and running soft kisses along the bare skin of her thighs.

She stopped him as his mouth reached her centre, laying her palm against his cheek as he looked up at her. 'I need you now, Duarte.'

Her voice was a husky whisper and he reacted instantly, pulling himself up over her and covering her with his big body.

The first contact of his bare skin flush against hers was almost too much. She spread her palms over his powerful shoulder muscles and just looked up at him for a long moment. She knew that this was real, not an instrument of anger, control or manipulation. And he felt it too, this intense connection between them. She could see it in his eyes as he slid into her in one sharp thrust, his hand splaying roughly through her hair to hold her in place.

It felt far too intense, locking eyes this way as their bodies began to move in a rhythm that managed to be both frantic and heartbreakingly intimate. Nora felt words in her throat, the need to tell him what she felt. But she closed her eyes, burying her face into his shoulder and focusing on the pleasure he gave her. On the way he touched her, the care he took in ensuring she found her pleasure...

Maybe that was his way of showing love. Even if trust could never truly exist between them, perhaps she could be happy so long as they had beautiful moments like this. Maybe that would be enough for her.

They made love hard and fast, barely able to catch their breath by the time they both fell in a pile of limbs on the carpeted floor. Duarte gathered her against his chest and let out a sigh that she felt deep within herself. A sigh of relief, as if he were coming back into the warmth of home after battling through a freezing storm.

But as she lay in the silent afterglow of their passion the silence crept over them once more and reality flooded back in.

She excused herself to go to the bathroom and stared at her flushed face, wondering how something that felt so wonderful could make her feel so hollow inside afterwards. She closed her eyes, wishing that loving him didn't have to hurt quite this much.

Duarte had spent the night in her cabin, in her bed, his warm body curled around hers. Despite her sadness, she'd slept well in his arms and had awoken at dawn to find him sitting back on the pillows, feeding their son.

After breakfast, he'd said he needed to run some errands for the day before the event that evening. She'd already told him she wasn't sure about attending the event, using her lack of appropriate clothing as an excuse. But as he'd been about to leave he'd kissed her softly and said he had asked his sister to offer her services to help her get ready.

Nora had not been prepared for Daniela Avelar to arrive an hour later, with a full entourage in tow. Though Daniela had made sure to double-check that her presence was welcome before she'd ushered in the small team of stylists, with racks of dresses and cases of hair and make-up.

Now Nora felt overwhelmed, but excited at the prospect of being pampered for an hour. She had always enjoyed dressing up for her father's events—she just hadn't enjoyed his authority over her appearance.

This wasn't the same, she told herself sternly as she felt her anxiety rising. Duarte had done this *for* her, not *to* her. It was not the same.

Her inner turmoil must have been apparent, because Daniela gave her a moment to collect herself and asked if she could hold Liam. Duarte's sister seemed thoroughly enamoured by the tiny infant, and only reluctantly returned him when Nora said he needed to sleep.

She settled him near the open balcony doors in his crib and immersed herself in looking through the expensive gowns on the racks in the makeshift dressing area that had been set up on the opposite side of the saloon.

'If you don't want to attend the event, you can move to my yacht,' Daniela spoke quietly beside her.

Nora turned to the other woman, noting the question in her golden eyes. 'I wasn't sure if I wanted to attend,' she said, clenching her hands together. 'But now I think I do want to be here for the celebration. I just haven't been very sociable of late.'

'Because of the baby?' Daniela asked.

'Even before that. I've been hiding myself away for a long time. I'm not sure I know how to be the kind of woman who wears gowns like this anymore.' She gave a weak laugh.

Daniela seemed to measure her words for a moment, becoming serious. 'Valerio told me who you are. Who your father is.' Golden eyes met hers earnestly.

Nora stiffened, looking away towards where her son slept. She wondered if Duarte had told his sister what her father had done. Why their beloved parents were no longer alive. She felt shame creep into her, clogging her throat.

Daniela stood up and closed the space between them. 'He also told me that you risked your father's wrath to try to save his life on that terrible night, and most likely saved my own fiancé's skin too.' She reached out to take her hands. 'I want to thank you.'

Nora shook her head, finding herself unable to find the right words to protest at the other woman's gratitude. Clearly Daniela didn't know the full story, because if she did she'd bet that this would be a very different conversation.

'I'm sorry you had to go through all that,' Daniela continued. 'I just want you to know I don't judge you for who your father is.'

Nora pressed her lips together, hearing the kindness in the woman's words but hating that they had to be said at all. She felt the reminder of her father's influence like a weight in her chest.

'When my brother came back from that place...' Daniela sighed, reaching out to examine one of the dresses on the rack. 'He was like a shell of his former self. I've never felt so helpless. But now here he is with you...with a child.'

'It's a lot to take in,' said Nora, pursing her lips.

'He hasn't said exactly what you are to one another, but I can tell that he's different. He looks more...alive.'

Nora frowned, remembering that this woman had believed her brother dead for six months, just as she had. They had both experienced grief and mourning over him, only to have him reappear in their lives.

'He proposed to me,' Nora blurted out, feeling the sudden urge to confide her turmoil in someone. To try to sort through her own tangled mind.

'Of course he did.' Daniela rolled her eyes. 'I bet he told you it was a practical solution too. I often wonder how a man can manage to run a multi-billion-dollar empire, with all its intricacies, and yet be utterly clueless when it comes to the workings of his own brain.'

'It's a rather complicated situation...' Nora hedged.

'With the Avelar family, it always is.' Daniela laughed. 'But if you do decide to marry him, I would be honoured to have you as my sister-in-law.'

Nora smiled, feeling some of her misery lift a little, despite herself.

Daniela walked over and laid a hand on the crib where Liam slept peacefully, taking a moment to gaze down at her infant nephew. Nora felt her heart swell a little, watching the obvious love this woman already had for a child she'd just met.

And as she sorted through the beautiful gowns, feeling the silk and the embroidered tulle, she wondered… Would it be so bad to be a part of their family?

Nora stood in front of the full-length mirror in her cabin, taking in the wondrous transformation Daniela's styling team had achieved in just a few short hours. Her hair had been swept back from her face and made to sit in graceful waves over one shoulder. Smoky make-up had been expertly applied to enhance the colour of her eyes, and her lips had been painted a perfect nude pink that seemed to make the roses of her cheeks glow.

She'd selected a pale blue strapless gown that accentuated her narrow waist and skimmed over her stomach. The material was a gauzy silk, embroidered with tiny delicate flowers that had glittering diamonds in their centres. She hadn't been quite brave enough to choose anything tight fitted, even though, at only seven weeks post-partum, her body had begun to feel normal again—if perhaps a little wider and less solid. This gown was comfortable, and light enough for the warm Florida evening, and the colour was perfect for her pale complexion.

She'd enjoyed every moment with Daniela, from selecting the colour for the polish on her now perfectly manicured nails to stepping into the expensive diamond-encrusted heels on her feet. For the first time in years she felt ultra-feminine and glamorous and…*happy*.

She had a small smile on her lips when Duarte appeared in the mirror behind her. He was impossibly handsome, in a simple black tuxedo with a pale blue handkerchief tucked into his pocket in exactly the same shade as the dress she wore.

'You look amazing.' He moved behind her, watching her

in the mirror as he lowered his lips to press them lightly against her neck. 'But there is just one thing missing.'

Nora watched as he revealed the small black box in his hand and held it in front of her. His eyes flicked up to hers in the mirror as he opened the box to reveal a stunning square-cut diamond ring that sparkled and played in the light.

'Duarte...' she breathed, feeling time slow and then spin around her as she turned to face him.

Her eyes were glued to the ring as he took it from the box and slid it onto the third finger of her left hand. It was stunning. It was the kind of ring any rational woman would dream of... And yet, when he slid it on and released her hand it felt cold and heavy on her finger.

She had told him she needed time. She had asked him to wait. He hadn't answered when she'd asked if he'd considered *her* plans for the future.

When she forced herself to look up at him she saw his eyes glowed with triumph and happiness.

'It fits.' He smiled, pressing a kiss to her fingers.

She forced herself to smile back, not wanting to ruin the moment. They had made love last night and fallen asleep in one another's arms; she knew they had more than just a passing attraction. It was only natural that he would assume he could introduce her as his fiancée, wasn't it?

Unease swirled in her gut, ruining the easy delight she'd felt moments before.

But he was about to celebrate the biggest moment of his career, she rationalised. His sister was here, his best friend and other family members. She didn't want to ruin this night for him, to cause him more pain. She had already hurt him so much with her poor choices in the past. He had said he wanted to be a family...maybe she owed him the chance?

The idea of a night of glamour suddenly seemed less appealing. The prospect of walking onto the entertaining deck on his arm and being introduced as his future wife was more than she could handle. She felt her insides shake, but steeled herself against the panic, telling herself to be grateful. To accept what he was offering and not dwell on what was missing between them.

Like trust…and love…

She closed her eyes and reached up to kiss him, hoping she would be able to get through the rest of the night without losing her composure completely.

Duarte was on edge. Maybe it was the single glass of champagne he'd allowed himself, or maybe it was the effect of having Nora by his side in that showstopping dress with his ring on her finger.

Every man on the yacht had turned to watch her when she'd arrived at the top of the steps. She always glowed with natural beauty, but after the added pampering and styling she bordered on ethereal. And yet no matter how much he'd tried to relax and enjoy the celebrations he knew something wasn't right. On the surface Nora was calm, and gave him reassuring smiles in between shaking hands with the various acquaintances and business associates he introduced her to. But every now and then he caught her looking off into the distance, with the faintest glimmer of unhappiness in her eyes.

Daniela had looked after Liam while Nora was busy getting dressed and was yet to return him to his mother. Duarte met Valerio's eyes across the crowded deck of the yacht and gave him a silent salute, wondering how long it would be before he was gifted with little nephews and nieces of his own.

A flurry of movement nearby caught his eye and he

smiled as he saw Valerio's parents and older brother arrive. He gestured to Nora to join him and soon he was embraced in the warmth and smiling faces of people who had been part of his extended family since he was a teenager.

Valerio's mother Renata immediately took Liam in her arms and began crying, and when she saw the ring on Nora's finger the tears started anew. The rest of the Marchesi men were more stoic, clapping him on the back and quietly offering parenting and marriage advice to both Duarte and Valerio.

'He is very like Guilhermo,' said Renata. She smiled, her face relaxed and serene as she looked down at the infant in her arms. 'His name is fitting…'

'I chose it in memory of Duarte's father,' Nora said quietly. 'He hasn't been christened yet, but his name will be Liam Duarte… Avelar.'

Duarte looked at her, not missing the way she'd hesitated over the last name. He was surprised at this revelation of the connection of Liam's name to his father's. He'd never made it himself. Liam was short for the Irish for William, she'd said on that first day in hospital, what felt like a lifetime ago. Something softened within him, knowing that even then—even when she had been unsure of him—she had chosen to honour his father that way.

'Little boy, you will break hearts,' Dani chimed in from his side, and they all raised their glasses in a toast to the oblivious baby, who promptly fell asleep and was placed in his pram.

'Duarte, you must tell us the story behind this beautiful family who have appeared with you out of the blue!' Valerio's father boomed.

'How did you two meet?' asked his mother.

Renata had directed her question to Nora, who immediately began to worry at her lower lip.

'It's a…a long story…' Nora began uncomfortably.

'We met in a samba club.' Duarte spoke over her and fixed a smile on his face, tightening his grip on Nora's hand as he felt the sudden tension in her body beside him. 'Very stereotypical for Rio, but there it is. I spotted her across the dance floor and whisked her away before any other man could steal her.'

Nora looked up at him, a glimmer of surprise in her eyes.

'Sounds like it was love at first sight,' said Renata, and smiled as she reached out to place a hand on Nora's with a dreamy sigh.

Nora stiffened and recoiled, and Duarte winced as he watched the older woman's eyes flash with confusion.

'Were they with you while you recovered on the Island?' asked Rigo, Valerio's older brother.

'No… Nora was actually busy finishing the final year of her degree in architecture,' Duarte hedged, avoiding the way Nora's gaze had flashed up to him. 'She's hoping to find an internship when we move back to England.'

'Such a long way for you to move…' Renata's face softened as she clearly mistook Nora's hostility for sadness. 'Have you family in Brazil?'

'My mother runs an animal sanctuary in the north, near the Amazon. My father is…is in Rio at the moment.'

Across from him, Duarte saw Valerio and Dani watching with furrowed brows. He felt the need to end the conversation, to take Nora away and protect her from having to talk about what had passed between them.

If they ignored it for long enough, maybe it would become less of a looming presence in their lives. He saw the shadows in her eyes when they were together; he knew they had both said and done things to one another that would be hard to come back from. He hoped someday it would be easier. But right now things were fragile between them, too fresh.

'I look forward to meeting both your parents,' the older woman continued, oblivious to the tension surrounding her. 'I've always considered the twins to be part of our family. Now we have two weddings to look forward to.'

'You won't be meeting my father, unfortunately.' Nora straightened as she spoke, suddenly pulling her hand from Duarte's. 'He's a notorious crime boss who is about to be put in prison for corruption, blackmail and murder.'

Everyone fell silent. Everyone except Dani, who took a deep, whistling intake of breath and as usual did her best to try to lighten the mood. 'Murder too? He was a busy man.'

'Yes, he was.'

Nora's voice was rough with emotion as she looked from Dani to Duarte. She opened her mouth to speak again and Duarte found himself shaking his head, urging her to stop while he swiftly changed the subject.

As he launched into a description of their time in Paraty he felt Nora shrink beside him, the tension rolling off her in waves. After a few minutes she quietly excused herself and turned to move through the crowd away from them.

'Have I said something wrong?' Renata looked to Duarte for assurance. 'She seems upset.'

Duarte cursed under his breath and quickly asked Dani to watch Liam while he followed his runaway fiancée.

He tracked her down to the rear viewing deck of the ship, which was quiet and empty of any guests. She faced away from him, her arms braced on the rail as she looked out into the distance. He stood beside her, taking her chin between his fingertips to turn her face towards him. Tears streaked her cheeks.

'Is this because of your father?' he asked softly. 'I know it must be hard to think of him. To answer questions.'

She pulled her face free of his grip, folding her arms across her chest and shaking her head softly. 'I know who my father is. I've had a lot of practice in what it feels like to be Lionel Cabo's daughter.'

'Then what's wrong?' He frowned.

'You and me. That's what's wrong.' She took a deep breath, wiping the remaining tears from her cheeks before she turned back to face him. 'I can't marry you, Duarte. I can't be a wife you're ashamed of.'

'I'm not ashamed,' he growled.

'You're lying.' She threw the words at him. 'I'm not prepared to skim over the gritty details of my life just to avoid judgement. You can't avoid everyone's questions and hide our history for ever. Your family deserve the truth.'

'I will give it to them…eventually. I want them to get to know you first.'

'You're trying to control everything—to manipulate them into liking me just so they don't show the same bias you did when you found out the truth about me. The first time *and* the second.' She shook her head, turning away from him. 'I may have made mistakes, and I may be the daughter of a crime boss, but I refuse to live another day feeling ashamed and hoping that one day you might truly trust me or love me. I refuse to accept the scraps of your affection.'

'That's what you think of me proposing to you? Trying to create a life with you? That you're getting the scraps?'

'If Liam hadn't been a factor in all of this you never would have considered marrying me…' She spoke quietly, twirling the diamond ring on her finger.

'Of course I would have, eventually.' he said quickly, frowning at her words and at the dark cloud that seemed intent on pulling her away from him. 'In Paraty, I felt the connection between us.'

She shook her head. 'That was before you found out about everything that had passed between us.'

Duarte let out a sharp huff of breath, feeling the situation getting away from him. They were both aware that this marriage was to secure his rights over his son, but he knew that wasn't all. He knew he felt more for her than he allowed himself to admit. But the idea of laying himself bare…

It wasn't something that came easily to him. Not after all they'd been through, and not with the swirl of emotions he felt whenever he thought of how she might have left him.

'I know that what I feel for you is more than you're offering me,' she said sadly. 'When I'm with you, I can't think straight. I think I fell in love with you that first night on the beach in Rio and it terrifies me.'

'You make it sound so terrible.' He looked away and steeled his jaw against her words, against the bloom of pleasure and pain they created in his chest.

'It's unhealthy, Duarte.' She closed her eyes. 'It's like I have an illusion of you but you keep everything real locked away, out of my reach. It's hurting me.'

When he looked back at her she'd slid the ring off her finger. She took his hand and folded the diamond into his palm. 'You said you wouldn't force me.'

'I won't.' He heard himself speak as though from far away. He curled his hands into fists by his sides to stop himself reaching out and making her take back her words.

'I'm sorry, Duarte,' she said quietly, and she walked away, leaving him alone in the darkness of the empty deck with nothing but the sound of the waves lapping against the side of the ship to accompany his turbulent thoughts.

CHAPTER TWELVE

NORA STARED BLANKLY out of the open balcony doors of her cabin and watched as the first glimmers of dawn filtered across the waves. She had barely slept, and her tears had continued to flow long after she'd silently collected Liam and returned to her bedroom to hide for the remainder of the party.

Daniela had come to knock on her door at one point, asking if she needed to talk. She'd remained silent until the woman's footsteps had disappeared back along the passageway, then she'd let the tears continue to fall.

She forced herself to get up when the morning light was bright enough. She grabbed her suitcase and began packing her clothes and Liam's into her small suitcase, inwardly planning what she would say to Duarte when she told him she wanted to leave. She knew she was doing the right thing. She knew she couldn't live the life Duarte was offering her, no matter how much she wished she could.

It would only make her grow to resent him. They would hate each other, and she couldn't raise her son in a home without love and trust. They both deserved more.

A knock on her door startled her. It opened to reveal Duarte, still wearing his trousers and shirt from the night before. His eyes were haunted and grim as he took in the sight of her and the suitcase open on the bed. She held her breath as she waited for him to speak, her heart bursting at the sight of him, with the need to take everything back and fall into his arms.

But she stayed still, her hands still holding the clothes she'd been folding.

'You're leaving.' It was a statement rather than a question.

'I'm going to stay with my mother,' she said firmly, feeling her insides shake. 'She hasn't met Liam yet. After a week or two I'll get in touch and we can discuss how to manage things going forward as co-parents.'

'I'll take you there,' he said quickly, his eyes sliding to where Liam lay kicking his feet. 'I'll have the jet readied by lunch.'

'No,' she said resolutely. 'I meant what I said last night. I can't think straight when I'm here...when I'm with you. I need to do this alone.'

He was quiet for a long moment, his jaw as tight as steel as he ran a hand over the scar on the side of his head. Then he seemed to measure his words, looking at her with a silent question before slipping his gaze away to stare at the open sea behind her.

'If you need anything...' He spoke the words on a low exhalation of breath, as though he had just finished waging a silent battle within himself. 'Promise me you will call.'

She heard the words and knew what it must have taken for him to speak them. He was trusting her to take his son. She felt another pitiful bloom of love for him in that moment, for this broken, scarred man who was giving her such a simple gift and likely didn't even know how much it meant to her. The gift of freedom.

It was the first small moment of trust between them as parents.

'I promise.'

She spoke softly, meaning every syllable. She wouldn't keep Duarte from his son. She would find a way to make this work.

With one final kiss on Liam's forehead, Duarte nodded at her once and left, closing the door softly behind him.

The rain had finally stopped falling when Nora drove her rented Jeep through the gates of the wildlife sanctuary, her eyes strained from hours of concentrating on the dirt road that followed the bank of the Amazon. She took in the familiar sprawling fields and the tidy rows of fruit trees on the hills. To her, this place had always felt like a world of its own—probably because during the eighteen years she'd lived here she'd rarely left.

She'd spent years hating her mother for keeping her here, and the irony was not lost on Nora. She was now returning to beg her mother to let her stay.

Her mother's house was a beautiful wooden structure that fitted in perfectly with the tall trees that surrounded it. The architecture student in her took a moment to appreciate her surroundings, how utterly flawless it was in its design.

Dr Maureen Beckett was a fiercely intelligent woman who could talk for hours about the animals she rescued, studied and reintroduced to the jungle. Yet when it came to her only daughter Nora had always found her mother to be distant and far too heavy-handed with criticism. She was not an unkind woman—quite the opposite—but she was known for her matter-of-fact approach and the fierceness with which she protected the large sprawling animal sanctuary she had founded three decades before.

Nora knocked on the door, readying herself for a reunion she knew would be anything but joyous. Likely there would be shock, and judgement of her situation. There might even be anger or, worse, that same cool detachment her mother had shown the day she'd announced she was leaving to live with her father all those years ago.

But when the door opened her mother took one look at her, and the small baby she carried in her arms, and promptly burst into tears, embracing them both in a hug filled with nothing but love.

Once she was safely inside, Nora finally allowed herself to fall apart, telling her mother everything.

Maureen was silent, one hand cradling her tiny grandson in her sun-freckled arms as she listened.

When Nora had finally stopped crying her mother took the seat beside her and drew her into her arms too. Just being held as she cried…being allowed the space to *feel* everything and not run away…it seemed to make her feel better and worse all at the same time.

And the thing that finally broke her was her mother revealing the thick envelope that had been delivered there a week before.

Nora's results from university.

She had forgotten that she had given the address of the sanctuary once she'd known she needed to leave.

She opened the envelope with shaking fingers to see that she had passed. She had her degree.

Her tears began all over again, until she thought she might never stop crying.

They talked all night, about all the unspoken things that had stood between them for years. Her mother explained how she'd attempted to follow Nora to Rio, but her father had caught up with her and told her if she ever sent so much as a letter to her daughter she would wake up to her sanctuary in flames. She'd had no choice but to come back and wait, hoping that Nora would get away and come home, even as her absence tore her apart.

Nora felt a fresh wave of love and understanding for this woman who had raised her—along with enormous guilt that she had compared her situation with Duarte to that of her and her mother. Duarte would never threaten to hurt her that way.

She found herself telling her mother everything that had happened between her and Liam's handsome billionaire father, expecting her to be horrified and warn her off.

Instead, her mother was thoughtful for a long moment. Then, 'Do you love him?' she asked.

Nora shook her head sadly. 'I do, but he doesn't love me.'

'Men don't always know how to say what they feel.' Her mother pursed her lips. 'I find his actions are usually the best way to gauge a man's devotion.'

That night Nora lay in bed, listening to the gentle sounds of rain on the roof above her, and thought of Duarte. Had his actions shown that he felt love for her?

Memories of how he'd courted her at the beach house in Paraty made her insides feel warm. He might not have known the truth about Liam then, but he'd known virtually everything else. And even after her revelation, when he'd been consumed with hurt and anger, he'd still shown her small unconscious gestures of affection—making sure she slept well, ensuring she wasn't uncomfortable around his family. When he'd kissed her, she'd felt love.

She closed her eyes and sent up a silent prayer that she hadn't just made the biggest mistake of her life by walking away from him. She knew she was doing the right thing in taking time alone to figure out what she wanted, but it didn't make being away from Duarte hurt any less.

Birds sang overhead and the smell of moist earth hung in the air from yet another heavy morning rain. As the sun peeked through the clouds the rain turned to a gentle mist over the fields. Nora paced herself, feeling the burn in her shins and silently thanking her mother for lending her the sturdy walking boots she wore. Even in her white cotton T-shirt and cargo shorts she already felt the effects of the heat.

In the week since she'd arrived at the sanctuary she'd fallen easily back into the simple life there. Now she reached the office and set about using the computer there to send some more emails, as she had done every day since the first morning she'd woken here.

She already had some offers of internships in London, but one stood out more than the others. It was near to the town where Duarte's home was.

She'd told herself she was tempted to take it for Liam, to make it easier to co-parent. She'd ignored the sound of her foolish heart beating away in the background of her mind. Of course she missed him; she woke up every day and wished he was by her side, but she needed to think practically.

On her way back to the house, she stopped to talk with some of the staff and once again gently avoided the subject of where she'd been and how long she'd be staying. It was a small community, and she wasn't eager to become the local source of gossip.

She took her time, stepping off the track to pick some fresh acai berries. The noise of the animals around her was so loud that she almost missed the sound of car tyres, making their way along the road at a pace much faster than any local would dare to drive. She turned just in time to see a large black Jeep barrel past her, turning at the fork in the track in the direction of her mother's home.

Her berries were scattered on the jungle floor, abandoned as she began to walk and then run in the direction of the house. She reached the fence at the end of the driveway just as a tall, dark man stepped out of the Jeep and turned to face her.

'Duarte,' she breathed, shock clouding her thoughts and rendering her unable to say anything more.

He looked terrible: his eyes were dark-rimmed, his shirt was wrinkled, and the trousers of his suit had mud splatters on them. But even though he looked utterly out of place, she'd never seen anyone look more imperious as he stood to his full height, looking down at her.

She came to a stop a few steps away from him, wrapping her arms around herself to avoid jumping into his arms.

'What are you doing here?'

'Do you want the polite answer or the truth?'

His voice was a low rasp, his eyes haunted as he raked his gaze over her with burning intensity.

'I think we've moved past politeness, don't you?' Nora said quietly.

Duarte nodded, running a hand along the untrimmed growth on his jawline. 'I've been a mess since you left. I told myself I wouldn't try to push you, wouldn't try to force you to come back to me, and I won't.' He closed his eyes and shook his head. 'But I've missed you, Nora. I've missed you both so much it feels like I've lost a limb. I decided that even if I drove all this way and you told me to leave, it would be enough…and I was right. Because seeing you right now, I'm not sorry.'

Nora felt a blush creep up her cheeks at the heat in his gaze. She took a step towards him, like a magnet being pulled towards its true north.

He held out a hand to stop her. 'You said you can't think straight around me, and I know what you mean.' He shook his head. 'I promised myself I wouldn't start throwing my feelings around and negating the very real concerns you had. But we've always had this intense chemistry between us, right from the start. That was never the issue. You were right to leave me. I was… I was the world's biggest fool.'

He took a step away, clearing his throat before he looked back at her and went on.

'I can see now why you wanted to come back to this place.'

His voice was warm, caressing her skin.

'It really is a paradise.'

'I never appreciated it until I left.' She took in a deep fortifying breath. 'But I've figured out a lot of things since I came back. Reconnecting with my mother was easier than I expected.'

'I'm glad you got what you needed.' His voice was rough. 'I took some time to re-evaluate things too. You leaving gave me the push I needed to make some hard choices. I told Dani the truth about our parents. It was a difficult conversation, but necessary. She asked me to pass on a message to you, to say that she misses you and Liam and she will come and find you if you keep her from him for too long.'

Nora felt tears build behind her eyes, thinking of Daniela and her wry sense of humour. 'That must have been hard,' she said softly, turning to face him.

'I'm just sorry I'd avoided it.' Sincerity blazed in his golden eyes. 'I'm sorry for how I handled everything, really.' He bit his lower lip, shaking his head. 'I wanted to tell you in person before word spread that I've resigned as CEO of Velamar.'

Nora gasped. 'Why would you do that?'

'I want to be free to work remotely, with less travel and less of that life in the spotlight, so I can focus on being with Liam. So we can create a parenting plan that considers both our needs and not just mine. Valerio was very understanding; he suggested I become a silent partner so I can focus on my own design firm.'

'That's…that's amazing, Duarte.'

'I don't know if you've thought about where you plan to live…?'

'You're *asking* me?' she said dumbly, hardly believing that he was here, that he was offering her everything she'd never thought possible.

Everything except himself…

Suddenly, his earlier words struck her. 'You said you'd told yourself you wouldn't use your feelings to make me come back. What *are* your feelings, Duarte?'

'Apart from feeling like a fool for letting you go?' He shook his head softly. 'I realised that the anger I felt when I got my memory back was so strong because I was in love with you. I never stopped being in love with you—even when your father came to me, even when I lay on the ground with you holding me and begging me to live. And when I found you again those feelings were always there, drawing me back to you. Back to where I belonged. Once I'd worked past my own stubbornness, and once I'd realised how much I hurt you by telling your father you meant nothing to me, I saw that my anger was only towards myself, and I saw how blind I'd been to what I'd had. And I saw that I'd had the kind of second chance that most people can only dream of…'

Nora felt her breathing become shallow as she took a step towards him, flattening her hands against his chest and feeling the steady beat of his heart under her fingertips.

'I don't want you to jump back into my arms,' he said. 'I know you have every reason to wait and see if I can keep my promises. But if you give me another chance I will do everything right this time. I will show you every ounce of love I possess.'

Nora claimed his lips then, unable to wait another moment to be in the warmth of his embrace. They kissed for what felt like hours, her heart singing with joy at his words, at how his body moulded around hers in a mirror of the relief and longing she felt.

When they finally separated he still held her close and breathed in the scent of her hair. He laughed. 'I think I might have to go back on that promise to leave.'

'I think so.' She smiled. 'I know we have a lot of plans to discuss, but about your proposal—'

He cut across her. 'I was wrong to make that proposal. I wanted to force you to stay with me, to be mine. If we do this now I want you to be with me because you *want* to. I don't care if we never get married, as long as we're together.'

'And if I say I want to live here in the rainforest for ever…?' Nora breathed, keeping her expression deliberately serious.

His eyes widened slightly. 'Well, it would be a hell of a commute, but I would make it work somehow.'

She closed her eyes, laughter bubbling in her chest along with an intense euphoria such as she had never experienced before. 'Well, if that isn't love I don't know what is.'

He lowered his mouth, nipping at her neck with his teeth and making her shiver. 'You are a cruel negotiator, Nora Beckett.'

The kiss that followed was even steamier than the first, leaving both of them out of breath and her shirt wrapped around her waist by the time she had the sense to break away.

'I don't really want to live here,' she said quickly. 'I've spent all week applying for internships in London. I want a fresh start. I want to create a family with you and turn your big house into a home. *Our* home.'

Her hands travelled over his chest, feeling a bump under his shirt. He smiled self-consciously, revealing a chain around his neck and on the end of it…her diamond engagement ring.

'I spent hours that day, picking this out.' He pulled it over his head, placing it in her palm. 'It doesn't need to mean anything. It can just be a symbol.'

'You know, I always dreamt of having my wedding here, in the local chapel, surrounded by the friends of my youth, my mother and our little community.'

Nora held the ring in her palm for a moment, watching it glitter and sparkle in the light. When she finally met his eyes again she felt a wave of emotion so strong it took her breath away. She placed the ring back in his hand.

'I want it to mean something, Duarte. If you'll still have me.'

He needed no further encouragement, getting down on one knee right there in the rain-soaked mud and taking her hand in his.

'I didn't give you a proper proposal the first time and I won't make that mistake again.' He looked up at her, the ring glittering in the light between them. 'Will you marry me?'

'I thought you'd never ask,' she breathed, getting down on her knees with him as he slid the ring onto her finger.

'I never thought I'd be so grateful for almost dying,' he murmured against her lips. 'If that pain was what I needed to go through to bring us back together I'd go through it all again right now, just to have you here in my arms where you belong.'

'Please don't,' she said. 'I was quite looking forward to celebrating our engagement somewhere private before we're interrupted.'

He laughed, standing up and scooping her into his arms to carry her into the house in search of the nearest bed.

'Lead the way, my love.'

'I always will.'

EPILOGUE

As a young girl, Nora had dreamt of her wedding day. She'd imagined herself walking down the aisle in a flowing gown to the sounds of a classical melody. As an adult, once she'd learned the truth of her parents' history, she'd stopped seeing marriage as something to celebrate. But now, as she walked down the planks at the sanctuary's wooden dock, hand in hand with the man she'd just vowed to love and cherish for ever, she felt her heart swell with joy.

They'd spoken their vows in the old chapel in the village, taking Liam into their arms between them towards the end of the ceremony when he'd begun to fuss. Nora wore a simple white strapless dress, with flowers from her mother's garden woven through her hair. Duarte looked effortlessly handsome in a tux, the shirt collar unbuttoned. She'd chosen the colour scheme, even convincing him to tuck one of her favourite purple orchids into his lapel.

They reached the small speedboat at the end of the dock and Nora turned to her husband, looking over her shoulder at the small crowd of their loved ones, still enjoying the wedding reception and dancing on the bank of the Amazon behind them.

'What is this surprise you've kept so secret?' she murmured against his lips, smiling at the sound of cheers erupting behind them.

'It's not a surprise if I tell you first.' He took her hand, helping her into the boat and getting behind the wheel. 'We'll only be away for a bit.'

She smiled as he manoeuvred them away from the sanctuary and along the river at a gentle speed. She placed her hand over his on the wheel, looking at the matching rings on their fingers and feeling herself smile even wider as the sun danced through the trees.

When he began to slow, she looked around.

'I read about this place a long time ago.' Duarte turned to face her. 'Do you know where we are?'

She shook her head.

'We're at the meeting of the waters. It's where two separate rivers finally meet and become one after running side by side for miles. Look down.'

He pointed to the river around them and Nora blinked. Sure enough, ahead of them the water seemed to cleave into two different shades. The dark, almost black waters of the Rio Negro ran seamlessly alongside the coffee colour of the Amazon before blending into one behind them.

They stood in silence for a moment, taking in the remarkable feat of nature.

'I can't believe I've never seen this before,' she breathed.

'Today has been perfect.' Duarte turned and took her hands in his, gently sliding her wedding ring from her finger and holding it up to the light. 'But I have one last surprise.'

She frowned, looking down at the inner circle of the ring. A soft gasp escaped her lips. Despite them having barely a week to plan their small civil ceremony, he'd somehow managed to have the platinum band engraved with the date and time of when they'd first met. The moment he'd asked her to dance and she'd lost her heart to him.

'I wanted us to make our own vows here, because I feel like it symbolises everything I love about you. About us.'

'Darkness and light,' Nora murmured, smiling as tears filled her eyes.

'I love you, Nora Avelar.' He slid the ring slowly back onto her finger, his eyes never leaving hers. 'I love everything you have been through, and everything that makes you the woman you are today. I promise to love and honour you for the rest of our lives.'

Her hands shook as she removed Duarte's ring and pressed it gently to her lips. 'There's nowhere else I could imagine making my vows to you than here on the water. This is beyond perfect.'

She slid the ring back onto his finger, smiling as she looked up into his brilliant golden eyes. 'I promise to love and honour you, Duarte Avelar. *Para sempre.*'

'*Para sempre,*' he echoed, sweeping her into his arms to show her just how good for ever could feel.

* * * * *

MILLS & BOON

Coming next month

PRIDE & THE ITALIAN'S PROPOSAL
Kate Hewitt

'I judge on what I see,' Fausto allowed as he captured her queen easily. She looked unfazed by the move, as if she'd expected it, although to Fausto's eye it had seemed a most inexpert choice. 'Doesn't everyone do the same?'

'Some people are more accepting than others.'

'Is that a criticism?'

'You seem cynical,' Liza allowed.

'I consider myself a realist,' Fausto returned, and she laughed, a crystal-clear sound that seemed to reverberate through him like the ringing of a bell.

'Isn't that what every cynic says?'

'And what are you? An optimist?' He imbued the word with the necessary scepticism.

'I'm a realist. I've learned to be.' For a second she looked bleak, and Fausto realised he was curious.

'And where did you learn that lesson?'

She gave him a pert look, although he still saw a shadow of that unsettling bleakness in her eyes. 'From people such as yourself.' She moved her knight—really, what was she thinking there? 'Your move.'

Fausto's gaze quickly swept the board and he moved a pawn. 'I don't think you know me well enough to have learned such a lesson,' he remarked.

'I've learned it before, and in any case I'm a quick study.' She looked up at him with glinting eyes, a coy smile flirting about her mouth. A mouth Fausto had a sudden, serious urge to kiss. The notion took him so forcefully and unexpectedly that he leaned forward a little over the game, and Liza's eyes widened in response, her breath hitching audibly as surprise flashed across her features.

For a second, no more, the very air between them felt tautened, vibrating with sexual tension and expectation. It would be so very easy to close the space between their mouths. So very easy to taste her sweetness, drink deep from that lovely, luscious well.

Of course he was going to do no such thing. He could never consider a serious relationship with Liza Benton; she was not at all the sort of person he was expected to marry and, in any case, he'd been burned once before, when he'd been led by something so consuming and changeable as desire.

As for a cheap affair…the idea had its tempting merits, but he knew he had neither the time nor inclination to act on it. An affair would be complicated and distracting, a reminder he needed far too much in this moment.

Fausto leaned back, thankfully breaking the tension, and Liza's smile turned cat-like, surprising him. She looked so knowing, as if she'd been party to every thought in his head, which thankfully she hadn't been, and was smugly informing him of that fact.

'Checkmate,' she said softly and, jolted, Fausto stared at her blankly before glancing down at the board.

'That's impossible,' he declared as his gaze moved over the pieces and, with another jolt, he realised it wasn't. She'd put him in checkmate and he hadn't even realised his king had been under threat. He'd indifferently moved a pawn while she'd neatly spun her web. Disbelief warred with a scorching shame as well as a reluctant admiration. All the while he'd assumed she'd been playing an amateurish, inexperienced game, she'd been neatly and slyly laying a trap.

'You snookered me.'

Her eyes widened with laughing innocence. 'I did no such thing. You just assumed I wasn't a worthy opponent.' She cocked her head, her gaze turning flirtatious—unless he was imagining that? Feeling it? 'But, of course, you judge on what you see.'

The tension twanged back again, even more electric than before. Slowly, deliberately, Fausto knocked over his king to declare his defeat. The sound of the marble clattering against the board was loud in the stillness of the room, the only other sound their suddenly laboured breathing.

He had to kiss her. He would. Fausto leaned forward, his gaze turning sleepy and hooded as he fastened it on her lush mouth. Liza's eyes flared again and she drew an unsteady breath, as loud as a shout in the still, silent room. Then, slowly, deliberately, she leaned forward too, her dress pulling against her body so he could see quite perfectly the outline of her breasts.

There were only a few scant inches between their mouths, hardly any space at all. Fausto could already imagine the feel of her lips against his, the honeyed slide of them, her sweet, breathy surrender as she gave herself up to their kiss. Her eyes fluttered closed. He leaned forward another inch, and then another. Only centimetres between them now…

'Here you are!'

The door to the study flung open hard enough to bang against the wall, and Fausto and Liza sprang apart. Chaz gave them a beaming smile, his arm around a rather woebegone-looking Jenna. Fausto forced a courteous smile back, as both disappointment and a very necessary relief coursed through him.

That had been close. Far, far too close.

Continue reading
PRIDE & THE ITALIAN'S PROPOSAL
Kate Hewitt

Available next month
www.millsandboon.co.uk

COMING SOON!

We really hope you enjoyed reading this book. If you're looking for more romance, be sure to head to the shops when new books are available on

Thursday 4th February

To see which titles are coming soon, please visit

millsandboon.co.uk/nextmonth

MILLS & BOON

MILLS & BOON

THE HEART OF ROMANCE

A ROMANCE FOR EVERY KIND OF READER

MODERN

Prepare to be swept off your feet by sophisticated, sexy and seductive heroes, in some of the world's most glamourous and romantic locations, where power and passion collide.
8 stories per month.

HISTORICAL

Escape with historical heroes from time gone by. Whether your passion is for wicked Regency Rakes, muscled Vikings or rugged Highlanders, awaken the romance of the past.
6 stories per month.

MEDICAL

Set your pulse racing with dedicated, delectable doctors in the high-pressure world of medicine, where emotions run high and passion, comfort and love are the best medicine.
6 stories per month.

True Love

Celebrate true love with tender stories of heartfelt romance, from the rush of falling in love to the joy a new baby can bring, and a focus on the emotional heart of a relationship.
8 stories per month.

Desire

Indulge in secrets and scandal, intense drama and plenty of sizzl hot action with powerful and passionate heroes who have it all: wealth, status, good looks…everything but the right woman.
6 stories per month.

HEROES

Experience all the excitement of a gripping thriller, with an inten romance at its heart. Resourceful, true-to-life women and strong, fearless men face danger and desire - a killer combination!
8 stories per month.

DARE

Sensual love stories featuring smart, sassy heroines you'd want as best friend, and compelling intense heroes who are worthy of the
4 stories per month.

To see which titles are coming soon, please visit

millsandboon.co.uk/nextmonth

MILLS & BOON
DARE

Sexy. Passionate. Bold.

Sensual love stories featuring smart, sassy heroines you'd want as a best friend, and compelling intense heroes who are worthy of them.